Patricia Burns is an Essex girl born and bred and proud of it. She spent her childhood messing about in boats, then tried a number of jobs before training to be a teacher. She married and had three children, all of whom are now grown up, and she recently became a grandmother. She is now married for the second time and is doing all the things she never had time for earlier in life.

When not busy writing, Patricia enjoys travelling and socialising, walking in the countryside round the village where she now lives, belly dancing and making exotic costumes to dance in.

Find out more about Patricia at www.mirabooks.co.uk/ patriciaburns

Also available from
Patricia Burns

WE'LL MEET AGAIN
BYE BYE LOVE

Follow Your Dream

Patricia Burns

29 MAY 2010

MIRA

MIRA is a registered trademark of Harlequin Enterprises Limited, used under licence.

First published in Great Britain 2010.
MIRA Books, Eton House, 18-24 Paradise Road,
Richmond, Surrey, TW9 1SR

ISBN 978 0 7783 0344 2

54-0410

MIRA's policy is to use papers that are natural, renewable and recyclable products and made from wood grown in sustainable forests. The logging and manufacturing processes conform to the legal environmental regulations of the country of origin.

Printed in Great Britain
by Clays Ltd, St Ives plc

To the Swanwick Fun Club –
for their wit, wisdom and silly emails.

CHAPTER 1

LATE one January night in the bitterly cold winter of 1947, Lillian's Aunty Eileen made a break for freedom.

Lillian woke up when Eileen crept out of the bed they were sharing. One side of her felt suddenly cold from the space her aunty had left, while the other was still warm where her older sister Wendy was curled up with her back against her. Moonlight was shining into the attic room through the crack between the threadbare curtains. It outlined her aunty as she pulled on two layers of clothes and carefully lowered the old suitcase from on top of the wardrobe.

'What are you doing?' Lillian whispered.

Eileen started. She caught her lip between her teeth as she stared at the little girl. Then she tiptoed over to the bed, bent and kissed Lillian on her chilly cheek.

'I'm escaping, sweetie-pie,' she breathed. 'I'm going to follow my dream. I'm going to be happy! Don't tell anyone, all right? Not a word. It's our secret, just you and me.'

'Can I come?' Lillian asked.

Beside her, Wendy stirred. Eileen put a finger to her lips. They both held their breaths, willing Wendy to stay asleep. They both let out a sigh of relief when she turned and settled. Eileen smoothed back a lock of hair from Lillian's forehead and kissed her again.

'Bye-bye, my darling little Lindy-Lou. Not a word, remember! And listen, you make sure you follow your dream too, when the time comes. Don't let them stop you.'

'I won't,' Lillian breathed, though she hardly knew what she was promising.

Eileen propped a note up on the washstand and tied a scarf over her hair. Then, with her shoes tucked under her arm and the suitcase in her hand, she carefully turned the doorknob and slid out onto the landing. The door closed behind her with a creak from the carefully released handle, and she was gone.

Lillian lay for a long time, wondering what it was all about. Where had her aunty gone? How could you follow a dream? Dreams disappeared as soon as you woke up. Even she knew that, and she was only six-and-three-quarters. It didn't make sense. Of one thing she was sure—there was going to be big trouble in the morning. Worrying about what Mum and Dad and, most of all, what Gran would say when they found out kept her awake for what seemed like half the night.

Yet at some time in the early hours she must have fallen asleep, for the next thing she knew was Wendy sitting up beside her and shaking her shoulder.

'Where's Aunty Eileen?'

Lillian looked at the space beside her in the lumpy double

bed. Where *was* Aunty Eileen? Strange memories stirred. Aunty Eileen in her outdoor clothes. Aunty Eileen kissing her. But it was a dream. There was something about a dream.

'Dunno,' she said.

'Oh, you! You never know anything. I s'pose she's got up early. Go and get my undies.'

Lillian growled and pulled the blankets tight round her. She was lovely and warm in bed, and in the room it was freezing.

'You get 'em.'

Wendy reached under the sheets and pinched her hard on the bottom. Lillian squealed and kicked backwards with her hard little heels, catching her sister on the shins.

'Ow! Kick donkey! Go and get my undies, go on! And my shirt. Or I'll tell Gran you kicked me.'

'I'll tell her you pinched me,' Lillian countered.

But she knew it was useless. Wendy was three years older than her, three years bigger and stronger and far more than three years more ruthless. She always won the arguments in the end. Lillian slipped out of bed, scampered across the room to the chest of drawers, pulled two sets of vests, knickers and liberty bodices out of the left-hand top drawer and two blue cotton school shirts out of a lower one. Just as she was about to run back and shove the clothing under the sheets to warm up, another memory surfaced, of Aunty Eileen carrying a suitcase. She pulled open the right-hand top drawer, the one that belonged to her aunt. It was empty.

She caught her breath. At that moment, Wendy piped up, 'What's that on the washstand? Is it a letter?'

Lillian stared at the envelope. So it wasn't a dream. Aunty Eileen had gone out in the middle of the night. She had kissed her and said goodbye. Fear, grief and a sense of betrayal began to churn inside her. Slowly, as if it might bite her, she reached out and picked it up, dropping the school shirts as she did so.

'Give it here,' Wendy demanded.

'It ain't for you,' Lillian told her.

Oblivious now of the cold air that was bringing her arms and legs out in goosebumps, she stood gazing at the writing. It was Aunty Eileen's all right. Just one word, in pencil, in her unmistakable sprawling hand. *Mum.*

'Give it,' Wendy repeated.

'No.'

Lillian clutched it to her chest. This was her link with Aunty Eileen. Wendy was not going to have it. Her sister bounced out of bed and tried to snatch it from her. Lillian squealed and held on tighter. Wendy twisted at one corner. There was a rip and the cheap paper gave way. Both girls stood still, aghast.

'Now you done it,' Wendy said.

'It wasn't me, it was you! You shouldn't of grabbed it.'

'You should of let me have it.'

'It's for Gran,' Lillian told her.

They both went silent, thinking of their grandmother's wrath.

'You better give it her, then,' Wendy said.

'No. You wanted it. You tore it. You give it to her.'

'Finders keepers,' Wendy said, taking her underclothes from Lillian and jumping back into bed with them. From the warmth of her cosy nest she added, 'You better take that to Gran straight away. She'll be cross if you don't.'

The thought of facing Gran first thing in the morning with bad news, and bad news in a torn letter at that, made Lillian feel quite sick. Shaking now with nerves and cold, she opened the door of the dark oak wardrobe. All Aunty Eileen's clothes were gone. All that was left was a faint smell of the scent she used.

Wendy started nagging at her again. Lillian pulled on her baggy navy knickers, tore off her nightie and pulled on her woollen vest as fast as possible, then struggled with the fiddly rubber buttons of her liberty bodice. Next came her school shirt, her gym slip, her cardigan and the knee length grey socks with elastic garters to stop them from falling down. Every single item had once been Wendy's. Some of them had been Eileen's before. She couldn't remember ever having had a new piece of clothing.

'Hair,' Wendy said.

It would never do to appear before Gran with untidy hair. Lillian looked on the washstand. The hairbrush that she and Wendy shared with Aunty Eileen was gone. She picked up the comb, dragged it through her straight hair and shoved a couple of hairgrips in to hold back the side-parted curtain. Lillian had similar colouring to most of the family, who had hair ranging from fair to mousy and eyes of greyish blue. Wendy was the lucky exception. She had inherited her mother's wavy blonde hair and clear blue eyes. Wendy was pretty and she knew it. She was her daddy's darling. Lillian was just Lillian, the smallest and the skinniest.

At last there was nothing more she could do to delay the moment.

'Go on,' Wendy ordered.

Lillian stepped out onto the cramped landing. All the family except Gran slept on the attic floor, the girls in one room, the two boys in another and Mum and Dad in the third. She went down the steep narrow stairs to the second floor landing. This was reserved for the PGs—the paying guests. At this time of year there were no PGs at all, nor likely to be any, since nobody came to Southend in the winter except a few commercial travellers, but still Gran insisted that the family stayed in their cramped quarters.

'You never know when someone might knock at the door. We don't want to have to turn money away just because we haven't got a room ready,' she stated.

And because the house belonged to her, they all had to agree, even Lillian's dad. The PGs' bathroom, however, was not out of bounds. Lillian dodged in, used the toilet and gave her hands and face what her mother called a lick and a promise. It was far too cold to wash properly, but she didn't dare appear before Gran without washing at all. That done, she went down the main staircase with its gloomy brown paint and narrow runner of threadbare carpet held in place by brass rods. They were stairs that Lillian knew intimately from having to clean them every day with a dustpan and stiff brush. Down she went again to the ground floor, where she hesitated in the hall. At the end of the long corridor with the step halfway along it was the kitchen. Her mum would be in there, stirring the porridge, cutting the bread, boiling the kettle for tea. But first she had to face Gran.

Biting her lip, Lillian knocked on the door of the front room, the room that was the best parlour in most houses, used only for funerals and Sunday visitors.

'Come in,' came a gruff voice from inside the room.

Lillian took a deep breath and opened the heavy brown-painted door. It was gloomy inside the room, even though the rust-coloured curtains had been drawn back. Heavy furniture, a black marble-effect fireplace, green and brown leaf-patterned wallpaper and a brown patterned carpet square with a fawn lino surround made it look wintry on the brightest of summer days. Now, on a grey January morning, it was downright depressing. Lillian saw little of the detail. What took all her attention was the woman sitting up in the iron-framed single bed by the wall opposite the bay window.

Whenever the teacher read fairy tales to Lillian's class, the princess in the story always had Wendy's face in Lillian's imagination, while the wicked witch or the evil stepmother always looked just like her gran. The same tight steel-grey curls held in place, as Gran's were now, with a hairnet, the same hard hands, the same piercing grey eyes and grim mouth.

At least Gran had been given her early morning cup of tea, Lillian noted with relief. And she had had her first cigarette of the day. There was a smell of fresh smoke in the room and a mangled fag end in the ashtray by her bed. All this was good. It meant that Gran would be more approachable. But still Lillian's stomach churned with fear.

'Well?' Gran said. 'What is it? What are you bothering me with at this hour of the morning?'

Lillian came into the room and shut the door behind her as she had been taught. There was a dark red chenille curtain hanging behind it to keep out the draughts. She stepped forward and stood by Gran's bed, the letter clutched to her chest. Reluctantly, she held it out.

'It's for you. I'm sorry it's torn. It was Wendy, she tried to take it from me, but I said no, it was for you, not for her.'

'Don't blame others for your crimes,' Gran told her, taking it. She stared at it. 'There's no stamp, no address. Where d'you get this? Give me my glasses, girl.'

Lillian did as she was told. Gran settled the steel-framed spectacles on her nose and peered again at the pencilled writing.

'"Mum",' she read out loud. 'Who's this from?'

'Aunty Eileen,' Lillian mumbled, looking down at her feet.

'Eileen? What's Eileen doing writing me letters? What's all this about?'

Lillian didn't dare suggest that she open it and find out. Instead, she just muttered, 'Dunno,' and kept her eyes downcast. Through her lashes, she saw Gran rip the envelope and take out a single sheet of cheap lined paper. The only sound was Gran's laboured breathing as she took in contents. Then came the eruption.

'What? Gone? How dare she—? What do you know about this? Where's she gone? What did she tell you?'

Lillian shrank back. 'N-nuffing,' she stuttered. 'I don't know nuffing. Honest.'

Gran glared at her. 'You must know something. You and her are thick as thieves. What did she say? When did she go?'

'Last night. But she didn't say nuffing to me,' Lillian lied desperately.

'You saw her go?'

'No!'

'Then how do you know she went last night?'

'She—she—she wasn't here this morning. Just that letter. She left that letter.'

'Didn't you hear anything? You must have. You share a bed.'

Lillian shook her head emphatically. It seemed less bad than actually telling a lie.

'What about Wendy?'

'She didn't neither.' That at least was the truth.

Still Gran's eyes bored into Lillian's. She could feel herself going red.

'You know what happens to liars, don't you?'

Lillian nodded. Liars' tongues shrivelled up and dropped out. But she had promised Aunty Eileen not to tell.

Gran made a disbelieving sound in her throat. 'There's something you're not telling me. Go and get your dad.'

Relieved to be let off the hook, if only for the moment, Lillian turned and trotted out of the room. Her father rarely had a kind word to say to her, but he wasn't as frightening as her grandmother. She carefully closed the door behind her and went down the chilly passageway to the kitchen. There she found her mother at the sink and her father sitting at the table with a bowl of porridge in front of him, reading the *Mirror.*

'Gran says you're to come,' she told him.

Her father sighed and turned slowly to look at her. 'What?' he said, as he always did, to gain time.

Lillian repeated her message. Her mother started drying her hands on her floral apron.

'Oh, dear, what's the matter? What does she want?' she asked, nervous as a bird.

'She wants you,' Lillian told her father. She didn't want to be accused of repeating the message incorrectly. She was in enough trouble already, covering for Aunty Eileen.

Doug Parker sighed again and stood up. He was a tall man, but already he had an apologetic stoop which made him look older than his years. His once handsome face was marred by lines of discontent and his right arm hung awkwardly, the result of a fight with his brother long ago in the butcher's shop the family had once owned.

'S'pose I better go,' he said, as if he had some choice in the matter. They all knew he was just deceiving himself. In this household, when Gran said jump, you asked how high.

Lillian and her mum waited as he went down the passageway and into the front room. Neither of them suggested that Lillian might start eating her breakfast. They needed to know whether Gran would want them next. From the front room came Dad's voice, raised in anger and dismay as he heard what his little sister had done.

'Gone? Gone where?'

Nettie Parker flinched. 'What is it?' she whispered to Lillian. 'What's going on?'

'Aunty Eileen's gone,' Lillian told her.

'Oh, my Gawd!'

Nettie put her two hands to her thin cheeks. 'Now we're for it,' she predicted. 'Eileen! The silly girl. How could she do this to us?' She pulled out a chair with a shaking hand and sat down. 'What are we going to do?' she asked. 'Your gran'll go mad. It's terrible, terrible.'

Before Lillian could work out whether she was supposed to answer this, her father put his head round the front room door and yelled for her to come back in. Reluctantly, Lillian obeyed. As she walked back towards Gran's room, she saw Wendy sitting on the stairs grinning at her through the rails. She put her tongue out at Lillian as she passed. Lillian did the same back. At that moment her two big brothers, Bob and Frank, came clattering down the stairs.

'What's up?' Frank hissed. 'What's going on?'

'Aunty Eileen's done a bunk,' Wendy said, her blue eyes as big as saucers with the excitement of it all.

Frank whistled and sat down beside her. 'She ain't? What, done a midnight flit?'

Wendy nodded. 'She's taken everything, even the hairbrush. She just left a letter for Gran.'

'Wow!' Frank was fond of American expressions. 'She's got a nerve, ain't she? You got to hand it to her.'

'She's a very silly young woman, if you ask me,' Bob said from his lordly position of oldest son and the accepted clever one of the family.

'Nobody did ask you,' Frank told him.

Their father's head appeared round the door again. 'Lilli—! Oh, there you are. Come in here when you're told, girl.' He caught sight of Wendy and his voice softened. 'And you better come as well. She can't of gone without either of you hearing nothing.'

This time it was Wendy's turn to look alarmed and Lillian's to make a face before both of them lined up by Gran's bed. It was easier with Wendy there, as she vehemently denied knowing anything and Lillian just stood beside her, agreeing with everything she said. But Gran still had her suspicions.

'You and her, you was like blooming Siamese twins,' she said to Lillian. 'I can't believe she'd go and not say nothing to you, whatever she might do to the rest of us, the ungrateful little madam. Walking out in the middle of the night like that! I never knew the like—'

Gran went off on a long tirade. The two girls stood silent, knowing better than to make any comment. Their father nodded and agreed with everything. But eventually Gran came back to her original point.

'So come on, what did she tell you?'

Lillian shook her head. Despite her concern not to give anything away, the full impact of what had happened was finally getting through to her. Aunty Eileen had been more like a mother to her than her real mum, who was worn down with housework and miscarriages and trying to please everyone. Aunty Eileen had always stuck up for her and put her first. Out of nowhere, tears welled up and spilled over.

'I don't want her to go!' she wailed. 'I want her to come back!'

Try as they might, her father and grandmother could get nothing more out of her. A sharp smack round the ear from her father only made her cry harder.

'Get her out. I can't hear myself think with all this racket going on,' Gran ordered. 'You get off to work early, Douglas, and on your way ask at Madame Pauline's if they know anything. She must of told them; she can't just walk out of a decent job. And, if they don't, there's only one thing for it—we'll have to go to the police.'

Lillian found herself pushed out into the hallway again, where Frank and Bob grabbed her and demanded to know what was going on.

'The police!' Bob said. 'Gran's never going to ask them to come here, is she? She'd never do that. It'd give the neighbours a field day.'

'You're such an old woman,' Frank scoffed. 'But come on, Lill, spill it. Where has Eileen gone?'

He loomed over her, his pale face gleaming with the excitement of it all. Nothing as dramatic as this had happened in their family in their lifetimes.

Lillian stamped her foot with frustration. 'I don't know! I don't know! She's just gone. She went in the middle of the night—'

She was saved by her father putting his head round the door.

'Clear off into the kitchen, you lot. Your gran don't want all this row outside her door. Go on, get!'

It was the beginning of a difficult time. The police were sympathetic but, with nothing to work on, they were unable to do more than suggest that the family get in touch with the Salvation Army. Gran continued to rant and rave about the situation, but all her bad temper couldn't bring back the daughter who had escaped her heavy rule. Gradually, they all came to realise that Eileen really had gone for good.

Her absence was felt by all the family, though to different

degrees. One fewer wage coming in made a difference to all of them, so did one fewer ration book. Mum missed a strong pair of hands to help with the many chores involved in running a guest house. Wendy missed having her blonde curls tamed into cute ringlets. They all missed Eileen's cheerfulness. Her stories of difficult customers at the hairdresser's where she worked had livened up the tea table no end.

But Lillian felt it most of all. She had lost her friend, her ally, her source of love and security. There was nobody now to give her a big hug and ask how her day at school had been, nobody to take her on their knee and tell her how sweet she was, nobody to stop the others from treating her as a general dogsbody. Lonely and miserable, Lillian would creep inside the wardrobe and breathe deeply through her nose, taking comfort from the lingering remnants of Evening In Paris. But there came a day when even that had gone, and Aunty Eileen with her ready laugh and her unquestioning love seemed to have disappeared from her life for ever.

CHAPTER 2

'YOU'RE not going to wear that tie, are you?' James's sister Susan nagged.

James looked at the tie in the spotted mirror over the fireplace and adjusted the knot. 'Why? What's wrong with it?' he asked.

'Can't you see? It's too loud.'

James laughed with sheer disbelief. Who could possibly say that dark red with small interlocking yellow squares was 'loud'?

'What you mean is, it's not the sort of thing that Boring Bob wears,' he said, and waited for the explosion.

Susan's pretty round face went quite red and her eyes glittered. She clenched her fists. 'Will you stop calling him that? Bob is my young man and he is not boring!'

James grinned at her. At seventeen, he was taller than her now and able to look down at her, which she hated. She was the elder by two years and had bossed him around when they were children.

'Not if you like watching grass grow,' he teased.

'You—! You're just so hateful! Mum! Mum, James is being horrible.'

Cora Kershaw came out of the bedroom that she and Susan shared in their tiny flat. Her blue frilly blouse was not yet tucked into her pleated skirt, and her thin hair was all over the place. Her soft face looked even more anxious than usual.

'Children, please—Jamie, darling, you mustn't—'

Susan took in her mother's appearance and found a new target.

'Mum! You can't wear that blouse with that skirt!'

Cora looked mortified. 'Oh, darling, really? Are you sure? Only I thought—Mrs Jefferson gave me this blouse, you know, and she buys her clothes in London. But if you think— I don't want to let you down. Not when we're going to tea with the Parkers.'

James went and put an arm round her. He faced his sister.

'Leave Mum alone, Suse. She looks perfectly all right. More than good enough for the flaming Parkers. Anyone would think we were going to Buckingham Palace.'

Tears of frustration were gathering in Susan's eyes.

'Can't you see? This is *important* to me. The Parkers have invited all of us to go round and meet all of them. I want it to be *perfect*. I mean, look at this place—' She gestured at their home, three rooms and a kitchenette on the first floor of a small terraced house, with an outside toilet that they had to share with the people downstairs. 'The Parkers live in that great big place just off the seafront.'

'It's a guest house,' James stated. 'They don't live in all of it.'

'But it's theirs. They own it. They don't rent it.'

Their mother sighed. 'I know it's not what you want, darling. You deserve better than this, both of you. It's so poky in here. When I first got married, I never expected to still be living somewhere like this, all these years on. Never in a month of Sundays. We had such dreams, you know. We were going to have a big house with a garden and a garage and everything, one of those lovely places down in Thorpe Bay. If only your poor dear father had survived…'

Her voice trailed off. James and Susan were silenced, as they always were, when their mother started on this subject. The words 'If only…' had threaded all through their childhood. There was nothing meaningful they could say, for it was true, things would have been completely different for them if their father had not been killed in the war. The eyes of all three of them turned to the photograph in pride of place on the mantelpiece, showing a tall man in cricket whites with dark hair and eyes and a narrow, clever face who looked back at them with a sunny smile. As James grew older, it was becoming ever clearer that he was the image of his father.

James gave Cora another hug. 'You won't live here for ever, Mum. I'll buy you a house with a garden one day, you'll see.'

He might be the youngest of their little household, but he was the man of the family, had been since he was five years old, and it was up to him to provide.

Cora reached up and patted his cheek. 'You're a good boy, Jamie.'

He could tell that she didn't really believe him. How could a boy who worked in a garage ever get to buy a house?

'And anyway,' he said, returning to the argument that he and Susan were having, 'just because the Parkers live in their own place down by the seafront, it doesn't mean they're better than us. So stop having a go at us, Susan. We're not going to let you down.'

'I didn't say you were. I just said I wanted it to be perfect, and you—' Susan broke off, catching sight of the clock. 'Look at the time! We'll be late if we don't set off in five minutes. Come on, Mum, I'll help you do your hair.'

After a brief flurry of activity they set out, James and his mother arm in arm, Susan walking just ahead of them.

'Doesn't she look a picture?' Cora said, smiling proudly at her daughter's back.

'Lovely,' James agreed, to keep her happy.

Susan was tip-tapping along in her polished court shoes, neat and proper in the powder blue suit that she had made herself on the old hand-cranked Singer sewing machine. She wore a little blue felt hat perched on top of her head and new white gloves. Her black handbag hung from her arm. The whole outfit had taken months and months of saving from her wages as a junior in the office of a department store in the High Street.

'Just like something out of a magazine.' Cora sighed. 'You look just like something out of a magazine,' she called ahead to Susan.

Susan turned her head and smiled back at her. 'Really?'

Even James had to admit that his sister was looking pretty. Plenty of men would be delighted to go out with her. Why she was so stuck on Boring Bob was a mystery to him.

'I do hope the Parkers will like us. This is so important to Susan,' his mother said.

'Mum, the Parkers aren't as wonderful as Suse likes to make out, you know. Has she told you how they came to be living here?'

'No, but—'

'Susan told me one day. She says that Gran Parker's husband once had a butcher's shop in Upminster, but he died of a heart attack and his elder son, Norman, took over. Norman was useless, and what profits he did make he spent at the races. On top of that, he had a nasty temper. Bob's father, Doug, was the younger son and he thought he could make a better fist of it and said so, and one day when they were having a row Norman picked up a knife and attacked Doug. His arm was so badly injured that at one point they thought it was going to have to be amputated. Norman walked out, joined the army and died in India of malaria, the butcher's went bust and, with what money was left, Gran moved to Southend with Doug and his family and put a deposit on the guest house. Which was fine until the war came and that business nearly went bust too. From what I can make out, they're just about hanging on now, with people wanting to go on holiday again. So you see, they're not a grand family living in a big house. They're ordinary people who've had a lot of bad luck, just like you have.'

'Oh—yes—I see. Dear me, what a terrible story! Fancy one brother attacking another like that. How dreadful.'

Going over the tale kept them occupied as they made their way along the depressing back streets with their rows of almost identical houses till they could see the grey gleam of the Thames estuary, finally emerging on to Southend seafront just past the gasworks. All three of them paused to take in the scenery. Susan gazed at the dome of the Kursaal, where she had met Bob at the dance hall. Cora looked mistily at the pier, marching out across the grey mudflats to the shining river. She and her late husband had taken many a romantic stroll along its mile and a quarter of decking. James looked at the Golden Mile of amusements and longed to be there with his friends, playing the machines and eyeing up the girls, instead of being stuck with this gruesome family tea with the Parkers.

It was still too early in the year for many day trippers to be about, but the sunny weather had brought out plenty of locals to walk off the effects of their Sunday lunches. Young couples wandered hand in hand, families marched along in groups, elderly people stopped to look at the fishing boats or across the water to the hills of Kent, dogs ran around barking at the seagulls.

A brisk walk along the promenade in the spring sunshine brought the Kershaws to the Sunny View Guest House, set a few houses back from the seafront on a side road. There was not much to set it apart from any of the others in the terrace. They were all three storeys high with square bay windows, grubby brickwork and dark paint. All displayed 'Vacancies' signs. James couldn't imagine wanting to stay in any of them. They looked most unwelcoming.

The front door of Sunny View was opened by a skinny kid of thirteen or so with long plaits. She looked about as pleased to see them as James was to see the Parkers.

Susan put on her grown-up voice. 'Hello, Lillian dear. How are you today?'

'All right, I s'pose. You better come in.'

Bob came to meet them in the hall, took Cora's coat and gave it to the kid to hang up, then opened the door to the front room.

'We're in Gran's room today,' he told them, in a tone of voice that made it clear they should think themselves honoured.

The entire Parker clan was gathered in the gloomy room. After the fresh sea air it smelt stale, a mixture of cigarette smoke, polish and cooking fat. James found himself introduced to each family member—Bob's grandmother, parents, younger brother Frank and the kid Lillian. But none of them made any impression on him, for there, sitting amongst them, was the most stunning girl he had ever seen.

'My sister Wendy,' Bob said.

She was a natural blonde, her hair in soft curls round her lovely face. Her eyes were big and blue and her lips were luscious, while her body was as alluring as Marilyn Monroe's. She wore a pink jumper that showed off her magnificent breasts to perfection, and a wide belt emphasized her narrow waist. James was mesmerised. There was a general shaking of hands, during which James got to grasp hers.

'Pleased to meet you,' he managed to say. He felt hot all over.

Wendy kept hold of his hand a few telling moments longer than necessary. 'Likewise,' she said with a cool smile.

James was horribly aware that she knew just what effect she was having on him and, what was more, she was enjoying it.

He sat on the dining chair nearest to where Wendy perched on the arm of her father's seat. Around him, the two families were making polite small talk. The words buzzed about him but made little sense. Then he realised that Susan was hissing at him.

'James!'

'What?' he asked, disorientated.

'Mrs Parker is asking you a question.'

With difficulty, he focused on Bob's grandmother. She was a grim-looking old bat, dressed entirely in black with a large cameo brooch at the neck of her blouse.

'Yes, Mrs Parker?' he said, trying to sound intelligent.

From across the room there came a snigger. James glanced over. It was Frank, a lanky young man of about twenty with a shadow of a grin on his face. He understood just what the problem was.

'I asked what you did for a living, young man.'

James looked back at the grandmother.

'I'm an apprentice mechanic at Dobson's garage,' he told her.

'Hmm, well, it's a good thing to have a trade. Our Bob has a position at the bank, of course.'

'Yes, Mrs Parker,' he said. Nothing on earth was going to make him sound impressed.

'It's such a comfort to have an office worker in the family. Bob takes after his grandfather. He has the brains of the family.'

There was a murmuring of agreement from the older members of the family.

James couldn't help glancing at Bob. He was sitting there looking like the cat that got the cream, and there was Susan, gazing at him with her face glowing.

'Susan has an office job,' James pointed out. Nobody was going to make out that the Parkers were better than the Kershaws.

'But not in a bank,' the old bat stated. She shut her mouth in a tight line, to show that she had said the last word on the subject.

'It's a good job though, for a girl,' James argued. Susan had let slip how Gran ruled the roost round here, but she wasn't his grandmother and he wasn't going to let her shut him up like she did the others.

Mrs Parker turned her stony glare on him. 'When are you going for your national service, young man?'

'July.'

Mrs Parker gave a satisfied nod. 'That'll knock the cheek out of you. You won't know what's hit you.'

'Make a man out of you,' Bob's father said.

Bob and Frank both agreed. They had done their national service. They sat there with the superior expressions of those who had been through the mill and survived it. James was conscious of Wendy, sitting there watching the fun and waiting for his reaction.

'I've been the man of our family since I was five,' he said.

Gran made a harumphing noise in her throat and looked at Bob's mother, who had so far said nothing.

'Time to put the kettle on, Nettie. And you, Lillian, go and help her.'

Susan, her voice brittle with strain, steered the conversation into a discussion of the weather. Everyone seemed relieved when tea was ready and they could move into the next room. In the hallway, Susan caught hold of James's arm.

'How could you?' she whispered accusingly.

'What?' he asked.

'Be so rude to Mrs Parker.'

'I'm not. I'm being perfectly polite.'

'James, *please.*'

He relented. She was his sister, after all, and she wanted to make a good impression on these awful people. 'OK, sis.'

They went into what was usually the guests' breakfast room, where the small tables had been pushed together to make one large one. Plates of sandwiches and dishes of shrimps and cockles and whelks were set out all along it. James made a beeline to where Wendy was sitting, but found himself outmanoeuvred. She was flanked by her father on one side and Frank on the other. The only spare seat was between Bob and the kid. James sat down, resigned to being bored.

Eating, making polite remarks about the food and discussing the best place to buy fresh seafood took up most of the meal. James let them get on with it, while he tried not to stare at Wendy. He was surprised to find Lillian speaking to him.

'You work in the garage, then?' she said.

'Yup.'

'So you're good at fixing things?'

'Yes. Why?'

'Only I've got this bike, see. I bought it at a jumble sale but it won't go properly.'

Despite himself, James was interested.

'If someone's sent it to the jumble, it must be pretty bad. How rusty is it?'

'Quite a lot,' Lillian admitted.

'And do the pedals go round?'

'No.'

From the other side of the table, Frank joined in. 'It's a heap of junk. Best thing to do with it is to give it to the rag-and-bone man.'

'It's not a heap of junk,' Lillian said.

Frank gave that sneering grin of his. 'Junk,' he repeated.

'Have you had a go at it for her? Given it an oiling or any-thing?' James asked.

'Got better things to do with my time, mate.'

'Pig,' Lillian muttered.

James felt sorry for her. It must be pretty grim having Frank and Bob as big brothers, and that old hag ordering her around all the time.

'I'll have a look at it for you, if you like,' he offered.

Her sharp little face lit up. 'Would you? Really?'

''Course. After tea, if you like.'

'Oh—I got to do the washing-up.'

'After that, then,' James offered.

So he found himself half an hour later in the back yard.

Lillian disappeared into a rickety shed and wheeled out a rusty ladies' bike. James was pleasantly surprised. It wasn't as ancient as he had thought it would be.

'It's a Raleigh, and that's good for a start,' he said, trying the brakes, examining the chain. 'The parts will be easy to get. You know what I think? This has been dumped in someone's back yard for years in all weathers. The tyres aren't very worn—see, there's plenty of tread on them—but they're cracked from neglect. There's even quite a bit of wear in the brake blocks, once I get the brakes going again.'

'They will work, then?' Lillian said.

'Oh, yes, nothing that a good clean and a bit of oil won't fix. That saddle has had it, but you could put an old beret over it for now, if you've got one. You'll have to buy new tyres and inner tubes, though. Can you afford that?'

'I'll save up my paper round money.'

'Good, well, if you get on with getting rid of all this rust—' He explained what to do, while Lillian listened and nodded. 'You don't mind getting your hands dirty, then?' he asked. It wasn't a job that Susan would have considered tackling.

'Oh, no. Not if it means I'll have a bike to ride. But what about the brakes and the chain?'

'I can't do it now 'cos I've got my best stuff on and I haven't any tools with me, but I'll come back and do it next weekend, if you like,' James offered.

'Would you really?' Lillian sounded amazed. She was looking at him with glowing eyes. 'You'll come back and do it for me?'

James didn't like to tell her that it was worth it to have the chance of running in to Wendy again.

''Course,' he said.

'Wow! That's the nicest thing anyone's ever done for me.'

For a moment he thought she was going to fling her arms round him, but instead she veered away and turned a perfect cartwheel, allowing a glimpse of her long slim legs and her navy knickers.

James clapped and Lillian laughed with pleasure.

'I was dreading this tea party, but now I'm really glad you came,' she confided.

'Me too,' James agreed.

He never thought he would admit it, but Boring Bob's family had turned out to be much more interesting than he'd expected.

CHAPTER 3

'WHERE are you off to, squirt?' Frank demanded, barring Lillian's way downstairs.

'None of your beeswax,' Lillian told him, making to dodge under his arm.

She wasn't quite quick enough. Frank caught hold of her wrist.

'Not so fast, squirt. You're supposed to be helping.'

It was the time of the dreaded spring clean. All the paintwork had to be washed, all the windows cleaned, inside and out, the curtains taken down and washed, the carpets and rugs taken outside and beaten, the floors scrubbed, the fireplaces scoured and the furniture polished. Everyone, even the men, was supposed to be helping. Gran, of course, was organising it all. She didn't actually do any physical work.

'I've done mine,' Lillian said. Her hands were red and raw from the sugar soap solution she had been using to wash the paint in all the first floor rooms. It was now all clean and shining, but nothing could disguise the fact that it was chipped.

'No, you ain't, because the back room floor's got to be done yet.'

'That's yours. You was on floors,' Lillian protested.

Frank's grip tightened. He bent her arm up behind her back. 'I got better things to do. You can finish it for me.'

'What's in it for me?'

'You'll be sorry if you don't, that's what.'

He pushed her arm a bit further up. Lillian bit back a squeal of pain.

'I'll tell Gran you've bunked off,' she threatened.

'You wouldn't.'

'Try me.'

Another hitch of her arm. Lillian gritted her teeth.

'Sixpence,' she managed to say.

Despite the fact that he was by far the bigger and stronger, Frank was forced to bargain. He didn't dare risk Gran knowing he had wriggled out of part of his task.

'Thruppence.'

'Fivepence ha'penny.'

'Fivepence, and not a farthing more.'

'Done.'

Frank released her and she held her hand out for the money. Her back and arms and knees were all aching from the cleaning she had done already, but five pence was not to be sneezed at. She needed a lot more than that before she could buy the new tyres and inner tubes for her bike. With a sigh, Frank fished four pennies and two ha'pennies out of his pocket, slapped them into her palm and went clattering downstairs, whistling the latest Johnnie Ray number. Lillian knew just where he was off to; he was going to join his mates and hang about down at the amusement arcades on the sea-front. She was doing him a favour, taking some of his cash off him. He would only go and lose it all on the machines.

Half an hour later, Lillian emptied the now filthy cleaning water into the first floor toilet and lugged the bucket and scrubbing brush and block of green Fairy household soap downstairs. The whole house smelt of damp floorboards and polish and the vinegar that had been used to shine the windows. The windows and doors were all open to give the place a good airing. On her way through to the yard, she met her dad coming in from work in his lift attendant's uniform.

'You finished already?' he asked.

'Yup.'

He looked at her suspiciously. 'You done it all properly? Your gran'll be up there to check.'

Gran was sure to find some fault, but Lillian knew she had made a good job of it. She had been well trained.

'Yup, every bit.'

'Right, well, you can go down the newsagent's and get me a packet of fags.'

Lillian groaned inwardly. She wanted to go out in the yard and get her bike out. James was coming to see what she had done when he finished work today.

'All right,' she sighed, with as good grace as she could manage. After all, there was no getting out of it. She was the youngest, the runner of errands.

Her father counted the exact amount into her hand, so there was no chance even of being given the change. Lillian went out of the back door—nobody ever used the front—wheeled her bike out of the shed and leaned it against the fence, then went through the rickety gate and along the alleyways, emerging into the street six houses up from her own.

Outside, it was warm in the spring sunshine, even though it was now late afternoon. Freed from the day's chores, Lillian felt light and happy. Today was the day that James had said he would come—lovely James who treated her as if she was somebody. She had to stop herself from putting a skip into her step. After all, she was fourteen now, not a little kid. Next year she would be leaving school.

At the newsagent's, a woman was buying sweets. The paper bags were lined up along the top of the counter, half pounds of toffees and pear drops and humbugs. Now she was hesitating between mint creams and nut brittle.

'Oh, I'll have a half of each,' she decided.

Since sweet rationing had been taken off in February, people had been going mad for sweets. Lillian drew in the sugary smell, her stomach rumbling. In her pocket was the five pence that she had extracted from Frank. She gazed at her favourite, Fry's Five Boys chocolate. But then there was nougat as well. She loved nougat, and it lasted longer. She jingled the money, sorely tempted. No, she mustn't. Every penny brought those tyres nearer, and with them the day she could get on that bike and ride it.

As she stepped out of the shop with her father's Player's Navy Cut, she saw James just rounding the corner into her road on his bike. She let out a shriek.

'James! Wait for me!'

He skidded to a halt as she raced towards him, amazed that he had actually stopped. No one in her family would wait for her like this. She pounded down the road, her plaits bobbing on her back as she ran.

'Oh—' she panted as she joined him. 'You've really come. I didn't know if you would.'

James looked faintly puzzled. 'I said I would, didn't I?'

'Yes, but people don't always do what they say they will,' she pointed out.

'I do,' James told her.

And she knew absolutely that this was the truth. He was not the sort of person who would let you down. It gave her a strange glow inside.

'You're not like my family,' she told him as they started towards her house. 'But never mind them. I've been working really hard on my bike. Just wait till you see it! It's shiny as new.'

He actually listened to her and asked her sensible questions. Lillian could hardly believe it. She led him in through the back way to where the curtains were still drying on the washing lines in the yard.

'We've been spring cleaning,' she explained.

'Oh, yes. My mum goes mad on that each year for a bit, but she never gets very far. Susan and I usually finish it. But we've only got a little flat to clean. It must be a big job doing all this place,' James said, looking at the back of the house as it reared up above them, the bare windows gleaming. 'Do you all help? Wendy as well?'

'Even Dad'll have to tomorrow, when he's off work,' Lillian told him. 'Oh—I got to go and give him these cigarettes. Would you like a cuppa?'

James said that he would.

'You can see what I've done to my bike while I'm making it,' she suggested.

When she came back out with a large cup of tea and the biscuit she'd dared to take, he was already busy with his tool kit and oil can. He admired what she had done and for a while they talked cogs and chains and brakes. Lillian soaked up all the information.

'You're very clever,' she said.

James shrugged. 'I enjoy getting things working. Bikes are easy. Cars take a lot more skill. Some of the blokes where I work, they do the job but they don't think about it. If something's a bit tricky, they just adjust a few things and get it moving but they don't make it sing. If a car's going well, you can hear it, it speaks to you.'

He gave an embarrassed smile. 'I suppose that sounds daft.'

But Lillian knew just what he meant. 'No, no, it doesn't. I know when a movement is just right. It's the same thing. Look.'

She stood up, took a pose, then executed a series of pirouettes across the concrete yard, finishing by the door. James grinned and clapped, but Lillian hadn't finished.

'No—that's what I mean. Anyone could do that if they practised. Now watch.'

She came back again the other way, this time making every part of her body as graceful and fluid as possible. Everything had to be right—the angle of her head, the way she held her arms, the expression on her face—as well as doing the steps perfectly.

'See?' she asked.

James was looking at her in amazement. 'Where did you learn to do that? Do you go to ballet classes?'

Lillian sighed. If only. It was her dearest wish.

'No, my best friend Janette does, and she shows me.'

'Well, you're very good at it. It was different again, the second time. You looked like a proper dancer.'

Delight coursed through her. No one had ever said that to her before.

'Really? Do you think so?'

She gazed at him, desperate for approval.

'Yes, but—well, I don't know much about it—'

Of course he didn't. He was a boy and they weren't interested in things like dancing. But he hadn't laughed at her. That was the important thing.

'At least you watch properly. None of my lot do.'

Lillian sighed and squatted down beside the bike as it stood upside down between them. Her sense of the unfairness of life, never very far from the surface, welled up. Here was someone who might understand. 'You're the youngest of your family, aren't you? Don't you think it's horrible being the youngest?'

James appeared to consider this. He adjusted a nut on the rear wheel and gave it a turn, nodding as it ran smoothly.

'I suppose it's different for me. There's only the three of us, and Mum—well, it's hard for her, being a war widow. Susan and me, we've always sort of looked after her as much as she's looked after us. She's not strong, you know. When we were little, she used to go out and do cleaning jobs because what they give her for a pension doesn't go very far. But she always found it very difficult to manage working and seeing to us. Now we're both working she doesn't have to any more. We made her give up the last job she had a year or so ago. If she could have carried on, we might have been able to move to a better flat, but it was making her ill. That's why I left school at fifteen. I had to get out and get earning.'

Lillian understood this. 'Yeah, I've got to leave next year. My gran says education is wasted on girls because we're only going to get married. It's Bob who got to stay till he was sixteen. He's the brains of the family, so they're always saying. He passed his eleven plus, so he got to go to the grammar and get his school certificate and his wonderful job at the bank. You should see him in the morning, making a fuss about his clean collar and his tie and his shoes, like he's the bank manager or something, instead of a clerk. I'm the one who has to do his blooming shoes, not him. He's too important. And Gran looks at him and goes on about at least someone in this family is doing all right. It makes me sick.'

'Boring Bob,' James said.

Their eyes met through the spokes of the bicycle wheel. They both smiled, knowing that the other one felt exactly the same.

'You got it,' Lillian agreed, revelling in the warm glow of understanding. The intimacy of the moment propelled her into further revelations.

'Everything'd be different if my Aunty Eileen was still here. I suppose—like it'd be different for you if your dad hadn't been killed. She used to be on my side. She was lovely.'

'Eileen? Susan's said nothing about an Aunty Eileen,' James said.

'Oh, they never talk about her. She's our black sheep, or at least that's what Gran says. A black sheep, or a viper in the bosom. Isn't that a horrible thing to say about someone—a viper in the bosom?'

'It's from the Bible. But what did she do?'

'She ran away from home when I was six. She went in the middle of the night.'

Lillian sat back her heels, looking back down the years to that bitter night when her aunty had left her.

'She told me she was going to follow her dream, and I didn't know what she meant 'cos I was only a little kid, but later I thought she meant she was going to do something amazing, like being a film star. I was so sure she was going to be a film star that I looked at all the posters outside all the cinemas to see if her picture was there.'

She glanced at him, worried suddenly that he would laugh at her for being so stupid, but there was no hint of it on his face.

'What had happened, then?' he asked.

Lillian hesitated. It was so lovely to talk like this, so seriously, like grown-ups. It was intoxicating just to have him listen to her without making fun. But, however much she was drawn to confide in him, still this was a family secret.

'Promise you won't tell?' she begged.

''Course not.'

'Not even Susan? Only I haven't told anyone, not even my best friend Janette. And Gran'd kill me if she knew.'

'Cross my heart,' James said.

She thought she did see a shadow of a smile then in his eyes, but it was soon gone, and the need to draw him in, to make him a confidant, was too strong for her to resist. She lowered her voice.

'She ran away with one of our guests, one of the regulars, a travelling salesman. Only the thing is, he was a *married man.*'

Which meant that her Aunty Eileen, her wonderful, funny, loving aunty was a wicked woman living in sin. It simply didn't match up with her sunny memories. She felt sick suddenly. She had betrayed her aunty, and all for a moment's attention. She wished with all her heart that she could take the words back, but it was too late now. They were out, and it was all her fault. She wanted to shrivel up into the ground.

James gave a low whistle. 'That was brave of her,' he said.

Lillian stared at him, hardly daring to believe it. It was all right. He understood. It was a miracle. Relief lit up her face.

'It was. You see, she had to do it, 'cos Gran would never have allowed it.'

'No, well, she wouldn't, would she?'

Lillian knew what he meant. To have a family member living in sin was a terrible disgrace ordinarily. But Aunty Eileen was different.

'Like I said, she was following her dream. And I'm going to do the same. I'm going to be a dancer.'

Once again, she wished she had not said it. She couldn't understand what was getting into her, giving away all her closest secrets like this, baring her heart to this boy. This time he really was going to laugh at her. After all, lots of girls wanted to be dancers, but they ended up working in shops and getting married, just like everyone else. No one else could see that inside she knew she was different.

She stole a look at James from under her thick lashes to see what his reaction was. His serious face gave away nothing as he worked at loosening the brake callipers. Then he stood up, turned the bike the right way up and squeezed the brake levers on the handlebars to see if it was all working properly. The pause before he replied seemed like a hundred years to Lillian.

'Well,' he said finally, 'I don't know anything about it, but they do say it's a hard life.'

'I don't care. I'm used to working hard, and it'd be working at doing something I love,' Lillian told him.

James stopped fiddling with the brakes and looked at her. 'That's what makes the difference, isn't it? I don't mind how hard I work when I'm trying to get a car going. But I'm not doing that for someone else all my life, slaving away to make them money. I want a garage of my own.'

Lillian felt quite breathless. He was offering her his secrets.

'Is that your dream?' she asked.

'That's my dream. I'll have a business of my own with people working for me, and a car of my own, and I'll get a decent place for my mum to live with a proper kitchen and bathroom, so nobody can look down their noses at her any more—'

He broke off, gazing over Lillian's shoulder, a rapt look on his face. Where a second ago his attention had been all hers, now it was as if she was no longer there. Slowly, he straightened up.

Lillian didn't have to turn round to know who was there. She was seized with such a storm of rage and jealousy that she thought her chest might burst open. She didn't know where it had come from or how to deal with it. She gritted her teeth and growled, only just stopping herself from leaping up and attacking her fascinating sister with teeth and nails and feet.

Wendy stopped a couple of feet away. Lillian picked up one of James's spanners and started jabbing it into the sour earth for all she was worth. In spite of herself, her eyes were drawn to her sister. Wendy was still dressed in the old skirt and blouse she had been wearing for the spring cleaning, with a spotted scarf over her hair. Anyone else would have looked scruffy and bedraggled after the hard day's work. But Wendy had stopped to apply bright red lipstick to her full mouth, her waist was cinched in with a wide black elastic belt, her blonde curls escaped from beneath the scarf and the blouse was undone at the neck just enough to give a tantalising glimpse of cleavage. She stood with one hand on her hip and flicked James with a cool assessing glance.

'So you came to see to the famous bike, then? She's been going on about it all week.'

'She's made a good job of it. I've just done a bit of maintenance.'

'Yeah, I can see that. Your hands are covered in oil.'

James flushed. 'It's honest dirt. You like men with soft white girly hands, do you?'

Wendy gave a knowing smile. 'I like a man who can take me out dancing and show me a good time.'

'I can dance,' James said.

'They all say that. Then they tread all over your feet. I can't bear being trampled on.'

'No danger of that with me.'

For a moment their eyes locked, each of them challenging the other. It was as if Lillian didn't exist. She wanted to leap up and scream *Look at me!* but something held her squatting by her bike, raging inside.

Wendy raised her eyebrows and turned away. 'I don't think I'll take a chance on it.'

She walked back into the house. James's eyes were fastened on her opulent backside until the door shut behind her. Even then he didn't come back to Lillian immediately. He stood staring at the closed door.

'Idiot!' he muttered. 'What did you go and say that for?'

'What?' Lillian asked.

Slowly, he turned his head to look at her, his eyes seeming to adjust like someone who had just come indoors from bright sunshine outside.

'I went and told her I could dance. I can't, not properly.'

A whole beautiful new vista of opportunity suddenly stretched out before Lillian. She beamed at him.

'I can,' she said. 'I could teach you, if you like.'

CHAPTER 4

THE kid's bike was the perfect excuse to get in with the Parker family. Or, to be more precise, to get closer to Wendy. Wendy filled James's days and haunted his dreams. He had never met a girl like her before, not in real life. She was like something out of a film, what with her luscious body, her lovely face and her exotic natural blonde hair. And then there was the way she treated him. He knew she didn't take him seriously. He was only a few months older than her, and she was looking for men in their twenties with money in their pockets, so he knew she regarded him as a kid who hadn't even started his national service yet. But he was not without hope. There was something in the way she looked at him, a certain challenge in her big blue eyes and her mocking smile, that kept him coming back for more.

So when Lillian announced that she had saved up enough for the tyres and almost enough for the inner tubes, he offered to loan her the rest.

'The weather's getting almost summery. You want to get out on that bike as soon as you can,' he said.

She looked at him in total amazement. 'Would you?' she cried. 'You'd do that for me? Trust me with your money?'

If only it were so easy to please her sister.

''Course,' he said. 'I know you're good for it.'

'Oh!' she gasped. 'You must be the nicest person in the world!'

And as she often did when really pleased, she put her delight into action, crossing the narrow yard in two flick-flacks. James laughed and clapped. It was a pleasure to see her dance or perform gymnastics. She moved with such grace and athleticism that even someone like himself, who knew nothing about it, could see that she was good.

Once the bike was up and running, it was more difficult to find reasons to visit the Parkers. What was more, time was getting short. In July he would be eighteen, and then his call-up papers would arrive. But luck was on his side. He called in after work one Monday with the excuse of making sure that Lillian was managing all right, and found Mrs Parker in despair over the mangle.

'It's stuck,' she explained, practically in tears. 'And we've had PGs in over the weekend and there's all these sheets to get dry.'

She indicated the big galvanised tub full of wet bedlinen.

James had rather overlooked Wendy's mother in the past. There were so many large personalities in the family, what with Wendy herself, and little Lillian, and their old hag of a grandmother, as well as Boring Bob and Shifty Frank, as he thought of them, that Mrs Parker rather faded into the background. He smiled at her as she stood there in her floral overall, her wispy hair tied up turban-style in a scarf and her sleeves rolled up to reveal thin arms and red, work-roughened hands.

'Would you like me to take a look at it for you?' he asked.

Relief flooded her tired face. 'Oh, would you? I'd be ever so grateful.'

It was the work of a moment. Mangles were hardly difficult pieces of machinery to understand. Mrs Parker was so fulsome in her thanks that James was ashamed to earn so much praise for so little.

'Let me turn it for you,' he offered. 'You just feed the stuff in.'

Turning the heavy handle to squeeze the water out of the washing was easy for him, young and strong as he was. In no time the job was done. James carried the basket of damp sheets and towels and pillowcases into an outhouse, ready to be pegged out on the lines in the morning. Just as he had done this, Wendy's father arrived home. He looked at James with suspicion.

'You here again?' he asked.

There was something about the man that irritated James. Maybe it was the apologetic stoop to his shoulders, or the way he always seemed to be looking for a way to get at other people. James supposed he must be bitter about having a crippled right arm and just managed to bite back a sarcastic reply. After all, this was Wendy's father. He needed to keep in with him.

'Oh, Doug,' Mrs Parker said. 'James has been such a help to me. He got my mangle going and everything.' She turned to James with real warmth in her smile and for the first time he saw something of her daughters in her. 'Won't you come in for a cuppa, dear? Kettle's boiling.'

After that, he seemed to be accepted as the fixer of anything mechanical, just as he was at home. Mr Parker couldn't have done these tasks, not with his bad arm, but it amazed him that neither Bob nor Frank seemed capable of doing them. He was glad that they weren't, though. He now had the perfect reason to be calling in at the Parkers' whenever he liked. He soon found out what time Wendy got in from her job at the big department store at the top of the High Street, and timed his arrival to coincide with hers.

Of course, she knew perfectly well what he was up to.

'You're a regular little ray of sunshine, aren't you?' she commented. 'Fixing Gran's glasses, getting the clock going. Whatever would we do without you?'

'I'm sure I could fix something for you, if you let me,' James told her.

Wendy gave him one of her dismissive up-and-down looks. 'I don't think there's anything I need from you, sweetie.' And she teetered elegantly out of the room on her high heels.

Lillian, who always seemed to be around when he was there, launched into a savage take-off. She put her hand on her hip the way Wendy did and looked back over her shoulder with the same don't-touch-me pout.

'*I don't think there's anything I need from you, sweetie,*' she repeated, with exactly Wendy's intonation, and walked to the door with an exaggerated wiggle to her bottom.

Despite his disappointment at the brush-off, James had to laugh. 'You've got her to a T,' he said.

'Huh, she thinks she's so wonderful, but really she's such a cow.'

'Lillian, language!' her mother protested feebly.

'But she is,' Lillian insisted.

Her mother handed her a cup of tea and a plate of biscuits. 'Take these along to your grandmother, there's a good girl.'

Lillian sighed and went. A few minutes later, she came back through the kitchen and out of the back door.

'Got to go and get something for Gran,' she explained as she went.

Her mother hardly seemed to notice.

This was something that James had picked up on since he'd been spending more time at the Parkers'. Lillian hadn't just been whinging when she'd said it was horrible being the youngest. None of her family seemed to speak to her except to tell her off or get her to do something for them. She was forever running around doing errands. It had changed his view of what it was like to be part of a large family. Often when he was young he had yearned to have lots of brothers and sisters like the families he read about in adventure stories. Now he was beginning to realise that, though his family was a bit claustrophobic at times, at least they did all value each other. He certainly wasn't left out like Lillian seemed to be. He brought up the subject with Susan one day.

'Don't you think it's unfair, the way they all treat Lillian?'

His sister looked surprised. 'How do you mean?'

'Well, getting her to do all their jobs for them, like she's was some kind of servant.'

Susan didn't seem to think it was important. 'Oh, she doesn't mind. And it keeps her out of mischief. If she wasn't doing something useful she might be getting into trouble. She's got that wild look about her, don't you think?'

'No, I don't. I think she's rather a nice kid, and she's getting a raw deal from that lot. She does all this stuff for them, but do they do anything for her? No. She cleans your Bob's shoes for him every day, but it wasn't him who helped her with that bike, it was me.'

Susan just laughed. 'Oh, yes, and why did you do that, I wonder? Out of the kindness of your heart, or to get to see Wendy?'

She was right, of course.

'At least I did do it. Now the bike's roadworthy and Lillian can ride it,' he pointed out, not wanting to lose the argument.

He didn't like to admit that he was taking advantage of Lillian's good nature himself. The dancing lessons were a great success. There had been a problem to start with, because both of them wanted to keep it a secret. There was always somebody around at the Parkers' so going there was no good, but then Susan had started going out with Bob on Tuesday evenings as well as at the weekend, which just happened to be when his mother went to her Townswomen's Guild meeting.

'Won't your parents think it's a bit off, you coming round to mine of an evening?' James asked. His mother always wanted to know where Susan was and certainly wouldn't have let her go to an older boy's house when nobody else was there. After all, he knew his intentions were entirely innocent, but the Parkers might not look at it that way.

Lillian just shrugged.

'They won't notice. Or, if they do, I'll say I'm going round my friend Janette's.'

He had to take her word for it. And she was an excellent teacher. They didn't have a record player or much space, but they pushed back the furniture and rolled up the carpet square, then twiddled the tuner of the big Bush wireless till they found some dance music. Lillian showed him the basic steps to the waltz, quickstep and foxtrot, and soon he was moving round the floor with confidence.

'I can do it!' he said, as his feet began to obey the music.

Lillian beamed at him. 'It's fun, isn't it?'

'It is,' he agreed. 'I never thought it would be, but it is.'

She was a strict teacher.

'Don't look at your feet,' she told him. 'Head up—arm higher—elbow out—now glide, glide, don't just walk—think of Fred Astaire!'

'That'll be the day,' James said.

He asked her how she came to learn to dance herself. 'Did you say your friend taught you all this?'

'Yeah, Janette. Her parents have got the newsagent's on the London Road—you know?—and they let her go to lessons, lucky thing.' She sighed. 'She goes to everything—ballet, modern, tap and ballroom. It's so unfair! She's an only child and they let her do everything she wants. I wish I was her.'

James gave one of her plaits a little tug. 'I bet she's a spoilt brat. Not like you,' he said.

Her sharp little face flushed with delight. 'Do you like me?' she breathed.

He was shocked by the longing in her eyes.

'Of course,' he said, feeling uncomfortable. 'You're a good sport. Now, show me again how that reverse turn goes.'

By the beginning of June he felt he knew enough to venture onto the floor at the Kursaal dance hall on the seafront. He spent an evening steering various girls around, managed not to step on anyone's feet or bump into any other couples and even found he enjoyed himself.

'It was fun,' he admitted to Lillian afterwards. 'I think I might get to like this dancing lark. Now, the question is, am I good enough at it to ask Wendy out?'

The dancing lessons had been the highlight of Lillian's life. She could hardly believe her good fortune when James had actually taken her up on her offer. Here was her chance to be really useful to him, to do something for him that nobody else could. She was beside herself with excitement, imagining wafting round a ballroom with him like a film star. More than once she'd got into trouble at school for daydreaming, picturing herself in a wonderful gown, waltzing in James's arms. Mostly she'd managed to banish from her mind the fact that James wanted to do this because Wendy had said she liked men who would take her dancing. When she did remember, it sent her into such a pit of despair and hatred for her sister that she could hardly bear to be in the same room as her.

For once she was pleased that her family took no notice of her, for nobody remarked on her volatile state and nobody questioned where she was off to. But the pressure of all these new emotions was too great to be contained. She'd confided it all to her best friend Janette as they'd sat eating sweets in her pretty pink bedroom in the flat above the newsagent's.

'He's just the most wonderful person in the whole wide world,' she said with a sigh.

'Ooh—' Janette teased. 'Have you got a pash on him?'

'No! It isn't a pash—' Pashes were what first formers got on prefects, or even the young PE teacher. This was far more serious, far more painful. It was taking over her life. But she didn't know what to call it.

'P'raps it's love,' suggested Janette. She reached up to stroke the picture of Frankie Laine that she had cut out of a magazine and pinned on her bedroom wall. 'I'm in love with Frankie. I kiss him every night before I go to sleep.'

'That's only a picture,' Lillian scoffed.

'But he's much more handsome than your precious James,' Janette said, highly offended. 'And he's famous, and he's got a *won*derful voice. When he sings *Answer Me* I know he's singing it just for me.'

She sighed dramatically and gazed at her hero.

'It's not the same,' Lillian insisted. 'The days when I don't see James are like…like…a desert.'

She didn't admit, even to Janette, that she cycled the long way back from school each day just so that she could go down the street where James worked. The garage seemed the most wonderful place in the world, while the smell of petrol was sweeter to her than roses. She never got to see him there, although once she had heard someone call his name. She had waited to see if he appeared, but in the end whoever had called must have gone to seek him out. After hanging about outside the garage, she would cycle down the street where he lived, even though she knew he wasn't there.

'Do you think he's interested in you?' Janette asked.

'I don't know,' Lillian said miserably. 'He can be so kind, but—'

Burnt into her memory was the time when he had said she was a 'good sport'. Sometimes she managed to convince herself that this was a compliment, but mostly it brought her close to tears, for she knew in her heart that it was a brush-off.

She slid off the bed and went to study herself in the looking-glass above Janette's dressing table, adjusting the triple mirrors so that she could see all round. She twisted this way and that, hoping in vain to find someone more exotic than a fourteen-year-old girl with long thin legs and white ankle socks. Her skinny body was beginning to fill out a little. She had small rounded breasts and a proper waist. She dug her hands in above her bony hips to emphasize the curves, but she knew she looked nothing like Wendy. Wendy's vital statistics were a perfect 36-24-36, even before she wriggled into her elastic roll-on.

She undid the rubber bands at the ends of her plaits, shook

her hair out and gathered it up on top of her head, trying to look more sophisticated.

'D'you think I'm pretty?' she asked.

''Course,' Janette said loyally.

But Lillian turned away and flopped down on the bed, tears welling in her eyes.

'It's not fair,' she wailed. 'I'm never going to be as pretty as Wendy. You're just so lucky, being an only child.'

That had been last week, and now here was James asking if he was a good enough dancer to ask Wendy out. Lillian couldn't believe that something could hurt so much. It made her want to cry out loud.

'You—you don't really want to, do you?' she managed to ask.

James laughed, as if it was some sort of joke.

'But of course! That's the whole point. I've got to do it before I have to go off to national service. Now, come on, what do you think? You're her sister. Do you think I've got a chance?'

Lillian was torn. The last thing she wanted was for Wendy to get her claws into him, but neither did she want him to stop coming to their house.

'I dunno,' she muttered.

'You must have some sort of an idea,' James insisted.

Goaded, Lillian burst out with the truth. 'If you must know, I think you're much too nice for her. She only likes spivvy types with cars and patent leather shoes.'

'A car!' James was looking at her as if she had just handed him the Crown jewels. 'If she likes blokes with cars, then I'm her man.'

'You haven't got a car,' Lillian said.

'No, but I can get hold of one.'

'I didn't know you had a driving licence.'

'I don't, but who's going to ask? I can drive all right. Lillian, you're a genius! I'll come round your place and ask Wendy if she wants to go for a spin.'

Lillian wanted to cut her tongue out. Whatever had made her mention cars? That night she cried herself to sleep, convinced that all was lost.

Two days later, she happened to be in her grandmother's room at just about the time Wendy was due home from work. Gran's main occupation, apart from smoking and reading the newspaper, was making hooked rugs. Since wool was expensive, it was one of Lillian's jobs to go to jumble sales and find handknitted garments in the colours that Gran wanted for her projects. Now she was busy unravelling last Saturday's finds and winding them into hanks to be washed before use. Out of the corner of her eye, she saw a vehicle stop outside their house and turned to look. Gran was immediately on the alert. Plenty of delivery vans pulled up in their road, but only one family owned a car.

'What's that car doing by our front door? It's not that dreadful man that your sister wanted to go out with last week, is it? Go and look.'

Lillian did as she was told, pulling aside the net curtain so that she could see better. There at the kerbside was a smart black Morris, and inside it...

'It's James,' she said, unable to keep the distress out of her voice. He had done it. He had got a car to impress Wendy with.

'James? James who?'

'James Kershaw. Bob's Susan's brother,' Lillian explained.

'What's he doing here with a car?'

Gran's heavy footsteps thudded across the room. She leaned over Lillian's shoulder. As she did so, James got out of the car and looked up the road. Craning her neck, Lillian saw her sister walking towards him. Her heart thudded so hard in her chest that she could hardly breathe. James was leaning against the car as if he owned it. Wendy came to a stop beside him, looking it over. Lillian strained to hear what they were saying, but it was impossible with Gran keeping up a running commentary right by her ear.

'What's going on out there? What's he up to? I'll give her a piece of my mind, standing there as bold as brass in the street like that talking to a young man...'

Gran rapped on the window with her knuckles. James and Wendy both looked up, then Wendy walked down the street to the alleyway, leaving James staring after her. Something about the slump of his shoulders gave Lillian hope.

'Go and tell her to come in here,' Gran demanded.

Lillian went to meet her sister at the back door.

'Gran wants to see you. She wants to know what you were doing out there with James,' she gabbled.

Wendy cast her eyes to heaven. 'She needn't worry. I wouldn't be seen dead out with a kid like that, even if he has got hold of a car.' Muttering with irritation, she went off to obey the summons.

Lillian spun round and round, hugging herself with joy. James was safe! James was still hers! Everything was well with the world.

Or at least it was for a day or so. James did not appear at the house again. More days dragged by, long, achingly dull days with no James in them.

'What exactly did you say to him?' Lillian demanded of her sister.

Wendy examined her perfect nails. 'Oh, I told him to sling his hook.'

Two weeks went by, then three. The summer visitors were

flooding into the town now, and Lillian was kept busy help-ing her mother prepare bedrooms. But nothing could keep her heart from yearning to see James again. June turned into July. Susan announced that her brother's call-up papers had arrived. Lillian could bear it no longer.

'He is going to stop by and say goodbye to us, isn't he?'

'Oh, I expect so,' Susan said.

'Will you ask him to?' Lillian insisted.

'Stop nagging, Lill. Susan's got better things to do than pass on messages for you,' Bob told her.

Susan patted his arm. 'It's all right. I don't mind. I think James has got a bit of a soft spot for your little sister.'

Lillian could have kissed her.

For the next three days she lived in a state of nervous ex-citement. And then, when she had almost given up hope, there he was at the back door.

'James!' she squealed, leaping up and running to meet him. 'I thought you weren't coming.'

She just about stopped herself from throwing her arms round him.

'Oh, well—you know—couldn't go without saying good-bye,' he said.

As bad luck would have it, all the family were home and sitting in the kitchen having tea. Lillian could hardly get a word in as Bob and Frank vied to give James advice on how to survive his basic training. And then it was over, and he was shaking everyone's hand. When he got to Lillian he tugged at her plait and gave her a quick wink.

'Don't let them get you down, eh?' he whispered.

She nodded, too close to tears to speak. It might be weeks before she saw him again. The back door closed behind him, and he was gone.

Desperate to be alone, Lillian went down the yard to the shed where she kept her bike, the bike that he had helped to fix. As her eyes adjusted to the dim light, she cried out in amazement. There was a note propped up on the saddle. As she snatched it up, she realised that the saddle itself was different. The saggy old thing covered in a beret had been changed for a brand new one, red and black to match the paintwork. Lillian scanned the note, almost too excited to take in the contents.

Thanks for all the dance lessons. Good luck. J.

Lillian clasped it to her chest.

James had done this for her, had taken the trouble to think of what she really needed and quietly fitted it on without making a fuss in front of her family. Life was worth living after all.

CHAPTER 5

LILLIAN cycled along the seafront with the wind in her hair. The tide was in, the sun was sparkling on the water and the seagulls were soaring in the blue sky. It was a warm July Saturday and everyone had their summer clothes on, the women in cotton dresses and straw hats, the men in short sleeves and open-necked shirts. Everyone seemed to have a smile on their face. Everyone but Lillian, whose heart was broken.

The summer season was practically at its height. Not so many people came to Southend for a whole week any more, but the day trippers were out in force. After years of war and then of austerity, people were sick of rations and restrictions and making do and general dreariness. It was a new age, there was a new young queen on the throne, and they wanted to have fun again. Hundreds of families came down the Thames on steamers, landed at Southend pier and streamed down its mile and a quarter to spread out along the seafront. Others came by train from the City or the East End. The quieter people got out at Leigh or Chalkwell or Westcliff, looking for more genteel pleasures. The rowdy ones stayed on for Southend and headed for the Golden Mile. Clubs and workplaces booked coaches which trundled down the main roads, stopping off at pubs along the way, till they arrived at the huge coach park behind the Golden Mile, their passengers happily drunk and ready for a good knees-up.

As she approached her own street, Lillian slowed down. She had already cycled all the way along the seafront to Shoebury and back and she ought to turn in and go home. But at Sunny View there was Gran and a whole list of chores. She couldn't face it. She hated her family and she hated doing chores. Past the top of her road she went, past the Kursaal with its fairground and its dance hall and its famous dome, along the Golden Mile and all the amusement arcades and finally under the pier and out the other side. Here she stopped at last and treated herself to an ice cream.

She leaned on the rail at the edge of the promenade and looked down at the go-karts roaring round the speedway. The whiff of petrol and exhaust fumes set off a wave of longing.

'Oh, James,' she said with a sigh.

She was missing him so much. He was a month into his basic training now, and it had seemed like the longest month of her life. Nothing was fun any more. Nobody cared. Even Janette was fed up with hearing her talk about him and refused to listen any more.

'Why don't you write to me?' she said out loud.

She still hoped against all logic that he would, but always she was sorely disappointed. She had to rely on Susan, begging her for news of her brother every time she came round to their house. Bob was often cross with her, telling her not to bother his girlfriend, but Susan was surprisingly nice.

'He says he's surviving it OK,' she told Lillian. 'He's not letting the NCOs get him down.'

Or, 'He's been square-bashing all week and he's got blisters, but at least he knows his left from his right, which is more than some of them do.'

Or, 'He's enjoying the rifle practice; he says he's quite good at it.'

Always he sent his regards to the Parker family. The family, not Lillian personally. It hurt every time.

There was still another two weeks until he finished basic training and got a weekend pass. Would he call in at Sunny View? He had to. She couldn't bear it if he was so close and she didn't get to see him. A small cold voice of realism told her that he might well come to see Wendy. She gripped the handrail, growling with jealousy. It wasn't fair! Why couldn't she be beautiful like Wendy?

Below her, the young men running the speedway showed off, jumping on the side bumpers of the cars driven by pretty girls and flirting with them. All these people enjoying themselves. For her, summer only meant more work to do at Sunny View. She finished her ice cream and sighed deeply. She didn't want to go home, but staying here was only making her feel more fed up.

She drew her eyes away from the speedway and looked at the pier pavilion with its theatre. A long banner advertised the summer show, with its singers and dancers. Dancers. An even deeper gloom settled on her. That was another thing. She was no nearer her dream of becoming a professional dancer. Then into her mind came something that James had said when they were discussing their futures.

'It's no good just waiting for fate to take its course; you have to do something yourself.'

'I am,' she had told him. 'I practise every day.'

'But that's no use if nobody sees you but me and Janette. We're not going to give you a job on the stage.'

Lillian had flared up at that, and asked him what he was doing towards becoming the owner of a garage with a car of his own.

'At the moment I'm learning all I can, not just how to fix cars, but how to run the business. There's all sorts of things that could be done better where I work,' he told her. 'Then I'll try to get into REME when I do my national service and get a bit more training there, and when I come out I'm going to start doing repair work for people on Sundays and evenings and build up a list of customers while I save up for equipment. Then I'll rent a small place and work my way up.'

Lillian had been very impressed. He really did have it all planned out. His was not just a dream, it was a real ambition. It made hers look like childish fantasy.

As she thought of this, her eye was caught by a poster with a dancer on it fixed to the railings just along from where she was leaning. She moved over to read it better.

Carnival Talent Contest—Children—Juniors—Adults—Big Prizes—Enter now!

A bubble of excitement formed inside Lillian. This was it! This was her chance to show what she could do! She grabbed her bike and pedalled up the steep hill to the Carnival offices to get an entry form, then freewheeled back down again and headed for home, her head buzzing with ideas of what she might do.

The moment she stepped in at the back door, she was in trouble. Bob was sitting at the kitchen table, studying for his banking exam.

'Gran wants to see you,' he said in a tone that made it sound like a threat.

Her confident mood evaporated. It was as if a heavy cloak had fallen over her shoulders, weighing her down, smothering her. Lillian went along to the front room and knocked. Gran didn't even call for her to come in, she opened the door herself.

'Where on earth have you been? Why are you never here when you're needed?'

'I...I didn't know...' Lillian stammered.

'That's no excuse. Your mother's ill or something—' Gran managed to imply that the illness was minor and probably imaginary '—and the sheets need to go on number five. What if we want to let that and it's not ready? Go and see to it straight away.'

It was no use Lillian suggesting that someone else might have done it. Wendy was still at work; Frank was probably out, Bob was studying and of course Gran herself couldn't do it. She was about to run upstairs when there was a ring at the front door. She hesitated. Usually she would have hurried to answer it, but Gran was just as near as she was and, as it was sure to be potential guests, she would want to look them over.

'What are you standing there for?' Gran demanded. 'Go and answer it before they go away. We can't afford to lose good money.'

Lillian did as she was bid. Standing on the doorstep were a young couple with a cheap suitcase each. The girl looked very nervous. She was half hiding behind the man. Lillian knew immediately what their fate would be but, with Gran listening to what she was saying, she didn't dare suggest politely that they tried elsewhere.

'If you'd like to come in, I'll just fetch the landlady,' she told them, using the formula that Gran required.

She put her head round Gran's door again, informed her that there were guests to see her and set off to get the sheets out of the airing cupboard. As she went up the stairs, she heard Gran's heavy footsteps crossing the hall floor and her icy voice.

'Are you married?'

The man answered, sounding offended. 'Yeah, 'course we are.'

'You don't look like it. Where's your wedding certificate?'

'At home, ain't it? We don't carry it around with us,' the man said.

'I don't have any funny business going on under my roof.'

'Here, what are you saying? You calling me a liar?'

The man sounded really truculent now. Lillian opened the airing cupboard door as quietly as she could, so that she didn't miss anything.

'I'm saying I have a right to say who I have using my rooms.'

The young woman spoke now, her voice squeaky with fear. 'Come on, Pete, let's leave it.'

'No, I'm not bleeding leaving it. This old bat thinks we're here for a dirty weekend. Bleeding cheek!'

'I will not be sworn at. Kindly leave.'

Lillian leaned over the banisters. She could see the top of the young couple's heads. The woman was edging towards the open door.

'Please, Pete—'

'Don't worry, love. I wouldn't stay here if you paid me. The cheek! I never heard the like. Come along, we'll find somewhere what's pleased to take our money.'

'This is a respectable house,' was Gran's parting shot, before she closed the door behind them.

Lillian changed the bedlinen in room five, making crisp

hospital corners as she had been taught, then ran up to the attic and tapped on the door of her parents' room. Her mum was often what she called 'a bit under the weather' but she very rarely took to her bed, especially not on a Saturday, their busiest day.

'Mum?'

She peeped round the door. Her mother was lying curled up in the high double bed. The green curtains were drawn, giving her face a ghostly tinge.

'Mum, are you all right? Can I get you anything?'

Her mother opened her eyes a little. 'Does your gran want me?' She sounded very tired.

'No, no, it's all right. I've done number five, and I can do tea if you like. What's the matter, Mum? Has the doctor been?'

'No, no, it's just—you know—women's troubles.'

Lillian did know about women's troubles now, but hers had not yet caused her to take to her bed.

'D'you want a cuppa or anything?'

'No, nothing. I just want to sleep.'

She closed her eyes again. Lillian crept away. It didn't even occur to her to wish that she had a mother she could confide in, someone whom she could share her hopes with and consult about what she might do for the talent contest. Her mother had always been too tired or too busy to give her any attention. But oh, if only Aunty Eileen were still around…

The rest of the afternoon passed in a flurry of work. Two more lots of guests arrived, passed Gran's stringent suitability test, were told the house rules and were shown their rooms. Lillian got on with buttering the bread and setting the table so that tea was ready for when for Dad and Wendy came in from work and Frank turned up from wherever he had been.

After tea she had the washing-up and clearing away to do. Wendy was supposed to help her, but she was getting ready for a date.

Lillian was dying to rush round to Janette's, tell her about the contest and sift through her pile of records to find a suitable one to perform to. But with Mum in bed and Wendy and the boys going out, there was nobody left but herself to make tea and cocoa, answer the door to any late guests and see to anything Gran might want. Lillian spent the evening humming tunes and trying out steps. A fast happy song or a slow dreamy one? Tap or ballet? She just couldn't make her mind up. And then there was the question of what she was going to wear. It was all a lot more complicated than she had first thought. One thing was clear, though, she now had something to prove to James that she was just as serious as he was about achieving her aim.

On Sunday morning her mother was on her feet again, though looking far from well, but Lillian still had to help prepare the breakfasts for the PGs, clear away and wash up afterwards and strip their beds when they had left. Then there was Sunday lunch, with more washing-up and the cooker to clean.

'Horrible, horrible thing!' she growled, scrubbing grease from the inside of the oven.

It was nearly three in the afternoon before she finally made it round to Janette's, and by then she was just bursting with impatience.

Her friend was thrilled with the idea of entering the talent contest.

'You are brave! I like doing shows with the dancing school, but I couldn't get up there and dance in front of judges.'

'It's a way to get noticed,' Lillian said.

'Won't your family mind?'

This had been bothering Lillian. There was no danger of their going to the contest but, if she won, she would be in the local paper. She couldn't imagine what the reaction would be.

'I'm not going to think about that,' she said. 'Let's decide what music I should choose.'

It took two days of constant mind-changing before she finally decided on *We're a Couple of Swells*. The music was jaunty but not too fast and gave her an opportunity to put some gymnastics into the dance. She and Janette cobbled together bits of routines Janette had learnt at her classes with new ideas of Lillian's that had been inspired by trips to the cinema and the variety shows she had watched on Janette's parents' television.

'It's no good trying to look like Grace Kelly or someone like that. My dance teacher says people like young girls to look like young girls, not sophisticated women. You need to be fresh and lively. People like lively. It makes them feel happy,' Janette said.

Lillian had to take her word for it.

'More like Petula Clark?' she suggested.

'Sort of. The gymnastics are good. They're your strong point. Nobody at my class can do cartwheels and handsprings and stuff as well as you.'

So they all went in.

Costume was easier—Lillian could get into Janette's pink taffeta party dress and her last year's ballet shoes, so all she needed was a pair of frilly knickers to wear underneath.

'Do I look all right? Isn't it a bit babyish?' she asked anxiously, peering at herself in Janette's mirror.

'It's very pretty,' Janette said, offended.

Lillian filled in her form and paid her entrance fee. She

came away from the Carnival offices feeling rather sick. She was committed now. It wasn't just a pipe dream; she really was going to get up there in front of people and perform. All she had to do now was to buy the sheet music for the pianist and practise until her dance was perfect.

James was due home the weekend before the carnival. Lillian stayed in all day on Saturday on the off-chance that he might call in. She whiled away the time practising her dance routine, but by late afternoon she couldn't stand being inside any longer and went out into the yard to oil her bike. After all, James had told her to maintain it properly, and she didn't want him to think she had been neglecting it.

She was busy pumping up the tyres, all the while keeping her ear tuned to any possible visitors to the house, when there was a pounding of footsteps in the back alleyway. Lillian looked up as Frank came crashing through the gate clutching a bundle wrapped in sacking. He dived into the shed, shuffled around a bit and then came out again without the bundle.

'If anyone asks, you ain't seen me, right?' he said to Lillian.

'Yeah, but—'

'Ain't seen me all day. You got that?'

'Right.'

'Mind you remember. It's life or death.'

At that, he disappeared out of the back gate again and could be heard running northwards, away from the seafront. Lillian was about to go and investigate the bundle when she heard men's voices coming from the other direction.

'Which is his one?'

'They all look the same.'

'Count—his is the sixth one up.'

The tall back gate wobbled and opened to reveal three young men in Edwardian-style jackets, bootlace ties and drainpipe jeans. They sported long sideburns and their hair was brushed back in James Dean quiffs. When they caught sight of Lillian they stopped and stared for a moment. Lillian looked stonily back, trying to control a lurch of fear. Teddy boys! They might look very smart, but they had a bad reputation. They always went around in gangs and usually carried knuckle dusters and flick knives.

'You Frank Parker's sister?' one demanded. He appeared to be the leader. The other two just stood there looking tough.

Lillian nodded.

'Where is he?'

Lillian swallowed. They did look very threatening. 'Dunno.'

'He indoors?'

'No.'

'You sure? Only he was heading up this way.'

They took a couple of steps towards her. Lillian stood up. Life or death, that was what Frank had said. He might be a pain, but he was her brother.

'I ain't seen him all day.'

It came out without a wobble. Lillian was proud of herself. The three men looked unconvinced.

'I been out here doing my bike for half an hour or more,' she elaborated. 'So I'd of seen him come in. We always use the back.'

'You're not lying, are you?' the leader asked.

All three of them pressed forward, surrounding her. Their faces were menacing. The leader pushed her in the chest with his hard fingers.

'Only you better not be lying. We don't like liars.'

One of them picked up her bike. 'This yours?'

Anger laced with fear came flooding through her. 'Don't you touch that! I ain't done nothing to you.'

The young man laughed and heaved it over the fence, where it landed in next door's yard with a clatter.

'You pig! You better not of damaged it!' Lillian cried.

What would James say if he found it was broken?

The leader poked her again. Lillian's heart beat with fear.

'That's just a warning. If we find out you're lying, you'll be over that fence next, see? Now, where's Frank?'

'I dunno!' Lillian repeated desperately.

She tried to turn and run inside, but one of the Teds grabbed her and spun her round to face the leader.

'You leave her alone!' A new voice rang out.

There was a blur of khaki and a smack of fist on flesh. First one then the other Ted yelped and Lillian found herself released.

'James!'

For it was him, in his uniform and very angry.

The third Ted, the one who had thrown her bike over the fence, yelled, 'Blimey, it's the army!'

James landed two more punches on the leader.

'Yeah, and you better scarper before my mates get out here. They'll make mincemeat of you,' he threatened.

For a long nerve-stretching moment, Lillian thought the Teds might set on James with bicycle chains or flick knives. James made a move towards the third one. It broke the deadlock. All three turned and ran.

Lillian's legs turned suddenly to string. She staggered and James caught her in his arms.

'Lillian, are you all right? What was all that about?'

'Where's your friends?' Lillian asked stupidly.

'What? Oh, there aren't any. I didn't want them to think it was three to one. Lillian, what's going on?'

Shakily, Lillian managed to explain.

'I don't think much of the company your brother keeps,' James said. 'Come on, let's get you inside.'

For once in her life, Lillian was the centre of attention.

'Oh, Lillian, thank God—' her mother gasped. 'Those dreadful Teddy boys—sit down, sit down—'

She found herself sitting at the kitchen table, clasped in her mother's arms.

'Hot sweet tea, that's what she needs for shock,' James was saying.

Susan filled the kettle. 'Did you take them on all by yourself?' she asked her brother.

'He did. There were three of them; they were looking for Frank,' Lillian explained.

'I don't know what the world's coming to, really I don't,' her mother wailed.

Gran appeared, alerted by the raised voices. 'What's going on here?'

Everyone tried to explain at once.

Gran laid a hand on Lillian's shoulder. 'You all right, girl?' she asked gruffly.

Lillian nodded. It was the first time she had ever been shown any concern from her grandmother.

'That boy; he's heading for trouble,' Gran stated. 'I'll have a few words to say to him when he gets home.'

A cup of hot sweet tea was put in front of Lillian. She sipped it, basking in her temporary star status.

Gran was fulminating about Frank bringing the family in disrepute while Bob agreed with her. Susan distributed more tea.

'What did they want Frank for, I wonder?' James said.

With a jolt, Lillian remembered the bundle. What was it, that caused so much trouble? And was it still in the shed? She wanted to go and look but, when she made to get up, James pressed her down into her chair again.

'You just stay there.'

And then she thought of something else. 'My bike! Have they damaged my bike?'

'I'll check in a minute. If they have, I'll mend it,' James assured her.

Nettie looked up at him. 'You saved my little girl,' she said. 'I'll never be able to thank you enough.'

By the time Dad and Wendy arrived home, James was the official hero of the hour.

'Fought them off single-handed, he did,' Nettie said.

'If I'd have known what was going on, I would have been there with him,' Bob explained.

'Of course you would, dear,' Susan agreed.

Even Wendy looked mildly impressed.

Everyone wanted to know all about James's basic training, and he kept them all entertained with stories of the hardships he had survived until Susan reminded him that their mother was making him a special meal.

'Nothing skimped now rationing's over,' she boasted.

And he was gone. Lillian had been rescued by him, but had had no chance to speak to him and tell him about what she was doing towards making her dream come true. It was very poor compensation to hear Frank getting a rollicking from Gran when he finally made an appearance close to bedtime.

CHAPTER 6

THE Wednesday of the talent contest was wet and windy. Janette came to call for Lillian and they cycled along the gusty seafront in their school macs carrying the party dress, ballet shoes and sheet music plus make-up that Lillian had stolen from the messy cache in Wendy's side of the chest of drawers. They were heading for the bandstand, which was at the top of the cliff gardens on the far side of the pier from where Lillian lived. As they went, Lillian kept her nerves at bay by telling her friend all about her brush with the Teddy boys and James's heroic rescue. Janette was awestruck.

'Weren't you terrified?' she asked, her bike wobbling as she gazed at Lillian.

'You bet I was! I thought they were going to pull me to pieces. They don't care, you know. They don't care about anything, Teds don't.'

'But what was in the bundle?'

'I don't know,' Lillian admitted. 'When I went back to have a look later, it was gone. Frank must've sneaked in and got it some time in the evening, 'cos he didn't come home properly till gone eleven. I think he thought everyone'd be in bed by then. Well, usually they are, but Gran and Dad stayed up. He didn't half get a telling off from them, I can tell you.'

'Serves him right.'

'Do you know something? He had a go at me the next day about it! Said I should of kept quiet about it with the family! I said to him, "You owe me, Frank. I didn't say anything to the Teds, and I didn't tell Gran and Dad about that stuff you hid and, if James hadn't come along, I'd of been chucked over the fence and landed on top of my bike." But he wasn't a bit grateful.'

'The beast,' Janette sympathised. 'But what a bit of luck, James arriving just at that moment.'

'Wasn't it?' Lillian agreed. The biggest bit of luck she'd had for a long time. The trouble was, she was going to have to live on that memory now, for she had seen nothing more of James that weekend. According to Susan, he had gone out with his friends on the Saturday night, stayed in for Sunday lunch with the family the next day and had set off back for Catterick by late afternoon. Now it would be another long, long six months before he got any more leave.

They had no breath left for talking as they laboured up Pier Hill, and from there it was only a short spin along the cliff top past the Never Never Land gardens to the band stand. The building was oval shaped, with a covered stage facing away from the sea and covered seating on three sides. In the centre was a large seating area open to the weather where on nice days people sat in the sunshine to enjoy the concerts and look at the view through the glass walls.

By the time Lillian and Janette arrived they were wet and dishevelled. Everyone else seemed to have come with their mothers, and the place was awash with loud-voiced women chivvying their children and insisting on somewhere decent to change. Lillian and Janette found the harassed-looking organisers and asked what they had to do.

'Who did you say you were, dear? Lindy-Lou Parker? Oh, yes. And you're doing what? Dancing? Have you got your music? You're number eleven on the running order. Off you go round the back there and get changed, then someone will tell you where to sit until it's your turn.'

Janette was snorting with laughter as they walked away.

'Lindy-Lou? Where does that come from?'

'It's what my Aunty Eileen used to call me,' Lillian told her.

'But you were only six then.'

'All the same, it's better than Lillian. More sort of stagey.'

'More sort of babyish, if you ask me.'

Still arguing, they found a damp corner of the cramped room beside the stage. Lillian stepped into the taffeta dress. As a party dress it would have been much too short for her, but it was fine for dancing as it showed off her long slim legs.

'You should have tights on underneath really, but your legs are nice and brown, so perhaps it won't notice,' Janette said.

'I did them with gravy browning, like they used to during the war. You don't think they'll go streaky in the rain, do you?' Lillian asked.

'Keep them covered, just in case.'

The night before, Lillian had borrowed some of Wendy's setting lotion, combed it through her hair, then made it into six tight little plaits. Now she unplaited them and brushed the now crinkly hair into two bunches, which she tied up with pink ribbons.

'What d'you think?' she asked.

Janette put her head to one side, considering. 'Well…'

Lillian's confidence plummeted. 'You think it's horrible,' she accused.

'No—'

Lillian peered into the hand mirror she had brought with her.

'You're right, it is horrible. Oh, if only Aunty Eileen were here, she'd of done it beautifully for me.'

'Well, she isn't, so it'll have to do,' said her practical friend. 'Sit down, and I'll do your make-up.'

Lillian submitted to Janette's efforts with the powder and lipstick. Once more, Lillian looked in the mirror.

'I look like a doll!' she exclaimed, horrified.

'It's stage make-up. It has to be like that,' Janette insisted.

Lillian looked about her. Some of the pushy mothers were applying real greasepaint to their little dears' faces. All of the performers looked like badly painted dolls. Reluctantly, she accepted Janette's word for it. After all, Janette had performed in dancing school shows. For all her ambitions, Lillian had never set foot on a stage before.

The time for the start of the competition drew near. The competitors were herded off into seats alongside the stage while the mothers and Janette had to sit in a different part of the bandstand. Day trippers and holidaymakers out for some entertainment huddled in the sheltered seats and the four judges sat at the table at the centre back. There was a huge gap of empty seats in the middle where nobody wanted to sit in the rain. A compère with an over-jolly voice came on and made a couple of feeble jokes, introduced the judges and the pianist, and the contest began.

First on was a boy of twelve or so who played *The Happy*

Wanderer on the accordion. He got a decent smattering of applause and went off again looking fairly pleased with himself. Next came a lumpy girl in a short frilly dress and ringlets who sang *On The Good Ship Lollipop* in a shrill voice. The girl sitting next to Lillian leaned close and commented, 'There's always someone who does Shirley Temple. Isn't she dreadful?'

'Ghastly,' Lillian agreed.

Nerves were really getting to her now. She felt sick and her hands and legs were shaking. Whatever had made her think that this was a good idea?

Two girls dressed up as twins went next and did a tap dance. Lillian couldn't really see them from where she was sitting, but she could hear that they weren't entirely in step.

'That was pretty crummy,' the girl beside her commented.

One by one the competitors went up. Singers, dancers, a conjurer, a violinist. Then it was the turn of the scornful girl next to Lillian. As she got up, Lillian started trying to warm up. It was difficult in such a restricted space. She could hear the girl singing *Oh My Papa* in a big brash voice. It was quite a crowd-pleaser, bringing in the most applause there had been yet. Lillian had a feeling of doom in her stomach like a stone. How was she going to follow that? It was obvious that the girl had been having lessons for ever and made a habit of going in for talent contests. She wished she could just run out of this place and keep running. But a motherly-looking woman with a clipboard was beckoning to her. Shaking, Lillian walked towards her. This was it.

'And next—' boomed the compère, 'we have little Miss Lindy-Lou Parker dancing to *We're a Couple of Swells.*'

The woman with the clipboard gave Lillian a little push. 'Go on, dear, it's you.'

Lillian took a deep breath and stepped onto the stage.

There was a smattering of applause. It seemed very high up and exposed, and the audience was an impossibly long way away, sheltering at the back. Facing her were rows of wet unoccupied chairs. Lillian wanted to jump off the stage and crawl underneath them.

But then the pianist struck the opening notes, thumping the piano with unforgiving fingers, and something happened to Lillian's body. The music, pedestrian though it was, told her what to do. She performed a perky stroll round the stage and launched into the routine she had practised with such persistence. The steps, the turns, the arm movements ran seamlessly one into the other. She began to actually enjoy herself. The smile she had pasted on her face became genuine as she projected her joy in dancing to the people huddled at the back at the bandstand. Before she could believe it, the last phrase was rolling out. Lillian executed a series of pirouettes, turned a perfect cartwheel and dropped into the splits on the last chord. She bowed and looked up, still with her legs splayed on the floor of the stage. They were clapping! They were clapping her! She bounced up and bowed again. There was more applause. This was wonderful. They liked her. She wanted it to go on for ever.

'Thank you, Lindy-Lou,' the compère was saying. 'Thank you. Off you go, now.'

He was ushering her off the stage. There was a sniggering from the wings. Lillian saw the next child waiting to come on and realised that she had outstayed her welcome. Scarlet with embarrassment, she ran off.

On the other side of the stage from where she had been waiting to go on, the competitors who had already performed were penned up together. The *Oh My Papa* girl spoke to her with grudging respect.

'Sounds like you were quite good,' she said. 'Better than most of this lot, anyway.'

'You were smashing,' Lillian said politely. 'You've got a—a big voice.'

'My teacher says I'm going to be the next Anne Shelton,' the girl said.

Lillian could believe it. The famous singer must have sounded similar when she was young.

As the excitement of performing drained away, Lillian found she was cold and hungry. She sat shivering as the long list of young people did their turns. The crowd in the seats on her side of the stage grew and grew. The scornful girl continued her commentary on everyone's efforts. Lillian had time to wonder how Janette was, waiting out there in the damp with all those mothers. And then at last it was over and the compère was telling jokes as the judges made up their minds. Nerves were gnawing at Lillian's stomach again. She chewed her knuckles. She really, really wanted to win a prize. First prize, preferably, but anything would do, just some recognition that she could do it, she could be a dancer if she tried hard enough.

'I can't bear it, this waiting,' she said to the girl next to her.

'They always make such a to-do about the judging. I don't know why, when it's obvious who's best.'

'It is? Who is?' Lillian asked.

The girl gave her a pitying look. 'Me, of course, stupid.'

'Bighead,' Lillian muttered.

Then the pianist played a fanfare and the carnival queen and her court came onto the stage to huge applause to present the prizes. A photographer from the local paper got ready to snap the winners. The head judge handed a piece of paper to the compère.

'Right then, ladies and gentlemen, boys and girls. Here are the results in reverse order. Highly commended—'

Two names were read out. Part of Lillian was disappointed, another part was still hopeful of even better things.

'Third prize—'

It was the accordion boy. He bounded up onto the stage, beaming all over his chubby face. Lillian felt she was going to burst with suspense.

Please, God, she bargained silently, *please let it be me. I'll be good for the rest of my life.*

'Second prize—Lindy-Lou Parker.'

It was her. They were saying her name. Lillian just sat there, confounded.

'Go on,' her neighbour said, poking her. 'That's you. You're second.'

Her head swimming with amazement, Lillian stood up. Somehow she made her way onto the stage. There was a polite round of applause. She walked across to the carnival queen, an impossibly glamorous young woman in a long white gown and a blue cloak with a crown of what to Lillian looked like sparkling diamonds on her head. Lillian curtseyed, which made some of the court ladies giggle.

'Well done, dear,' the queen said, handing her an envelope. 'Smile for the camera.'

She was directing a brilliant smile at the photographer. Giddy with delight, Lillian did the same. There was a flash, and then it was over. Once again, she was being ushered off stage. There was a shriek from the audience.

'Lillian! We done it! We done it!'

There, in front of the mothers' seats, was Janette, jumping up and down and waving both arms over her head. Lillian squealed and managed to wave back before she was grabbed and pushed into the wings. Somewhere behind her the winner was announced. It was the *Oh My Papa* girl. Lillian didn't care. She had got a prize! The judges thought she was good. She was really going to be a dancer one day. It was all just too wonderful to be true.

All the way home the girls went over every detail of the contest, but at Lillian's house they parted and Janette went on her way. Lillian was still buzzing with her success as she pushed her bike through the back gate. She did a couple of handsprings as she crossed the yard, out of sheer exuberance. As ill luck would have it, Gran was in the kitchen when she arrived, checking the state of the shelves.

'Time you grew up, young lady,' she said. 'Kicking your legs up in public like that. What would the neighbours think if they saw you?'

Any lingering hope Lillian might have had that her family might be interested, let alone pleased at her success, instantly died.

'Sorry, Gran,' she said.

'And what's all that muck on your face?'

'Oh!' Lillian's hand went to her cheek. In the excitement, she had forgotten to wipe the make-up off. 'Er—Janette and I were playing about with her mum's make-up. Her mum doesn't mind.'

'She ought to mind. Letting a young girl go out looking like a scarlet woman! Go and wash it off at once. And then you can go and get a loaf and a pound of streaky bacon. We're full tonight.'

Lillian had been too self-absorbed to notice the 'No Vacancies' sign up in the front window. Carnival week was the busiest of the year. There were two processions, one on Saturday and a torchlight one on Wednesday evening, a funfair at

Chalkwell park, dances and dinners on somewhere in the town every evening and various competitions and displays. It was no wonder they were full mid-week.

'That's good,' she said.

'Seems people have got money to waste,' Gran commented with a sniff of disapproval.

Lillian did not hang around to point out that surely it was not wasted if it came into Gran's pocket.

It was one of the PGs who gave her away. She was bringing the toast into the guests' breakfast room when a middle-aged man recognised her.

'Well, if it isn't Miss Lindy-Lou Parker!'

Lillian went cold. Gran was right behind her, making sure that the guests didn't pocket the cruets or fill their flasks from the teapot.

'Oh!' the man's wife exclaimed. 'So it is. Oh, we did enjoy the show, dear. You was ever so good.'

'Lovely little dancer,' her husband agreed.

'Lovely. Ain't she a lovely little dancer?' the woman asked Gran. 'You must be very proud of her.'

Lillian could feel her grandmother's piercing eyes on her, shrivelling her up inside.

'Yes,' Gran said.

Lillian knew she was only saying that to keep face in front of the guests. Sure enough, as soon as they were all safely out of the house, she was summoned to Gran's room.

'What's all this about dancing?'

Lillian glared back at her, her heart beating hard.

'I was in the Carnival Talent Contest,' she said, her voice loud with defiance. 'I got a prize.'

'You went up on a stage and made an exhibition of yourself in public?'

The way Gran said it, performing on a stage was something disgraceful. Anger overcame Lillian's fear of her grandmother.

'I wasn't making an exhibition of myself, I was dancing. What's so wrong with that? And I was good; I came second out of lots of people.'

This made Gran even angrier. If there was one thing she didn't like, it was people arguing with her.

'Don't you defy me, my girl. If I say you're not to go up on a stage, then you're not, and no questions asked. Understand?'

'No, I don't!' Tears of anger and frustration were gathering in Lillian's eyes now. 'Just tell me what's so wrong about it!'

'You lied to me. Lied by sneaking out and doing it behind my back. And I won't stand for liars. You're a disgrace to the family—'

Gran was off on one of her tirades. Lillian stared at a point above her shoulder and tried not to listen.

'—and you're not too big to be punished.'

Lillian came back from the place where she had been mentally sheltering to see that Gran had the stick in her hand. With a wicked swish, it came down hard on her calves, sharp and stinging, five times. She couldn't contain a squeal of pain.

'There—' Gran was looking at her with satisfaction now, breathing hard. 'Now say you're sorry.'

'Sorry,' Lillian mumbled, with huge reluctance.

'Let this be a lesson to you. No going out for two weeks.'

'But, Gran—'

This was a real blow. Lillian had been looking forward to going to the funfair with Janette and her other friends.

'No buts. Go and see if your mother needs some help.'

Sore, angry and resentful, Lillian did as she was told.

To her surprise, Wendy was completely on her side. In bed that night, she wanted to know all about the contest.

'Good for you, kid,' she commented. 'Don't you take any notice of what Gran says. Blooming killjoy! It's Eileen, you know. She thinks if she's hard enough on us we won't turn out like her.'

Light dawned in Lillian's mind. So that was it.

'But how could going in for a talent contest mean I'm going to run away with a married man?'

'Search me, kid. That's Gran, isn't it? Grumpy old bag. I always wanted to go in for the Carnival Princess, but I never dared. I bet I would of won, too. Maybe next year I'll go in for the Carnival Queen. That'd show them!'

Warmed by the thrill of sisterly solidarity, Lillian agreed. 'I think you should, if that's what you really want. Aunty Eileen said you should always follow your dream. That's what she did.'

'Bully for Eileen. I hope she's enjoying herself. She was right to escape from this family,' Wendy said.

Despite the gating, Lillian didn't regret her actions for a minute. It was more than worth it when she relived her short spot on stage, the heady thrill of performing, and the dizzy moment when her name had been called out.

Ten days or so after the event, support came from an unexpected quarter. As the family sat round the tea table, Bob made a pronouncement. 'I think we may have been a little hard on Lillian. After all, she did win a prize in that contest.'

Lillian gazed at him in astonishment. Her brother was sticking up for her! It was unheard of. Only Bob, with his status as the brains of the family with a respectable job, could have got away with saying such a thing. Even so, Gran did not look best pleased.

'What, for kicking her legs up in front of a lot of strangers?'

'But it was for the Carnival Fund. That's a very good cause, you know. They're building bungalows for deserving old folk. Mr Caraway supports the Carnival Fund. He said that our Lillian was a credit to us, giving her time and her talent.'

Mr Caraway was the manager at Bob's bank, and second only to God as far as Gran was concerned.

'Huh, well, that's as may be. I'm sure it is a good cause, though no one ever offered me a bungalow, but it still doesn't mean I want to hear of my granddaughter making an exhibition of herself in public,' Gran said, unwilling to concede the point, even to her favourite.

It was only later that Lillian found out how Bob came to be championing her. Susan had written to James about it, and James had written back in her defence. Susan had then used her influence with Bob. Lillian was overjoyed. Even far away in Catterick, James had thought to come to her aid. It was practically another prize.

CHAPTER 7

THERE were far better reasons for a forty-eight-hour pass than attending your sister's engagement party, James thought as he watched the lighted windows of the eastern suburbs of London trundle by. Especially when that sister was set on marrying Boring Bob Parker. The party itself didn't promise to be a bundle of laughs, either. His army pals had envied him his trip home, assuming that the celebration would be a big booze-up at the pub. James hadn't told them that it was going to be Saturday tea at the Parkers' place. Even with a cake made and iced by Susan, it was not his idea of fun. Still, family was family and Susan had insisted that the celebration be postponed until he could get leave, so here he was on the train to Southend, ready to be happy for his sister and his mother, both of whom appeared to be delighted with this turn of events. And, of course, there was the bonus of seeing Wendy again. Maybe she was an unattainable star, but he wasn't going to give up trying.

Homecoming was always special, engagement or no engagement, and as the train passed through Leigh-on-Sea James put away his book and stared out into the darkness, trying to see the estuary. Moonlight spilled through a gap in the clouds as he gazed, making a silver path across the Thames and emphasizing the dark shapes of the boats moored in the shallows, while across on the other side the flames from the oil refineries flared like beacons. It was good to be back.

Susan and Bob were waiting for him at Southend Central. An irrational disappointment dragged at James when he saw it was just the two of them. He hadn't expected Wendy to be with them to greet him. He hadn't even hoped. It was Friday night and she was sure to be out with some flash bloke enjoying herself. But, all the same… He pulled himself together and strode along the platform to meet them.

'Hello, you two! Congratulations—' He kissed Susan's cheek, shook Bob's hand. 'I hope you appreciate what a treasure you've got in my sister.'

'Oh, James—!' Susan exclaimed, embarrassed but pleased.

'But of course I do. She's going to be the perfect wife,' Bob assured him.

James could believe that all right. Susan had been in training for it all her life. She was an excellent cook, even with the limited facilities they had in their tiny kitchen, an accomplished needlewoman and a fanatical housewife. And she was used to managing on a limited income. There would be no overspending in their household.

Susan threaded her arm through her fiancé's and gazed up at him with pride.

'And Bob will be the perfect husband.'

This James doubted. How could his sister be in love with such a dull stick? It was still a mystery to him.

'How's your family?' he asked Bob, hoping for news of Wendy.

'Oh—fine, fine, thank you. All very well. They're looking forward to seeing you tomorrow. Lillian wanted to come with us to meet you this evening! But of course it was out of the question.'

Little Lillian. James smiled to himself. That put him in his place. He hoped for Wendy and got her kid sister. Well, at least someone was pleased he was back.

All the way home, he was treated to an account of how Bob and Susan were saving up for the deposit on a house of their own. Before they had crossed the High Street, he was bored almost to tears with the minutiae of percentages and repayments and surveyors and solicitors. It all seemed so dry compared with the active challenges he had been tackling every day on his army training. It was only when they arrived at the flat that his own achievement was recognised.

'My darling boy!' His mother gave him a welcoming hug. She seemed smaller than when he had last seen her. He could feel the frail bones of her back.

She held his upper arms to take a good look at him, then realised what was under her fingers.

'What's this? A lance corporal's stripe? You clever thing! Well done! Look, Susan, Bob—James has been made a lance corporal already!'

James gave a shrug. 'It's only one little step up the ladder, Mum.'

But he couldn't help sneaking a look at Bob, who he knew had only got his stripe a month before leaving the army.

'You're spending your time yelling at your platoon, then?' Bob said.

'Oh, yes, I got my drills one and two, and my marksman's. All helps put a bit extra in the pay,' James said, deliberately playing it down. They both knew that not everyone got these qualifications. He had spiked Bob's right to patronise him when it came to army service.

It wasn't until Susan had gone off to the Parkers' the next afternoon to help with the party food that James had a chance to speak to his mother about the engagement.

'Do you really think Susan's doing the right thing?' he asked.

His mother looked at him in amazement. 'But of course she is, darling. She's so happy! And Bob's such a steady chap, he'll look after her well. They're saving for a house of their own, you know. Bob has it all worked out—'

'Yes, I do know.' He had heard more than enough about it last night. 'But is that enough? I mean, is that all you need to be happy with someone?'

'Susan loves him, and he'll be a good provider. Not like some young fellows these days. The things you hear about those Teddy boys! I'm afraid his brother is one of them. Now, if our Susan wanted to marry Frank, I'd be very worried, but Bob's quite different. He's solid, is Bob.'

So that was all that women wanted? A house and a good provider? He was sure that Wendy wanted more than that. Unbidden, into his mind came the memory of Lillian telling him of her dream of becoming a dancer. She certainly wanted something out of the ordinary. But then she was just a kid. It was different for his sister.

The celebration tea at the Parkers' was slightly less gruesome than the one ten months ago when the two families had been introduced to each other.

After months of army food, just having a good tea was a treat for James. Now that rationing had at last ended, everyone was enjoying a more varied diet. Susan's cake took pride of place in the centre of the table, a fluffy sponge covered with royal icing and fancy piping, with her name and Bob's inside a sugar heart. It was resting on a green glass plate that James and Susan's parents had received as a wedding present. Around it were jam tarts and scones, and four different sorts of sandwiches—banana, egg and cress, corned beef and ham and mustard.

'What a feast!' James said, and earned grateful smiles from all the womenfolk who had been involved in providing the spread.

All, that was, except Wendy. She was looking more opulent and desirable than ever in a baby-blue fluffy jumper and a grey pencil skirt.

'Typical man, thinking about his stomach,' she remarked. It sounded dismissive, but there was that challenge in her eyes.

'I was thinking what a good party this is for Bob and Susan,' James said.

His hands ached to run down her spine and over her beautiful backside.

'We all helped,' another voice piped up.

A small part of his mind registered Lillian's presence, but his attention was still on her sister.

'Oh, yeah, the happy couple,' Wendy said.

For the first time, he realised that they thought the same about something. Wendy was no more delighted with the occasion than he was but, with both their families within earshot, they could say nothing more. One thing was for sure, though—he was determined not to be outmanoeuvred at the tea table this time. He pulled a chair out and invited Wendy to sit down. To his delight, she accepted. Swiftly, he sat on the chair next to hers. Mission accomplished. His knee was just inches from hers.

The rest of the family were sorting themselves out. The

older ones hadn't changed in the time since he had last seen them. Wendy's mum was still faded and anxious-looking, her dad still carried his dark cloud of resentment against the world, her grandmother still ruled them all. But the young people had changed. Bob looked practically middle-aged; he was even going a bit thin on top, though he was only twenty-five. Frank was sporting a DA and sideburns to go with his full Teddy boy rig of draped jacket, drainpipe trousers and brothel-creeper shoes. And Lillian—Lillian was sitting at the corner of the table furthest from him, in between her mother and grandmother. Her schoolgirl plaits were gone and in their place was a fashionable ponytail. She was wearing a white blouse and bright red cardigan with a full blue and grey checked skirt, and around her waist was one of those wide elastic belts that Wendy favoured. She would have looked surprisingly grown-up, had she not been in a huge sulk. James caught her eye and was given a glowering look. He couldn't imagine what he had done to upset her. Why, he'd hardly spoken to her, so what could he have said wrong? He gave her a grin and a wink across the table. She went red and looked away. James gave up on her. He had more important things to do than worry about a sulky kid.

As the conversation limped along at the table, James gradually let his leg sag sideways, until his knee touched Wendy's. He expected her to twitch her leg away in a huff but she didn't, so James moved his foot as well, so that it was resting alongside Wendy's. He could feel the warmth of her shapely calf against his as she talked to the others, natural as anything, not giving anything away.

When most of the food was eaten, Susan stood up to cut the celebration cake. Flushed and happy, his sister sliced into her white-iced masterpiece and handed it round the table to polite noises of admiration from everyone. James did not want to move from his delicious closeness to Wendy, but he had been planning a surprise for this moment and he didn't want to let it pass. The Parkers might have the big house to hold this party, but the Kershaws were not going to sit there playing the poor relations, not while he could do something about it. He reached behind him for the brown paper bag he had set down by the wall.

'Before we eat Susan's lovely cake—' he said.

Voices round the table fell quiet. Surprised eyes turned on him. Gran Parker looked affronted at his interruption, Susan's face was frozen in dismay. He smiled at his sister, trying to re-assure her that he was not about to ruin her big moment.

'—I thought it would be nice to have something a bit more exciting than tea to toast the happy couple with.'

He produced a bottle of sherry and a half bottle of Scotch. There was silence for a couple of heartbeats while the entire Parker clan looked at Gran to see what her reaction would be. The old woman pursed her lips, then, to everyone's surprise, she gave a nod.

'I wouldn't say no.'

There was a general letting-out of breath and happy cla-mour. Lillian was sent to fetch glasses and James poured sherry for the ladies and Scotch for the men, making sure that Lillian got a drop along with the others. Keeping a firm hold on the initiative, he stood up and raised his glass.

'To Susan and Bob—may they have a long and happy life together,' he said.

'Susan and Bob!' everyone chorused.

Glasses clinked, drinks were sipped, the cake was eaten, everyone relaxed for the first time that day. Across the table from him, James was glad to see his sister glowing with pleasure and his mother wiping away happy tears. The Parker men had a more complicated reaction. They were obviously delighted to be having a drink, but mortified that someone younger than them had had the courage to risk Gran's disapproval. One up to the Kershaws, he thought as Wendy's leg brushed against his.

When the meal was finally over and the smokers were lighting up, Gran gave Lillian a poke in the arm. 'Dishes, Lillian. And you, Wendy.'

Susan got up to help as well, but James stood at the same time.

'It's all right, Suse, I'll do it. This is your party.'

This time, though, his plan fell apart. Wendy helped clear the dirty plates but, once they were piled up in the kitchen, she made for the door.

'Won't be long,' she said.

Lillian slammed the cutlery into the sink.

'Huh. That's what she always says. That'll be the last we see of her. She'll only come back again if she thinks Gran's about to come and inspect what we're doing.'

James was torn. He wanted to follow Wendy to wherever she was off to, but a sense of fairness held him where he was. Everyone took advantage of Lillian. He didn't want to be the same. He gave her glossy ponytail a playful tug.

'What's up with you, Lill? You're like a bear with a sore head.'

She jerked her hair away. 'Don't call me Lill. I hate it.'

'OK, OK.' James picked up the tea towel. 'So what shall I call you? Lillian's a bit of a mouthful.'

Lillian didn't answer. She washed the cups and saucers and plates with swift efficiency and stacked them on the draining board for James to dry. He could tell just by the set of her shoulders that something was up.

'What do you think?' he persisted, while wondering where Wendy was. Probably the only places she could hide were the bathroom or her bedroom, neither of which he could go to.

'My Aunty Eileen called me Lindy-Lou. But don't you dare say that's babyish,' she growled.

It was babyish, of course. But he couldn't keep his mind on the subject. Supposing Wendy had been expecting him to follow her? Was he missing his big chance? But then, if he didn't follow her when she wanted him to, did that give him the upper hand? Perhaps, if he did try it on, she would just laugh at him... He wasn't used to this games playing. He wasn't even sure if it was games playing. Maybe Wendy simply didn't like washing-up.

He was roused from his reverie by the sound of a sob. He glanced at Lillian and was horrified to find that she was crying. He put a comforting hand on her shoulder.

'Hey—what's the matter? Whatever's wrong?'

No doubt her ghastly family had done something to upset her.

Lillian threw the dishcloth into the water and held on to the rim of the sink with white-knuckled hands. Her shoulders were shaking.

'Why are you so h-horrible to me?' she sobbed.

James was shocked. 'Me? What have I done?'

'You're ignoring me. You're treating me l-like I'm not here, just like they all do. You used not to. You used to be n-nice to me. You treated me like I was a p-proper person and you l-listened to me.'

'I am listening to you,' James protested.

'You're not! You're thinking about Wendy.'

This was so true that he was silenced.

'I hate her. She's so beautiful and everything, she just does what she likes. It's not fair! I saw what she was doing. Just 'cos I said you were going to be rich—'

'*What?*' James asked. He couldn't follow this at all.

Lillian bit her lip. For several moments she didn't answer. She just stood there, fiddling with the dish cloth. Finally it burst out of her.

'I told her you were going to be rich one day, and own a garage and a car and everything, and now she's sitting next to you and looking at you with those goo-goo eyes—'

Now it was James's turn to be angry. He didn't want to be seen as some stupid boy boasting about what he was going to do, when he knew no one would believe him. His own mother didn't believe him when he said he was going to get her out of that flat one day. It wasn't that he didn't believe it himself. He did, completely. But he knew how it looked to other people—just a pipe dream.

'You told her about that? Lillian, I told you in confidence. That was between you and me. I haven't told anyone about your dreams. I wouldn't even think of doing so. They're your private thoughts.'

'I'm sorry, I'm sorry—' Lillian was shaking her head from side to side as she listened to him. Now she looked up at him with anguished eyes, her face pinched and her mouth distorted. 'I didn't mean to, honest. It just sort of came out. We were talking, and we never talk usually and she was being nice for once and telling me what she wanted and about marrying someone rich and that and I just sort of let it out. Oh, now I've spoilt everything! I wish I was dead—'

Living with two women over the years had made him used to coping with emotional outbursts. He put his arms round Lillian and rocked her as she sobbed on his shoulder.

'Come on, now, you don't mean that. And I know you

wouldn't have let it out deliberately; you're not like that. It's not the end of the world—'

'Well, well, well! What a touching little scene!'

James looked round. There in the doorway was Wendy, standing with one hand on the frame and the other on her hip, smiling. James felt his face going red. This must look bad.

'She's upset,' he said.

'She's fifteen,' Wendy said, as if that explained everything. She strolled into the kitchen and picked up a spare tea towel. 'Good thing it was me and not Gran or Dad what came in.'

With a howl, Lillian backed out of his now loose embrace and ran from the room.

Wendy shrugged. 'She'll learn,' she said. 'You can finish the washing. I don't want to ruin my hands in that water.'

'But shouldn't we—couldn't you go after her, say something?'

'She's all right. Like I said, she's fifteen. She'll get over it.'

When everything was neatly stacked away, she leaned her back against the sink and gave him one of her slow, considering looks.

'You've made yourself really useful round here, haven't you? I wonder why?'

This time James didn't stop to think. He stepped forward and put his hands on her narrow waist, pulling her towards him. His mouth closed on her shining, mocking smile. For a second or two she resisted him, then her lips opened and responded and he fell into a whirlpool of a kiss. When Wendy pulled away, she almost looked impressed.

'My—you're quite good at that, aren't you?'

'Come out with me tonight,' James said.

Wendy put a hand to her head, smoothing an imaginary stray lock back into place. 'Oh, no—just because you've got a stripe up already, it doesn't mean I'll go out with you. Maybe if you get made a sergeant.'

She gave a superior smile. They both knew that national servicemen hardly ever got made sergeants.

She made for the door.

'Is that a promise?' James pressed. He knew he could get the trade qualifications needed. He already had the skills from his time at the garage. He could certainly get to be corporal. After that, being made even an acting unpaid sergeant depended on someone dropping out.

Wendy looked back at him over her shoulder. 'Maybe.'

He would make it, James resolved, if it was the last thing he did.

CHAPTER 8

'BUT I don't want to work in a shop!' Lillian protested.

Easter was fast approaching, and with it her last weeks at school. Now she was fifteen, she could leave and get a job. Staying on till the end of the school year was out of the question. Gran was annoyed enough that she had to stay on till the end of term. She was even more annoyed that Lillian should question her choice of a job.

'Don't want has got nothing to do with it, young lady. You'll do as you're told.'

'But I want—' Lillian hesitated. She wanted so much to be a dancer. The thrill of those precious few minutes on stage at the bandstand had confirmed everything she had always imagined. Hidden in an old chocolate box at the bottom of her underwear drawer was the newspaper picture of her receiving her prize from the carnival queen. She got it out and looked at it whenever she was feeling low, and it always gave her a boost. But it was no use even trying to explain this to Gran. In fact, it was important that she kept quiet about it. What Gran didn't know about, she couldn't forbid.

'I want to be a hairdresser,' she said, surprising herself. Her Aunty Eileen had been a hairdresser.

'That means a long apprenticeship with you earning next to nothing.'

'Well, if money's the thing, I'll work in a factory. I'd earn more in a factory than at a shop.'

'You'll do nothing of the sort. Our family has always worked in shops. We had a shop once, after all. We'd still have it now, if there was any fairness in this world.'

Lillian knew she was defeated once Gran referred to the shop.

'Yes, Gran.'

'Your sister says there's an opening at Dixon's, in the household department. You'll go and apply for it tomorrow.'

The last thing Lillian wanted was to be working at the same place as Wendy. After the way she had behaved towards James, Lillian could hardly bear to look at her. She muttered something that sounded like agreement, but in her heart she was refusing. She marched straight out of the house, fuming. Why wasn't her life her own? Why couldn't she do what she wanted? She walked to the High Street and went along looking at the shop windows. Halfway up, one of the shoe shops had a notice in the window—*Junior wanted*. Lillian went in and asked to see the manager. A tall man with thinning hair was fetched. He looked at her over his half-moon glasses.

'Yes?'

'I've come for the job. In the window,' Lillian said.

As the words came out of her mouth, she could hear that they sounded stupid. She should have planned this better.

'My name's Lillian Parker. I'm leaving school at the end of this term,' she explained.

'I see. Right. And what makes you think you are suitable to work here?'

'I…I'm very interested in shoes,' Lillian improvised. 'And I'm used to looking after people. My family has a guest house and so I'm dealing with the public quite a lot and I know how to be polite and find what people want.'

That sounded much better. She was surprised at herself. She gave a tentative smile. The manager did not respond.

'I take it you can make tea?'

'Oh, yes,' Lillian said. What had that to do with selling shoes?

'And can you handle money? Eighteen and elevenpence ha'penny, what's the change from a five pound note?'

'Four pounds, one and a ha'penny,' Lillian said promptly. That was easy. She had been doing shopping since she was five years old.

The manager nodded. He went and took a red stiletto from one of the displays and handed it to her.

'Go into the store room and find the other half of this pair,' he said.

Lillian went through the door at the back of the shop. It was dark and cold out here and the floor was bare, unlike the cosy carpeted brightness of the shop. She found the light switch and gazed at the shelves and shelves of shoeboxes, stacked right up to the ceiling. Where to start? She scanned the rows, looking at the pictures on the ends of the boxes. The nearest ones were all men's shoes. She found the ladies' section, dismissed the flat styles, scanned the stilettos. There— at the top! She grabbed a stepladder that was standing nearby, climbed up, checked the size, pulled out a box. Inside was just one shoe, the partner of the one she was holding. She scampered into the shop.

'There!' she said, triumphant.

The manager looked vaguely surprised. 'That was very quick.' He offered her a trial of a month.

It wasn't a very exciting job, as it turned out. On her first morning, the manager set her to dusting the shelves.

'Have you finished that?' He ran a finger over the surfaces. 'Yes, well, that's all right. You can go and put the kettle on now and start making tea for the mid-morning break.'

After that, she was set to sorting out the stand containing the shoelaces. By the end of the day, she had hardly touched a shoe. She certainly hadn't spoken to a customer. That set the pattern. As the junior, she was mostly cleaning and tidying, fetching things for the other staff and running errands for the manager. But it was her job and she made the best of it. It was nice to put on her own clothes in the morning instead of hand-me-down school uniform, and to be called 'Miss Parker' in front of the customers. It was lovely to get her little brown paper envelope of money at the end of the week, even if most of it did have to go to her mother for her keep. She was a grown-up now, taking her own place in the world.

A small corner of her heart hoped that this might help her when it came to seeing James again. Mostly she felt totally humiliated when she thought of their last meeting. However much she told herself that it had all been Wendy's fault, she knew she had behaved badly. Of course he was going to treat her like a child if she shouted at him then blubbed all over him like that. What had made her do that? She couldn't understand what had happened to her. Being with him seemed to bring on a sort of madness, making her lose all self-control. Every time she thought of it, she wanted to curl up and die. But then there had been that wonderful, wonderful moment when he'd taken her in his arms. She relived that a thousand times, making it end differently in her imagination. Maybe, just maybe, when they next met he would see this young woman who worked for her own living and not just a scruffy kid. The thought kept her going until the next blow fell.

'James had some worrying news in his last letter,' Susan announced one evening. Now that she and Bob were engaged and saving up for a house, they spent a lot of evenings at each other's homes rather than going out to the pictures or dancing. This particular evening, Lillian was sitting at the table in the kitchen reading a library book while Bob studied for his banking exams and Susan knitted him a jumper. Bob merely grunted at her statement, but Lillian was instantly alert.

'Did he? What was it?'

'Well, he's been made a corporal, which is good, of course, but he's got a posting abroad.'

A terrible chill struck Lillian, like an icy hand clutching at her entrails.

'Posting?' she managed to say.

'Yes, he's being sent to Cyprus. Poor Mum's beside herself. It's so dangerous out there with all those dreadful EOKA people letting off bombs and things. James is playing it down, of course, so as not to worry Mum. He says in Cyprus there are oranges and lemons growing on trees, which must look so pretty.'

'When they say you've got to go, you've got to go,' Bob commented, without taking his eyes off the page he was looking at.

'Well, yes, I know,' Susan agreed, ever the good fiancée. 'But poor Mum! It's brought it all back to her, you see, having James go off to a war zone. She can't help thinking about Dad.'

'It'll all blow over soon enough,' Bob said. He had never been further than Catterick on his national service.

'W-when's he leaving?' Lillian managed to ask.

'Next month. He'll be there till he's finished his time.'

A whole year! James was going to be away for a whole year! And to Cyprus, where guerrilla fighters were attacking British troops. It wasn't just a jaunt abroad, like being sent to Germany. He could be involved in real fighting. How was she going to bear it? She couldn't even spill it all to Janette the next morning like she used to when they were at school together, but had to wait all through a miserable day till she could cycle round to Janette's after tea.

'My life is finished!' she announced as she burst through the door to Janette's flat. 'There's nothing left to live for.'

'Oh, so you won't want to see this, then,' Janette said, waving a blurry carbon copied piece of paper in front of her.

'James is going to Cyprus. He's going to be away for— what's that thing?'

Despite herself, her eyes had lighted on the word *Dancers* on Janette's paper.

'Sure you want to see?' Janette teased, backing away from her with the paper held above her head.

'Yes—come on—what is it?'

'No more flipping James?'

'OK, OK.'

Eagerly, Lillian read the notice. *Do you like dancing?* it asked. *Are you fifteen or over? Come and audition for the Mamie Hill Dancers and help with our charity work dancing for Old Folks etc.*

Her excitement dimmed a little at the words *charity work*. This was not a professional troupe, then. But it was a start. It was dancing, up on a stage, in front of an audience. She made a note of the time and place of the audition and spent the rest of the evening discussing it with Janette. James wasn't forgotten, but she did have something to look forward to once more.

Mamie Hill turned out to be a tall lady with a cigarette in a long holder and rather too much make-up, who could have been any age from forty to sixty. She made an exotic figure in her bright dress and flowing scarves in the middle of a dusty church hall. What impressed Lillian was the fact that she had been a professional dancer—it showed in every movement she made.

After a word or two about the troupe, she got each of the dozen or so girls who had arrived to dance on the stage, accompanied on the out-of-tune piano by a woman who chain-smoked through the whole proceedings. Lillian did her *We're a Couple of Swells* routine, enjoying the thrill of it all over again. As she dropped into the final splits on the rough boarding of the stage, she felt a splinter ram into her thigh, but managed to keep the bright smile on her face. She got up and looked at Miss Hill. Had she liked it? So much was riding on this. This was more than just one contest, this was the chance to learn and perform.

Mamie Hill opened her notebook, her gold propelling pencil poised. 'What did you say your name was, dear?'

'Lindy-Lou Parker.'

'And have you been dancing for long?'

'Oh—ages,' Lillian said.

'Mm—well—I won't ask who taught you, but you've got a lot of rough corners to knock off. A lot. But you've got oodles of raw talent, and you can perform. That's the thing, dear—performing. You have to give out to the audience, you have to give all of yourself, and you do that. Now, are you prepared to come to two practices a week and be available whenever we're asked to perform?'

Was she? There was only one answer to that.

'Oh, yes, Miss Hill! I'd love to.'

'Very well, then. Be here at seven o'clock on Thursday.'

Lillian cycled home six inches above the ground. This was it! This was her start. Her feet were on the yellow brick road.

The only problem, and it was a huge one, was deciding what to say to the family. After the fuss about the talent contest, she feared that if she admitted to what she was doing it would be forbidden. Round and round her head went Aunty Eileen's last words to her—*Don't let them stop you.* Maybe the best way was simply not to tell them. But if she went ahead and did it, lying in the process, then there would be even bigger ructions when she was finally found out. She couldn't bear the idea of being stopped before she had started, so she opted for secrecy and said she was going to see friends when she went to practices. Maybe something would turn up to change Gran's mind. It was a long shot but she went for it, closing her eyes to the consequences.

Mamie Hill was a tough teacher. She treated the girls as if they were a proper dance troupe, picking up sloppy steps and lazy arms and making them all work really hard, going over each movement until it was right.

'Practice, practice, practice!' she insisted, gesticulating with her cigarette holder.

Some of the girls groaned and complained as they did a sequence for the tenth time. Two got so fed up that they left. But Lillian loved it. This was what she wanted. She could feel her body responding to the discipline. She welcomed the criticism and did everything that Miss Hill suggested. She got up early each day to do ballet exercises, using the chest of drawers as a barre and ignoring Wendy's complaints at being disturbed. She went over the dance routines in her head as she cycled to work and practised steps in the store room of the shop as she searched for shoes.

The troupe got their first booking, a request to entertain the Darby and Joan Club at their birthday party. Lillian was thrilled. Then Miss Hill started to talk about costumes. Lillian listened, appalled, as ideas for three different outfits were described. How on earth was she going to make these? Like all girls, she had learnt some basic needlework at school, but a sailor suit? A frilly satin dress? How was she going to make those? And the cost! It was going to take all the money she had left from her earnings after giving her keep to her mother.

'Now, I'm sure your mothers will be able to help you with this,' Miss Hill was saying. 'All mums are clever with their needles, and they love a pretty project to do. It makes a nice change from turning sheets sides to middle and mending trousers.'

Quite apart from the fact that she had not yet told the family about the Mamie Hill Dancers, Lillian could just imagine her mother's reaction if she asked for help. That weary, washed-out look would come over her face.

Oh—I don't know—really I don't—your grandmother wants me to—

There was always something that Gran wanted doing. And the summer season was looming.

It was no use asking Wendy. She hated sewing and, anyway, she never helped anyone if she could get out of it. If only her aunty Eileen were still here, she would be delighted to try. Turning it over in her mind, Lillian realised that they did have someone in the family who could sew. Susan. Asking her would mean having to admit to what she was doing, and then of course Susan would tell Bob and then the whole family would know. But Susan, on James's request, had come in on her side when she'd gone in for the talent contest, so maybe she would support her this time.

The next time Susan came round to their house, she waited till Bob was out of the room and broached the subject.

'Oh, that sounds interesting, dear. A stage costume! I haven't made a stage costume before. Let me see the pattern.'

Lillian showed her the sketches and the newspaper patterns that had been copied from the expensive tissue ones. Susan nodded and commented on the technicalities involved. Just as Mamie Hill had predicted, the project interested her. It was something a bit different from ordinary dressmaking. By the time Bob came back into the room, she was getting enthusiastic.

'Oh, Bob, dear, just guess what Lillian's been doing,' she cried.

Lillian held her breath. This was the crunch moment. If Bob disapproved, all was lost.

'She's been giving up her own spare time to practise for an entertainment for the Darby and Joan Club. Isn't that sweet of her? I'm going to help her make some lovely costumes. Won't that be fun?'

Lillian could have kissed her. She couldn't have broken the news better. Even so, Bob was not altogether happy about taking her side.

'I don't know what Gran's going to say. You know what she thought last time.'

'Oh, but that was different, darling. Lillian's doing this for charity. And I'm sure this Mamie Hill is a very respectable lady.'

'Oh, yes, she is,' Lillian said, wondering just what the family would make of Miss Hill and her theatrical air.

There was a row, of course. At first Gran seemed immovable. But then two things came to Lillian's aid. She found out that her sister was going out with one of the regular PGs, a commercial traveller. This was absolutely forbidden because of Eileen's having run off with a traveller.

'Gran's not going to like it,' Lillian said.

'Gran's not going to find out because if she does I'll know who told, and your life won't be worth living,' Wendy threatened. She had just come in from a date with the man. She smelt of cheap scent and cigarette smoke. 'God, my feet are killing me,' she said, plumping down on the bed and kicking off her high heeled shoes. 'Here, undo me, will you?'

Lillian pulled down the long zip. The skin-tight bodice of Wendy's dancing dress parted to reveal her warm flesh. Wendy stepped out of it and hung it up carefully in the wardrobe.

'Is he nice? Does he take you to posh places?' Lillian asked.

'Oh—lovely! We've been to this dinner dance. Wonderful band, and all this posh food. And wine—we drank real French wine. And there was all different knives and forks for every course! Imagine the washing-up!' Wendy started slapping cold cream over her face. She looked at herself in the mirror and flicked back the blonde hair that she was now growing long so that it curled over her shoulders. 'He says I look like Diana Dors. That's who I want to be like.'

'What, and be a film star?' Lillian asked.

'No, stupid. How am I going to get to be a film star? I want to marry someone really rich and wear fur coats and ride around in a Rolls-Royce.'

That was when Lillian realised that she did after all have something in common with her big sister. They both had ambitions.

'I want to be a dancer, but Gran won't let me. If you stick up for me, I'll keep quiet about your PG,' she bargained.

It took a while longer but in the end Wendy had to agree,

for she had the most to lose. They both knew that if Gran did find out about the commercial traveller, Wendy would be gated for at least a month.

Having Wendy speak up for her didn't make a huge difference but it did begin to tip the balance. And then *Blackboard Jungle* hit town. This was a film about a tough New York school, but what really got the audiences going was the music that played over the titles, a song called *Rock Around the Clock* by an American band called Bill Haley and the Comets. All over the country, teenagers were going crazy at the very sound of it. It was new, it was wild, it had a hypnotic beat. All the fuddy-duddies hated it, and that was the real attraction—it was music just for teenagers. They called it rock'n'roll and they loved it. Frank and his gang of Teddy boys went along to see the film and got up and danced and yelled the moment the music started. Other cinema goers tried to shut them up, Frank's gang got aggressive and a fight broke out. Frank was one of those unlucky enough to be hauled off to the cells when the police arrived.

Gran was outraged, Dad was sourly angry and Mum wept.

'A member of our family arrested! I don't know what the world's coming to. The shame of it! We'll never live it down,' Gran raged.

Beside Frank's crime, Lillian's wanting to get up on a stage and do some singing and dancing was small beer. Permission wasn't exactly given, but neither was it withheld. Lillian quietly got on with rehearsals and Susan fitted her costumes.

'That looks very nice,' she commented, as Lillian turned round in front of her in the calf-length yellow satin dress with its rows of black-edged ruffles. 'Very pretty. You're getting quite a nice little figure there, Lillian.'

Lillian blushed with pleasure. 'Am I?' She looked this way

and that in the mirror. She certainly didn't look like a school-girl any more.

'It's the dress that does it. You're so clever, Susan,' she said, genuinely grateful but wanting to please. She had a further favour to ask. 'Do you—I mean, have you told James about making the costumes, when you write to him? Does he know I'm going to be performing?'

'I did mention it, yes,' Susan said.

'And what does—did he say anything back?'

Susan made a last little adjustment to the shoulder.

'Why don't you write to him yourself and tell him all about it?' she suggested, through a mouthful of pins.

A new and wonderful prospect opened up before Lillian.

'Could I?'

'Of course.' Susan was quite matter-of-fact. 'I'll give you his address in Cyprus.'

'And would he—I mean, do you think he'd like it if I sent him a letter?'

'Why not? All soldiers like to get letters from home. It makes them feel like they're not forgotten.'

Forgotten! As if she could ever forget James. She thought about him every minute of the day. She listened to every bit of news about Cyprus on the wireless and devoured Gran's newspaper when she had finished with it. But for now Lillian was in heaven. She didn't care now how horrible Wendy and the others were to her, or how boring her job was, or how many chores she had to do for her mother. She sang *Rock Around the Clock* at the top of her voice as she cycled to work or changed sheets. She had Mamie Hill and the dancers, and she had letters from James to look forward to. She was on top of the world.

CHAPTER 9

FOR the young people it was like a bright light switching on, banishing the dreary post-war gloom. In dance halls around the country, decorous waltzes and quicksteps gave way to the loud beat and dizzying whirl and spin of rock'n'roll. It was their music, and they loved it. English boys, unable to afford expensive guitars and double basses, formed skiffle groups. Lonnie Donegan had his first skiffle hit with *Rock Island Line* in the first week of 1956.

Rock Around the Clock was followed by new hits.

'See you later, alligator!' Lillian would say as she parted from the dancers after a rehearsal, quoting from the latest Bill Haley number.

'In a while, crocodile!' they would chorus.

It was rumoured that even Princess Margaret and her set said it to each other.

Then in the late spring a new and irresistible talent burst

upon the scene. With curling lip and soulful eyes, bluesy voice and swivelling hips, Elvis Presley had arrived. For thousands of teenagers, life would never be the same again.

It was into this bright new world that James was finally released from his national service. He arrived home feeling slightly odd in his stiff new civvies to a tearful welcome from his mother.

'Oh, my darling boy! You're safe at last. I've not been able to sleep this past year, worrying about you.'

James returned her hug. She felt more birdlike than ever. He was afraid to hold her too tightly.

'Yeah, home now to plague you, Mum. You'll be wishing I was out from under your feet again within a week,' he teased, uneasy at the thought of her constant anxiety. If he had stayed in Britain for the two years, she wouldn't have been lying awake convinced that his life was in danger. But he had been eager for a foreign posting, wanting to get as much experience as possible out of his time, and he had landed himself in what was practically a war zone.

'Oh, darling, as if I would! It's just so wonderful to have you back, safe and sound. Let me have a look at you. Oh, but you've grown into such a fine young man! So handsome! Do you know, you're the image of your poor dear father. And you're looking so fit and brown. I can't get over it.'

'Plenty of sport and army food, Mum. And it's lovely and sunny in Cyprus,' James said, embarrassed at all the personal scrutiny. 'Here—I said I'd bring you oranges fresh off the tree. Look, they've still got their leaves on. You'll never taste anything as juicy as these.'

It was strange being back home. The flat seemed smaller than ever after living in army huts and, even though it was hardly luxurious, it was soft and feminine, a total contrast to the all-male regime he was used to. James set about getting on with the next part of his life. His old job had been left open for him and he took it up again as a stopgap. He'd learnt a lot in the army, and planned a great deal more. Working at Dobson's would keep the money coming in while he laid the foundations for his own business.

He picked up the threads of his social life too, looking up friends who like him had finished their national service. And then there were the Parkers. Susan insisted that he came with her to visit them.

'They're all dying to see you again,' she told him.

James doubted that. He and Bob tolerated each other for Susan's sake, Mrs Parker liked him because he was useful and Lillian—Lillian was a bit of an embarrassment. She'd written him several long and rambling letters while he'd been in Cyprus, saying how much she missed him. As for the others, he suspected that they disliked him as much as he disliked them. Except for Wendy. He did hope that Wendy might look at him more favourably now that he was no longer a kid. Now, if *she* had written him letters, that would have been altogether different.

He walked down to the Parkers' on Saturday evening with Susan, on his way to the Kursaal.

'So Wendy's not got engaged or anything?' he asked, as casually as he could.

'No, she's far too flighty to settle down. She never seems to go out with anyone for more than a few weeks,' Susan said.

'You don't like her much, do you?' he asked.

'It's not that at all. I like all of Bob's family. It's just that Wendy and I are very different, that's all.'

That was very true. Susan was perfect wife material, neat, loyal and domesticated. Wendy was—he hardly had the words to describe Wendy. Exotic, desirable, untamable. But not entirely beyond his reach. He still felt he was in with a chance.

When they reached the Parkers', most of them were in the kitchen. While the wireless burbled in the corner, Mrs Parker was ironing, Mr Parker was sitting at the table with his newspaper, Frank was combing his hair into an extravagant quiff, Bob was cleaning out his pipe and Lillian was putting away the newly washed dishes.

It was Lillian who spotted him first. 'James! James, you're back!' She rushed up to meet him at the back door, then stopped short, embarrassed. 'H-hello,' she said, holding out her hand for a formal shake. 'How are you?'

'Very well, thank you,' James responded automatically. He glanced over her shoulder, noted that Wendy was not there and brought his attention back to Lillian. What he saw surprised him. The leggy schoolgirl had grown into a tall young woman in a fashionable full skirt and tight waist, her shiny fair hair in a ponytail and her smile enhanced with pink lipstick.

'It's nice to see you again,' he said, keeping his voice cheerful and neutral, strictly older-brotherish. 'How's the dancing going?'

'Oh, it's fantastic! I've got loads of new friends and I'm doing a solo in a show next Wednesday afternoon. Miss Hill says I'm—'

From behind her in the kitchen came a chorus of, 'Lillian! Door!'

Lillian's face creased with frustration. With a dramatic groan, she went to answer the front door bell. Nothing had changed there, then, James noted. He stepped in to greet the rest of the family, and was soon busy answering questions about his time in Cyprus and his plans for the future.

'I'm going back to Dobson's for the time being,' he explained, 'and I'm hoping to get some work on the side. Repairs and services, that sort of thing.'

He didn't elaborate. He'd learnt that people tended to think he was just boasting if he said he was going to have his own garage one day. They'd see what he was up to soon enough.

'There's a lot more cars around than there used to be,' Bob said.

'I go for motorbikes, myself. Much more fun. Cars are for old men,' Frank said. 'Mate o' mine did the ton up the Southend Arterial the other day.'

'Young fool. Police'll get him if he's not careful,' his father commented.

Frank laughed. 'They'll have to catch him first.'

The men were arguing about the comparative merits of various cars when Wendy strolled in. She was wearing a crisp striped shirtwaister dress and she looked more stunning than ever.

'So you couldn't keep away, then?' she said to James.

'I wasn't going to miss seeing the prettiest girl in town.'

Wendy accepted this as nothing more than her due. 'You'd better look quickly, then, 'cos I'm going out right away.'

Her father spoke out then, trying to assert his authority. 'Where are you off to this evening? And who with?'

Wendy cast her eyes to the ceiling. 'Oh, *Dad*—I'm going to the pictures with Peter.'

'Is that the young whipper-snapper you went out with last week? You mind he brings you back by half past ten.'

'All *right,* I know. He knows too. You don't have to go on about it.'

The doorbell rang again and, for once, Wendy went to answer it. But Lillian was there before her. She flung it open and stood back, saying, 'Come in, they're all in the back.'

Wendy hurried down the hall, gathering her escort up and hustling him back outside, but not before James caught sight of a rather weedy-looking young man and, beyond him, a Morris Oxford parked at the kerb.

'He's got a car, then,' he remarked.

'It's not his, it's his dad's. He's some big noise out on the new industrial estate,' Frank said.

So that was what he had to compete with. To go out with Wendy, you had to have money and, since he was never going to be a rich man's son, he was going to have to earn it himself.

Wendy had her own ideas about what she was going to do with her life, and they didn't include James. If pushed, she would admit that he was rather good-looking, and he had done what he'd said he would and got as far as acting sergeant by the end of his national service, which was more than either of her brothers had done. Maybe if he'd achieved that, he'd go on and make himself rich one day, like Lillian said he planned to do, but Wendy couldn't wait that long. Leafing through the pages of *Picturegoer* and looking at the exotic lives of the film stars, she craved silk sheets, swimming pools, sophisticated parties and glamorous gowns. Or—if that was perhaps just too far out of her reach—at the very least she wanted to escape from life at the Sunny View Guest House. What she most feared was turning into a drudge like her mother, slaving away from dawn till dusk in a pinny and a headscarf, her hands getting redder and rougher by the day and no hope of any change for the better.

And here she was, nearly twenty years old and no sign yet of a rich husband. She'd had proposals all right, but none of the men had been up to scratch. She'd had some fairly rich boyfriends, but none of them had proposed, even though she'd led them on until they'd been begging her. She'd told them that she was a nice girl and she was saving herself for her wedding night.

Something had to be done before she was over the hill. She had to get herself noticed by the right sort of people. Then Lillian mentioned that she was going to enter the Carnival Talent Contest again.

'I don't care what Gran says, I'm going to have a go at it. I reckon I'll have a better chance this time. I've had so much tuition from Miss Hill, and I've performed in front of people lots of times,' she said.

'Only OAPs,' Wendy scoffed.

Lillian went on to say something else, but Wendy wasn't listening. The mention of the Carnival had revived an idea. If Lillian could go in for a stupid talent contest, then she could go in for the Carnival Queen. That would get her noticed all right. The Queen and her court went to all the events in town, and travelled to other towns in the area to take part in their carnivals. They got to go to dances and dinners and all sorts of things, and they met lots of people with influence. All the bigwigs in town supported the Carnival. The more she thought about the idea, the more she liked it. She saw herself riding around in a big car, arriving at nice hotels dressed in a white gown and velvet cloak with a sparkly crown on her head, shaking hands with rich men. Yes, that was definitely the answer. If she was honest with herself, she was never going to get to Hollywood, but she did have a good chance of becoming the Carnival Queen. She went to the Carnival offices.

'Do you have to parade in a bathing suit?' she asked the lady there.

'Oh, no, dear. It's not the Miss Lovely competition, you

know. The choosing of the Carnival Queen is very dignified. She has to represent our borough to the world.'

'Good. I'll have an entry form, then.'

That was all right. She would never hear the last of it if she got up on a stage in nothing but a bathing suit. She hung on to the word 'dignified'. Gran would like that.

Preliminary rounds were held in hotels around the town. Wendy was assigned to one in Southchurch. She got Peter, her latest boyfriend, to take her in his car.

'You'll be sure to win. It'll be a walkover,' he said.

'This is only the first round. Four girls from each group go forward,' Wendy told him.

She tilted the rear-view mirror so that she could check her lipstick. Yes, she did look good. Her hair was freshly set, her make-up was perfect. She practised her smile.

At the hotel, Peter went off to sit with the spectators in the ballroom, while Wendy joined a mêlée of excited young women in the cloakroom, all trying to make sure they looked their best. Wendy powdered her nose and shook out the skirts of her favourite dance dress, then followed the others to the lounge. A fat middle-aged man with a shining bald patch got up and spoke to them. Wendy disliked him on sight.

'He's the sort that looks down your cleavage,' she murmured to the girl next to her.

'Well, now, what a bevy of beauties we have here this evening! I'm sure every one of you deserves to be the Carnival Queen, but I'm afraid we have to choose just four to go to the next round. So you will all parade round the ballroom for everyone to see how lovely you are, and then you will be called up one by one to speak to me at the microphone. Is that clear?'

'Oh, dear, a microphone. I've never talked through one of them before,' the girl next to Wendy said.

'It's easy,' Wendy told her, though she had no idea really. It looked easy enough on the television.

When they entered the ballroom, they were met with a fanfare, bright lights and loud applause. Any nerves that Wendy had melted away with the attention. This was wonderful. This was like being a film star. She walked round in a line with all the other girls, head up, chest out, smiling for all she was worth. Everyone clapped politely. She caught sight of Peter, applauding for all he was worth. Yes, well, he was going the moment she found somebody better.

They were asked to line up along the back of the ballroom, facing the table at which the three judges sat. Wendy remembered films she had seen and stood slightly sideways with one foot in front of the other and a hand on her hip. She looked good and she knew it.

The fat man stepped forward and spoke into the mike. He was sweating copiously.

'Now, ladies and gentlemen, the Carnival Queen has to meet all sorts of people and make many speeches during her reign, so it is very important that she can speak clearly in public. I'm now going to interview each of these lovely young ladies and see how they shape up.'

The first girl did nothing but giggle nervously and wave at somebody in the audience. The second was very confident and talked easily about her job and her hobbies. That, Wendy saw, was the way to do it. When it came to her turn, she directed her smile at the judges before turning to the master of ceremonies.

'And now, who do we have here?' he asked.

'Good evening, I'm Wendy Parker.' It came out clearly enough. She was pleased.

'Tell me, Wendy, what do you do for a living?'

'I work in Dixon's on the High Street, in the ladies' separates department.'

It was all over far too quickly. Before she knew it, Wendy was back in the line waiting with the rest of the hopefuls. One by one the others were interviewed. A three-piece band played while the judges made their minds up and the girls were asked to parade round the ballroom again. Wendy smiled and smiled till her cheeks began to ache. At last the judges handed a piece of paper to the MC. He walked to the mike.

'Ladies and gentlemen, I now have the result of this evening's contest. It has been a very hard task for our judges, but a very pleasant one as well—'

'Get on with it—' Wendy muttered through clenched teeth. The man did like the sound of his own voice.

Finally, he announced the four winners. There was the confident girl, a tall brunette, a bouncy long-haired girl '—and last, but certainly not least, Miss Wendy Parker.'

Wendy squealed with delight. She was on her way!

She decided not to tell them at home yet. There was time enough for that if she got through to the final.

She had to get time off work on a Friday afternoon for the next round. It was held at the Palace Hotel, the huge prestigious place on top of the cliffs by the pier. The Carnival committee was there and the mayor, and this time there were two film stars in charge of events, David Kossoff and Julia Arnall.

'It's the first time I've met anyone famous,' she confided to the girl next to her.

It was so exciting. This was what she had entered the contest for.

Twenty-eight girls went through the same process as last time. Wendy was brimming with confidence now. The whiff of fame gave her a champagne lift. She chattered away to the stars as if they were old friends and strutted back to her place in the line as proud as a catwalk princess. But when the names were called, hers was not among them.

Wendy couldn't believe it. Dumbly, she watched the lucky five pose for the camera and speak to a news reporter. How could they be chosen and not her? She was prettier than any of them. She hated every one of them, and even more she hated the stars who had rejected her for this bunch of dumplings. Some of the other competitors were already melting away, their faces as disappointed as hers.

But then a whisper began to go round the big ballroom—'Too young! Too young!'

The mayor and the Carnival committee went into a huddle.

'What is it? What's going on?' Wendy demanded of a bystander.

'One of the girls is only seventeen,' she was told.

'What does that mean? Will she be disqualified?' Hope began to beat in her heart again.

'That's what they're deciding now. The rules are that the girls have to be eighteen to enter.'

The unfortunate winner was staring out of the window at the sea, biting her lip, while people round her comforted her. Wendy could feel nothing but triumph. She had another chance!

The committee came to a decision. The rules had to be obeyed. The girl burst into tears. Wendy smiled, hardly daring to breathe. Surely, surely—?

'—so our new contender for the crown is Miss Wendy Parker.'

'Yes!'

Wendy hardly knew whether she was laughing or crying. She was definitely in the Carnival Court, and she was in the running for Queen. As soon as the pictures were taken and the interviews done, she drew all of the money out of her Post Office savings account and spent it on the most spectacular evening gown she could find. This evening, she had to give it all she'd got.

By lucky chance, the first person she ran into when she got home was Bob.

'Look at this,' she said, displaying the dress. 'I'm wearing it to the Odeon this evening.'

'The Odeon? Isn't it the Carnival Queen thing there tonight? I thought all the tickers sold out ages ago.'

Wendy patted her hair. 'They were, but I'm not going to watch it—I'm in it.'

'In it? Are you saying that you might be the Carnival Queen? Gran might have something to say about that.'

At that moment, Lillian came bouncing down the stairs and stayed to admire the gorgeous gown. It tripped a half forgotten memory in Wendy's brain.

'I thought you said your precious Mr Caraway approved of the Carnival.'

'Well…yes…he does,' Bob admitted.

'So he would be very impressed by your sister being Carnival Queen and doing all that stuff for charity?'

Wendy was very impressed with herself. She couldn't have hit on a better argument.

'He would, yes. You're right.'

Lillian wanted to know all about it then, and pledged her support. Wendy wasn't interested in that. Nobody listened to Lillian. But, with Bob behind her, she was on her way.

She was right. Bob stressed what an honour it would be to have a member of the Parker family as Carnival Queen, and Gran actually agreed.

Wendy decided not to ruin it by actually showing her the gown. It was sensational, a strapless number encased in gold sequins that hugged her body from bust to knee, then flared out in a swishy skirt. For added glamour, she wore elbow-length white gloves. She looked a million dollars.

When Peter came to pick her up, he was practically speechless. 'Wow—!' he gasped, his mouth hanging open. 'M-Marilyn Monroe!'

It was just the effect she was aiming at.

The crowning of the Carnival Queen was one of the biggest events in town. Three thousand people were at the Odeon to see it. The foyer was decked with flowers and lights, the Mayor and Mayoress were there and there was a guard of honour formed by the Sea Cadets. Wendy felt like the film star she dreamed of being. This was what fame was like, and she loved it.

The five contestants were escorted to the dressing rooms at the back of the building. The other girls were surprisingly friendly.

'Isn't this fun?' one of them said. 'Whatever happens, we're all in the court. We're going to have such a good time.'

But Wendy didn't want to just be in the court. She wanted to be Queen. She eyed the other girls' dresses. They were pretty, but they didn't ooze glamour like hers did. She studied her face in the mirror, renewing her already perfect lipstick. Yes, she looked the goods. She couldn't fail.

Standing on the stage of the Odeon was different again from parading in a ballroom. The noise of three thousand people clapping was amazing. Wendy drank it in. Out there beyond the footlights, they were all looking at her. The thrill of it went right through her. She pouted and blew kisses.

So busy was she drinking in the attention, that she hardly listened to the first two girls as they were interviewed. When it got to the one before her, she started to pay more attention. David Kossoff and Julia Arnall were excellent at their task. They put her at her ease and got her talking naturally. Wendy felt a slight dip of confidence. This girl was good. You could see it. She spoke in a nice middle-class voice and she had plenty to say about her hobbies of amateur dramatics and netball and the Red Cross. She came back to her place in the line glowing.

'Don't be nervous—it's fine, they're lovely,' she whispered to Wendy.

'And next we have Miss Wendy Parker—'

The applause was just for her. Wendy moved forward. The gown was so tight round her upper legs that it forced a wiggle into her walk. She stopped between the two film stars and posed for the audience.

'Wendy, that's a lovely gown you're wearing for us tonight,' Julia said.

Wendy glowed.

'Well, thank you, Miss Arnall. I bought it specially. But yours is very beautiful too.'

They asked her about her work, and what she did out of work.

'I like going dancing down the Kursaal,' she said.

'And what's your favourite dance?'

'The tango. Only there's not many men can do it really proper.'

'And when you're not dancing, what do you like to do?'

'Well—er—' For a moment she was flummoxed. 'I like going round the shops, only that's difficult 'cos I work in one and I only get my lunch hour to look at the others. And I like reading—'

'Reading? What was the last book you read?'

'*Picturegoer.* I love looking at what the stars are doing.'

David Kossoff asked what her ambitions were.

'Oh, I want to be a film star, just like you and Miss Arnall.'

Right at this moment, she felt anything was possible.

'I want a great big car and a house with a swimming pool and lots of jewels and furs,' she elaborated.

'And are you looking for Mr Right to share all this with you?' Julia wondered.

'Of course, but he's got to be handsome and very rich.'

This brought laughter from the audience.

Wendy went back to her place in the line feeling she had done all right. The other girls smiled and nodded at her as she joined them. The last one went for her interview.

The MC came back on stage to remind the audience that they had one vote each, and that they were to bear in mind that the Carnival Queen not only had to look lovely, but be able to meet with all sorts of people in the course of her duties and speak in public. There was a murmur in the audience that grew to a buzz as everyone discussed their choice with the people next to them. Then the stars and the contestants left the stage to more applause, and the audience settled down to watch Jack Hawkins in *The Long Arm*.

'Can't we watch the film?' Wendy asked.

'I'm sorry,' one of the organisers told her, 'but once the votes are counted, the new Queen has to rehearse her speech.'

It was the longest wait Wendy had ever endured. The organisers tried to keep them all amused, but all Wendy wanted was to know the result. Over an hour went by.

'They're having a recount of the first two,' somebody said.

Wendy nearly screamed with frustration. Another thirty minutes passed. The chairman of the Carnival committee came in with a piece of paper in his hand.

'It was very close,' he said. 'Only ten votes in it between

first and second place but we now have a result—' He went over to the girl who had talked about being in the Red Cross. 'Congratulations, my dear. You are our new Carnival Queen.'

'No—' Wendy whispered.

Surely not. This couldn't be happening. They couldn't choose somebody else.

But they had. She was neither Queen nor deputy. She was merely a lady-in-waiting. And, what was more, she had to stand there with a false smile pasted on her face, being nice to the others when all the time her dreams lay around her in tiny pieces.

CHAPTER 10

LILLIAN stepped out of the shelter of the pier head station and into driving rain and wind. Carnival week was proving a disaster, weather-wise. The main procession had taken place in pouring rain. Wendy, sitting on a float only partly covered by a roof, had had to shelter under a large white umbrella as she waved to the crowds.

But it was not the rain that was bothering Lillian at the moment. She was shivering not from cold, but from nerves. Out of the blue, her big break had presented itself. She was going to an audition. Mamie Hill had heard from the producer's mouth that two girls had walked out of the end of the pier show. The producer needed replacements straight away. Several of the Mamie Hill girls had said they would like to try but, when it came down to it, only Lillian and one other had turned up.

'They've chickened out,' her friend said. 'They said if they did get it, it would only be for a month at most, just till the end of the season, and then what? It's always more difficult to get work in the winter when all the Golden Mile stuff closes.'

Lillian knew this was true in her heart of hearts, but she wasn't going to let it stop her.

'I don't care. If I get this, then I'll try to get another dance job after. I won't want my old job back,' she said.

Four dancers from London had also arrived, sent by their agents to audition. On the tram up the pier they discussed theatres and managements in a way that made Lillian feel very ignorant and sapped her confidence. These were real pros. They knew what they were at. What did she think she was doing, setting herself up against them? But then she remembered what James had said only a week or so ago when Frank had mocked his motor repair business.

'You should be out having a good time, mate,' Frank had said. 'There you are, every evening after work, every weekend, mending cars. And for what? I dunno why you do it.'

'Because I don't want to work for someone else all my life,' James had replied.

'Yeah, but it ain't exactly a Rolls-Royce dealership, is it?'

'Not yet. Everyone's got to start somewhere,' James told him.

Everyone's got to start somewhere—this was where she was starting.

A whole group of them had been on the same tram. As well as the dancers coming for the audition, there was a girl who was in the show already, an accompanist and, of course, the producer, Artie Craig. They all hurried up the steps to the top deck, waited while the producer unlocked the doors to the theatre and stumbled in, eager to get out of the rain. Lillian breathed in the smell of salt and damp carpet and cigarette ash. A theatre. She was in a real theatre. The producer switched the lights on, and with each click some more of the building was revealed. Lillian gazed round at green and white paintwork, green and brown tip-up seats and a plain proscenium arch with the safety curtain lowered, showing a picture of the pier as seen from the air.

Artie Craig lit a cigarette and took their names. 'You two Mamie Hill's girls?' he asked Lillian and her friend.

They both nodded. Lillian was mortified at how easily he had identified them. Was it so obvious that they were amateurs?

'You take the others to the changing rooms, Jenny,' he said to the chorus dancer. 'You girls give your music to Reg before you go. I want you all ready in ten minutes.'

Lillian didn't know whether she was more thrilled or terrified. It was so exciting to be putting on her dancing shoes in a real changing room, but so much was riding on this that she felt quite ill. She had had to pretend to be sick to get off work, and now it seemed as if her lies were coming back to haunt her.

'How did he know we were Miss Hill's?' her friend whispered.

'We must look as green as grass,' Lillian said.

'I suppose so. I'm ever so nervous.'

'Me too,' Lillian said.

It was an understatement. She was hot and clammy, her throat was dry, her legs seemed to have lost all their strength and she wanted to throw up. How could she possibly dance her best feeling like this? She changed into the shorts and blouse that Miss Hill had recommended, applied her greasepaint and brushed her hair. Around her, the London girls were talking to Jenny, the company dancer.

'What's he like to work for?'

'Who, Artie? OK. Thinks he's Busby Berkeley.'

'Don't they all? Does he keep his hands to himself?'

'Give me a break! He's bent as a hairpin. Can't you tell?'

'Well, now you mention it, I s'pose so. What's the rest of the company like?'

'All right. Us girls work well together. The comic's a pain in the backside.'

'I hate comics. They're such miserable bastards.'

Lillian felt completely out of her depth, but listened eagerly. This was a world she longed to belong to, and a language she wanted to understand. The girls all seemed strong and bright and confident, and she wanted to be like them.

'Have you been dancing long?' she asked Jenny.

'Since I was twelve, darling. Got my first job in panto as an elf. This your first audition?'

Lillian nodded.

'Well, give it your best. Artie's desperate to fill the gaps, and there aren't that many decent dancers available at this stage of the season. It's not as if we're a big line-up anyway. Losing two out of six is a disaster. And, what with all this foul weather, we've been doing great business, so we've got to have a full company.'

'Yes, of course,' Lillian said, trying to sound as if she knew what she was talking about.

'Come on, let's get on with it or Artie'll start getting his knickers in a twist,' Jenny called above the chatter.

The girls gathered in the wings, and one by one they were called on to the stage. It wasn't like watching the Mamie Hill Dancers. All of them knew exactly what they were doing and gave a competent professional performance. They could all sing, dance and do both at the same time.

'They're ever so good, aren't they?' Lillian's friend whispered.

'Mmm,' Lillian agreed, not taking her eyes off the girl who was performing at that moment. Another of James's sayings floated into her brain.

'If you want to compete, you've got to offer something extra.'

What did she have to offer? At first she couldn't think of anything, but then, as she watched the dancers, she began to realise that they were all rather mechanical. They could do the steps and sing the notes, but something was missing. They'd done it all before. They wanted the job all right, but not as passionately as she wanted it. What she had to offer was that she was fresh and keen. Whether that was enough, whether it was even a good thing, remained to be seen.

The other Mamie Hill girl was called on. Lillian could see that she was not in the same league as the London dancers. Artie Craig thanked her and told her she needn't stay. The girl burst into tears and rushed off the stage. Lillian had no time to comfort her because her name was being called.

'Lindy-Lou Parker.'

She skipped onto the stage and flashed her most brilliant smile in the direction of the producer.

'Good morning, Mr Craig!'

A weary voice came from the stalls. 'Just get on with it, sweetie. What are you singing?'

'Ready, Willing and Able.'

'I hope you are, sweetie, I hope you are. OK, Reg.'

The accompanist struck up the opening bars and Lillian launched into the jaunty Doris Day number. She sang it through, projecting every ounce of bounce and sparkle she could muster. Then she sang it again while dancing, ending with a flick-flack and the splits, which had never been in the original Mamie Hill version. She was greeted with silence. Disconcerted, she stood up and shaded her eyes against the footlights.

'Is that enough?' she asked.

'Quite enough, sweetie.'

Artie Craig's tone of voice had not altered in the least. Lillian felt utterly squashed. He hadn't liked it. He thought she was a silly little amateur. Shoulders slumped, she turned to walk off the stage.

'How old are you, sweetie?'

Lillian spun back to face the auditorium again, hope surging in her heart.

'Seventeen,' she lied.

'Right, well—stay there,' Artie told her. 'You other girls, let's have you back on stage. Jenny, stage front, and we'll run through the opening number. Music, Reg.'

Lillian hardly had time to take in what was happening as the dancers ran to form a line each side of her, Jenny stood in front of them and the accompanist struck up some opening bars. And then they were all singing and dancing to *I Do Like To Be Beside The Seaside*. Luckily, she knew most of the words and didn't have to think about them, as she concentrated fiercely on following the dance steps. *'Smile, girls, smile!'* she heard Mamie Hill say at the back of her head. Smiling was not easy when you were trying to pick up a routine, but she stuck one onto her face and carried on. The number ended in a group pose. Lillian found herself pushed out of the way by one of the London girls with arms stretched, leg forward and chest out. She leaned sideways precariously to make sure she was seen, her limbs trembling with the effort.

'Right, off you go, Jenny,' the producer called. 'From the top, Reg.'

'Bloody hell,' muttered one of the London girls.

Lillian swallowed. They were being asked to do the dance by themselves after just one run-through! At Mamie Hill's, they went through each section several times before putting the whole thing together, and even then they weren't expected to get it right. There wasn't time to panic. Already Reg was playing the opening bars again. Her body seemed to take over, taking its cues directly from the music. Twice she went wrong but managed to get back into it. She kept on singing and she kept that smile going. Never had a dance seemed so long.

This time she was ready for the ending. Dead on the beat, she dropped on one knee in the middle of the group, her arms out to each side. The others were forced to group round her. Her smile was bright with triumph. She had got through it!

Again there was that unsettling silence. The dancers stood up and waited for the verdict.

Artie Craig's flat voice floated out from the stalls. 'OK, you in the blue blouse—what's your name?'

'May.'

It was the one who had pushed in front of Lillian.

'May. Right, you're in. And you, Lulu or whatever you're called. Call me mad if you like, but I'll take a chance on you. Have you got an Equity card?'

Lillian shook her head. Membership of the actor's trade union was strictly for professionals only.

'Get signed up straight away or I'll have them on my back like a ton of bricks.'

Lillian tried to say, *Yes, Mr Craig*, but nothing came out. She had the job. She really had the job. She could hardly believe it. She was a real dancer in a real show.

There was no time to revel in her huge good fortune. Artie wanted the new girls in the line-up as soon as possible so, while the disgruntled failures went to get changed and go, it was down to work straight away for the newcomers. Jenny led them through the steps of the opening and closing numbers, while Artie came in with the finishing touches. The lethargic man slumped in the stalls seat was transformed into a slavedriver.

'Heads up, for chrissakes! Knees higher, May. Higher! Lulu, stop dragging that foot. Tighten up that turn. Clap! Clap! Look happy!'

Occasionally he would demonstrate what he wanted, and Lillian saw immediately that he was a very accomplished dancer himself.

She had never worked harder in her life. The concentration together with the physical effort was relentless. But she was young and strong and enjoyed every minute. This was real show business, the sweat behind the applause. This was what it was all about.

At midday there was a brief break for a snack.

'Haven't you brought a packed lunch?' Jenny asked.

'I didn't know I'd be staying. My mum's expecting me home for dinner,' Lillian confessed.

She was going to be in big trouble even before she confessed to getting a job as a dancer.

'Have some of mine,' Jenny said, offering a pile of chicken paste sandwiches wrapped in greaseproof paper. 'You got to keep your strength up. We've got two shows to get through this afternoon.'

Lillian found she was starving. She wolfed down the sandwiches, promising to give Jenny some of hers tomorrow. While she was eating them, an elderly lady with her hair tied up in a pink chiffon scarf pinned her and May into their costumes, ready to make some quick alterations. Those for the opening number were designed to be as bright as possible. The dancers all wore different coloured dresses with wide-brimmed matching hats. Lillian's was orange with black trim. The closing number called for showgirl-style outfits with bodies cut like corsets, fishnet tights, long gloves and feathered headdresses, all in pink and purple. Lillian scarcely recognised herself in this. She looked like a different person altogether.

The other three dancers, Val, Sue and Muriel, arrived, Lillian and May were slotted into their places in the line-up and the opening and closing numbers were rehearsed until they had it right.

'At least we can start and finish with a flourish. You other girls will have to carry on with just the four of you for the rest of the show. Tomorrow we'll get another couple of numbers in place,' Artie said.

Before Lillian had time to think about it, they were sent off to get ready while the first members of the public started coming in out of the rain. Sitting in the cramped little dressing room, putting on her greasepaint and listening to the other girls, stage fright set in with a vengeance. Her hands were trembling so much she could hardly get her lipstick on straight. What was she doing here? She felt a complete fraud amongst all these experienced performers. She was sure she was going to let everyone down and get thrown out of the theatre.

'Wish you hadn't done it now?' May sneered, as she applied her eyeshadow with professional ease.

'No,' Lillian said.

'Dunno why he chose you. You dunno your arse from your elbow, do you?'

'Lay off, May,' Jenny ordered. 'She's got the makings of a nice little dancer. Surprised me, how she picked up the numbers.'

Lillian felt ever so slightly better.

There was a rap on the door.

'Five minutes!'

The girls checked their hair, tied on their hats, straightened their dresses and warmed up their voices by running through some scales. Lillian wanted to go to the toilet, but didn't dare at this late stage.

'Overture and beginners!'

Jenny hustled the dancers out of the dressing room. In the wings the chatter died and they lined up in order of entrance. Lillian was shaking as she stood next to last between Val and Sue. It had all happened so fast that she was still half expecting to wake up and find it was only a dream. But then the medley of tunes from the first half faded and the opening bars of *I Do Like To Be Beside The Seaside* struck up as the curtains opened. Light flooded the stage, Muriel stepped forward and, before Lillian knew it, she was out in the full glare of the spotlights, giving it all she had.

The hours of rehearsal had not been wasted. Nerves or no nerves, her body remembered what to do. The first part of the dance was quite easy as they sang the song, then came a more complicated section where they danced to the music, including a tricky little bit where Lillian had got the timing wrong several times in rehearsal. She concentrated extra hard as they led up to it, but still her turn was half a beat behind what it should have been. There was no time for embarrassment, she picked up the step and completed the movement, hoping desperately that the audience and, more importantly, Artie Craig, had not noticed. And then it was back into the song again. A scattering of people in the audience started to clap along with the happy beat. More joined in. Lillian's heart lifted. They liked it. It was all right. The dancers took up the closing pose and applause broke out. Lillian smiled and smiled. She had done it! She had got right through her very first professional appearance without totally humiliating herself.

The curtain fell and the girls hurried off stage. Lillian was euphoric. This morning she had been a shopgirl skiving off work; this afternoon she was a professional dancer. Her chosen career had begun. *Look at me, Aunty Eileen,* she said in her head. *Look at me—I'm doing what you said, and I won't let them stop me!*

CHAPTER 11

JAMES cycled along the seafront towards the Parkers' place. Strong gusts of rain-laden wind blew off the shore, making him swerve dangerously and he thought longingly of the nice little Hillman he had just been offered at a knock-down price. He knew he could get it running sweet as a nut with a bit of work and then he wouldn't be out here in all sorts of weather, plus he would be able to offer Wendy a lift anywhere she wanted to go. But Wendy was now used to being chauffeured around in a limousine when on duty as part of the Carnival Queen's court, and he had made a decision to save all he could towards equipment for his own repair works. So he stood up on the pedals and battled on along the Golden Mile.

He almost rode straight past the slender figure hurrying along the pavement with her head down against the wind, until something familiar about her made him stop.

'Lillian!' He pulled into the side. 'What are you doing here? This isn't your way home, surely?'

'Oh, James—! Am I glad to see you! I've got such wonderful news, you'll never believe it, but right now I'm in so much trouble.'

Intrigued, he got off the bike to walk along with her. 'Come on, tell.'

She looked at him with shining eyes, a big grin of delight lighting up her wet face. 'I've got a job as a dancer in the end-of-the-pier show!'

'Congratulations! That's marvellous, Lillian. Clever old you; you've got what you wanted. Well done!'

Genuinely pleased for her, he gave her a hug, just as he would have hugged Susan or his mother. 'Tell me all about it,' he urged.

Out came the story of bunking off work, not telling the family, the audition process and the two shows she had been in that very afternoon. James immediately understood why Lillian was in deep trouble. This was not going to go down too well with Gran and the rest of the Parkers.

'I'll help you face the music,' he offered.

'Oh, would you? I'm scared stiff. But I'm not going to give it up. They can say what they like. They can throw me out and not speak to me again, but I'm not going to give it up. It's everything I've always dreamed of.'

'Good for you,' James said.

By now they were walking up the Parkers' road towards Sunny View. It had actually been freshly painted in the spring, but in gloomy brown and cream so it still looked as forbidding as ever. James couldn't imagine anyone wanting to stay there for a holiday, especially on a day like today, when they had to spend all day out in the rain and wind until Gran let them come back in at half past five. No wonder Lillian's show had been well attended. Holidaymakers needed to get out of the rain.

The whole family was sitting round the tea table as they came in. James found himself unnoticed in the outcry at Lillian.

'Wherever have you been?'

'I've been worried sick!'

'What do you think you're playing at? There'd better be a good explanation.'

'Most irresponsible.'

James stepped forward. 'Lillian has some wonderful news to tell you,' he announced. 'Now you have two stars in the family. Wendy's in the Carnival Queen's court, and Lillian's in the end-of-the-pier show.'

If anything, the babble was even worse at this. James took a big chance, depending on his sister's backing him up later.

'I'm sure Susan will think Lillian's really doing great things for the family name, Bob. She'll be extra proud now to be a Parker.'

Bob huffed and puffed at this, not knowing quite what to say, but it didn't seem to cut a lot of ice with the others. Gran drew breath to speak and everyone else fell silent. She fixed Lillian with her remorseless stare.

'Are you telling me, young lady, that you are making an exhibition of yourself to anyone who has the money to come and stare at you?'

She made it sound like some smutty peep show at the fair.

Lillian straightened her shoulders.

'It's a perfectly respectable show, Gran. Most of the people there this afternoon were families and OAPs. They were there to see some pretty dancing and hear some nice songs and enjoy themselves. There's nothing wrong in that, surely?'

'Plenty, if you ask me,' Gran countered.

If James hadn't known the Parkers so well he wouldn't have believed it. This was 1956, but Lillian's gran and dad still seemed to be living in Victorian times. Lindy might still harbour fond memories of her Aunty Eileen, but he suspected that she had her aunt to thank for the short rein she was kept on. They were terrified of her turning into another Eileen.

'And what about your job, might I ask? What happens about that? I can't see that shoe shop taking you back in the autumn if you throw up your place there now.'

Lillian didn't have an immediate answer to that but, before Gran could pounce on her again, Wendy spoke up.

'Why would she want a boring job in a shop back again? I'm sure I wouldn't. What's the money like, Lill?'

'More than I'm getting at the shop, and that's for two shows a day and three on Fridays and Saturdays,' Lillian told them.

There was a stunned silence.

'Blooming ridiculous, paying a young girl that much for so little,' Mr Parker growled.

James looked at him in disgust. How could a man be jealous of his daughter's success? He ought to be proud.

'Nice work if you can get it,' Wendy commented. 'Good for you, kid. Now, just in case you've all forgotten, I do have two engagements this evening. If I don't go and get ready now, the car will be at the door before I get my hair done.'

Her hair looked perfect already. In fact, she looked perfect altogether. James still couldn't make out why she hadn't been made Queen. And what a good sister she was, too. She had done a splendid job in defending Lillian and deflecting some of the interest onto herself. Lillian was often quite sharp and sarcastic when talking about Wendy, but James guessed that it was just jealousy.

Mrs Parker asked to be reminded where her famous daughter was going that evening. Wendy went on at some length about hotels and dinners and dances and bigwigs. She was sailing way beyond his reach, James realised. There was no way he could take her to places like that yet. One day he would be able to, but not now.

Lillian took the opportunity to slip into her seat at the table. 'Is there any tea left in the pot, Mum? I'm starving.'

The inquisition had not finished with her yet but, though Mr Parker and Gran were still outraged, Frank said he didn't see what all the fuss was about, and Bob, after prevaricating a bit, said he didn't think that there was any harm in it.

Through it all, Lillian devoured every scrap of bread, jam and cake left on the table, washed down with four cups of stewed tea.

'Of course, you'd have to put the extra money in the housekeeping,' Gran insisted.

It was the first crack. James tried to widen it.

'There's one easy way of settling whether or not this show is suitable for Lillian to be appearing in. Why not go and see it for yourselves?'

Mr Parker flushed and turned on him. 'What makes you think it's any business of yours? What are you doing here anyway? This is family business.'

James longed to hit him square on the nose. 'I came to fix a dripping tap in the scullery,' he told him.

'Oh, yes, he is, Doug. I asked him to,' Mrs Parker confirmed. 'It's been getting worse and worse and it's driving me mad—'

The doorbell rang and Wendy came downstairs ready for her evening of official appearances. She was dressed in her white lady-in-waiting gown and crystal tiara with a velvet cloak round her shoulders. The fuss around her departure gave

Lillian a break as the family gathered in the hall to wave her off. James watched with the others, envying whoever was going to talk to Wendy and dance with her that evening. She really did look like a film star, stepping into the big black car. One day, he would dress up in a tuxedo and take her out to a dinner dance. Then every man in the room would envy him.

The car drove off and the front door was closed. James was so engrossed with his daydream that at first he didn't realise that Gran was speaking to him.

'—a lot of sense, young man.'

'Oh—right—' he said.

'Yes. I might go to this place at the end of the pier. I haven't been up the pier since before the war.'

James was flabbergasted. He'd never expected Gran to take up his suggestion.

'Right, well, I'm sure you'll like it,' he said.

Gran disappeared into her room, effectively shelving the argument. The rest of the family dispersed around the house, while Lillian followed James into the scullery.

'Thanks ever so much for sticking up for me,' she said. 'You were wonderful. I don't know what I would have done without you.'

'Well, you've followed your dream all right today, haven't you? You got what you wanted and you held out against the family to keep it. I'm proud of you.'

'Are you?' Lillian said, her voice full of hope. 'Are you really?'

James busied himself with the dripping tap. ''Course I am,' he said. 'You're my little sister, remember? You believe in me and I believe in you. We're both going to make good.'

Wendy stood with the rest of the Carnival court, smiling and shaking hands and accepting compliments. A parade of middle aged people were lined up to meet them. The women were generally condescending and the men ogled her. Wendy did her bit and was charming to them, but all the while she was on the lookout for something better. She wanted a rich man, but she didn't want an old man. A bit older than her was fine, ten years or so was all right, but beyond that she wasn't so sure. She couldn't imagine kissing a man with a paunch or a bald head, however rich he might be.

This was the most important dance of the evening so the Carnival Queen and her court were due to stay until midnight, which left plenty of scope for assessing the talent. Before the girls were free to take to the floor, however, there were the usual speeches. The Mayor, with his gold chain of office over his dress suit, went on about what a great place Southend was and how wonderful its people were, then the chairman of the Carnival committee said what a success it was this year despite the dreadful weather. The amount raised so far that evening at the dance was announced and everyone clapped and cheered.

Then the Carnival Queen stood up and thanked everyone for coming and encouraged them to spend some more. Wendy stood there with a smile on her face and rage in her heart. It was all right for her. She had a nice accent and a confident manner. She knew how to talk at do's like this. She came from a family that was used to going to swish places and talking to posh people. That was what had clinched her crown. It wasn't fair.

Wendy caught a whiff of cigar smoke behind her.

'Is that hair natural?' a gravelly voice asked. Its owner was so close that she could feel his breath on her neck.

She glanced round, getting a brief impression of a man in his thirties with hard eyes and a sensuous mouth. She turned back, a shiver of arousal stirring.

'Of course,' she answered.

'That's good. I don't like bottle blondes,' the man said, for her ears alone. He had a London accent with a hint of menace in it.

'I'm the real thing,' Wendy told him, without taking her eyes off the Carnival Queen.

'I'll be back,' the man said.

Wendy wasn't sure whether it was more of a promise or a threat. She made the slightest of shrugs and felt his presence disappear, along with his cigar smoke. She felt slightly exposed, as if he had taken a layer of her clothing with him.

The speeches finished and the band struck up. The Mayor lead the Carnival Queen onto the floor; other dignitaries stepped forward to dance with members of the court. A portly gentleman who Wendy had danced with at one of the previous evening's events was making a beeline for her but, before he could reach her, a short man with powerful shoulders stepped in front of him.

'You going to introduce me?' he asked. It was the one who had been standing behind her.

The portly man looked put out, but did the honours all the same.

'Miss Parker, allow me to introduce Mr Terry Dempsey. Dempsey, this is Miss Wendy Parker. A very nice young lady,' he added, with undue emphasis.

Wendy found herself shaking a large hand and looking into a predator's face. Not a handsome face, but a commanding one, heavy about the jowls. Unlike the men around him, he did not have a severe short-back-and-sides. His thick dark hair was blow dried into a fashionable quiff and curled over his collar, with sideburns on his cheeks. Beneath his slickly tailored dinner jacket was a well muscled body.

'Pleased to meet you,' Wendy said, searching in her mind for where she had heard his name before. Terry Dempsey— Terry Dempsey—of course! He owned a hefty slice of the Golden Mile.

'Likewise,' Terry said. 'Care to dance?'

Here was money and looks and he was not too old.

'Don't mind if I do,' Wendy said, acting cool.

She stepped into his arms, trying not to show the thrill of excitement pulsing through her, laced with a delicious thread of fear. She no longer envied the Carnival Queen. She had snaffled the best man in the room. What was more, he had sought her out.

Terry Dempsey was not a wonderful dancer, but he led with decision. Wendy foxtrotted round the crowded floor with him, intensely conscious of his hand on her back, his legs guiding hers.

'D'you enjoy all this la-di-da stuff?' he asked.

'It's lovely,' Wendy said truthfully. 'All these dances and dinners and riding around in a big car.'

'What, with all these stiffs in penguin suits?'

'You're wearing a penguin suit,' Wendy pointed out.

'You gotta look the part, ain't you? You look the part. Mind you, you'd look better still in one of them off-the-shoulder numbers. Very nice.'

His thigh brushed her inner leg.

'Thanks,' Wendy said, just managing to keep a squeal of pleasure out of her voice.

'Don't mention it. I was about to leave. No lookers here at all. I'm glad I didn't now.'

It was all Wendy could do not to say, *So am I.*

'You can't leave before the Carnival court. We're the stars,' she told him.

The dance was over all too soon.

'Another?' Terry asked.

'Us ladies-in-waiting are supposed to dance with someone different each time,' Wendy told him.

'And do you always do what you're told, like a good little girl?'

'Only when I want to.'

'So how about another dance?'

It was the hardest thing she'd ever had to do. But years of coping with admirers had taught her never to appear too keen. You had to let them do the chasing.

'Sorry,' she said, treating him to her most brilliant smile. 'No can do.'

A couple of men were already heading her way with hopeful expressions on their faces. Wendy turned away to see which would get to her first. As she did so, she felt Terry rest his hand briefly on her buttock.

'We'll see about that,' he said in her ear, and was gone.

The rest of the evening passed in a blur. Whoever she was dancing with or talking to, Wendy was aware only of where Terry was and who he was with. Every time she lost sight of him she panicked, fearing he had left. Every time she glimpsed him again she flushed with relief. But all the time she took care not to let their eyes meet, which they nearly did many times. He was watching her just as closely as she was watching him.

At midnight, the MC announced that the Carnival Queen and her court were about to depart. Terry materialised at Wendy's side.

'How about letting me have your number, sweetheart?'

Wendy raised her pencilled eyebrows. 'That's for you to find out,' she told him.

The dancers had formed two lines across the dance floor to the door. Wendy joined the rest of the court and walked behind the Queen between the applauding revellers. She did not look back.

In the car, the girls laughed and chatted and compared opinions about the way the evening had gone. Wendy tried to join in, but her only thought was whether she had played it right. Had she been too cool? Would he bother to try and contact her? Had she blown it?

She need not have worried. The next morning a huge bunch of yellow roses done up in cellophane and bows was delivered to Sunny View. Nestling amongst it was a card that read, *To the most beautiful baby doll in the shop.*

CHAPTER 12

'I'M GOING to try for the panto in Wimbledon again. We had a really good run there last Christmas, and the producer was really hot on dance. We had lots of numbers.'

'Ah, but was he hot on dancers?'

'No, he had his eyes on the principal boy, but she was in love with the bloke what played the giant. It was all going on there, I can tell you.'

'I'm fed up with only doing pantos and summer seasons. I want to get a proper long-running job in a London show.'

There was a general sigh of longing.

'Don't we all? That'd be wonderful.'

Lillian listened as they all got changed for the first show of the day. There was just one more week left of the season, and all anyone seemed to be talking about was auditions and job opportunities. As always, she felt completely left out. Most of the other girls had been nice enough in the short time she had been with the company, but they still treated her as if she was not a real professional.

'What about you, Lindy?' Jenny asked her. 'Are you going back to your old job?'

'I don't think they'll have me. They got another girl in to fill my place, so they won't want me,' Lillian said.

'Oh, you'll find something. I'll have to get a fill-in job in a shop or something until the panto season starts,' Sue said.

Lillian wasn't so sure. The other girls didn't come from seaside towns, so they didn't realise how many jobs were about to close down. The illuminations kept the visitors coming into town in the evenings for a few weeks longer than the holiday period, but after that there would be a scramble for work as the cafés and pubs, amusement arcades and souvenir shops either closed for the winter or ran on a much reduced staff.

'She's not getting another dance job, that's for sure,' May said.

Lillian flared up. May was always getting at her for something. 'Why not? I'm as good as anyone here.'

May snorted. 'Was that a pink elephant I saw flying past?'

'I'm better than you,' Lillian asserted.

May simply laughed and went on applying her eyeliner.

'I'll get a dance job, you wait and see,' Lillian said.

They were interrupted by the five minute call for beginners. Later on in the afternoon, Jenny drew Lillian to one side. 'Look, kid, you're a good dancer, but p'raps it's best you don't go for another job just yet.'

Still annoyed by May's taunting, Lillian demanded why not.

'How old are you?' Jenny asked.

'Seventeen.'

Jenny just looked at her.

'Well—sixteen, actually,' Lillian admitted.

'I thought so. Listen, it's a tough old world out there. Not every company's like this one. This is a nice little set-up here. Artie's no trouble and if you think May's a bit sharp, she's nothing to what some girls are like. And you're still living at home. Being in digs in some godforsaken place with people who enjoy being nasty to you is no joke, believe me. Give it a year or two, all right? Or at least only go for jobs where you can stay living with your family. Promise me?'

Lillian pouted. 'Why?'

''Cos you're a nice kid and I wouldn't like to see you get hurt.'

It seemed as if everyone was out to thwart her ambitions. Lillian complained about it to James the next time she saw him. To her horror, he agreed with Jenny.

'I know you want to dance, but you are a bit young to leave home.'

'But dancing is all I want to do! I've loved this job, I've just loved it. It's been everything I ever wanted.'

She searched his face for a reaction. Surely he knew what she meant?

'Every morning since I started I've got up happy, just bursting to start the day. I've never felt like that before. It's been wonderful! I thought you'd understand. Nobody else does.'

'I do understand. I do know what it's like to have to do a job you don't like all day long, but sometimes it's best to wait until it's the right time to do something.'

Lillian was deeply disappointed. 'You've always been on my side before,' she croaked through her tight throat.

'I am on your side, Lindy!' James sounded exasperated. 'If you want to be treated like a grown-up, then don't act like a spoilt kid. Look, I could leave Dobson's now if I wanted. I could easily get enough work repairing cars at the roadside. I'd be working for myself, which is what I want, but I'd find it hard to get any further. I want a proper workshop and, since nobody's going to lend me any money, I've got to stay on at Dobson's and earn enough to set myself up. See what I mean? Sometimes it's better to wait.'

'I can see that it's better for you, but I don't need to save up. I'm a professional. I've got my Equity card. I can apply for a dancing job anywhere.'

It gave her such a sense of power to be able to say that.

'You can still dance with the Mamie Hills,' James pointed out.

'But it's not the same! I love Miss Hill, I really do, but it's just playing at performing with her dancers. It's not the real thing. Oh, why can't I make you see?'

A shout came from inside the house. 'Lillian! Door!'

Lillian sighed and got up. At the theatre she was a professional dancer with an Equity card. Here at home she was still just Lillian, the family dogsbody.

'See?' she said to James as she went to answer the door. 'This is what I want to get away from. None of them would miss me at all, except they wouldn't have a servant any more.'

'I'd miss you,' he said.

Lillian stopped still and turned back to look at him. 'Would you? Would you really?'

'Course.'

For a long moment she gazed at his narrow face, his dark eyes. He looked back at her steadily. He wasn't teasing. James didn't tease. He meant it. He really didn't want her to go. Her heart seemed to turn over in her chest, and suddenly the world was a wonderful place again. Lillian sang as she hurried to open the door to a couple of prospective PGs.

In bed that night she thought it over. She still wanted to dance. She wanted it more than ever now that she had had a taste of it. But she knew that if she left home now the family would regard her as being almost as bad as Aunty Eileen. She weighed family disapproval against doing what she wanted. However much she hated them all at times, they were still her family. But would they ever let her go? Would they always want her here to run errands and do housework? She ran the little scene from that day over and over in her head, reliving that delicious moment when James had said he'd miss her. It made her feel quite odd inside, happiness mixed with a huge aching yearning. If James wanted her to stay, then maybe she would leave it a while before leaving home for another dance job.

'Where are you going tonight, Wendy?'

Three of Wendy's fellow workers stood round her in the staff cloakroom as she applied her lipstick. Wendy smoothed the colour on, pressed her lips together, then blotted them with a tiny bit of powder.

'Dinner dance at the airport restaurant,' she said casually, while inside she felt a thrill of excitement. The airport restaurant! It sounded so sophisticated, as if she was one of the jet set.

She looked at herself critically. Did she look like Diana Dors? She was just as pretty, she was sure of that. Her mouth was just as full, her nose and eyes just as attractive. Maybe her hair didn't wave over her shoulders quite so luxuriantly but, unlike Diana, or Marilyn Monroe, for that matter, Wendy's was natural blonde. More than ever now she wanted to live the film star life and ride around in a Rolls Royce. Terry didn't have a Rolls, but he did have a Jaguar, a great grey and black monster that smelt of leather and cigars inside. Just thinking about it made her feel like a queen.

Around her, the other girls were twittering with envy.

'You're so lucky—the airport restaurant! What are you going to wear?'

An older woman came out of one of the cubicals and walked over to wash her hands. 'You want to watch it, my girl, going out with someone like that Terry Dempsey.'

Wendy immediately flared up. 'What d'you mean by that?'

'I mean he's a crook, that's what.'

It wasn't the first time someone had said that to her, but Wendy refused to believe it.

'He's not. He's a very successful businessman. People just say that because they're jealous of him, 'cos he's made more money than they'll ever have.'

The woman faced her with her fists on her hips.

'You listen to me, young lady. Me and my husband had a nice little shop down on the Golden Mile until Terry Dempsey's thugs came and demanded protection money. At first we refused to pay it and our windows got smashed in, so we paid up. Then the amount went up and up, and we refused again, and this time the door got broken down and the stock was ransacked. In the end my husband had a nervous breakdown and we had to leave, and guess who bought it at a knockdown price? Your Mr Terry Dempsey, that's who.'

Wendy turned away from her and concentrated on powdering her nose. 'That wasn't Terry. It was someone using his name. My Terry don't need to do things like that,' she said.

Terry had told her that there were hard men out to blacken his name. This tale was proof of it.

'You'll see,' the woman said. 'You carry on going out with him, and you'll be no better than a gangster's moll.'

Wendy laughed. 'You been watching too many Al Capone films, you have.'

'I don't need to. I've seen it first-hand. You just remember what I say—you'll live to regret knowing Terry Dempsey.'

She marched out of the cloakroom. There was a second or two of stunned silence, then Wendy's three friends burst out talking.

'Ooh, Wendy, you want to watch it!'

'I have heard about that before—'

'You'd never believe something like that happening here in Southend, would you?'

'I don't believe it, 'cos it ain't true,' Wendy said. 'She's just a poor old jealous cow. She and her old man went bust and she blames my Terry. It's all a load of hogwash.'

She wasn't going to let rumours like that spoil her fun. She was on her way to where she wanted to be, and nothing was going to get in her way. Now that the Carnival and the illuminations were over, there weren't so many official functions for the Queen and her court to attend, but there were enough to feed her need for celebrity. In between these, she went out with Terry Dempsey, who took her to restaurants and dances and even drove her up to London to go to nightclubs or a private casino.

The family weren't happy about her going out with him.

'He's a shady character. There's all sorts of whispers about what he's got his fingers into. He's not the right man for my little princess,' her father said.

'He's most unsavoury. I'm not at all comfortable with my sister's name being linked with his,' Bob added.

'This is a respectable family, we don't go about with gippos from the seafront and riff-raff like that, however much money they flash about,' Gran stated.

But, short of locking her up, they couldn't stop her, not when she told them that Terry would not be at all pleased if they tried. They let her go, but with misgivings. They were afraid of Terry Dempsey.

So Wendy closed her eyes and ears to the warnings and had the time of her life. Terry bought her gowns and jewellery so that she looked the part at the places he took her to, and all she had to do was hang on his arm, laugh at his jokes and be nice but not familiar with his friends. She'd had to fend him off a few times, of course, but a girl expected that from a man who was so obviously a real man, as Terry was. He didn't like having to keep his hands above her waist, but she knew that he respected her for insisting. No man liked a girl who was easy.

It was while they were outside the airport restaurant that evening that she got her first shock. Terry was talking to a business friend and Wendy was waiting to one side for him when a glamorous dark girl in an air hostess's uniform came hurrying up to him and threaded an arm through his.

'Terry, darling! You should have told me you were going to be here this evening. I would have brought a dress to change into. That's the trouble with this job; I'm never in when you phone me. But if you don't mind me coming in in my uniform—? I know you like a girl in a uniform—'

Jealousy surged through Wendy like an acid tide. Who was this girl? Why was she talking to him like that, as if she was close to him? But then, to her delight, she realised that Terry was not pleased to see her. Not at all. There was no smile, no mention of a name. Quite the opposite. His face went dark, his body shifted subtly to become aggressive. He caught hold of her wrist and pushed her away from him.

'I told you before—don't interrupt me when I'm talking business.'

The girl's eyes widened with shock. 'But, Terry darling—'

'Just shut it, right?'

He let go of her abruptly and she staggered a little, still staring at him in disbelief.

'Terry, what is this? What have I—?'

'I told you, it's business. Now, sling your hook.'

The girl turned to go, but as she did so she caught sight of Wendy, waiting by the doorway in her gold cocktail dress with her fluffy stole about her shoulders. For a long moment their eyes met and each recognised her enemy. Then Wendy smiled, for she knew that she was the winner. She was here ready to be taken in to dinner by Terry, while the air hostess had been dismissed. The other girl shot her a look of pure hatred and clattered off on her high heels.

Terry, meanwhile, had returned to his discussion. It appeared to end amicably with laughs and claps on the shoulder, then he finally turned his attention to Wendy.

'Right then, doll, let's go in. I fancy a nice bit of rump.'

His hand closed round her satin-covered bottom, giving it a hard squeeze. Wendy squealed and slapped him playfully on the arm.

'Ooh, Terry, you are naughty!'

But she couldn't quite put the air hostess out of her head.

'Who was that?' she asked.

'Business friend, darling. You don't need to know.'

They were going in to the restaurant now. They were known here. The head waiter greeted them and took them to the best table. Menus and drinks appeared—whisky for Terry, Babycham for Wendy. She sipped her drink and stared at the menu while the head waiter told them about today's special—Dover sole.

'Nah, can't stand fish,' Terry said. 'Give us a nice steak. Rare. What about you, doll? You want a steak? Or a bit of chicken?'

They were both treats for Wendy. She'd never had a steak before she'd met Terry. The nearest they got to it at home was steak and kidney pie, while chicken was just for special occasions. But this evening she was finding it difficult to concentrate on food.

'Oh…yes…' she said.

Terry cast his eyes up. 'She'll have the chicken,' he told the waiter.

'That girl—' Wendy began as soon as he had left with their order.

'What girl?'

'You know—outside—'

'Oh, her. Flaming nuisance. Don't know her place.'

And that was all she could get out of him. When she persisted, he went very still and gave her his stony look.

'Drop it, doll.'

She knew that tone of voice. She dropped it. But it wouldn't drop out of her head.

And then someone at work came up to her at tea break and ever-so-casually mentioned that they had seen Terry Dempsey getting out of a car with a girl.

'Very glamorous, she was. Dark girl. Hair up in a French pleat.'

Wendy felt quite ill with anger and jealousy. The rat! She knew there was something going on there. She managed to shrug and appear unconcerned, but it churned around inside her for the rest of the week. She wasn't due to see Terry again till Saturday, so she had plenty of time for it to fester.

On the Friday evening, she had a Carnival appearance. She and the rest of the court were attending a charity concert in aid of the Carnival fund.

'Are you still going out with that Terry Dempsey?' one of

the others ladies-in-waiting asked as they sat in their prime seats in the stalls. 'Only I thought I saw him at the Overcliff the other night. He was dancing with a girl in a red dress. I noticed because she looked so different from you. Dark-haired and sort of skinny.'

The next act came on. It was the Mamie Hill Dancers. They did two numbers, one of which featured Lillian in the star spot.

'That's your little sister, isn't it?' the lady-in-waiting on the other side of her whispered. 'She's very good, isn't she?'

'Mmm,' Wendy said.

Though she was looking at the stage, she was hardly seeing it. Rage filled her heart. How dared he two-time her like that? She was Somebody in this town. She was part of the Carnival Queen's court. People rushed to see them wherever they went. Sometimes they even recognised her when she wasn't in her gown and tiara. He ought to be proud to be seen out with her. Well, two could play at that game. There were plenty of other men dying to go out with her.

She mulled it over half the night and all the next day at work. She needed someone striking, someone who would make Terry jealous. It wasn't until she got home to find Bob, Susan and James all drinking tea in the kitchen that it came to her. She'd always rather dismissed James in the past as Bob's girlfriend's brother, a mere mechanic with some stupid idea that one day he was going to be Mr Big. She had flirted with him a bit, just because she enjoyed seeing the reaction she got. Now she looked at him with new eyes. He was taller than Terry and better-looking. She knew he looked good in a suit and moved well on the dance floor because she had seen him at the Kursaal ballroom. And he seemed to be able to get hold of a car to take her around in.

Wendy went into action.

'Hello, James,' she said, favouring him with her best smile. 'I don't seem to have had time to speak to you properly for ages. I'm just so busy these days.'

She sat down opposite him and peeled off her jacket slowly, revealing her magnificent bust in its tight pink sweater. James could not keep his eyes off her.

'I think it's about time we put that right,' he said.

Wendy leaned forward and cupped her chin in her hand, gazing at him across the table.

'I think so too,' she said.

CHAPTER 13

IT CAME as a complete shock to Lillian. Wendy had said nothing about it at tea time; she had simply gone up to change for the evening, leaving Lillian to clear away the dishes and wash up. Wendy had been excused all chores during Carnival week, and it seemed to have become permanent. At seven o'clock there was a ring at the bell and the usual cry of, 'Lillian! Door!' went up. Lillian put down the tea towel and went to answer the bell.

'James! What are you doing at the front?'

He looked heart-stoppingly handsome in a dark suit and narrow tie, his gleaming hair brushed into a fashionable quiff.

'You look just like James Dean,' Lillian said.

'I hope not. He's dead.'

Lillian laughed. 'Silly! You know what I mean. But what—?'

As had happened so many times before, his attention suddenly switched to a point over her shoulder. Behind her, she could hear her sister tip-tapping down the stairs. Lillian whipped round. Wendy was wearing one of the dance dresses that Terry Dempsey had bought her, a yellow and white number with sequins that swirled over the bodice and spilled onto the full skirt. Even in the poor light of the hall lamp, she sparkled and glittered as she moved. Lillian looked back at James. He was gazing at Wendy like a man who had just been given the Crown jewels.

'You look fantastic. Like a film star,' he said.

The full reality of the situation came home to Lillian in a shattering shaft of pain.

'You—you're not—you can't be—with Wendy—are you—?' she stammered.

This couldn't be happening. Not her darling James with her sister.

'We're just popping down the Kursaal,' Wendy said, as if it hardly mattered at all. She looked past James to the street, where a large Sunbeam car was parked outside their house. 'Oh, good, you've got a car. I wasn't going to walk.'

'No one would expect you to. It's not like what you're used to, but it's quiet and comfortable.'

Gran poked her head round her door to see what was going on.

'Who's that you're going out with, Wendy? Oh—it's you. Oh, well, you'll do all right. You should know what the rules are in this house by now, young man. You'll get her back home at a decent time.'

'Of course, Mrs Parker,' James assured her. He offered an arm to Wendy and they stepped out into the street. 'Bye, Mrs Parker. 'Bye, Lindy!'

Lillian said nothing. Gran went back into her room while Lillian stood rooted to the spot, watching as James opened the car door for Wendy to get in, closed it carefully after her, got into the driving seat and set off. Like an automaton, she shut the front door and leaned back against the wall. Huge sobs were tearing at her chest. A howl of rage and pain wrenched from her throat as she slid down the wall to curl up in a ball of misery on the floor, sobbing and cursing. Somewhere beyond her, she heard Gran's door open again and self-preservation kicked in. With manic energy, she sprang up, launched herself at the stairs and ran up to the sanctuary of her room. There she flung herself on the bed and wept, thumping uselessly at the pillows.

'Why?' she cried out loud. 'Why him? You could have anybody. Why him? I hate you. I hate you both!'

But she knew inside that she didn't hate James. That was the trouble. She loved him.

Nobody bothered to come and see if she was all right. After the first terrible storm had subsided into hiccups and sniffs, Lillian felt the overwhelming need for sympathy and soothing. She crept downstairs again on feeble legs. Keeping her head down so that her long hair hid her swollen face, she muttered something about going to Janette's as she passed through the kitchen, grabbed her bike and wobbled off towards her friend's place. All the energy seemed to have drained out of her, and it was all she could do to make it to where Janette's parents' shop stood on the London Road.

Janette took one look at her and led her into her bedroom. She was in the throes of first love herself, though she was more successful, having fallen for one of the boys in the table tennis team at the youth club she went to. He thought she was wonderful and took her to coffee bars and played her favourite records on the jukebox for her.

'You poor darling,' Janette said, her arms round Lillian as they sat on the bed. 'Oh, the cow!' she exclaimed, as Lillian told the story through fresh tears. 'How could she do that?

Your own sister. Surely she knows how much you love him? I thought she was going out with that Terry Dempsey person.'

She disappeared downstairs to collect supplies of Tizer and sweets.

'This'll make you feel better,' she said.

Lillian swallowed down a random selection of chocolate and pear drops and felt sick.

'Oh, and I got you this. Someone ordered it and never came to collect it. I thought you might be interested.'

Janette passed her a magazine. Lillian glanced at it. It was a copy of *The Stage*. She burst into tears again.

'I didn't go for another dance job because he said he'd miss me,' she sobbed.

By the end of the evening they hadn't solved anything, but at least it had all been well chewed over. Lillian felt calmer, although her poor heart was still in pieces. She went home to face a night sharing a bed with Wendy. Her sister, happy from an evening spent dancing in James's arms, fell asleep almost immediately. All the good work that Janette had done fell to pieces as Lillian lay awake churning with envy and hatred. It was a very long night.

Some time before dawn Lillian slid out of bed, unable to stay there any longer. She picked up her threadbare dressing gown—a hand-me-down from Wendy—and made for the bedroom door. As she did so, her bare feet met with a wad of paper on the floor, which she picked up without thinking. It was only when she reached the bathroom and put the light on that she realised that it was the copy of *The Stage* that Janette had given her. Shivering in the November cold, she leafed through the pages, listlessly at first and then with increasing interest. Soon she was engrossed. Here was the world she longed to be part of, of productions large and small, of stars and support artists, of directors and producers, stage crew and technicians, musicians and singers and variety acts— and dancers. And here too were audition calls. Lillian forgot she was cold, forgot even that her heart was broken. The panto season was fast approaching. Performers of all types were needed.

Eagerly, she read the small print and, as she did so, she realised with rising excitement that she could apply for some of these. She was qualified, just. She had done a summer season, or at least she had done half of one, and she had her Equity card. She could leave all her problems behind her. She could do what her Aunty Eileen had done. Somewhere out there, Eileen was living the life she had chosen instead of being told what to do all the time.

At this point she paused as she realised just what she was contemplating. She had lived in this house, in this town, all her life. Out there in those places mentioned in the adverts she knew no one. She would have to live in one room, like a PG. It was frightening, but it was also exciting. She looked round at the bathroom she had cleaned so many times. No more cleaning! No more 'Lillian, door!' Guilt gnawed at the edges of her mind as she thought of her mother being left to do everything. But it was quiet now. Apart from the odd commercial traveller, there would be no PGs until next summer. And who else here cared if she stayed or went? Nobody. But, however cold they might seem, still they were her family and this was her home. The prospect of leaving was daunting. Then she thought of James. James had said he would miss her, but that plainly wasn't true. The pain of it spurred her on.

What should she try for? She scanned the places and the

dates. The magazine was two weeks out of date and already some of the calls were past. She looked at those in the London suburbs. She could apply to Hornchurch or Lewisham. But something made her reject them. She needed a grand gesture. If she was going to go away, she wanted to go far away. Once again, she pressed on the bruise by remembering James and Wendy going out to the car arm in arm. She never wanted to see them together again. She whittled the productions down to two—*Snow White* in Bristol or *The Sleeping Beauty* in Sheffield. As she had always preferred the story of *The Sleeping Beauty*, she decided on that and lay awake beside Wendy until daylight, worrying.

She had a day to find out how to get to Sheffield and arrive in time for the audition. It was all such a big rush that she hardly had time to think of the enormity of what she was doing until she finally got on the train at St Pancras and settled down for the long journey. Then it really started to dawn on her just how rash she was being. She was all alone, for the very first time in her life. She couldn't concentrate on the book she had brought with her, couldn't even take an interest in the scenery going by. She almost got off at the first stop in order to go straight home again, but thinking of James made her stick it out. She would show him.

Early evening found her on Sheffield station, with a suitcase borrowed from Janette in her hand and a duffel bag over her shoulder. She struggled down the platform with the heavy case, gave in her ticket and stood in the concourse. People swirled around her. They all seemed to know where they were going.

'All right, lass? You lost?'

It was her first encounter with a Yorkshire accent. The man speaking looked all right. He was middle aged and neatly dressed. But she had heard plenty of scare stories about wicked men who hung about stations preying on young girls.

'No, I'm meeting someone. My brother,' she lied and, picking up the suitcase again, she set off for the entrance. She had a plan in her head. It wasn't a very detailed one, but it was a plan. She approached a youngish woman with a couple of children.

'Excuse me, can you tell me where I can find a decent guest house for the night?'

The woman was a bit vague, and again she had a strong accent, which Lillian found difficult to follow, but she managed to understand the directions and the street names. Ten minutes later, her arms and shoulders were aching, it had come on to rain and she hadn't reached the street the woman had mentioned. After the stress of getting her things out of the house unseen, parting from Janette, spending a good part of her savings on the train ticket, finding her way through the London underground and brooding over James and Wendy and leaving home all the way up to Sheffield, she felt as if she had been through an emotional wringer. And now she was all but lost in a strange city. Tears were very close to the surface.

'You can't give up now, girl,' she told herself out loud. 'You got to find somewhere for the night.'

Eventually, after asking twice more, she found the street and knocked on the first place that had a 'Vacancies' sign in the window. She knew what to expect. Young girls on their own were always turned away from Sunny View, so she was not surprised when two landladies shut the door in her face. The third looked her up and down and finally decided that she looked respectable enough. Lillian was shown up to a little back bedroom furnished with a narrow bed, a large gloomy wardrobe and a washstand.

'The necessary's out t' back, no visitors in the room, front door's locked at ten, breakfast's at seven,' the landlady informed her.

'Thank you,' Lillian whispered.

Being on the receiving end of the rules made her feel more detached from home than ever. She plumped down on the bed, relieved just to take the weight off her feet. Now what? Her brain seemed to have stopped working. For a long time she just sat, staring at the wardrobe. She had never felt so lonely in her life.

Why was she here? Why had she done this? Were they missing her at home, or was there just an almighty row going on with everyone saying what a wicked girl she was and arguing about which side of the family such bad blood had come from? Whatever happened tomorrow, she couldn't go back now as she hadn't enough money for the train fare. She was stuck here in this place where she knew nobody and they all spoke with funny voices. The tears that had been threatening for some time now ran down her face unchecked.

Eventually she was forced to go downstairs and use the toilet in the yard. Coming inside again to wash her hands in the kitchen, she smelt toast and realised that she was ravenously hungry. She remembered passing a fish and chip shop not far away and went out. After the cold dreary streets, the chippy was a haven of warmth and cheerfulness and lovely fatty smells.

'You new round here, lass?' a large woman in a headscarf asked her.

'Yes, I've just arrived. I'm from Southend-on-Sea,' Lillian said. It was a pleasure to talk to someone.

Her accent was chuckled at and heads were shaken over such a young girl being all on her own so far away from home.

'What's tha' doing in this neck of the woods?' an old man asked.

'I've come for an audition at the theatre,' Lillian explained. Inside she glowed with pride. Now she was a real professional, striking out on her own.

Some of the people in the queue were mildly impressed, others dubious. Copious advice was given; she was wished good luck. Lillian paid for her saveloy and chips with almost the last of her savings, and scoffed the lot before she reached the guest house. Pleasantly full and warmed by the concern of the people in the chippy, she got into the chilly bed, only to be struck anew by the emptiness all around. It was the first time she had been away from home on her own. She was in a house full of strangers, who didn't care a hoot whether she lived or died. The loneliness was overwhelming. The darkness seemed to press in on her. But eventually a full stomach and the exertions of the day worked their magic, and she slept the sleep of exhaustion.

The theatre was alive with hopeful performers the next day. Lillian hid her suitcase behind the last row of the stalls and stood at the back of the auditorium looking at it all going on. People were greeting and kissing each other, singers were warming up their voices, friends were shrieking and waving at each other across the rows of seats, groups were deep in conversation. There was a frantic tide of voices, and nobody noticed her at all. It seemed to her that she was doomed to feel confused and alone, totally left out of things. Lillian took a deep breath and approached the one person who was not talking nineteen to the dozen, a woman with a broom, a scarf turban and a cigarette.

'Excuse me, but I'm here for the dancers' audition. Who am I supposed to see?'

The woman took her cigarette out of her mouth. 'Dancers, love? Tha's way too early. They won't be doing dancers till this afternoon.'

'This afternoon?' Lillian wailed. 'If I'd of known it was this afternoon, I could of got the first train this morning and not spent all that money at the guest house last night.'

The woman clucked sympathetically. 'Your first audition, is it?'

'Second,' Lillian said proudly. She wasn't a complete beginner.

'Oh, aye? But your first time here, I take it? You'll like it here—'

The woman, whose name turned out to be Elsie, then proceeded to give Lillian the lowdown on everybody working in the place. As she talked, which she seemed to be able to do without stopping, Lillian looked about her. The building was an ornate Victorian one decorated in dark red and cream, with plaster cherubs gambolling amongst forests of plaster foliage all over the walls and ceiling. Fat boxes swelled out from the side walls and the proscenium arch was a riot of pillars and swags and comedy and tragedy masks. It was all very different from the wooden structure at the end of the pier. As Elsie went on about the management's shortcomings, the safety curtain went up, then the heavy crimson and gold stage curtains parted to reveal the set for the production that was playing that fortnight.

The producer, a heavy man with a florid face, stood up and called for quiet.

'That there's Harvey Goddard. Produces the best panto in Yorkshire, he does,' Elsie informed Lillian.

The principal boys were called, the footlights came on with startling brightness and an attractive girl with long legs encased in fishnet tights strode onto the stage, announced her name and launched into a spirited rendition of *Somewhere Over The Rainbow*.

'I'd best get some work done,' Elsie said to Lillian. 'If you fancy a nice brew, love, just come and find me over at the stage door.'

Lillian thanked her profusely. She no longer felt so lonely. She had a friend in the theatre now. She settled down in a plush seat to watch the other hopefuls. As the day wore on, the prince and princess, king and queen, good and bad fairies and comedy parts were chosen. Lillian's stomach began to rumble. The solid breakfast at the guest house seemed a long time ago now. Girls in their teens and twenties began to arrive in ones and twos and give their names to the producer's assistant. Lillian jumped up and spoke to one of them.

'Are you here for a dance part?'

''Sright, love.'

'So am I. I'm Lindy.'

'Maggie.'

She picked up her duffel bag and gave her name and music to the assistant and then followed Maggie round the maze of dark dusty passageways to the female dressing room. The room was a heaving mass of girls in various states of undress, all busy changing, doing their hair, putting on their make-up and talking , talking, talking nineteen to the dozen. It was easy to see that this was going to be a different game altogether from her last audition. Artie had been desperate for two replacement girls mid-season. Harvey Goddard had his pick of all this lot. Lillian took a deep breath and broke in on the nearest conversation.

'Hello, I'm Lindy. It's a madhouse, this, isn't it? You played here before?'

A willowy girl with very pale skin answered her. 'Hello,

love, I'm Diane. Yes, I was here last year. I was hoping Harvey'd let me in on the nod. He knows I'm OK. But no, I've got to go through all this cattle market again.'

While Lillian grilled Diane for inside information about what Harvey Goddard was looking for, the dancers were called out in lots of six. Some came back looking either tearful or angry and began changing back into their street clothes. Amongst then was Maggie, whom she'd spoken to earlier.

'He gets rid of the ones he really doesn't like, then there's a second round to choose who gets the parts,' Diane explained.

The familiar sweaty sickness of stage fright gripped Lillian as her batch was called out to wait in the wings. The first two girls in her group didn't even get halfway through their audition numbers before a bored voice called, 'Thank you, dear. Next!' from the darkness beyond the footlights. Supposing that happened to her? Whatever was she going to do? It wasn't going to happen to her, she told herself. She was going to be chosen. She had to be. She shook out her arms and legs, keeping her muscles supple.

Diane was called on, and chosen to stay.

'Next!'

Lillian held her breath as she skipped onto the stage. Miss Hill had told them that this gave the eyes an extra sparkle. She stopped in the centre and smiled winningly at where the bored voice was coming from.

'Lindy-Lou Parker.' Her voice came out as a stupid squeak.

The pianist struck up the opening chords of her music. Lillian assumed the starting position and the stage fright miraculously dissolved. Her body obeyed her perfectly as she used the whole width of the big stage, exuding bounce and confidence out across the lights towards the jaded producer. To her delight, she got right through her number without the dreaded *Next!* being called.

'Right. Well. Where was your last engagement?' Harvey Goddard asked.

'The end-of-the-pier show at Southend,' Lillian told him, proud to be able to sound like a pro. This time her voice rang out clear.

'Southend. Hmm. OK, Lindy, we'll take another look at you.'

Bubbling with excitement, Lillian rushed offstage to join Diane and the other girls who had got through the first cull.

'Oh, he'll take you all right. He likes fresh meat, as long as it's got a bit of talent,' one of the other dancers said.

Lillian didn't know quite whether this was good news or not.

Soon about twenty of the original fifty dancers were left. In two batches of ten, they had to perform a high-kicking Til-ler Girl routine. Lillian was delighted. She could do this. She'd been doing it all summer.

The dancers gathered on the stage as Harvey's assistant read out the final list of twelve. Diane's name was second. One by one, the chosen girls squealed or clapped or merely nodded as they heard their names. Eleven had got parts. The assistant paused a moment, then said, 'And Lindy-Lou Parker.'

As those around her groaned with disappointment, Lillian jumped up and down for joy, then rushed up to Diane and hugged her.

'We did it, we did it!' she cried.

'Yeah, well done, kiddo,' Diane said. 'C'mon, get changed before you get cold.'

Walking on air, Lillian went back to the dressing room. It was only when she was back in her ordinary clothes that she came down to earth. She asked Diane for advice.

'Do you know anywhere I can stay? The landlady at the place I stayed last night said she didn't do theatricals.'

Diane sighed. 'You really are a tyro, aren't you? You ask the management. They always have a list of theatrical digs.'

'Oh, right, thanks,' Lillian said. Now that she had a job, she felt ready to tackle anything.

'I tell you what,' Diane offered, 'I'll take you to where I stayed last year. Ma Frazer's a nice old girl and she likes dancers. She used to be one herself.'

'Oh, would you? Thanks ever so, you're a real pal,' Lillian cried, giving Diane another hug. 'Look, do you mind waiting a bit? There's something I got to do first.'

'That's OK. I've got to phone my aunty so she can tell my mam I got the job,' Diane said.

Lillian went off to find Harvey Goddard. She was still on such a high that she hardly felt nervous at all about what she had to do next. If he wanted her as a dancer, how could he refuse to give her an advance on her wages? She found him sitting in the bar going through a pile of paperwork with a glass of something clear with ice in beside him. He looked at Lillian over the top of his half-glasses.

'Yes?'

'I…er…' Now that it came to the point, what she was about to ask did sound rather cheeky. Gran had always drummed into them that they should neither borrowers nor lenders be. 'You see, the thing is, Mr Goddard, I haven't got enough to live on till we're paid, so I wondered if I could possibly have a sub off my wages. Please. If that's all right with you. Only—'

'A sub, eh?'

Harvey Goddard took his glasses off and looked her up and down. Something in the way he did it made Lillian blush and feel uncomfortable. She fidgeted from one leg to the other.

'Yes. You see, I've come all the way from Southend and it's cost me nearly all my savings and I didn't know the call for dancers was for the afternoon so I had—'

'All right, all right.' He cut through her nervous gabble. A smile lifted his lips, showing his yellowing teeth. Close to, Lillian could see that his hair, which curled romantically over his collar, was in fact thinning on top. 'I think I might be able to accommodate that. If you're willing to accommodate me.'

Lillian had no idea what he meant. She was just grateful that he appeared to be agreeing.

'Yes, yes, of course.'

Harvey's eyes travelled over her again. They lingered on her small breasts, then travelled down to rest on her crotch. Then he stood up and caught hold of her wrist.

'Come on, then,' he said, and led her out of the bar.

Mystified, Lillian followed him into the backstage area, till they came to a dressing room with a faded gold star on the door. Harvey took her inside and locked the door behind them. He flung himself down on the easy chair and gestured at her impatiently.

'Come on, then, take them off. I'm not doing the work.'

'What?' Lillian said.

'Your clothes, sweetie. Take them off. Nice and slowly.'

'But—I don't understand—No! Take my clothes off? I'm not—you said—'

Harvey's face took on a very unpleasant look. This time there was an edge to his voice. 'We've a good old-fashioned saying round here, love. You don't get owt for nowt. If you want to eat between now and payday, you'd better start stripping.'

For a long moment, Lillian stared back at him. 'I—I can't—' she whispered.

'Oh, yes you can. Come on. I haven't got all day.'

Lillian looked at the door, then back at the producer. She wanted this job, but—take her clothes off? And it swept over her with horrible clarity that this was why the family didn't want her to leave home. They knew about the Harvey Goddards of this world.

'No. I—I can't—I don't—'

Harvey groaned. 'You're a bleeding virgin, aren't you?'

Lillian nodded. She knew what a virgin was. It was someone who hadn't done It. According to gossip at school, It involved a man putting his Thing in you. Just where in you, she had no idea, except that it was between your legs.

'All right—' Harvey's voice was rough with something between anger and resignation. 'I'm not a bleeding monster. Just come here and sit on my lap.'

Slowly, reluctantly, Lillian went to him and perched on the very end of his knees with her back to him.

'Not like that. Closer. Sit back. Let's have a feel of that nice tight little arse.'

With strong hands, he clasped her hips and pulled her towards him. She felt something hard against her backside.

'That's better. Now move. Like that. Yes—'

Feeling sick and soiled, she did what he asked, thankful that at least she didn't have to look at him. His breathing went harsh and ragged, and then he groaned and released her.

'All right. You can stop now.'

Lillian stood up. Harvey sat spreadeagled in the chair, looking limp and crumpled. He reached inside his pocket for his wallet, extracted a couple of notes and held them out to her.

'Not the best I've ever known, to put it mildly. There you are; take that and consider y'self lucky. There's not many that would let you off lightly like that. I'm too soft by half, I am.

Now scarper, and remember, one word about this and you're out. Understood?'

'Yes, Mr Goddard.'

Lillian was ready to agree to anything just to get out of that room. She snatched the notes from him, unlocked the door and escaped.

CHAPTER 14

JAMES discussed Lillian's disappearance with Susan as they
drove round to the Parkers' place in a borrowed car.

'They all seem so angry. Much more angry than upset or
worried,' he said.

'Oh, I don't know. Sometimes being worried makes people angry,' Susan replied.

James wasn't so sure.

'If you did something like that, poor Mum would be beside herself. She wouldn't be going on about what a wicked
and ungrateful girl you were; she'd want to know why you'd
gone and whether you were safe.'

'I know, but—the Parkers are different from us.'

'You can say that again.'

'Except for Bob, of course.'

'If you say so.'

Personally, he thought Bob was as bad as any of them, except for Wendy.

'She did say she wanted to go off and get a dancing job somewhere. But she's only a kid, she's much too young to be leaving home. I thought I'd managed to persuade her not to,' he said.

'Ah, well, of course she talks to you,' Susan said in a knowing tone of voice.

'What d'you mean by that?'

'Wake up, Jamie! She's got a huge crush on you.'

'What, still? That was before I went on my national service.'

'You've only got to see her face when you come into the room.'

'But—' James refused to believe it. 'No, you're wrong there. I've always treated her like a little sister. Nothing more.'

'I'm not saying you haven't, but that's got nothing to do with it. You know what I think? I think she's run away because you're going out with Wendy.'

'You're kidding.'

'I'm not.'

'But they're sisters—'

'Exactly. Lillian's jealous.'

'But I never gave her any idea that I might go out with her. I mean, she's just a kid—'

'She's sixteen.'

'Well, I think of her as a kid.'

They arrived at the Parkers' before they could discuss it any further. There, they found that a letter had arrived from Lillian, apologising for running off and assuring them that she had a job and digs and was quite all right. James ignored Gran and Doug and looked at Lillian's mum. She was sitting at the kitchen table with her head in her hands, looking weak and pale. With Susan's suspicions still fresh in his head, James was beginning to feel very guilty. If she was right, then he was at least partially responsible. He sat down by Nettie.

'At least you know she's safe now, Mrs Parker.'

'Yes, yes—' Nettie seemed to dismiss this thought. 'What did she have to do this for? I don't know how I'm going to manage with her gone.'

James stared at her, appalled. He hadn't believed Lillian when she'd said that her family would only miss her as a servant. But maybe she was right after all.

Wendy appeared, looking stunning as usual and insisting that they went dancing at the Queen's Hotel. This was more expensive than the Kursaal and meant that no savings would be going into James's account that week, but he brushed that to one side. What Wendy wanted, Wendy got. She was worth it. He escorted her to the car, leaving his sister to chew over the Lillian situation with Bob and the rest of the Parkers.

The Queen's was a big Edwardian place with a grand ball-room.

'I'd like a drink first,' Wendy said, heading for the bar.

She perched on a high bar stool, her shapely calves showing beneath her frothy skirts, and sipped the Babycham that James bought for her. He asked her about her latest Carnival court engagement and she chattered on, but her attention was not fully with him. All the time she was speaking, her eyes were ranging over the crowd in the bar.

'Are you expecting someone?' James asked.

'What? No—not at all. I'm bored sitting here, let's go into the ballroom.'

The average age of the dancers was much older at the

Queen's than it was at the Kursaal. If James hadn't been there with Wendy, he would have thought it a dead loss. Everyone seemed to be in couples. It certainly wasn't a place to find new dates.

'Not exactly a bundle of laughs here, is it?' he remarked to Wendy.

'I think it's very elegant,' Wendy said. 'And there's room to dance properly.'

But it wasn't long before she was asking to go back into the bar. On their third visit, he saw her recognise someone in the crowd and quickly look away. Then she deliberately leaned towards him and laid a possessive hand on his arm, smiling into his eyes.

'I think they're playing a tango,' she said. 'I just love to tango. Come on.'

She slid gracefully off her bar stool. James put his drink down and followed her.

As they prowled and flounced their way round the floor, he became aware of a brooding presence just inside the door of the ballroom. He looked over Wendy's shoulder. There, glaring at them with his arms folded across his chest, was Terry Dempsey.

'Your ex-boyfriend's here,' he said.

'Is he? Really? Where?'

'By the—'

But there was nobody there.

'Well, he was. He's gone now.'

'Oh, well—' Wendy's voice was deliberately offhand '—who cares where he is?'

James had the uneasy feeling he was being used. But it didn't stop him from asking Wendy for another date at the end of the evening.

* * *

Now that the Parkers had Lillian's address, James and Susan expected that one of the family would be dispatched to bring her home. But no, it seemed that the general view was that she had made her bed, so now she could lie on it.

'I'll have to go,' James decided. 'We can't just leave her up in the north all by herself. Anything might happen to her. I'll borrow a car and drive up there on Sunday. It's a helluva haul, there and back in one day, but it can be done.'

Susan gave him a hug. 'That's really good of you, Jamie. Look, I'll come with you, and I'm sure Bob will too. If we all go, she's sure to listen to us.'

The last thing James wanted was Bob as a travelling companion, but he supposed that somebody from Lillian's family ought to come, so he reluctantly agreed. Better Bob than Frank or Mr Parker, and he knew Wendy would never get out of bed early enough to go with them.

He got the loan of a small Austin for the day, in exchange for giving it a full service for free. He filled up the petrol tank and put three extra two-gallon cans in the boot. They smelt a bit, but he couldn't risk running out of fuel on a Sunday evening with no petrol stations open. It was dark when they started out, a wet December day that never really appeared to get light, even at midday. The A1 seemed to go on for ever, rolling under their wheels. Bob began to complain that it was a stupid idea and they should never have come, but was pacified when Susan produced neatly wrapped packages of cheese and pickle sandwiches and home-made Victoria sponge, together with a flask of tea. It was gone one o'clock by the time they got to Sheffield and the rain was bucketing down. After asking for directions at the police station, they finally found Lillian's digs in a long terrace of identical houses climbing up a steep hill. Stiff, weary and irritated with each other, they climbed out of the car and knocked on the door.

A tall thin woman let them into her narrow hall. There was a smell of roast meat and gravy in the air that made all their stomachs grumble.

'Lindy!' the landlady called. 'Visitors for you.'

A door opened along the passage and Lillian's face appeared, pale and suspicious. When she saw who it was, she squealed with delight. 'James! And Susan—and Bob! I don't believe it! Is it really you?'

She ran down the hallway and flung herself at them, hugging each of them in turn. She turned to the landlady, pink with pleasure.

'Oh, Mrs Frazer, this is my brother Bob and his fiancée Susan and her brother James. They've come all the way from Southend. You don't mind if they come up to my room, do you?'

'You've come from Southend today?' the landlady asked.

'We drove. It's taken us well over six hours,' Bob said, speaking for all of them.

Mrs Frazer insisted on giving them all tea and biscuits, then Lillian led them upstairs. Hers was a small dark room at the side of the house which appeared to have been made by dividing a larger room down the middle so that she only had half a window. It had faded wallpaper that must have been put on before the war, cracked lino on the floor and cheap Utility furniture. Lillian whipped a pair of damp stockings off the back of the only chair, and insisted that Susan had that while she and the men sat on the bed.

James shivered. He had been freezing in the car, despite wearing a winter coat and gloves, and this room wasn't much warmer. He sipped thankfully at the strong tea while Lillian asked Bob for news of all her family and Bob told her what a furore she had caused. Already Lillian was beginning to look mutinous.

'So this is where you're staying,' Susan interrupted, looking round with distaste.

James knew what she meant. Their flat might be cramped and shabby, but it was homely. This room was depressing.

'Yes. It's wonderful to have a room of my own at last. No more sharing a bed with beastly Wendy! It's a real treat—' Lillian broke off and looked at their serious faces. 'You haven't come to take me home, have you? Because I'm not going. You can say what you like, but I'm not going.'

Bob opened his mouth to speak, but Susan got in before him. Leaning across to pat Lillian's knee, she said, 'You know, dear, your mother is so worried about you. So are we all. We only have your best interests at heart.'

Lillian flared up. 'Excuse me, Susan, but you don't know what my best interests are! All I want is to be a dancer, and now I am. James knows that, don't you, James?'

Her eyes sought his, large and pleading. James knew she was relying on him to side with her, to understand her. He was torn. He knew all about ambition, and he had always encouraged Lillian. But she was only sixteen and a very long way away from home.

They were all looking at him now.

'The thing is, Lindy—' he began.

Lillian's eyes grew hot with disappointment. He could see that she felt betrayed. He, of all people, should have seen things her way.

'—it's like I said to you when you finished at the pier; you're a bit young to be leaving home.'

'I'm old enough to be married!' Lillian retorted.

'Married? You're not here with a man, are you?' Bob interrupted. 'Because, if so, I want to meet him. I shall have a thing or two to say, I can tell you.'

'That's not what I meant!' Lillian cried, exasperated. 'I meant if I'm old enough to be married, I'm old enough to leave home. I've got these digs. Mrs Frazer's very nice. She used to be a dancer, and she knows what it's like. My friend Diane's got the room next door and two of the courtiers have got the front room and it's all very jolly—'

'Courtiers?' Susan asked.

'Yes. At Sleeping Beauty's court. We're all theatricals here, you see.'

This was said with something between pride and defiance. James looked at her as she sat very upright on the bed, flushed and bristling. He had to admire her. Not many kids of her age would go to these lengths to achieve what they wanted in life.

'Theatricals!' Bob said with distaste.

'It's a good job. This is a big production. The comics were top of the bill at Blackpool in the summer, and the Wicked Fairy's played in the West End. And it's a good run, too. We're opening on Boxing Day and going right through till halfway through February. So you can say what you like, Bob, but it's not some little tinpot show. I got chosen out of more than thirty dancers to be one of twelve.'

James whistled. 'Well done, Lindy.'

Bob and Susan both glared at him. He realised that he was letting the side down. But it was true; Lillian had done well. It was just her age, and her vulnerability. He had found going away for national service a shock to the system, and he had been eighteen. To be sure, it had made a man of him, as everyone had said it would. He was fitter and tougher mentally and physically, he had learnt how to get on with people and had seen different places and cultures. It had broadened his view of life beyond all measure. But was being in a pantomime in Sheffield going to do the same for Lillian? There she was, fresh-faced and leggy and innocent. She knew nothing of what the world might throw at her. She had to be rescued.

'Look,' he said, 'you've proved you can do it. You know you're good enough to be a professional dancer. You've got all your life ahead of you, Lindy. A year or two's waiting won't hurt. Come back with us now and take it up again later, when you've grown up a bit—'

'No!'

Lillian jumped up. She was shaking and her breath was coming in big gulps.

'If I back out now, I'll get a reputation for being unreliable, then nobody will take me on. I'll be finished before I've hardly started. I can't do that. Can't you see, James? I thought you'd understand. They don't—' she gestured contemptuously at Bob and Susan '—they can't see anything more than mortgages and saucepans and curtains. But you—I thought you knew what it was like, having a dream. This is my dream and I'm going to follow it, just like Aunty Eileen said, and nothing any of you can say is going to stop me!'

Tears ran down her face and she brushed them away angrily as she glared at all three of them.

Bob stood up to face her, partly blocking James's view. 'This has gone far enough,' he stated. 'Now, you listen to me, Lillian. We've come all this way today to take you home with us, and that's what we're going to do, whether you like it or not.'

He reached out to take hold of her arm. Lillian screamed, 'No! No!' and slapped him hard across the face. Bob yelped and Susan gasped and, before any of them knew what was happening, she was out of the door and running downstairs, her feet pounding on the lino-covered steps.

'Lindy!' James pushed between his sister and her fiancé, who seemed to be rooted to the spot, and charged after Lillian. Bedroom doors flew open as he passed and curious faces watched the show.

'Lindy, stop, please!'

He ran behind her along the downstairs passage, through a breakfast room and a kitchen where the dishes from Sunday lunch were still stacked in the sink. He almost reached her as she wrenched open the back door, but then she whipped through it and slammed it in his face. James followed her outside. He found himself in a small dark yard with the rain slanting down in stair rods. Where had she gone?

'Lindy?' he called. 'Lindy, where are you?'

There was no reply. Surely she hadn't run off through the back gate? Not on a day like this with only her indoor clothes on. Already the rain was soaking his head and shoulders. Then he saw a small building in the far corner. Of course. The khazi. He ran across the yard and tapped at the door.

'Lindy? You in there?'

From inside came a stifled sobbing.

'Lindy, please—'

'Go away and leave me alone!'

He had to do something drastic before Bob and Susan found them. He lowered his voice. 'For my sake, Lindy.'

There was a long pause. The rain beat down upon the slate roof of the privy. James tried in vain to find shelter. He was getting soaked to the skin.

'Lindy?'

Finally a small voice came from within. 'Are you still going out with Wendy?'

James closed his eyes and sighed. He couldn't lie to her. It wouldn't be right. 'Yes,' he admitted.

'Then I'm staying here.'

At that point there was a clattering at the back door of the house and Bob and Susan could be heard. Then Bob loomed beside him, grumbling at the weather.

'She in there?'

James almost denied it, but there didn't seem to be any point in that. If he said Lillian had run off, then they would simply wait for her to come back. Nobody could stay out in weather like this.

Bob thumped on the door. 'Come out, Lillian! Come out at once, I say!'

'Go away!' Lillian screamed. 'Just go away and leave me alone! I hate you! I hate you all!'

It was Bob who gave in. After five minutes of fruitless orders, he issued an ultimatum. 'I'm going back indoors, Lillian. If you are not out of there within five minutes, then we are going home without you, and you can take the consequences.'

They waited five minutes, then ten, then fifteen, while Mrs Frazer complained about the noise and the mess all over her clean floor. Lillian did not appear. Bob was in high dudgeon, calling his sister stubborn and wicked and irresponsible. Susan was trying to calm him down while not crossing him. James felt sick at heart. They had now made everything ten times worse. He knew Lillian. She would stick to her purpose. Maybe she would never speak to any of them again.

'Right,' Bob said, 'that's it. We're going. On her own head be it.'

James couldn't leave it at that. He borrowed a piece of paper and a pencil from Mrs Frazer and wrote a quick note to Lillian.

Dear Lindy,
   Please try not to be too angry. We did it because we care about you.
   The best of luck with everything. I hope your dream is everything you wanted, but if you do have any problems, please, please get in touch.
Yours,
James.

He ran upstairs to leave it on her chest of drawers. After that, there was nothing to do but to face the long weary journey home again, dogged by the knowledge of failure.

CHAPTER 15

JAMES was due to see Wendy again on Tuesday. He hurried home from Dobson's and put off the servicing of the Austin that had taken them all to Sheffield and back in order to give himself enough time to get ready. Cleaning up after a day's messing around with the insides of cars took some time, since he took pride in looking as sleek and polished as any of the rich boys she had been out with.

When he got to the Parkers', Wendy, as usual, was not ready for him. He took a seat at the kitchen table. From the front room came the sound of the television that Gran had recently bought. Despite the lure of entertainment in her room, still the rest of the family sat in the uncomfortable kitchen.

'I went to that new serve-yourself shop today,' Mrs Parker announced.

James looked at her in surprise. He couldn't remember her ever having started a subject of conversation before.

'How does that work, then? Sounds daft to me,' Mr Parker said.

'You pick up this wire basket thingy at the door and you go round and there's all open shelves and you just pick what you want off them and put it in the basket. It was ever so strange. I felt like I was stealing.'

'There will be people stealing, won't there? What's to stop them putting stuff straight into their own bags?' Mr Parker asked.

'I dunno. Nothing, really. I mean, it would be quite easy—'

'And where do you pay? You do have to pay?'

'Oh, yes, you have to pay. You can't get out without passing the tills. They take all the stuff out of your wire basket and ring it up and then you put it into your own bag.'

'Don't see the point of it,' Mr Parker said, dismissing the whole idea.

'It's American, ain't it?' Frank said, without looking up from his motorcycle magazine. 'Yanks of got all the best ideas. It's quicker, see? Instead of waiting around for people to serve you with this and that, you just get it yourself.'

'Sounds a very bad thing to me. It'll do a lot of people out of jobs. The unions ought to get on to this.'

'I don't think I'll go again,' Mrs Parker said. 'I didn't like it. There's no one to talk to except the girls at the tills. I think I'll just stick to the Co-op.'

'It won't last, you mark my words. Stupid American idea.'

'I think it's good,' Frank said.

James tapped his fingers impatiently on the table top. He really couldn't care less about shops.

'Have you heard from Lillian?' he interrupted.

'Not a word,' her father said. 'Flighty little madam. Don't know what side her bread's buttered, that's what.'

'Have you written to her?' James persisted.

Frank shrugged. Mr and Mrs Parker looked amazed that he had asked the question.

'No need, is there? 'S obvious she don't give a monkey's about her family.'

It was obvious to James that her family didn't care very much for her, either. Poor Lillian.

At that point he heard Wendy's high heels tip-tapping down the stairs and sat up straight, ready to stand when she came in. As always, she was worth waiting for. She was wearing an electric blue satin dance dress with a tight bodice, scoop neck and wide skirt that rustled as she moved. Long white gloves, a little envelope handbag and a sparkly necklace completed the outfit. She looked a million dollars, and he was the lucky man to be taking her out.

The one downside was that she didn't appear to be pleased to see him.

'Oh,' she said. 'You're here. Come here a minute.'

She took hold of his arm. Over her shoulder, James could see Frank grinning at them in a particularly unpleasant way. He followed her into the chilly PG's breakfast room, a faint but definite feeling of doom gathering in his guts. As soon as she had shut the door behind them, Wendy turned to face him.

'I got something to tell you,' she announced.

He knew what it was before she said it.

'You can't come out with me tonight,' he guessed, hoping against hope that this was all.

Wendy looked almost put out that he had pre-empted her. 'Right. Well, it's more than that. I don't want to go out with you at all. Ever.'

James could feel himself dropping into the great black

chasm that was the future without Wendy in it. For several long moments he just stared at her, stunned, as if she might change her mind.

'Well, that's it, then,' she said, turning to go.

'No—' The word was wrenched out of him. Wendy paused and looked at him, but nothing sensible seemed to form in his head. Finally, he managed to say, 'Why?'

Wendy shrugged. 'Terry found out. He don't like sharing me with anyone else.'

'Terry? Terry Dempsey? I thought you said you weren't going out with him any more.'

She definitely had said that. He remembered it clearly.

'Well, now I am again, all right?'

'No, it's not all right,' he burst out. 'He's a cheap crook, Wendy. You're much too good for him.'

The future without Wendy in it was bad enough. The future with Wendy in it but going around with that man was a hundred times worse. It made him feel sick to the stomach.

Wendy drew herself up and faced him, her big blue eyes glittering.

'He's not a crook. That's just a filthy lie. He's a very successful businessman. He's got more money than you'll ever see in your life.'

With those words, something of the shine came off. There she was, as lush and desirable as ever. He still loved her and wanted her, but now, reluctantly, he could see the flaws beneath the beguiling surface.

'And money's what matters, is it?' he asked.

In his heart he had known it all along. He had simply closed his eyes to any imperfections.

'Of course,' Wendy said, as if he were an idiot. 'You don't think I want to live in a dump like this all my life, do you?'

'So you'll sell your soul to the likes of Terry Dempsey?'

Wendy's beautiful mouth took on an unattractive pout. 'I haven't got time for all this. I'm going out.'

'With Dempsey?'

'Yes, as a matter of fact. Not that it's any of your business.'

'Well, I hope you don't live to regret it.'

'Oh, I shan't,' Wendy assured him, and swept out of the room.

James stood staring at the door. Amidst all the turmoil of anger and heartbreak a small clear thought surfaced. If only she had said this on Saturday, he might have had a better chance of persuading Lillian to come home.

The next day, as he was cycling home down a quiet back street, a grey and black Jaguar drew up alongside him, so close that he had to leap off his bike and pull it up on the pavement. The passenger door swung open and a gravelly voice ordered, 'You! Get in.'

James knew just who it was. Getting into a car with Terry Dempsey was not on his list of wise things to do.

'You want to speak to me, mate, you get out and do it here,' he replied.

At that, the rear doors opened and two beefy men with crew cuts got out. James swung a leg over his bike, but the men moved surprisingly fast. Before he could get going, a punch in the stomach had winded him and he was being dragged over to the car.

'When Mr Dempsey says get in, you get in,' one told him, and they bundled him inside, knocking his head on the doorframe as they did so.

Terry Dempsey sat behind the wheel of the Jaguar, regarding him sardonically as he gasped for breath. 'I hear you been bothering my girl,' he said.

'I went out with her,' James managed to say. He almost added that they'd had a good time, but stopped short. A remark like that might rebound on Wendy.

'That weren't very clever of you. My girl don't like being bothered by nasty little punks like you. So in future you'll keep clear of her, all right?'

James looked at Wendy's boyfriend. There was hand-stitching down the lapels of his suit and the hand that rested on the steering wheel sported a gold sovereign ring but, despite the trappings, his face was that of a thug.

'I hear you,' he said.

Dempsey poked him in the chest. 'That's not what I asked.'

James swallowed. He was still breathing like a landed fish. He didn't exactly have the upper hand here, but it went right against the grain to give in to this bully.

'She said she didn't want to go out with me again, so I shan't,' he said.

'No, you won't, not if you know what's good for you,' Dempsey said. 'Remember that. Now get out.'

James reached for the door and found it already being opened by one of Dempsey's men.

'You mind you treat Wendy right,' he said as he was pulled out of the car.

The two henchmen flung him against a wall, threw his bike after him and got into the Jaguar. Furious, James picked himself up as the big black and grey car pulled away. His head was ringing from colliding with the wall and his nose was bleeding where the handlebars had caught him, but he was more bruised in his mind than his body. It was humiliating to be dictated to by a man like that. He felt he should have put up more of a fight against the henchmen. It had all been so unexpected and it had happened so quickly. Another time, he would be more on his guard. But at least he had got the last word in. That gave him a small glimmer of satisfaction.

He straightened up the bike and carried on home, still fuming. What was Wendy doing going out with a villain like that? Was she completely blind? He had to come to the conclusion that she saw only the car and the clothes and the fancy places he took her to. It frightened him to think of what might happen to her if she got on the wrong side of Terry Dempsey.

He tried to talk about it to Frank when he came to him with the motorbike he had bought, a gleaming Norton.

'Wendy? Oh, she knows what she's doing,' he said. 'Now, what do you reckon? Can you tune it up a bit for me?'

'But does she?' James asked, ignoring Frank's question. 'Does she really know what sort of bloke Dempsey is? Is she safe with him? I wouldn't like my sister to be going out with the likes of him.'

'Look, mate, she's got what she wants, ain't she? Swanning off every night done up to the nines to all these posh places. She likes that sort of thing. Besides, it might be useful, having someone like Dempsey sort of part of the family. I mean, he's Mr Big round here, ain't he?'

'Useful?' James thought of the warning he'd been given. 'Useful as a time bomb, if you ask me.'

'Nah, you just want Wendy back, don't you? Everyone does. Now, what about tuning this beauty up?'

James gave up. It was clear that Frank admired Dempsey. And, yes, he did want Wendy back, but he certainly didn't want to talk about that with her brother.

'You got plenty of power there already,' he said.

'Yeah, but I want to get a ton out of it, don't I?'

'You'll get a ton out of it all right.'

James allowed himself to be seduced by the beauty of the machinery. It was a very fine bike. They talked engines and power for a while.

'Must've cost a bob or two,' James remarked.

'Got it on the never-never, didn't I?'

Even on hire purchase, this bike was going to be expensive and Frank never seemed to hold a job down for more than a few weeks. He had worked for two or three places along the seafront during the summer, and now he was at some factory out at the back of town. But that was Frank's headache, not his.

Over the next couple of weeks he was busy both at Dobson's and with his own burgeoning business, servicing cars that were due to take families on Christmas visits across the country. Working all the hours he could soothed the ache in his heart just a little. The money in his savings account was mounting up, and so was his list of customers. Soon he would be able to buy the equipment he needed and open up his own workshop. Then he would show Wendy what he was made of.

CHAPTER 16

THE long cold days of rehearsing in church halls were over. They were on stage at last. Lillian skipped joyfully through the village green scene that preceded the King's men coming along to confiscate all the spindles. It was a complicated set piece, with the courtiers, who doubled as villagers, coming in to do some of the dance with them. Harvey Goddard dropped his mask of weary boredom and went into a frantic rage as yet again someone turned the wrong way.

'For Christ's sake! How many more times? What is wrong with you people? It's not difficult. One-two-three away, one-two-three back and turn *in*. A kid of three could do it. A bleeding monkey could do it. We are two days away from dress rehearsal—*two days*—and still you can't get a simple thing like this right...'

The offending villager dissolved into tears and was comforted by the man next to him, while the rest of the cast waited for the rant to run its course. Lillian scratched the bites on her legs; Mrs Frazer's cats had fleas. She looked out into the rows of red velvet seats and up to the circle and the gallery. Next week these would all be filled with excited people wanting to be entertained. Next week she would be doing this for real. She could still hardly believe it. The thrill of it buoyed her up through rehearsals that left her so exhausted that she could hardly crawl into bed, through feeling perpetually hungry and at times so lonely she wanted to cry. This was all part of show business, she kept telling herself. You had to suffer before you got the glory.

'From the top—' Harvey was saying. 'And this time get it right.'

Once more, Lillian danced faultlessly through it. This one was easy. The one she had difficulties with was the fairy scene at the baby princess's christening, which involved dancing on points. She had not done a great deal of this in the past, certainly not as much as the rest of the dancers, so she'd put in extra practice in her room for an hour or so a day till she'd got to be reasonably proficient. Her toes were bruised and bleeding as a result, and her ankles painful.

This time everyone managed to get through it. The scene ran its course, the dancers left the stage and huddled into shapeless cardigans and robes to keep warm. Lillian drank a glass of water, Diane handed round sweets.

'Harvey's got his knickers in a right twist, ain't he?'

'Yes,' Lillian agreed.

'But he's all bark and no bite. He's all right, is Harvey.'

'Mmm.'

Lillian hadn't told anyone about what had happened the day of the auditions. She was too ashamed. What made it even worse was the fact that she had since learnt that Harvey wasn't even the person to apply to for a sub. She should have gone to the theatre manager. It made her feel like an idiot on top of the humiliation of what she had been forced to do. She still couldn't look at Harvey, or even hear his name spoken without suffering agonies of fear and shame.

'You heard from your family yet?' Diane asked.

Sadly, Lillian shook her head. It was as if she no longer existed.

'You'd best come over to us for Christmas, then. My Mam won't mind. The more the merrier.'

'If you're sure—'

The thought of spending Christmas Day at the lodging house with Mrs Frazer and her cats was pretty dismal.

''Course I'm sure. It's not far, and my uncle can run us both back on Boxing Day.'

Diane lived in Bradford in what sounded like a big happy family. Lillian envied her her easy relationship with her parents and siblings. It all seemed very different to her own lot.

'Thanks a million,' she said, giving Diane a hug. 'You're a real pal. I don't know what I would've done without you.'

'Oh, you'd of managed,' Diane said. 'You're a tough kid.'

Lillian wasn't so sure.

When they got back to Mrs Frazer's that evening, there was a letter waiting for her. All the weariness dissolved from her body as she looked at the writing on the envelope.

'James!' she cried. 'It's from James!'

'Someone's happy now,' Diane said knowingly. 'I'll leave you to it.'

Lillian raced upstairs, clutching the letter to her heart. She burst through her door, flung herself on to the bed and tore it open.

Dear Lindy,

I thought it was about time somebody wrote to you. I hope everything is going all right for you up there. Everything is much the same as usual here. I'm very busy doing last minute services and Susan and Mum are making mince pies and icing cakes and all that. Your lot are coming here for tea on Christmas Day so you can imagine what a flap they're in. I've still got to find some time to do a bit of Christmas shopping. Susan and I have clubbed together to buy Mum a television for Christmas. It's second-hand, but it's working well. We know she's been wanting one for ages so I think she'll be really pleased.

Lindy, you really ought to try to get home for Christmas. I know the show opens on Boxing Day and it would be impossible to get back up to Sheffield in time by rail, but if you can get yourself down here on the train, I can drive you back on Boxing Day morning. Think about it and let your family know. I'm sure you could patch it up with them if you came back.

Hope to see you Christmas Day.

All the best,

James

The euphoria of receiving the letter sank into a small trough of disappointment. Part of her had hoped for more— the part that daydreamed about him all the time, thinking up wonderful stories where he came roaring up to the stage door and swept her away to live happily ever after. *All the best, James* was practically an insult when what she craved was, *All my love, James.* But he had written, and he had thought about her and solved a huge problem for her. She had been trying to tell herself that she didn't care about not getting home for

Christmas, but the truth was that she did care, very much. Diane's family might be wonderful, but they were strangers. Her own lot might seem cold and unfeeling, but they were still her family. She was suddenly overcome with longing to see them again, even Wendy. She found a pencil and some paper from the back of a script and wrote a long letter back to James, telling him about the company and the rehearsals and thanking him from the bottom of her heart.

Home looked just the same as ever, when she finally arrived back.

'Oh,' her father said. 'So you're here. I didn't think you'd have the cheek to show your face.'

Lillian swallowed, forcing down the painful lump in her throat. It had been a long journey on crowded trains and she was tired. She had hoped for something of a welcome from her family.

'Hello, Dad,' she said. 'Happy Christmas.'

'You'd best go straight in and see your gran,' he replied.

Had this been such a good idea, after all? Lillian set down her overnight bag and her bulging carrier of presents, then took a deep breath, squared her weary shoulders and went into Gran's room.

The familiar fug of warmth and cigarette smoke met her. Gran was sitting by the fire in her armchair, watching the TV. Over her knee was the latest hooked rug she was making. Her cold eyes swept over Lillian from head to toe.

'So you've come crawling back, have you?' she demanded.

It was as if the years had rolled back and she was a little girl again, accused of some shortcoming.

'I—I wanted to see you all for Christmas,' she stammered.

'Did you? And what makes you think that we want to see you?'

Tears prickled at the back of Lillian's eyes. 'You're my family,' she said. She could not stop her voice from wobbling.

'Yes, we are. The trouble is, my girl, you seem to have forgotten that,' Gran said. 'You seem to have forgotten what you owe us. You go off prancing about on a stage, bringing disgrace to the Parker name. Do you really expect to come back here and find that all is forgiven?'

She didn't expect it, but she had hoped.

'I—I don't know—I thought—as it was Christmas—'

'Christmas? You thought that would make a difference, did you?'

'Well, yes—'

Gran leaned forward. She thumped the arm of her chair to lend emphasis to her words. 'Well, let me tell you, young lady. I shall never, never forgive you for running off like that. The shame of it! A girl your age, living I don't know where amongst wicked stage people? I don't know what the world's coming to that my own granddaughter should even think of such a thing.'

'They're not wicked!' Lillian cried but, even as she did so, Harvey Goddard's face swam before her eyes, stopping her from saying anything else.

'Don't you contradict me. I read the papers. I know what these actors and actresses get up to. And to think that you have been living amongst them—!'

Anger finally came to Lillian's aid.

'You don't know a thing about it,' she protested. 'It's not like the *News of the World*, you know. We don't have wild parties and get drunk. I've been working so hard rehearsing that all I do in the evenings is go back to my digs and go to sleep.'

'Digs! A girl from a nice family living in digs, at your age?'

Gran said. 'My granddaughter should be living here at home where her family can keep an eye on her and know she's behaving. God knows what sort of reputation you're getting. No decent young man's going to look at you now.'

Lillian hardly knew whether to laugh or cry. 'This is nineteen fifty-six, Gran. Just in case you hadn't noticed, it's Queen Elizabeth on the throne, not Queen Victoria.'

Gran's eyes bulged. 'How dare you talk to me like that? Where's your sense of duty, answering your elders back? You should be crawling on your knees to me, thanking me for letting you back into this house after all you've done to disgrace us. So you realise just how upset your mother has been? You've broken her heart, you have.'

She had finally attacked Lillian's weak point.

Lillian bit her lip. 'I never meant to, honest I didn't.'

'She's not been the same since the day you left.'

Lillian knew just how much her mother depended on her. 'I'm sorry, but—'

'Sorry's not enough. Sorry's easy to say. What are you going to do about it?'

Lillian gaped at her. 'I—I—'

'You'll go and say you're sorry to her, of course. And tell her that you'll not do it again. I shouldn't be letting you back over the threshold of this house, wicked girl that you are, but, for her sake, I am. I'm letting you off scot-free. So go on, get into that kitchen and apologise.'

'But—I—'

Not do it again? Did Gran think she was back home for good?

'Go on, before I change my mind.'

Lillian went. Her legs felt like string. She hardly knew whether she was more angry or upset. And there was still the prospect of another row when Gran realised that she was going back to Sheffield first thing Boxing Day morning.

She tottered back up the passageway to the kitchen. Her father was sitting at the table smoking and drinking a cup of cocoa while her mother grated breadcrumbs.

'Hello, Mum.'

'Lillian, love—'

The kind word did what Gran could not. Lillian burst into tears. Her mother patted her shoulder and put a cup of cocoa in front of her. When she was able to talk again, Lillian asked where the others were.

'Frank's out with his mates, Bob's round at Susan's and Wendy's out with Mr Dempsey.'

There was nothing that could have cheered Lillian up more.

'So that's back on again, is it?'

'Yes, more's the pity,' her father said.

James was safe.

Lillian finished her cocoa and reached for the grater. 'I'll do that, Mum,' she offered.

Her mother passed the task over to her.

It was as if she'd never been away. On Christmas morning she got up early, put the turkey in the oven and walked down the road to the seafront, taking in deep breaths as she went. It was wonderful to smell the salt in the air again. She broke into a run until she reached the promenade rails. There it was, the great brown glistening stretch of Southend mud, and beyond it the steel-grey gleam of the Thames. She hadn't realised just how much she had missed the sight of it, and that smell of salt and seaweed and shellfish, the scent of home. She stood there for a few minutes, taking in the wheeling seagulls, the boats lying on the mud, the black tracery of the pier, making sure she had it all well fixed in her mind for when she was back in Sheffield again, miles and miles from the sea.

When she got back, the family were surfacing for breakfast. Mum was in the kitchen frying bacon, Bob was polishing his shoes and Dad was drinking his first cup of tea of the day. Frank slouched in and then Wendy appeared, pale without her make-up and looking tired.

'You'd think we could have a lie-in today. It's supposed to be a holiday,' she complained. 'No cooked breakfast for me, Mum.'

When they were all sitting at the kitchen table, Gran made her entrance.

'So—we're all here at last. All the family together,' she said, accepting the plate of bacon and eggs that Mum put in front of her. She looked round the table, her eyes coming to rest on her granddaughter. 'And that's how it's going to stay.'

Lillian was eating a big mouthful of bacon and fried bread. She had been hungry after her early morning walk. Now her appetite deserted her. If she had hoped to postpone this part of the argument till later, she was doomed to disappointment. She looked round the table in a vain bid for support. The rest of the family sat there stolidly chewing, avoiding her eyes. She cleared her throat.

'I'm sorry, Gran, but I have to go back. I'm under contract. That's a legal binding agreement.'

She wasn't sure whether that was so, but it sounded good. Across the table, she saw Frank grinning. He was expecting fireworks. He was right. Gran went off on one of her long tirades about family and duty and not knowing what the world was coming to. Lillian sat poking at her rapidly cooling breakfast.

'I'm really sorry, but I've got to go back, and that's an end to it,' she repeated.

To her infinite surprise, Bob spoke up. 'Actually, I think Lillian's right, Gran. If she's under contract, she can't renege on it. She'd be in trouble if she did.'

Lillian could have kissed him. But the Parkers weren't in the habit of showing affection to each other, so she just shot him a look of profound gratitude.

'Yes, I would,' she agreed.

Gran didn't back down immediately. She had a lot more to say on the subject of ungrateful young girls. But then she suddenly changed tack. 'I'm not happy about it and I never will be, but if there's the law involved, I suppose you'll have to obey it,' she said. 'But I'll expect you to send some of your earnings home each week. If you're not going to be here, you have to contribute in other ways,' she said.

Lillian was so relieved at being let off the hook that she agreed to do it.

After surviving that argument, it was a pleasure to spend the rest of the morning helping her mother with the Christmas dinner.

The Parkers never made a great deal of fuss about Christmas. A sad-looking tree and a few paper chains were the only decorations, but at least now that Gran had vented her displeasure over Lillian's rebellion, there was a display of family unity. They all ate dinner together at one o'clock and afterwards they exchanged presents.

The highlight of the day was tea at the Kershaws'. Shoehorning all of the Parkers into their small flat was something of a feat but, once there, Lillian could admire the effort they had made for the occasion. There were paper garlands across the ceiling, tinsel over the pictures and the mirror, mistletoe hanging from the central light and a pretty little tree with baubles and a star on top on the sideboard. They all exchanged gifts—

Lillian was touched and delighted to get a boxed set of writing paper and envelopes from Susan and a fountain pen from James—then Mrs Kershaw and Susan produced a feast of a meal with a beautifully iced cake as its centrepiece. 'Susan made it all herself, icing and everything,' Mrs Kershaw said proudly.

'She's a fine little housewife,' Gran approved. 'Not like some of these girls these days. Do you know what I saw advertised on the telly the other day? Packets of mashed potato mix! Fancy being too lazy to peel a potato. I don't know what the world's coming to.'

They couldn't watch Mrs Kershaw's new television as it didn't yet have an aerial, so they played Animal, Vegetable or Mineral and What's My Line. Lillian couldn't remember ever having enjoyed a Christmas more. And there was still the ride back with James to look forward to.

They set off at seven o'clock in the morning.

'It's really, really kind of you to do this for me,' she said as she got into the car.

She settled down into the front seat and looked about her. She had hardly ever ridden in a car, and certainly not for a long journey like this was going to be.

'That's all right. Did you enjoy your visit? Have you sorted things out with your family?'

'Sort of. Gran went on at me, of course, but in the end she gave in, except that she said I must send money home each week.'

'What, even though you're not living there?' James questioned.

'Well, it's winter, isn't it? Only the odd commercial traveller staying and the bills to pay.'

'But Wendy and Frank and Bob and your dad are all earning and paying in.'

'I know, but that's what Gran said I had to do.'

What she didn't tell him, because she didn't want him to think badly of her, was that she had lied to her grandmother about how much she was earning. She wasn't going to be made to send every last penny home.

'Doesn't seem fair to me,' James said.

A warm glow started inside her. He did understand. He was on her side.

They drove through the silent streets, past locked shops and dark houses. It seemed as if they were the only people awake in the world, just the two of them enclosed within the car with the engine humming and the road swishing under the tyres. They talked about their families, carefully skirting round the subject of Wendy, then James asked about her life up in Sheffield and the people she was working with and the panto and rehearsals. Lillian tried to describe to him the atmosphere of a theatrical company gradually forming out of a disparate group of people—the rivalries and friendships, the love affairs and the rows, the fun and the frustrations.

'It was really confusing at first, 'cos I didn't know anyone and being in the end-of-the-pier show was nothing like being in this production. It's such hard work, and sometimes you wonder if it's ever going to be ready or if you're ever going to be good enough, but it's wonderful when it's all going well, and then you finally get on to the stage and you're in a real theatre and there's the lights and the costumes and the sets and the music—you'd be amazed how different it is when you've got a proper orchestra playing and not just a piano! And this afternoon we're opening! It's really strange to think that there are loads of people up in Sheffield looking forward to coming and seeing us this afternoon. I still can't believe it's true.'

'You really love it, don't you?' James said.

'I do.' Lillian struggled to put what she felt into words. 'It's like…like magic. When it all goes right it's a whole magical world and people will come and, for that time when they're in the theatre, they'll believe in our magical world and we'll make them happy. That's a good thing to do, surely, to make people happy?'

'It is,' James agreed. 'There's not enough happiness in the world.'

For those few hours, Lillian was suspended in a little bubble of happiness, fragile and precious. They trundled through London and set off up the A1, all the while talking together, sometimes seriously, sometimes pulling each other's legs. Apart from Wendy, there wasn't anything they couldn't discuss. They didn't always agree, but they did respect each other's opinions. The cafés along the road were closed for Boxing Day, but they found a pub and had a drink and a packet of crisps each. Lillian sipped her orange juice and felt like a queen. Everyone in the pub must think that James was her boyfriend, and she couldn't have been more proud. He was definitely the most handsome man in the room, and she knew he was the kindest and the cleverest as well.

As they crossed the border to Yorkshire, her happiness had a hollow quality to it. If only they could just go on and on like this, travelling together. As it was, it was as if she were on the crest of a wave. All too soon, that wave was going to crash on to the shore.

'I wish you could stay and see the show,' Lillian said.

'I'd love to, Lindy, but won't it be sold out?'

'I suppose so, but you could ask at the box office. There

might be a spare place at the last minute, someone sick or something. Please, James, won't you try? I know it'd make you ever so late getting home, but I just so want you to see it.'

There was nothing else in the world she wanted so much at that moment.

'If I can get to see it, Lindy, I will.'

James took her to Mrs Frazer's to drop off her suitcase and pick up her stage make-up and dancing shoes, then they drove to the theatre. They parted at the stage door.

'What's it I'm supposed to say? Break a leg?' James asked.

Lillian felt as if she might burst into tears at any moment. This might be the last time she saw him for weeks. She flung her arms round him and kissed him on the lips. She wanted to hold on to his warm, strong body and never let him go.

'Thank you, thank you, thank you for everything!'

James disengaged her arms and gave her shoulders a squeeze.

'It's been a pleasure, kiddo.'

Kiddo! The tears did spill over then. Lillian broke away and made a bolt for the door.

When she arrived at the female dressing room, at least half the dancers and most of the courtiers were there already in various states of undress. The noise was tremendous as they exchanged accounts of their Christmases. Lillian slid into her place beside Diane and listened as she told her all about what her family had done as they put on their make-up and pinned up each other's hair. Had James been able to get a seat? How would she know if he had? There was no way she could go to front of house now and find out. The familiar gripes of stage fright caught at her, leaving her sick and weak.

'You're quiet,' Diane commented. 'Not like you, you're usually the big chatterbox. What's up?'

'Stage fright,' Lillian admitted.

'They say all the best performers have it.'

'Mmm.'

They got into their costumes for the first scene. Around them, the noise level was going up and up. If anyone else was suffering, they certainly weren't doing it in silence. Lillian could think only of James. Was he already on his way home? Or waiting till the last minute to see if he could get a seat? Or sitting in the auditorium with a programme and an ice cream?

The ten minute and five minute calls came round, and then it was overture and beginners. Lillian lined up in the wings with the rest of the dancers. From where she was standing, she could see the curtains and part of the set. The orchestra was playing a selection of jolly tunes and, beyond that, on the other side of the curtain, she could sense the audience, rows and rows of families rustling and shuffling, impatient for the show to begin. There was a small disturbance behind her, a whispering further down the line.

'Lindy-Lou Parker?'

'Yes.'

One of the scene shifters put a piece of paper into her hand. Surprised, Lillian moved to where the light was better.

I'm in the gods. Go for that dream. J.

Lillian almost squealed out loud. But there was no time to think about it. The curtains were opening. She shoved the note down inside her bodice. There was an 'Ooh' of appreciation from the audience as the hall of the castle was revealed, and then it was their cue. Onto the stage Lillian danced, into the blaze of the footlights and the heat of the crowded theatre, a great big beam on her face. This was it. This was what she wanted to do and, out there, James was watching. It was a perfect moment.

CHAPTER 17

'WHO'S it from this time?' Diane asked.

'Oh, only Bob,' Lillian replied.

Of the three people who wrote to her—Bob, James and Janette—James was, of course, her favourite correspondent. His life was full of change. He had started his own garage, just as he'd said he would. After a slow start, it was now doing very nicely and he was thinking of moving the Kershaw family to a bigger and better flat. Something with a bit of a garden for his mother to look after and sit in, he said. All this Lillian enjoyed reading about. What she hated was hearing about where he had been with his latest girlfriend, especially if they had been dancing. She suffered agonies of jealousy, picturing him leading some girl round the Kursaal dance floor. What did soften it a bit, though, was the fact that none of these girls seemed to last long. No sooner did Lillian decide that Audrey or Val or Maureen was the name she hated most in the world, than he wrote and said that they had broken up and he was going out with someone else.

There was no danger of that kind from Bob's letter. It was full of details of houses that he and Susan had looked at, and why they were unsuitable. At the end was the information that their mother was very poorly. Lillian thought of the big spring clean coming up. How was her mother going to manage? Wendy might be dragooned into helping, despite being too grand these days to be doing anything useful, but, if not, it was just Frank and Bob, plus Dad when he came home from work. Oh, and Susan. Susan would be a big help to her mum. That stopped Lillian from feeling quite so guilty at not being there.

'You coming out?' Diane asked.

'Yes, why not?'

There was no matinée this afternoon, so they were free till the evening.

'Only those lads who took us out last night are downstairs offering to take us to lunch.'

'Ooh, lunch. That's a bit posh, ain't it?'

After the panto had ended in Sheffield, they had both got jobs with a touring company. This week they were in Preston. Lillian was getting the hang of assessing new towns now. The first concern was the quality of the theatrical digs, then the facilities, or lack of them, at the theatre, then came the cafés, shops and after-hours drinking holes. The last were essential if you wanted somewhere to wind down after the high of performing, and there were always men ready and willing to take the girls along to them. So far, Preston was doing rather well in her eyes. The digs were clean, warm and comfy and the landlady nice, the theatre was OK, and the place they'd gone to last night had not been a dive at all. In fact, it had been quite classy and the young men who had taken them there had not tried to take liberties with them just because they were dancers.

Lillian quickly flicked on a dash of lipstick and eyeshadow and backcombed her hair into a fashionable beehive. She pulled on the smartest things she could find that weren't creased from being in a suitcase, checked that the seams of her stockings were straight, and was ready to go.

Diane banged on the door of the room next to theirs as they passed. 'You all right, Bren?'

'No,' came a muffled voice from within.

Lillian and Diane looked at each other. The question of should they go in, and the answer that yes, they must, passed between them unspoken. Diane opened the door. Brenda, one of their fellow dancers, was curled up in bed with her back to them.

'Has it started?' Lillian asked hopefully. 'You want me to get you a hot-water bottle?'

'No,' came the anguished reply. 'It still hasn't.'

'You might feel better if you got up,' Diane suggested.

'What do you know? Go away.'

'But you—'

'Just go away and leave me alone!'

Diane and Lillian exchanged glances again.

'We'll look in again when we get back,' Diane said.

There was no reply. Lillian closed the door behind her.

'How long is it now?' she asked

'Six weeks. She's missed two.'

'Oh, Gawd.'

Lillian had learnt a lot very quickly in the last few months; quite enough to know the significance of two missed periods. The dancers in the touring company she was now part of had all been on the road for two years or more and constantly gossiped about each other and chewed over their male conquests. There was a sharp divide between Those Who Did and Those Who Didn't. The virgins thought the other girls gave all dancers a bad name, while the more experienced girls taunted them for being frigid little goody-goodies. But Brenda had taken Lillian aside soon after she'd joined the company and given her a talking-to.

'Don't give it away to just anyone,' she advised. 'The first time ought to be special. It was for me. I was head-over-heels and I thought he was too. Trouble was, it turned out he had somebody else all along and I was really cut-up about that for ages. It made me go off the rails a bit. So don't do what I did, right?'

Lillian thought of Harvey Goddard and shuddered. That had been a very lucky escape. How could she ever have looked James in the face again? It was bad enough having to live with what he had done.

'Right,' she agreed.

'Oh, and don't tell anyone what I just told you, either, or I'll have your guts for garters.'

As the girls came downstairs after leaving Brenda, two young men were waiting for them in the hall, both smartly dressed in long coats with their hair slicked back. They looked up and gazed with admiration.

'That's a right pair of little crackers we got there!' one said.

Lillian smiled and tried to remember the name of the one she had paired off with. Was it Alan or Andy? She knew it was something beginning with A. They made useful escorts for the week, saving Lillian and Diane quite a bit in meals and drinks and accepting with good grace the fact that they weren't going to get more than a kiss and a cuddle in return.

'They'll boast to their mates for years about the dancers they went out with. They think we're exotic,' Diane said.

'They wouldn't if they saw us in the mornings.' Lillian laughed, thinking of how they all slopped around in their tatty dressing gowns with no make-up and their hair up in rollers.

On Saturday night all the girls went to the late night club after the last performance. Brenda accepted drinks from who-ever would buy them for her and was maudlin drunk by the time they got back to their digs. Lillian woke twice in the night to hear her staggering to the toilet to throw up. In the morning she looked dreadful, ashen-pale and hardly able to stand up.

'I can't move,' she moaned.

'You've got to. We're getting the train to Liverpool at two o'clock,' Diane told her.

'I'll bring you up some tea,' Lillian offered.

Brenda just groaned.

Lillian brought her some anyway and, as she walked across the room, she nearly tripped over an empty gin bottle lying under a discarded skirt.

'What's this?' she asked.

'What's it look like?' Brenda retorted.

'You never drank all this by yourself? No wonder you feel bad.'

'Oh, go and boil your head,' Brenda growled. 'I just want to die.'

'She was trying to get rid of the baby,' Diane said when Lillian reported her find to her.

'*What?*'

It was the first time that Brenda's problem had actually been referred to as a baby.

'Drinking a bottle of gin's supposed to shift it. But I think it's just an old wives' tale.'

Lillian was shocked. All the intimate talk amongst the girls had not prepared her for this. She couldn't adjust to it at all and could hardly bring herself to speak to Brenda, who had to be made to get up, pack and move on.

The trains were delayed and the weather very unspringlike, with gusts of cold wind bringing heavy showers. All the company seemed bad-tempered. The comic who headlined the show had a car and didn't travel with them, which made for resentment. Sometimes he invited some other member of the cast to ride with him, but this caused even more bad feeling. Today the girl singer was the lucky one, and everyone else spent the time waiting around on cold platforms in slagging them both off. Lillian had to work very hard at not wondering whether this really was the sort of life she wanted.

Diane seemed to be having the same thoughts. 'If I was at home now, we'd have had my mam's lovely Sunday roast and we'd all be sitting around having cups of tea and listening to the wireless,' she said.

'I'd be cleaning up after the Sunday roast, and Gran'd be telling me I wasn't being thorough enough with the oven,' Lillian said.

The thought of it made her feel a little less bad about her present situation.

'And I'd of spent the morning changing beds and cleaning rooms if we'd had any PGs in,' she added.

Diane was still thinking of her family Sundays. 'My cousins usually come round of a Sunday afternoon, or we go to theirs. We all have tea together and my Aunty Evie plays the piano and we sing.'

Lillian sighed. If she had a lovely family like that, maybe she wouldn't have left home.

'Susan comes round to ours. And James, sometimes...'

'Ah, the gorgeous James,' Diane teased.

'Mmm.'

She missed James terribly. At least once a day she would think she saw him, in the street or sitting in a café or jumping off a bus. Her heart would turn over and she would cry out and start to run towards him, only to find it was someone who looked a little like him. Then came the disappointment, bitter after the leap of hope. While her heart was still so bound up with James, the boys who swam briefly in and out of her life meant nothing to her.

They arrived in Liverpool at last. Half a dozen of the dancers got digs with a Mrs Reeves in a narrow three-storey house close to the theatre. Lillian disliked the place from the start. It was gloomy and smelt damp and musty, and Mrs Reeves had bad teeth and a sharp manner. What was more, this was to be a two-week run. But the others were fed up and just wanted to get settled with the minimum fuss. It was either go along with the majority or find somewhere else by herself.

It was on Thursday that Brenda came into her room uninvited and dropped down onto her bed. 'I got to talk to someone,' she said.

Then she lit a cigarette and sat there puffing at it with quick, nervous movements, not saying a word.

'You've not come on, then,' Lillian said, to get the ball rolling.

Brenda shook her head. 'I been getting morning sickness.'

'Oh…dear…'

Even Lillian knew what this meant. 'What are you going to do?' she asked.

Brenda took another drag at her cigarette. 'I've heard of someone who can help.'

'Help? How? In what way?'

Brenda stared at the wall above Lillian's head. 'Get rid of it.'

'What? How can you do that? How can you even think of it? Your baby—'

'It's not a baby; it's just a blob, a thing.'

Lillian's knowledge on this point was vague in the extreme. 'But it will be,' she said.

'I've got to,' Brenda insisted. 'I won't be able to go on working once it shows, and then what'll I do?'

'You could have it adopted.'

'No. It ruins your figure. I'd never get work again. And if my parents found out, they'd kill me. They'd never let me in the house again.'

Lillian could understand that. If she were to get pregnant, Gran would turn her out for sure.

'What about the…the father?' she asked.

Brenda waved her cigarette in a dismissive gesture. 'Oh, yeah, can't you just see it? I find the bloke I was with two months ago and he says prove it—it could have been the one the week before, or the week after. They'd wriggle out of it.'

'You mean—you don't know who it is?'

'No, I don't know. Wicked, ain't I?' Brenda glared at her, challenging her to agree.

'That does…well…make things difficult,' Lillian said.

'Difficult? It makes it bleeding impossible.'

Lillian was way out of her depth. She fell back on knowledge gleaned from the problem pages of magazines.

'There are…places…you know, homes for…for…'

'Unmarried mothers? They treat you like dirt in them. Friend of mine had to go to one. She was never the same after. No, there's only one way out. It's lucky we're in Liverpool. The Irish girls all come over here to have it done.'

'I still don't like it.'

'It's not you that's got to choose.'

'I know, but—' Lillian sighed. This was dreadful. She didn't know what to say or do. 'If you've made your mind up, why are you asking me?'

'I'm not. I just want you and Diane to cover for me. I haven't told anyone else, and you might be a kid that knows nothing, but you're not a snitch.'

Lillian wasn't sure whether to be pleased at this or not.

'If I get it done tomorrow, I can go sick tomorrow night and Saturday, and we're off Sunday and Monday, and I might be OK to go back to work on Tuesday. You'll have to say I got the screaming runs and I can't possibly go on stage. Then nobody'll know I had it done, and I can just forget about it.'

Forget about it? Forget she ever had a baby growing inside her? Lillian put her hands to her stomach, trying to imagine a baby there.

Brenda was looking at her, expecting an answer.

'OK,' she agreed, because she couldn't very well refuse. The girls might all bicker and gossip but, when it came to the point, they stuck together.

Brenda did not come down to breakfast the next morning and nobody noticed her slip out some time before midday. Early in the afternoon, a taxi arrived at the digs. Lillian heard the driver speaking to Mrs Reeves at the door.

'Someone come and get this girl out of my cab. I don't want her messing up my seats.'

She put her head round the bedroom door. 'Come on, quick,' she said to Diane. 'It's Brenda.'

She was so shocked when she saw Brenda that she gasped, her hand flying to her face. She had never seen anyone look so pale. It was as if there was no blood left in her body. Her face was drawn with pain, making her look ten years older, and she could hardly stand. Lillian and Diane got one each side of her and supported her. They then started the slow and awkward climb up the narrow stairs.

'Here!' Mrs Reeves shouted after them. 'You can't take her up there.'

'You can't stop us,' Diane shouted back.

'Look at her! I know what she's been up to, the wicked girl. She'll bleed all over my mattress.'

'Good job. It needs replacing,' Diane retorted.

They had nearly reached the top of the stairs. Lillian, looking down at her feet to make sure she didn't trip, realised that blood was trickling down Brenda's legs and into her shoes.

'Oh, my Gawd,' she muttered.

She and Diane manoeuvred Brenda into her room and sat her down on the rickety wooden chair.

'Get some STs,' Diane said. 'I'll hold her up.'

'I wanna lie down. Jus' lie down,' Brenda slurred.

Mrs Reeves appeared with a rubber sheet and an armful of newspapers and whipped the sheets off the bed.

'There, she can lie on those,' she said. 'And that's more than she deserves.'

Lillian and Diane got Brenda into her nightdress and onto the pad of newspapers, where she lay trembling, curled up round her pain. Lillian offered her tea, which she refused, and aspirins, which she swallowed. Then she closed her eyes and refused to answer any of their anxious questions. The only reaction they could get out of her was when Diane suggested sending for a doctor.

'No,' Brenda whispered. 'No doctors.'

When the other girls returned from their trip to the shops, Diane and Lillian kept them out of Brenda's room, saying she had a bad case of the runs and didn't want to see anyone. But when the time came round to go to the theatre, they didn't know what to do.

'We can't leave her, she's still bleeding an awful lot,' Diane said.

'Is that normal?' Lillian asked. The whole situation terrified her. The responsibility was crushing. She wanted desperately to hand Brenda over to someone who knew what they were doing.

'How do I know? I've never had anything to do with this before either.'

They both looked at Brenda. It was bad enough that she was having time off, without one of them staying away as well. Being ill was simply not allowed. They were all expected to be 'troupers' and carry on, no matter what.

'If we say one of us has got the runs as well—bad enough not to be able to get out of the house—they'll have to accept it,' Lillian said.

'I don't know. There'll be a terrific row.'

From the bed, Brenda suddenly joined in. 'Go,' she croaked. 'Both of you. Not so many questions that way.'

'But we can't leave you,' Lillian insisted.

'I'm OK. Go. Please.'

After some more discussion, they reluctantly agreed. It would certainly be much easier to cover for one than for two.

Lillian found it impossible to join in with the usual banter in the dressing room. The image of Brenda lying groaning on a heap of newspapers kept getting in the way of any normal chat, filling her with guilt. They shouldn't have listened to her. They should have stayed. She went through her part in the performance like a puppet, making the right moves from long practice, but not projecting any of her usual verve into it. She just wanted to get it over with and rush back to check on Brenda.

When the curtain came down, she and Diane changed at

lightning speed and rushed back to Mrs Reeves's. They ran up the stairs, paused at Brenda's door, then softly opened it and looked in. A small amount of streetlight came through the open curtains. Brenda was lying perfectly still on the bed in exactly the position she had been in when they'd left her.

'She's asleep,' Diane whispered. 'Best leave her.'

Lillian was sorely tempted to agree, but something about Brenda shot fear right through her. She was too still.

She walked quietly into the room. 'Bren?' she whispered. 'You all right?'

There was no reaction from Brenda. An unpleasant smell hung about her. Lillian couldn't suppress a squeak of rising panic. She stepped back and felt for the switch. Light flooded the room and both girls cried out in horror. A great patch of red stained the bedclothes and Brenda's face was dead white. Even to two girls who knew nothing about medicine, it was clear that Brenda was not asleep but unconscious.

'Oh, my God, oh, my God, what shall we do? We never ought to of left her—' Diane wailed.

'Ambulance,' Lillian answered, and bolted from the room.

She leapt down the stairs two at a time, trying to remember where the nearest phone box was. On the corner—yes—on the corner by the theatre. She raced up the silent street, past darkened houses where people were peacefully asleep, reached the phone box and wrenched open the door. Panting now, she picked up the receiver and punched 999. A calm male voice with a strong Liverpudlian accent took her gabbled details.

'Please, please hurry! There's so much blood—'

The image of Brenda's still white face shimmered in her mind's eye. She could hardly keep from sobbing.

'An ambulance will be with you as soon as possible, miss.'

It was there at the door within ten minutes, but it felt like ten hours. Lillian and Diane clung to each other, not knowing what to do to help their friend, hating their ignorance. Mrs Reeves, alerted by the voices and the clatter of Lillian's feet, stood in the doorway of Brenda's room and talked non-stop about how nothing like this had ever happened in her house before.

'Oh, shut up, you old witch!' Diane snapped.

'Don't you talk to me like that. You're no better than she is. I knew it the moment I saw you lot—'

'Please!' Lillian cried. 'Please, stop it!'

They were prevented from descending into a full-scale row by the arrival of the ambulance.

The ambulance men took in the situation at a glance.

'When did she have it done?' one asked.

'Early this afternoon,' Diane told him.

'And she's been bleeding like this since then?'

'No. It—it wasn't quite so bad at first. She was awake—'

'She is going to be all right, isn't she?' Lillian begged.

The men gave away nothing.

'They'll do their best for her in emergency, miss.'

'You two coming with her?'

Diane and Lillian didn't even have to look at each other.

'Yes,' they chorused, and followed the men and the stretcher downstairs, with Mrs Reeves close behind them, still complaining.

Brenda was hurried away from them as soon as they arrived at the hospital. Lillian and Diane gave what few details they knew about her and were sent to wait.

It was a long, long night. They huddled together on an uncomfortable bench, every so often trying to assure each other that Brenda was going to be all right, and bewailing the fact that they hadn't got her to hospital earlier. Nothing they could say could take away the helplessness they felt, or the worry that ate away at their insides. At some point a nurse informed them that their friend had been taken down to Theatre for an emergency operation. Then, some time after that, a young doctor came to see them. His face was grim.

'You're the young ladies who are with Miss Tyler?'

They both nodded. Lillian could feel something unravelling inside her. The words *no—no—no*—pounded through her, but she didn't know whether she said them or not.

'Do you know who did this to her?'

They both shook their heads.

'You're sure? Because if you're withholding information, you're party to a crime.'

'Crime?' Diane squeaked.

'Abortion is illegal.'

Both girls flinched. It was the first time the word had been used.

'Sh-she didn't want us to go with her,' Lillian managed to say.

The doctor was incandescent with fury and frustration. 'It's disgusting what these people do. They're butchers. Butchers! Hanging's too good for them. They should be made to come and see the results of what they do.'

All the time he was speaking, Lillian felt a dreadful cold certainty creeping over her.

'Brenda—' she whispered. 'Is she—?'

The doctor closed his eyes briefly. His anger vented, he looked defeated and desperately tired. 'I'm sorry,' he said gently. 'We couldn't save her.'

CHAPTER 18

JAMES escaped early from the flat. Having to listen to his mother and sister talking wedding dresses and household goods morning, noon and night was beginning to get on his nerves. He paused at the gate to look back at his new home and felt a small glow of pride. The Kershaws were on the up. The flat was in a pleasant tree-lined street on the Westcliff side of town. It had its own small front and back garden, nice light rooms and a proper kitchen and bathroom. His mother was absolutely delighted with it and seemed to have gained a new lease of life, enjoying arranging the furniture and polishing all the surfaces when before she'd never seemed to have enough energy to get round to everything.

Satisfied that all was well at home, James set off for Kershaw's Auto Repairs. There was plenty there now to keep him busy. He fitted a new clutch for one customer and renewed the brake linings for another, breaking off to answer the phone to three new customers. After that he had an hour before the next car was due in, so he made a cup of tea before spending some time on the Riley that was his latest do-up-to-sell-on project.

He took Lillian's latest letter out of his pocket and studied it as he waited for the kettle to boil. He was worried about Lillian. Her last two or three letters had lacked her usual enthusiasm. He was sure there was something wrong and had written to ask her. She had assured him that she was all right, but he was not convinced. He was thinking about this when Frank turned up.

'Wotcha, mate,' he said. 'Got a minute?'

'Yeah, I'm just having a break,' James said. 'Tea?'

Frank accepted a cup and wandered round the workshop, fiddling with the tools and running a hand over the Riley. James watched him, sure that this was not just a social visit. He and Frank had never really hit it off.

'Doing all right, then?' Frank asked.

'Yeah, OK,' James said.

'How much d'you think you'll make on this, then?'

'Enough. Not a huge amount when you count the hours I've spent on it.'

'But you got a bit of money coming in?'

James could see which way this was going.

'Enough,' he repeated.

'Then you'd be able to help me out with a bit of cash, then? Just to tide me over, like?'

'I don't know about that.'

Frank was the last person he would consider lending money to. As almost-family, he would be last in line to be repaid.

'Oh, come on, mate,' Frank said. 'It's only till the end of the week. I'll give it you back on payday.'

'Been throwing it away on the gee-gees, then?' James guessed.

'Bleeding dogs. They fix it on that track, you know. I was on to a dead cert and it came in fourth.'

'If they fix the races, then why do you bet on them?'

'They don't fix all of them. Look, mate, I need fifty quid to pay the HP on the bike or they'll come and take it back.'

'Fifty quid? It'll take a lot more than a week for you to pay that back. How far behind are you?'

Frank shrugged. 'Not much. But they're sharks, these people. Won't let you get away with anything.'

'I'm surprised they let you run it up that far.'

James suspected there was more to it than just the HP. Frank must have borrowed from his friends already, and needed to pay them back too. His fifty pounds would be added to a long list of debts and, since Frank wasn't earning much, it was unlikely he would ever see it back.

'Oh, well, they don't care, do they? They can always get the bike back.'

The phone rang again. It was someone with starter motor problems. Frank mooched around the workshop while James took the details. He was just about to carry on about a possible loan when there was yet another phone call. This time it was someone looking for a runabout for his wife. Did James know of anyone who had one for sale? As it happened, James did and, what was more, he knew it was in good running order because he had recently serviced it himself. James undertook to negotiate a fair price and anticipated a nice little bit of commission.

'You're busy, then?' Frank said.

That couldn't be denied.

'Look, mate,' James said. 'I may be busy but that doesn't

mean I've got a spare fifty quid lying about. I'll tell you what I can do, though—if you'd like to come and work with me two or three evenings a week you can earn the money, and while you're working you won't be out spending, so you'll be gaining both ways.'

He knew Frank wasn't much of a mechanic but he could do the unskilled work, leaving James free to do the difficult stuff.

Frank huffed and puffed over this. 'Dunno about that. I got a job already. I don't want to be working evenings an' all. And, in any case, I need the money now.'

'Suit y'self,' James said. 'That's my offer.'

Frank gave him a sly look. 'Wendy wouldn't like it if she knew you wouldn't help me out.'

But James was familiar with how things worked in the Parker household.

'Wendy's not going to know, is she? Because if you tell her you're strapped for cash, she'll tell your gran, and then there'll be hell to pay.'

'I don't care what Gran says,' Frank lied.

'Like I said, take it or leave it,' James repeated. 'Now, I got work to get on with.'

Frank kicked at the back tyre of the Riley. 'There's other blokes that're not as tightfisted as you. They'll lend it me no trouble, you'll see.'

'That's all right then, isn't it?'

'Yeah, Terry Dempsey, for one. He's got plenty.'

Alarm bells rang in James's head. He might not like Frank, but he didn't want to see him mixed up with Dempsey.

'You don't want to owe Dempsey. He'll call in favours when he chooses, and you won't be able to refuse.'

'I'm not scared of him,' Frank boasted.

'Neither am I, but he's bad news. If you've got any sense, you'll stay away from him.'

Frank snorted. 'You're just jealous 'cos he's got Wendy. And he's got more money than you'll ever have.'

'At least my money's honestly earned,' James retorted.

Frank went off in a huff. James was left to admit to himself that yes, he was jealous of Dempsey. Every time he saw him with Wendy, he wanted to smash his face in. But jealousy wasn't going to get Wendy back, and neither was attacking Dempsey. He needed to follow his sister's advice and find himself somebody else. He resolved to go back down to the Kursaal on Friday.

Bob was due to come to tea at their house that evening. James wasn't sure he could stand a whole evening of being polite to him and decided to go back to the workshop to work on the Riley. The way the repair jobs were coming in, he wasn't going to have much time to get it done during the day and it wasn't earning him anything standing there. First, though, he had to get tea over with.

His mother always made a big fuss of Bob and, now that they had a more spacious home to entertain in, James knew that she really enjoyed having a guest. Sure enough, when he got in from work, there was a fresh baked chocolate sponge cake on the table, along with a choice of egg and cress or liver sausage sandwiches. Bob was already there, going on about some fuss at the bank.

Over the meal, Wendy's name came up.

'We're still not happy about what happened at the weekend,' Bob said. 'Gran can't get over it.'

'No wonder,' his mother said. 'I must say, I'm surprised at Wendy. If Susan had behaved like that, I'd have been very upset. Very upset indeed. Not that she would, of course, and you're too much of a gentleman to even suggest such a thing, Bob.'

'Behaved like what? What happened?' James asked.

Susan and his mother exchanged glances. He suspected that this was something they had decided to keep from him.

'We were talking about it yesterday when you were out, Jamie,' Susan said. 'Wendy went up to London with Mr Dempsey on Saturday night—'

James frowned. That was another thing that irritated him. They all referred to the man as Mr Dempsey, never by his first name.

'They were going to some nightclub or other so they weren't expected back till late, and Mr Parker didn't wait up for her. But, in the morning, they found that she hadn't come home.'

'She'd stayed the night up in town with Dempsey?'

This really was the end.

Bob nodded. 'Of course, I had to tell Susan. She and I have no secrets from each other. But it's not something that I want other people to know about my sister, so I'd like you to keep it to yourself, James.'

'Of course,' James said, annoyed that Bob should even ask such a thing. 'I don't go gossiping about people's private lives, especially W—anyone in your family.'

'It would ruin her reputation if it got out,' Susan said.

She sounded very sober, but her eyes were round with the excitement of discovering that Wendy, who'd always totally eclipsed her, had proved herself to be a bad girl. She would never be as pretty as Wendy, but she was more virtuous. The moral high ground was hers.

'Whatever was Mr Dempsey thinking of, keeping her out all night?' their mother asked.

James knew perfectly well what Dempsey had been thinking of.

'She did say that they stayed in separate rooms in the hotel,' Bob said. 'And of course I wouldn't like to think the worst of my sister. I know she wouldn't agree to staying all night with a man.'

James wanted to believe that as well. He held on to it when reason told him that Dempsey wasn't going to bother staying up in town if they slept in separate rooms.

'It's not as if he's got the excuse of missing the last train. He's got that flashy Jag,' he said. 'He could drive her home at any time.'

'I know. That's what's upset Gran. She says he's got no respect for Wendy or for us.'

This was all too true. It wasn't as if Wendy didn't have a family. She had a father and two brothers to look out for her, but the fact was that the Parkers were scared of Dempsey. His reputation as a hard man stopped them from laying down rules about when Wendy should be in. Dempsey could do what he liked.

'He's got no respect for anyone,' James said.

Gloomily, Bob agreed with him. 'He's not the sort of person we like seeing Wendy with, but she's dead set on him. Gran tried to stop her from seeing him any more, and Wendy just refused.

'"You can throw me out if you like, but I'm not giving him up." That's what she said.'

Susan shook her head at this.

'She's a very headstrong girl,' she said.

'She's had her head turned,' their mother said. 'That's the trouble. What with all this Carnival Queen business, riding around in a big car and wearing a cloak and a tiara and having everyone fuss over her, and then all those places Mr

Dempsey takes her to—! I was amazed when Susan told me about them going to Belgium in an aeroplane for the day. I mean, that's the sort of things film stars do, isn't it? Not ordinary girls like her who work in a shop. When you've done things like that, you can't want to go back to the everyday world and go out with decent ordinary boys.'

'Lillian once told me that Wendy wanted to be like Diana Dors,' James said.

Bob pursed his mouth like an old lady. 'I don't know what's happening to our family. There's Lillian touring all over the North with that dancing troupe and Wendy running around with a man like Terry Dempsey. I think it's something to do with all this rock'n'roll stuff. That American music rots the moral fibre. I don't know what the world's coming to when girls from a respectable family like ours behave like that, doing whatever they please.'

'It is fun, though,' James said. He loved rock'n'roll. 'Little Richard and Jerry Lee Lewis, they're amazing. You just got to get up and move when you hear their music.'

The others looked at him as if he were speaking a foreign language.

'Well, at least you and Bob are being sensible and doing everything the right way,' his mother said to Susan.

Susan smirked and looked at Bob, who patted her hand.

'Yes, at least we're keeping the standards up,' he agreed.

And the conversation turned to the subject of their wedding. James decided not to go to the Kursaal on Friday, but instead to one of the pubs where they had rock and roll bands and skiffle groups playing all night.

CHAPTER 19

'THIS ain't a bad place, all in all,' Diane decided.

'It's OK,' Lillian agreed.

Since the shock of Brenda's death, she hadn't been able to summon up any enthusiasm about anything.

They had been in their new digs for a week now. It was a good thing they were all right, because this was their home for the rest of the summer. The company had settled in Blackpool for the season, playing five afternoons and six evenings a week. It was a gruelling schedule, but it was not that that concerned Lillian. She just wasn't sure she wanted to be here at all. Imperfect though home was, she often found herself wishing she was back there. She worried about her mother, now that the season was starting and the PGs were beginning to arrive. She missed her brothers, annoying though she had always found them when she'd been living with them. She even missed Wendy, much to her own surprise. But there was more to it than that. She tried to explain it to Diane.

'It's this thing about being a stranger all the time,' she said. 'I liked it at first. I felt sort of—free, I suppose. I liked it that I didn't know anyone in whatever town we were in. But now…I don't know…it'd be nice if you went to the corner shop and they knew your name, and you didn't have to ask where things were all the time.'

'Everyone gets fed up of being on the road,' Diane told her. 'But we're here for the summer now. We can make this place feel like home, you know, have a few knick-knacks and stuff around. And Blackpool's a super town; there's loads going on. We'll get ourselves fixed up with a couple of nice boys for the summer.'

'Yeah, maybe.'

There were three things wrong with that statement, as far as Lillian was concerned. First, the digs were just like all the others, cramped and gloomy with old-fashioned furniture and a view of roofs and backyards. Her own room at home might be no better, but it was hers, or half hers anyway. Then there was Blackpool. It was a big jolly resort with lots going on and she had to admit that the beaches were better than back home, but there had always been a big rivalry between Blackpool and Southend, especially over which town had the best illuminations. Lillian felt she was being a traitor to her home town, being part of the attractions at Blackpool. Most of all, it was the boys. She didn't want to go steady with someone for the summer because there was only one boy in the world she really wanted to be with.

She touched James's latest letter as it sat in her pocket. He had written that he had been out dancing.

I'm really getting good at the rock'n'roll. You'd be proud of me,

*Lindy. I can spin my partners round like tops, and even do the
under the legs thing. You really taught me well.*

It was nice that he was grateful for her lessons, but she envied every girl who danced with him. If she were to go home,
would he take her out dancing with him? What a brilliant
partnership they would make. They would blow away everyone else on the floor. It was her favourite daydream.

'…out down the seafront before we go to the theatre?'

She realised that Diane was talking to her.

'Oh—yeah—all right.'

There was a sharp wind coming in off the Irish Sea. Bat-
tling against it made Lillian feel alive again. Before she knew
it, her cheeks were rosy and she was laughing and chasing
Diane like a kid. Crossing the road back towards the theatre
with the wind shipping her hair into her eyes, she suddenly
caught sight of someone who made her stop in her tracks.

'Eileen?' she gasped. 'Aunty Eileen?'

She dashed over to the pavement, narrowly missing a tram.
The woman she had seen was walking away from her with her
hands in her pockets and her head down. Her heart thumping in her chest, Lillian ran to catch her up.

'Aunty Eileen?' she yelled. She caught the woman by the
arm. 'Aunty—oh—!'

The disappointment was crushing. A stranger was looking
at her with something close to annoyance.

'I—I'm sorry. I thought you were someone else. I'm sorry,'
she gabbled.

The woman looked at her for a moment, then just shrugged
and walked on, leaving Lillian standing staring after her.

Diane caught up with her. 'You're daft, you are. You nearly
went under that tram.'

Lillian explained her mistake.

'Your Aunty Eileen? The one who was like a mum to you?'

'Yes. Only it wasn't.'

'Never mind. Maybe you still will find her one day. She might see you dancing in the show and come and say hello.'

'Yeah, maybe.'

Lillian allowed herself to be marched along the road to the theatre. She breathed in the smell of the dressing room, the mix of dust and greasepaint and cheap scent and female sweat. This was why she was here. This was why she didn't just leave and go home. She still loved the theatre, and she still revelled in being a dancer.

The afternoon audience was quite sparse. The season had hardly begun and most of them were elderly people. Everyone in the troupe assured her that it would be quite different when the wakes weeks started. Then all the mills in a town would close for the holidays and half the population would arrive in Blackpool. Every seat in the house would be full then, especially if the weather was bad.

Lillian was half changed after the show when the messenger boy put his head round the door. 'Lillian Parker? Anyone here called Lillian Parker?'

'No,' several girls chorused.

'Yes!' Lillian called above the noise. 'That's me.'

Heads turned in her direction. Everyone here knew her as Lindy-Lou.

'Phone call for you at the stage door.'

Lillian pulled her stained dressing gown on over her underwear and hurried to the stage door keeper's cuddy. Her heart was thumping painfully. What had happened? Was it bad news from home?

She was surprised to hear Wendy's voice. 'Oh, Lill, thank goodness. Lill, I got to talk to you.'

'What is it? Is Mum ill?'

'No, no—it's me.'

'You're ill?'

'No, not ill. Not…I…I'm…oh, Lillian, I don't know what to do. I can't ask the girls at work; they're all so jealous of me. And if the Carnival committee find out, I'll be sacked, and if Dad and Gran—Oh Lillian, they'll kill me. So I rang you.'

Lillian could feel herself going cold. She had heard this before. Fear and horror crawled over her. Not Wendy. It couldn't happen to Wendy as well. Not her sister.

'Listen,' she said. 'Are you…I mean…'

From his cuddy hole, the stage door keeper, an elderly man in a grey collarless shirt and a muffler, was tactfully sorting through some papers. But he could hear every word she was saying.

'—pregnant?' she whispered.

'Y—oh, damn and blast—the pips—'

Wendy sounded desperate. There were various clonking and whirring noises on the line, then her voice came back. 'Lillian? Are you there?'

'Yes, I'm still here.'

'I've put lots of money in now. Yes, I think I must be. I mean, I've missed two—'

It was Brenda all over again. Lillian couldn't believe this was happening.

'I don't know what to do,' Wendy wailed.

Lillian tried to think. The responsibility was crushing. Then she realised that, unlike poor Brenda, Wendy did know who the father was.

'Have you told Terry?'

'No! I couldn't—'

'Why? Aren't you going out with him any more?'

Self-interest intruded. Was she going out with James again? Please, not that. If James was the father… A moan escaped from her throat.

'Yes, of course I am, but—'

'And it's his? I mean, he is the—?'

'Of course he is!' The old Wendy surfaced, sharp and truculent. 'Whatever do you take me for?'

'Sorry. Only I can't see why you can't tell him.'

'He's not a baby sort of person, is he? I mean, it doesn't go with his way of life, does it? Nightclubs and things. He couldn't be bothered with babysitters and all that. And if I get all fat and ugly, he won't love me any more and oh, Lillian, I couldn't bear it if he didn't. It'd be the end of the world.'

'But you got to, Wend. It's the only way. You got to tell him, and if he really does love you, then he'll marry you.'

If he was any sort of a man, he would marry her anyway, whether he loved her or not, simply to give his child a name. But Lillian had her doubts about Terry Dempsey's sense of what was honourable.

'I don't dare, Lill. I can't risk it. What if he just chucks me?'

'He won't,' Lillian said, but she failed to get the right amount of conviction into her voice.

'No, it's no good, I got to get round it.'

'Get round it?'

The fear and horror were back again, increased a hundredfold.

'Yes—you know—make it go away. There are people who will do it. Then everything will be the same as ever.'

'Wendy, don't. You mustn't. You got to promise me you won't. Promise!'

There was a surprised silence at the other end of the line. 'Why? You not gone all bleeding religious, have you?'

'No. But you mustn't go to one of those people, Wendy. Anything but that. They're butchers, that's what the doctor at the hospital said. Listen—' She glanced again at the stage door keeper, but by now she hardly cared whether he heard or not. She had to save her sister. 'One of the girls here had it done. She bled to death. She was in such pain, and when we went in to see her she was unconscious, and we called the ambulance—you should have seen the blood, Wendy! It was horrible, horrible—I get nightmares—so you mustn't. Promise me. You must promise me.'

'But I—'

'Promise! I don't want you to die, Wendy!'

'Well, I suppose—'

'Cross your heart.' In her desperation, childhood phrases came into play.

There was a sigh at the other end of the line. 'All right, all right. Cross my heart.'

The relief made her quite limp. 'And go and tell Terry. It's the only thing you can do. Tell him.'

'I suppose—' Wendy sounded resigned now. 'I suppose you're right. It is the only thing. Oh, hell—'

There was a series of loud pips, then the line went dead.

'Wendy?' Lillian shouted. 'Wendy, are you there?'

But she had gone.

Still not fully convinced that her sister was going to listen to her, Lillian hurried back to the digs and wrote her a long letter, repeating everything she had said about Brenda, with more detail, and begging Wendy to tell her what Terry's reaction was. After that, she could only wait.

Wendy had hung on to her virginity for six months after she'd met Terry. After all, it was the only thing that an ordinary girl had to trade for a wedding ring. And a wedding ring was what she wanted. More than anything else in the world, she wanted to be Mrs Terry Dempsey. Then she could be sure of him, and of the way of life that he led.

But it had been very hard to say no.

'If you won't, babe, then there's plenty of other girls who will,' he'd told her.

'I'm not other girls,' Wendy had retorted.

Then she'd worried all night about the dark-haired air hostess, and all the glamorous women Terry seemed to know at the late night bars and gambling clubs they went to. Were they just waiting to get their hands on Terry?

'If you loved me, you'd do it,' he'd said.

'I do love you. I love you with all my heart,' Wendy had declared. 'But—'

But if she gave in, would he chuck her the moment he'd got what he wanted? She couldn't risk it. To keep him happy, she did go a bit further each time, until her body felt as if it was on fire and she desperately wanted to give in and be consumed by it. In her bed afterwards, she would lie awake, aching and unsatisfied.

She had finally given in one evening in his huge open-plan bachelor flat high above the Golden Mile. After that, there had been no stopping her. Everything was wonderful. Terry did not chuck her. Quite the opposite; he called her the hottest thing on two legs and delighted in teaching her a new sexual trick every time they made love.

And then the world had fallen apart.

After the phone call to Lillian, Wendy tried to imagine herself telling Terry. Just how could she break it to him?

There was the coy approach—*I got a lovely little secret I been meaning to tell you about.*

Or the practical one—*You know that time the thingy split when we was in bed?*

And then there was the defensive tack—*Now, Terry, darling, don't be cross, but there's something I got to tell you.*

However hard she tried, she couldn't see herself actually saying the words. None of them sounded right. But it had to be done. Lillian's account of the death of her friend had scared the life out of her. So there was no alternative.

She put on Terry's favourite dress and drank heavily through an evening out with one of his business friends and his wife. She couldn't concentrate on anything anyone said and, driving back afterwards, she was so consumed with nerves that she could hardly speak. They arrived back at his flat and, instead of falling into his arms as she usually did, Wendy walked over to the big picture window that looked out over the dark estuary. Below her on the Golden Mile, the pubs were turning out, while further on a garland of looped lights marked the pier as it marched out into the water. Beyond that, a liner was making its way down river from Tilbury, all lit up. Wendy didn't see any of it.

Terry came up behind her and put his arms round her. 'What's up, doll? You been like a cat on a hot tin roof all evening.'

Wendy's throat was so dry she could hardly speak. 'Well…I…I…'

'Have a drink.'

Wendy shook her head. The very thought of more alcohol made her feel ill.

'Blimey, that's a first. Come on, cough up. You're not giving me the elbow, are you?' He laughed at his own joke. No woman ever dared give him the elbow.

'No—course not—'

'What is it, then? You up the duff?' This time he didn't laugh.

Wendy went cold. This was it. This was the moment.

Slowly, she nodded. She closed her eyes, waiting for an eruption of anger.

'You are? You got one in the oven? You sure? You been to the doctor?'

Terry turned her round. Helpless as a rag doll, Wendy hung her head.

'No,' she admitted. 'But I missed two—you know—and I feel sick all the time.'

Still the explosion didn't happen. Instead, Terry looked totally expressionless, like he did when someone paraded a business idea in front of him.

'It don't show,' he commented. 'When's it due?'

'I—I don't know—'

Maths never had been her strong point. She counted the months on her fingers.

'January, I think,' she whispered.

'Blimey. January.'

There was a pause, during which Wendy died a thousand deaths. This was it. This was when he told her to get out.

'We better get a move on, then.'

'What?' she asked, confused.

'Get hitched while you still got a figure.'

'*What?*'

Wendy looked at him properly at last. She couldn't believe what she thought he had just said.

Terry was grinning. 'You heard. Better get the knot tied PDQ.'

She had been wallowing in a swamp of despair for so long that it was difficult to understand that the worst had not happened after all.

'We're—you mean—we're getting married?' she faltered.

'Yeah, well—' Terry actually looked slightly embarrassed. ''Bout time I got spliced. Makes me look more legit, like.'

It wasn't the most romantic proposal, but to Wendy it was better than all the moonlight and roses in the world.

'Oh, Tel—' she squeaked. She flung her arms round him and burst into tears on his shoulder.

'Bloody hell, turn the tap off,' he told her, holding her away from his expensive suit. 'It ain't the end of the world. Now, we better get one of them special licence jobs. We'll have it done at St Mary's and have the knees-up at the Westcliff. They'll fit it in for me, short notice or no short notice.'

The leap from misery to joy was so sudden that Wendy could only cry the harder. St Mary's was the largest church in town, with the longest aisle to parade down; the Westcliff was the poshest hotel. It was all going to be hers. She was going to be Mrs Terry Dempsey and have diamonds and furs and live in this flat that looked like something out of a magazine. Her wildest dreams were coming true.

CHAPTER 20

JAMES still couldn't accept it. Here he was, all dolled up in his best suit, sitting in St Mary's with his mother on one side and his latest girlfriend on the other, waiting for Wendy to arrive for her wedding. In front of him in the pews reserved for family were the Parkers and his sister. On the other side of his mother was the young man who had introduced himself as Lindy's boyfriend. James was surprised to find that he was disturbed by this. Somehow, he had always thought of Lindy as a girl pursuing her dream of being a dancer, not as a young woman with a boyfriend. But it was a small matter compared with the disaster that was Wendy's wedding. He could see part of Susan's profile from where he was. She was looking very po-faced. He was not the only one to be upset by this event.

Across the aisle were the Dempsey family. Everyone had been amazed to find out that Terry did actually have a mother and father. There they were, a typical little East End couple, old before their time and looking slightly bemused by their surroundings. Grouped round them were a collection of aunts, uncles and cousins, and sitting at the end of the front pew was Terry himself, stiff and ostentatious in a morning suit with a best man who looked more like a bodyguard. James clenched his fists. It was all he could do to sit there looking normal.

There was a flurry of movement at the back of the church. People turned round and stared. The bridesmaids had arrived and were sorting out each other's dresses. Anticipation mounted. James found himself hoping against hope that Wendy would realise what a big mistake she was about to make and not show up. After all, she had gone out with him before when she'd split up from Terry. If she chose to again, no amount of threats from that bully would keep James away from her. He closed his mind to the huge clues to her current condition. He just did not want to grapple with the decisions he would have to make if he really did have a chance with Wendy.

'It'd be a shock for Dempsey if Wendy did a bunk,' he said to Maggie, his girlfriend.

'Why would she do that?' Maggie asked.

'If she had any sense she would. Why does she want to marry a thug like him?'

'I think that's pretty obvious.'

That was what hurt so much. He didn't want to believe that Wendy was grasping enough to be marrying for money, so if this had happened in a more leisurely way the only other reason was that she must love him, which would have been even worse. But now there was the added factor—the baby. Nothing had been said, but everyone knew that you didn't have a rush job like this if time wasn't pressing. Whether it might have been love or money behind this marriage, the baby changed everything. Wendy had to marry its father, and that was the worst thing of all. Whichever way he looked at it, her choice made him sick with pain and anger.

There was another bustle in the porch. James felt a terrible sinking in the pit of his stomach. There was a rustle of expectation, a whisper of 'She's here!' that passed from pew to pew like a breeze. The organist struck a chord and everyone stood up. This was it. Wendy had arrived. All hope was over.

The well known notes of *Here Comes The Bride* rolled through the church. Everyone turned round to watch Wendy process up the longest aisle in Southend. James couldn't help it, he had to watch too. Holding on to her father's arm, a vision in white satin was walking to the altar, her face covered with a bouffant veil, the front of her dress obscured by a vast bouquet of red roses and green ferns.

'Doesn't she look lovely?' Maggie breathed as she passed.

'Lovely,' James agreed.

At that moment, Dempsey and his best man stepped out of their pew and stood waiting. Dempsey's brickwall face broke into a small possessive smile. James could only see the back of Wendy's head, but he knew that she was smiling back. Then she turned to give her bouquet to Lillian, the wedding party lined up at the chancel steps and the service began. It took all James's self-control to keep his face impassive as he was forced to stand and watch his golden girl being given away.

The wedding breakfast seemed to go on for ever. As chief bridesmaid, Lillian was stuck at the top table with the best man, whose name was Dennis. Through soup, melon, roast beef and trimmings, trifle and coffee, Lillian had to listen to his off-colour jokes and keep him at bay without sounding downright rude. As she looked left and right along the table, she could see members of her family and Terry's having similar problems in making any real contact with each other. Gran, as usual, was looking grim, her mum was still having difficulty containing her tears, her dad was being talked at by Terry's mum. None of them looked comfortable in their stiff new clothes and both sides looked as if they thoroughly disapproved of the other family.

But one person was totally happy. Now that the wedding ceremony was over and she was officially married, Wendy was beaming with joy and relief, gazing at Terry as if she had got the biggest box of chocolate in the sweetshop. As for Terry, he was letting Wendy have her big day, but he knew he had provided a show that nobody else there could match, and it showed.

'Wish I was in Terry's shoes tonight. Reckon she knows what she's doing, eh?' Dennis remarked.

'That's my sister you're talking about,' Lillian said.

'Yeah, and a right little goer she looks too. Always did think so. Bet it runs in the family, eh?'

'No,' Lillian told him.

She wished she could feel happy for her sister, but she had severe doubts about Terry Dempsey. You only had to look at him to know that he was a brute. But at least he had done the right thing, admitted the baby was his and married Wendy. The baby was still alive, and so was Wendy. She had not had to suffer like poor Brenda.

'Can't believe that. We'll see when the dancing starts, eh?'

'I don't think so.'

She wished this pig would shut up. She certainly didn't want to be reminded that she had to dance the first dance with him. For the hundredth time that day, she looked across the room to where James was sitting. Anxious though she was about Wendy, still she couldn't help being glad that her sister hadn't married James. Of course, she loathed that girl he was with, but James's girlfriends seemed to come and go quite quickly. They weren't the threat that Wendy had been. She wondered what he thought of Geoff, the boy she had come with. She knew that they must have met, because they had been placed in the same pew in church. Was James at all jealous? That had been her intention in bringing Geoff along. She had been going out with him for only three weeks and wasn't that struck on him, but he had been very eager to come with her to the wedding and she had decided to let him, just to see what James's reaction would be.

At last the speeches and the telegrams and the cutting of the cake were over. A five-piece band began setting up on the small stage while people wandered about stretching their legs and chatting to friends on other tables. Lillian got up with just one thought in mind, to go and speak to James, but she was waylaid by Geoff.

'This is quite a do,' he said. 'Bit different from my sister's wedding. We just had beer and sandwiches at the local.'

'I told you, Terry's Mr Big on the Golden Mile,' Lillian reminded him.

Where was James? He had left his table, but his girlfriend was still sitting there. She looked round the big room.

'He must be, if he's paying for all this lot. A big sit-down meal and now a band! D'you think they play rock'n'roll?' Geoff was asking.

Lillian looked at them. They were all over forty.

'Oh, yeah. They're the next big hit,' she said with heavy sarcasm.

'Hello, there, Lindy. Enjoying yourself?'

Lillian spun round with a gasp, her heart beating so hard she could hardly breathe. 'James!'

'You look like a fairy tale princess in that dress.'

'Oh—' Lillian held out the full skirts of pale blue satin supported with layers of net and curtsied. 'Thank you, kind sir,' she said.

There had not been time to make dresses for the six brides-maids, so they had been bought off the peg. Luckily for Lillian, she was a standard size and hers fitted her almost perfectly.

James and Geoff were chatting. Lillian tried to read James's reaction. Disappointingly, he seemed perfectly friendly towards Geoff.

'Lindy taught me to dance, you know,' he said. 'I owe her a lot.'

'She's a terrific dancer. She'll be the best on the floor here by a mile,' Geoff claimed. 'I'm not up to her standard at all, but she's very patient with me.'

'Well, I'm claiming a dance with her, that's for sure,' James said.

Sunshine broke out over the day for Lillian. It was worth the long journey, the nerve-cracking tension within the family, the endless meal with Dennis by her side, worth all of it just for this moment. For the first time, she was going to dance properly with James.

The big moment didn't arrive for a while. First Terry and Wendy took to the floor while everyone clapped, then Lillian had to endure being pulled around by Dennis. After that, Geoff came and claimed her, which was a relief after Dennis, but she spent most of the time she was dancing with him in watching out for James. How would he hold that girlfriend of his? Were they happy and laughing together? Did they behave like a real couple? To her chagrin, she found that James was spending most of his time following Wendy with his eyes. It wasn't the girlfriend who was the problem. Her big sister might have married Terry, but that didn't mean that James had stopped thinking about her.

At last, the MC announced a quickstep and James walked across the floor towards her. Lillian couldn't keep the smile of delight off her face. She stood up, took his outstretched hand and there she was, where she wanted to be, in his arms. For a minute or so they just danced, their bodies perfectly in tune, moving together as if they had been doing this every day of their lives. Lillian was in heaven. She didn't need words; it was enough just to live in the moment. His arm was at her back, her hand was in his, his breath was on her neck. She had only to lean her head a little and her cheek would be next to his.

And then he broke the spell. 'What do you think of this marriage, Lindy?'

Lillian could have cried. So this moment wasn't special to him like it was to her.

'Wendy's happy, so I suppose that's what it's all about,' she managed to say.

'Yes—she does look happy,' James agreed.

There was a world of longing in his voice. It tore at Lillian's heart.

'Terry might be a crook, but he has done the decent thing,' she said.

'So she is…I mean…there is…'

'She's pregnant. Yes,' Lillian told him.

After all, it was an open secret. Soon it was going to be obvious, and then everyone would know.

'I see.'

For the length of the room, James was silent. Lillian couldn't bear it.

'You must have suspected it,' she said.

'Yes, I did. I just…well…I hoped it wasn't true.'

They were dancing past the door into the main part of the hotel.

'Look—do you mind if we go outside for a bit?' James asked. 'This whole thing is getting on my nerves.'

They walked through the hotel and out onto the clifftop gardens. It was a perfect summer's day, warm and bright with a slight breeze. James and Lillian stood together looking out over the colourful beds and green grass of the gardens to the sparkling water of the Thames estuary, sprinkled with the dark red and white sails of boats.

Away from the claustrophobic atmosphere of the wedding party, Lillian felt free to change the subject. 'It's nice to be home,' she said.

'Do you miss it?' James asked.

'Yes. I didn't think I would, but I do. At first I really liked travelling to a new place each week, and then I got fed up with it and I was glad to be settling down in Blackpool for the summer, and now—'

She hesitated, for she wasn't really sure herself whether she liked the way of life she had chosen.

'What about now?' James prompted.

'I don't know. I don't want to just come back here and work in a shop again.'

'Are you still enjoying being a dancer?'

'Oh, yes.' Of this she was sure. 'I love it. It doesn't matter that we're doing the same thing every day; each time I'm in the wings I get nervous, and then when I get on the stage it's like…like something takes hold of me, you know? I turn into a different person. Everything else drops away, like everything that's worrying you, and the only thing that matters is the music and the steps and doing it right and making the audience love you. And they do love you, you know—you can feel it coming over the footlights. Some days it's better than others. Some days they sort of hold back and you can't get through to them, and other times it's a great big warm…oh, I don't know—a warm hug, an embrace.'

She stopped and looked up at James. 'That sounds really stupid, doesn't it?'

'No, I think I know what you mean. I haven't been on the stage, of course, but there is something special about going to a live performance. It's very different from the cinema.'

Without thinking, Lillian slipped her arm through his. 'I can't talk to anyone else like this,' she told him. 'D'you remember the first time we talked, when you fixed my bike for me?'

'And you told me about your Aunty Eileen, and following your dream?'

'She was right, Aunty Eileen, wasn't she? Nobody else would have believed we'd get what we wanted, but we did.'

'Yeah—look at you, only seventeen years old and doing what you set out to do.'

'And you've got your garage, and it's doing well.'

'Yes, but—Lindy, do you mind if I bend your ear for a bit? Only there's this idea I've had, and you're the only person I know who won't laugh at me.'

Lillian would have jumped off the pier for him at this point. Here was the old James back again, the friend who confided his secrets to her. They sat down on a bench. Seagulls sailed overhead in the blue sky.

'Come on, then,' she said. 'What's this big idea?'

'Exhaust systems.'

'Exhaust systems? You mean, the pipe that the smoke comes out of? What about them?'

'Well, they're always wearing out, even on a well serviced car, and they're quite simple to fit. It's not more than a forty-five minute job, generally, but you've got to have the right one for the car so you have to order it in, and then the car's owner has to leave it at the garage for half a day while it's done, so what should be a quick job becomes longer and more expensive than it should be. But what if I was to specialise in exhausts? If I had all the well-known makes in stock, I could practically do the job while the owner waited, and cheaper than an ordinary repair shop could.'

For the first time that day, James was his old eager self again. Lillian could see a light in his eyes where before there had only been pain and defeat. She tried to come up with an intelligent answer, more than just unthinking support for his idea.

'It sounds good to me. Geoff had to have the exhaust done on his car last week and it took three days. He was beginning to think that it wouldn't be done in time to get down here for the wedding. But how much would it cost? I mean, what about all this stuff you'd have to stock?'

'You've hit it right on the nail. That is the expensive bit. I'd have to borrow money to set it all up, and then there's no guarantee that it'd take off straight away. But I really think I'm on to something here. If I stay doing general repairs, I'm always going to make a living but I'm never going to be rich. With this exhaust thing, I could go bust or I could be really successful. It's got to be worth having a try.'

'It's follow your dream again, isn't it?' Lillian reminded him. 'It is.'

'And it worked last time.'

'It did. You're right. I'm going to do it. Oh, Lindy, it's so good to be able to talk to you again. There's nobody else who seems to understand the way you do. I've really missed our chats.'

A big bubble of happiness was swelling inside Lillian as he said this. It was almost too good to be true. He did care about her. In spite of Wendy and the wedding and everything else, she was special to him.

'So have I,' she said.

James put his hand over hers and squeezed it.

'We'll always be best friends, won't we?'

The bubble burst.

'Yes,' Lillian croaked through a throat aching with tears. 'Yes, we will.'

James walked back into the ballroom feeling much better. His love life might be a disaster, but at least he saw the way forward with his new business idea now that Lindy had approved it. He knew it was illogical, for Lindy knew nothing about either cars or running a business, but somehow he felt that having her support made all the difference. She had believed in him when he had just been a kid with big ambitions. She still believed in him now. And that, he suddenly realised, was what he had been craving—someone who believed in him as a person. Never mind the idea. Lindy knew he could make it work, whatever it was, and if Lindy thought so, then he would live up to her expectations.

When he arrived back at his table, he found that Maggie was not happy.

'Wherever have you been?' she demanded. 'I've had three of Terry Dempsey's mates asking me to dance, and they didn't want to take no for an answer.'

'Sorry,' he said. 'I didn't mean to leave you unprotected. I was talking to Lindy.'

'Oh, and what did you have to say to her that was so important?' There was a distinct edge to Maggie's voice.

'Nothing,' he lied. 'This and that. Just catching up, you know.'

'Just catching up? And you had to go outside with her to do that?'

'For heaven's sake, Maggie, I've known Lindy ever since Susan started going out with Bob. She's like a little sister to me. Now, do you want to dance or have a row?'

Still only partly convinced, Maggie opted for a dance. As they went round the floor, he noticed his sister dancing with Bob. Nothing unusual in that, of course, except that Susan had a face like thunder. Surely they hadn't had a row? They never fell out. He soon found out. When Bob went off to the Gents, Susan came and plumped herself down beside James and Maggie.

'What do you think of all this?' she asked, waving a hand at the room in general. 'Doesn't it make you sick?'

'It does,' James agreed, looking at Wendy, who was now dancing ever so slowly with both arms round Dempsey's neck. Dempsey had his hands on her bottom. It turned James's stomach.

'I mean, it's just so unfair,' Susan went on. 'Wendy goes out with that thug and gets herself in the family way and she gets all this—a wedding at St Mary's and a dress with a train almost as long as the Queen had when she got married and six bridesmaids and everything, and now this great big do with a sit-down meal and real French champagne and dancing and everything. It's not fair.'

'No, it's not. You're right.'

Dempsey could afford all this at the drop of a hat. But one day…one day he would be rich enough to be able to run something like this, and his money was going to be honestly earned.

Susan hardly heard him. She was incandescent with righteous indignation.

'She behaves badly and I do everything right. I shan't be getting in the family way before I'm married, and not for a while afterwards, either. We can't afford to have children straight away. And we've saved and saved to put the deposit on our house. We've given up all sorts of things. We only go out once a week, and then it's only to the cheap seats at the pictures, and I've sat in making things for my bottom drawer, and I shall make my own wedding dress, and we've only bought what we can afford, we haven't got anything on the never-never—'

'I know, but Suze—'

Susan swept on. 'We've done all this, and *she* goes and marries that man and gets everything. A TV and a radiogram and a washing machine and a fridge. He's got a great big fridge like you see in American kitchens in films, Mr Dempsey has, did you know that? And a cocktail cabinet. I've always dreamed of having a cocktail cabinet.'

'But you don't drink,' James pointed out.

'That's not the point. And now all this—why does she get all this when I shall only have sherry and sandwiches at the Parkers'? It just isn't right.'

Tears of frustration and jealousy trickled down Susan's face. James had to admit, it was unfair. Getting married was all his sister had ever dreamed of, and now she was being totally upstaged by her future sister-in-law.

'I think this whole affair is extremely vulgar,' Maggie commented.

'Vulgar?' Susan exclaimed.

'Yes. It's common and showy. Just what you would expect from a man like Terry Dempsey.'

'Oh—' Susan sat open mouthed for a few seconds, the wind completely taken out of her sails. 'Common. Yes. Well, I'm not saying that I would want a reception like this, just that Wendy seems to have had everything given to her.'

'I'm sure yours will be a much more tasteful wedding,' Maggie said.

James squeezed her hand in silent thanks. There was more to her than he had realised. She was a nice girl, boosting Susan up like that.

'And let's face it, Suse, who would you rather be marrying—Bob or Dempsey?'

'Bob, of course. That's a stupid question,' Susan said.

At which point Bob himself appeared, carrying a tray of drinks from the free bar.

'Here's to the next wedding,' James said, raising his beer glass. 'To Bob and Susan.'

'Bob and Susan,' Maggie repeated, while Susan smiled and blushed.

James looked at his sister as he downed his beer. He understood her outburst. She wanted Bob, but with Dempsey's money. That was his trouble too. He wanted the impossible.

CHAPTER 21

SHE had got what she wanted; that was the main thing. Wendy reminded herself of this every morning. She wasn't that shameful thing, an unmarried mother. She was Mrs Terry Dempsey. She had a wedding ring on her finger and she had the key to this incredible apartment. Once Terry had gone off to work she would clear up the breakfast things and make the huge bed, then wander round running her fingers over the radiogram, the big TV, the American fridge, the cocktail cabinet, still amazed to find herself here. She didn't feel at home. There was nothing of herself in this place; it was all Terry's. She didn't even have to clean it. The woman who had always cleaned for Terry, a squat middle-aged lady called Mrs Riley, came in every day to dust and hoover and polish. She took the dirty clothes away with her and brought them back washed and ironed. It was the film star life Wendy had always yearned for.

'I don't have to lift a finger,' she boasted to her mother when she went back to Sunny View to visit.

'Really? What, not housework nor cooking nor nothing?' her mother asked with outright disbelief.

'Nothing. Mrs Riley does all the cleaning and washing.'

What she didn't admit to her mother was that she found Mrs Riley disconcerting. Used all her life to being expected to help with chores, she didn't know how to react to having someone do them for her. That was why she made the bed each day before Mrs Riley arrived. She didn't want the woman's sharp little eyes spotting evidence of the previous night's activities. It disturbed her that Mrs Riley appeared to know more about what her husband liked than she did.

'Mr Dempsey likes it done like that,' was her answer to any of Wendy's suggestions for even the slightest of changes.

'Well, I like it done like this,' Wendy would retort to save face. But, after Mrs Riley went home, she always put things back how Terry apparently wanted. After all, it was his place and she wanted to please him.

Her mother didn't know this, though. She just saw Wendy living a life of unimaginable ease.

'All the cleaning and washing,' she repeated, awed.

It cheered up Wendy no end, reminding her of her own good fortune.

'That's right, and no dinners to cook, either. We eat out every night,' she boasted.

'Every night? What, in a restaurant?'

The only meals her mother ate away from home were on the occasional formal visits they made to the Kershaws'.

'That's right,' Wendy said.

Her mother shook her head, lost for words.

The lack of cooking added to Wendy's feeling of not belonging in the apartment. Producing a good English fry-up for breakfast was her favourite part of the day. She was good at breakfasts. After all, you couldn't grow up in a guest house without learning how to do a decent plateful of eggs and bacon. But proper wives always had a meal waiting for their husbands when they got in, and she wanted so much to be a proper wife. After a week of eating out, she had offered to cook for Terry. He had seemed quite taken with the idea.

'All right, doll. Get us a nice bit of steak. Steak and chips with some mushroom and tomato.'

Glad of something to do, Wendy went shopping for the first dinner she was to cook as a married woman. She had never bought steak before.

'Rib-eye? Fillet? Or a nice bit of rump?' the butcher asked.

Wendy tried to think what it was that Terry ordered when they ate out.

'Um—have you got T-bone?' she asked.

'We certainly have, my darling. How much would you like?'

'Er—enough for two,' she said vaguely.

The butcher carved two enormous slices and displayed them on a sheet of shiny white wrapping paper.

'That do you?'

'Er—lovely—' Wendy agreed.

She paid what seemed like a huge amount of money. What would her gran say to this? She could feed the whole Parker family for two days on that much. Wendy sailed out of the shop past women who eyed her with envy. This was the life. They were probably waiting to buy sausages or a bit of liver and bacon, and here she was with her T-bone steaks. She felt like a queen.

When it came to cooking the meal, she was not so sure.

Chips were all right. She knew how to do them. And frying mushroom and tomato held no fears for her. But these huge hunks of meat—how long should she do them for? She had no idea. She put them in the pan, then started on the chips.

Terry was at the big picture window, glass of whisky in his hand, staring down at the street below.

'That dinner ready yet?' he demanded.

'Nearly,' Wendy said, flustered.

She wanted so much for this to be perfect. She poked the nearest steak with a fork. Blood oozed out. Not nearly done. She turned the heat up.

'Come on, girl. Me belly thinks me throat's bin cut,' Terry grumbled.

'It's coming.'

She fussed around straightening the knives and forks on the table. Steak knives, they must have steak knives. She knew that much from eating out. She found some and put them on the table, then went back to the cooker. At last the chips were done. She lifted them out of the seething fat two or three at a time with the fish slice and piled them upon the two plates with the mushrooms and tomatoes. The T-bones looked all right now, thank God, really nice and brown on both sides. They had shrunk quite a bit but, even so, they still filled up the plates. Proudly, she carried them to the table.

'Ready!'

''Bout bleeding time too,' Terry said, and sat down.

Wendy watched him anxiously as he tried a couple of chips.

He nodded. 'Not bad,' he said, his mouth full. 'Yeah, all right, doll.'

Wendy felt pleased, but the big test was still to come. Her own meal untasted, she watched as Terry cut into his T-bone.

'Bit tough,' he commented as he sawed at it. 'Blimey, girl,

what've you done to it? It's ruined. It's like leather. I like my steak rare. You know that, you heard me order it enough times for Chrissakes. This is bleeding cremated. I can't eat this.'

He flung down his knife and fork and sat back in his chair, glaring at the meat as if it were poison.

Wendy was mortified. 'I'm sorry, Tel. I tried, only I didn't know how long to cook it for—'

'For Chrissakes—' Terry got up and strode over to the phone. 'Chuck that lot in the bin,' he ordered as he dialled.

A defensive anger kindled in Wendy. 'It's not that bad,' she protested. She stuck her fork into the meat on her plate and began cutting at a corner. There was no doubt about it, it was tough. Doggedly, she put the piece into her mouth and chewed. 'It tastes all right.'

Terry stared at her. His face, his body were still as he held the phone, but the very stillness exuded threat. Wendy felt a clench of fear. She couldn't swallow the meat.

'You contradicting me?' Terry asked. Into the phone, he said, 'Send us up some cod and chips and some mushy peas. And a coupla pickled eggs. Yeah, of course it's Mr Dempsey; who else do you think it is, you stupid cow? Yeah, I do want it straight away. Like now.'

He slammed the receiver down, his cold eyes still fixed on Wendy. 'You hear me?' he said. 'It's muck. Chuck it away.'

Wendy could defy him no longer. Miserably, she scraped the two platefuls of food into the bin, along with the half chewed mouthful she had attempted to eat. Terry switched on the TV and dropped on the sofa, ignoring her. Fighting back tears of humiliation, Wendy stayed in the kitchen area scrubbing at the dishes until a ring at the door heralded the arrival of the fish and chips.

The rest of the evening was a chilly stand-off, until they

went to bed. Then Terry slid his hand under her sheer nylon nightie and fondled her magnificent breasts, even fuller now with her pregnancy. Wendy gave a moan of pleasure. She wasn't sure whether she most hated or loved him at that moment, but whatever it was, she still wanted him. She turned towards him, reaching for him. Terry gave her a hard slap on the buttocks that both stung and roused her.

'You ain't much use in the kitchen, but you're still a hot little handful in bed,' he said.

Everything was all right again.

The biggest problem Wendy faced was boredom. She was unused to doing nothing. It was fine at first. No more rushing off to work, no more being on her feet all day, no more trying to avoid the Sunny View chores. She leafed through magazines, did her nails, went to the hairdresser, strolled round the shops. But shopping wasn't much fun on her own, and all her friends were at work during the day. She ambled up and down the High Street, fingering garments and occasionally trying them on until she fancied that the shop assistants were getting to know her and the fact that she never bought anything. The trouble was that now she was no longer working, she had very little money. Terry gave her a bit of housekeeping, enough for her to buy breakfast ingredients and get her hair done, but not enough to run to dresses and shoes.

At last, fed up with forever window shopping, she dipped into her meagre savings. There was a blouse she particularly fancied, tight and low-cut and bright red. She wanted it now, before she had to start wearing shapeless maternity smocks. She bought it and put it on ready for when Terry came in that evening. He took one look at it and exploded.

'What the hell is that you're wearing?'

Wendy could hardly believe what she was hearing. 'Don't you like it?' she asked.

'Like it? Like it?' Terry repeated. 'It's disgusting. You're my wife, the mother of my kid. You gotta look good when we go out. You gotta look like you're quality. You know what you look like in that? You look like a whore.'

Wendy gasped. It was not just the word, it was the venom with which he had said it.

'That's horrible!' she wailed. 'How can you say that?'

Terry grabbed a handful of the red satin blouse and pulled her close with such a jerk that she felt a seam rip at the back. Wendy gasped. Now they were eye to eye.

'You're my wife. I can say what I like to you,' he stated.

Wendy froze. Her mouth gaped open, but nothing came out. Her throat contracted with fear.

'You hear me?' Terry asked.

Wendy nodded.

Terry released her with such force that she staggered.

'Go and put on something decent,' he ordered.

Wendy went into the bedroom and started pulling things out of the wardrobe. Her head was in such a mess now that she couldn't make a decision. Terry came and stood in the doorway watching her with his arms folded and his shoulder propped against the frame.

'That one,' he said, as she looked at a pale blue and white Chanel-style suit.

'—get into it,' Wendy mumbled.

'What?'

'I…I can't get into it any more. B-because of the baby.'

She hadn't put on much of a stomach yet, but she had lost the lovely twenty-four-inch waist that she had been so proud of.

Terry's filthy mood evaporated as quickly as it had started. 'Why didn't you say so, doll?'

The next day he took her to the maternity department of the best store in town and bought her a whole new wardrobe.

Wendy kept telling herself that it would all be different once they moved into their new house. It was the fact that they were still in his bachelor flat that made her feel so awkward. Once they were in their proper married home she would feel she belonged. She would no longer be a glorified visitor. Terry was already negotiating with a business acquaintance who was selling a place in Thorpe Bay, but the legal process was going to take a few weeks. He had taken her to see it, and it was lovely, a huge solid detached property with a semi-circular driveway. She could hardly believe she was going to be living in such a posh place. It was a hundred times better than the cramped little semi in Southchurch that Bob and Susan were buying. She was a very lucky woman.

One day when Mrs Riley made her feel particularly superfluous, Wendy went for her usual stroll up the High Street. She looked good, she knew that. She was wearing a loose checked dress with a tie at the back that still gave her a bit of a figure despite her pregnancy. She was wearing high heeled shoes that emphasized her shapely legs, her face was carefully made-up and she had had her hair set the day before. Glancing at her reflection in the shop windows, she felt pleased. Looking down at the wedding and engagement rings on her left hand, she felt proud. She had got what she'd set out to achieve, a rich husband. She endeavoured to ignore the emptiness inside.

She spent half an hour choosing a new lipstick, then she went into her favourite coffee bar and ordered a hot chocolate. This place had an amazing continental jukebox that showed films of the singers as well as playing their songs. They weren't the songs she knew—no Elvis Presley or Cliff Rich-ards—but she like Johnny Halliday and watched him as he sang to her in French. She hadn't a clue what he was singing about, but it made her feel very sophisticated to listen. After that she went into a newsagent's and leafed through all the magazines, finally choosing the one with the most stories in it so that she had plenty to keep her occupied later in the day. She looked at her watch. It was only half past eleven. Terry had said that he might be back about one, but there was an awful lot of time to fill until then and Mrs Riley would still be at the flat. She considered going to visit her mother, but she had seen her only a couple of days ago and anyway she didn't particularly want to have to speak to Gran. She paused at a side road and something about it tugged at a memory. Wasn't James Kershaw's garage off here somewhere? She set off in search of it.

It was further than she thought, quite a way along the road and down a further side turning. It was a warm day. Her feet began to ache in her elegant stilettos and she was thirsty. She wished she had had a Coke instead of a chocolate at the cof-fee bar. But she was set on her course now and determined to find this garage. By the time she got there, she was ready for a sit-down.

A middle-aged man in greasy overalls was leaning over the engine of a car with a spanner in his hand. He looked up as she entered.

'Can I help you?'

'Is James around?' Wendy asked.

'Gov!' the man shouted. 'Lady to see you.'

Wendy hadn't realised that James now employed someone. She remembered Lillian boasting that one day he was going to be rich.

James appeared from the back of the workshop, wiping his hands on a piece of rag. His face broke into a wary smile when he saw her.

'Hello, Wendy. This is a surprise.'

Wendy just couldn't help it. She had to flirt with a good-looking young man. She gave him an arch look. 'A nice surprise, I hope.'

'But of course,' he responded. 'What can I do for you?'

'Oh, I was just passing, so I thought I'd call in and see you.'

'I'm honoured. I can't offer you much, I'm afraid, but how about a cup of tea and a biscuit?'

That was just what she needed.

'That'll have to do, I suppose,' she said, 'seeing as you haven't got any champagne.'

'Next time,' James promised.

He produced a clean towel from a drawer in his desk and spread it over one of the wooden chairs.

'Madam,' he said with a bow.

'Thank you kindly, good sir.'

They laughed and joked together while James boiled the kettle and made tea. Wendy was enjoying herself no end. It seemed such a long time since she had had an exchange like this with a man. She could see from his expression that James still found her attractive.

The other man closed the bonnet of the car he was working on and looked at his watch. 'That's that finished. Oughta be fine for another five thousand. It's quarter to one, Gov. All right if I go on my lunch break now?'

'Ok, Tony. We'll start on the MG when you get back.'

'Quarter to one?' Wendy squealed. How could it have got that late? It would take her a lot more than fifteen minutes to get back to the flat.

'James, sweetie—' She laid a hand on his arm and gave him her best smile, all glistening lips and big blue eyes. She saw the instant response in his face and thrilled inwardly. She still had it. She could still make a man do what she wanted, even though she was married and pregnant. 'You couldn't possibly run me home, could you?'

'It'd be a pleasure,' James said, as she knew he would.

When they arrived in the service road at the back of the Golden Mile, she was relieved to see that Terry's Jaguar was not there. It was all right. She had made it back in time, James stopped the car and came round to open the door for her. She got out, thanked him and hurried inside. She had hardly got to the top of the stairs when she heard the street door open behind her.

'Wendy!'

She turned round. Terry's bulk was silhouetted against the daylight.

'Oh—!' she said with a nervous laugh. 'Tel—there you are—'

'Who was that?' Terry demanded.

He was thundering up the stairs two at a time. Wendy fumbled with the inner door. She stepped inside the flat just as Terry got to the top. He grabbed her arm and spun her round to face him.

'Who was that?' he repeated.

'Terry—stop it—you're hurting me—' Wendy begged.

The look in his eyes terrified her. He was blazingly angry. Angry and jealous. He shook her. 'Who?'

'J-just my b-brother-in-law—'

'What brother-in-law? You ain't got no brother-in-law.'

'I will—I mean—when Bob gets married—' Wendy gabbled.

'Kershaw? What's he doing giving you rides in his car?'

'I—I—' Wendy's head was swimming. She couldn't think.

Her head snapped sideways as Terry's hand slammed into it just above the ear.

'You never take rides with other men, you hear me?' he demanded. 'Never. Never. Never.'

With each 'never' he hit her again. Her brain felt loose inside her skull. His face blurred in front of her.

'You hear me?'

'Yes,' she squeaked.

'Yes, what?'

'Yes, Terry.'

He held her upper arms and thrust his face into hers.

'Just remember that, right? No woman makes a fool of me.'

He flung her away from him. Wendy staggered to the nearest sofa and collapsed in tears, her world shattered around her.

CHAPTER 22

'TEA for the bridegroom! How are you feeling, Bob? Nervous?' Lillian asked as she plonked the teapot on the kitchen table.

Her big brother was pacing around the room looking pale and drawn.

'I am, actually. Terribly nervous. I don't think I can face breakfast,' he admitted.

'I feel like that every time I go on stage,' Lillian told him. 'I feel sick and wobbly and sometimes I even get stomach cramps. But it passes the moment I start performing. And you'll be all right too. Once you see Susan coming up the aisle towards you, everything will be fine.'

'Do you think so?' Bob asked doubtfully.

'I know so. Now, you sit down here and pour yourself some tea and have some of this toast I'm just making. You've got to eat something to keep your strength up. And I'll tell you something else, if any couple are destined to be happy, it's you and Susan. Anyone can see that you're made for each other.'

Bob managed to crack a smile. 'Thanks, Lillian. And you're right, of course. Susan's absolutely the girl for me. She always has been, right from the start.'

Lillian smiled back as she put toast fresh from the grill in front of him. 'I know. And she feels just the same way about you too.'

Bob reached out and caught her wrist, giving it a quick squeeze then releasing it. 'Thanks, Lillian. It's nice to have you back. The place isn't the same without you.'

Lillian flushed with pleasure. It was the first time Bob had ever said anything so nice to her. It brought tears to her eyes. 'Thanks, Bruv. It's nice to be back.'

Up till that moment, this hadn't been strictly true. She had got home in good time for this wedding. The summer season was over and the dancers were on a month's unpaid break. Lillian was glad of the rest, for the long weeks of touring followed by the twice-daily performances all through the summer months had sapped even her energy, and after Brenda's death nothing had seemed quite the same any more. She had looked forward to seeing her family again, only to find that nothing had changed at Sunny View. Her dad was gloomier and more cynical than ever, Frank was acting Jack the Lad and Gran still ruled with a rod of iron. Her mother looked washed out and weary.

'Thank goodness you're back. I don't know how I'm going to manage this wedding,' were her first words to her daughter.

Lillian found herself back in her old position at the bottom of the heap again. Within half an hour of arriving the doorbell had rung and the cry went up of 'Lillian! Door!' and she knew her so-called break was going to be one long round of chores. But Bob's declaration softened her. Perhaps her big brother did have a heart.

The last couple of days had been busy with last-minute dress fittings with Susan and the buying of food for the wedding breakfast. In complete contrast to Wendy's extravaganza, Bob and Susan were having a buffet reception at Sunny View for a limited number of guests. Lillian had spent the Friday making dozens of sausage rolls and getting the PGs' breakfast room ready, helped by Susan, Bob and James.

Now, on the morning of the wedding, she had got up early and was busy making plates of sandwiches. James came round at midday with trays of cocktail sausages on sticks and savoury bridge rolls which his mother and sister had been preparing in their kitchen and, of course, the wedding cake, which Susan had baked and iced herself. Together with Bob, they laid the food out on the tables, watched by Gran, who wanted it all done differently.

'We've got to do it how my sister says, Mrs Parker. She's given me a plan,' James told her, and refused to listen to anything she had to say.

'Susan's in a right old state,' he confided to Lillian. 'I've never seen her so nervous before. Are you going to be able to get to ours by two? She's got everything planned like a military operation, and if you're not there by then, the whole thing will fall apart.'

'Don't worry; it's all under control,' Lillian assured him.

True to her word, she arrived at the Kershaws' flat on time with her hair all pinned up and her make-up perfect. Just as James had said, Susan was crippled with nerves, which took the form of her being very pale and very quiet. Mrs Kershaw and the other bridesmaid, a cousin of Susan's called Pam, made up for this by fluttering and fussing non-stop like a pair of starlings. James and Lillian looked at each other. It was clear that as the cool-headed people, they had to take charge.

'Your hair looks lovely, Susan. Now, shall Pam and I get our dresses on now? And then we can help you with yours. And perhaps you'd like your mum to get ready now, too?'

'Yes. Yes. Mum, I told you to get dressed half an hour ago,' Susan said between clenched teeth.

'P'raps you'd like a hand, Mrs Kershaw?' Lillian suggested.

'I'll make some tea,' James volunteered. He was all ready and looking heart-breakingly handsome in his hired morning suit.

Order emerged from the confusion. Susan looked wonderful in the elegant dress she had made herself, Lillian and Pam were pretty in pale pink and Mrs Kershaw striking in raspberry-pink with a veiled hat. Everything went like clockwork, exactly to Susan's masterplan. They all got to the church in time in cars arranged by James who, in the absence of a father, was giving his sister away. The service went without a hitch and soon Bob and Susan were marching down the aisle, man and wife. As they all lined up for the photographs, James leaned to whisper in Lillian's ear.

'I reckon we did a good job there, eh?'

'We did,' Lillian agreed, looking at the shining faces of the bride and groom. 'For all their planning beforehand, they would have fallen apart if we hadn't been here.'

'What a team.'

'Yes, we're the best.'

But, even as she said it, she was crying inside. They were a perfect team, she and James. If he could see that, why couldn't he see her as a potential girlfriend? She pulled her face into a smile for the camera.

At the reception, the wedding party were no longer separated from the guests. James's girlfriend marched straight up to him and slid an arm through his, claiming him assuredly as pinning a badge on him marked *hands off*. For a while, Lillian kept herself busy handing plates round and making tea and pouring drinks. Her mother was sitting on a chair looking unwell, Mrs Kershaw was still in a flap and Wendy was too pregnant to help, and of course Susan was the bride and had only to stand and be congratulated by everyone, so Lillian organised Pam and the two of them hurried round making sure everyone had a full plate and glass.

Before the cutting of the cake, Frank, as best man, made a short speech with several off-colour jokes that nobody laughed at. Then James, in his role as replacement father of the bride, spoke fondly about his sister as a child and as a young woman, and how she and Bob were perfectly suited to each other. Lillian dragged her eyes away from him to glance at his girlfriend. She was gazing at him with pride on her face, as well she might. He looked and sounded confident and at ease, a man to be admired and relied upon. No wonder she kept close to his side. Perhaps she was hoping to be the bride at the next wedding. Lillian felt tears thickening her throat.

'Hear, hear!' she called, to stop herself from crying in front of everyone.

James smiled straight at her, as everyone clapped his speech.

'A toast—to Mr and Mrs Robert Parker—may their marriage be a long and happy one!' he said.

'Mr and Mrs Robert Parker!' everyone chorused.

The cake was cut, Lillian and Pam took the pieces round, more tea was made. James and Maggie were standing side by side, eating cake from the same plate. Lillian went to speak to her sister.

'Bit different from your wedding, isn't it?' she said.

'Yeah,' Wendy agreed.

'Not a patch on ours, eh, doll?' Terry said.

'No,' Wendy agreed.

'No band, no champagne, nothing but a few measly sandwiches—'

Terry elaborated on the shortcomings of Bob and Susan's arrangements for some time. Wendy just stood there agreeing with a faraway expression on her face. Lillian almost suspected that her sister was secretly wishing that her wedding had been a cosy home-made do like this. But she dismissed the thought as soon as it occurred. Wendy had adored the razzmatazz of her big day. She had been treated like a film star. Diana Dors herself couldn't have asked for more.

'How are you feeling?' Lillian asked.

'Oh—not so bad now—' Wendy ran a hand over her expanding belly. 'It's very lively. I can feel it kicking.'

Unbidden, the picture of Brenda lying unconscious and bleeding on the pile of newspapers slid into Lillian's mind. The contrast between her poor broken body and Wendy, beautiful and blooming, was almost too much to bear. Lillian gave her sister a hug.

'You look after yourself,' she said.

Terry gave her a hard look.

'What you say that for? She's got me to see after her now, ain't you, doll?'

'Yes,' Wendy agreed.

'See?' Terry said.

'I was only saying,' Lillian said, and left them to it.

Once the cake had been eaten, Susan and Bob disappeared upstairs to change into their going away outfits. Then everyone went outside to wave them off as James drove them to the station to catch the train up to London and on to Bognor for their honeymoon. After that, the party petered out. James came back and picked up Maggie to take her home and, in ones and twos and small groups, the rest of the guests departed.

'Hmm, that's that, then. What a lot of fuss. Put the kettle on, Lillian,' Gran ordered, and retreated to her room to watch the television. Lillian's dad went to join her. Frank went out. Lillian's mum hauled herself to her feet. She looked exhausted.

'I'm sorry, but I've got to go and have a lie down. I'll come down and help with the clearing up later,' she said.

Lillian, Pam and Mrs Kershaw were left standing in a room littered with debris.

'Well, I guess it's just us,' Lillian said.

She felt almost cheerful. She had known all along that she would be left with this task. To have two people to help her was a big bonus. She took tea up to her mum, who was lying on top of her bed fully clothed, staring at the ceiling.

'You all right, Mum?' she asked.

'Yes, dear. It's the usual, you know. I'll be better soon.'

As far back as Lillian could remember, her mum had been tired.

'You have a little sleep. We'll get cleared up downstairs OK.'

'Thank you.' Her mother's voice was a faint mumble, as if she hadn't the energy even to speak properly. Lillian left her to rest.

Downstairs, she handed out aprons and the three of them got busy, chatting about how well the day had gone as they worked. They were about halfway through the washing-up when James reappeared.

'Sorry to leave you in the lurch, but I had to take Maggie home. Can't expect her to help; she's not family, is she?'

Lillian felt a great lift of hope. Maggie wasn't family. She turned a bright smile on James. 'You're right. It's best with just us.'

When everything was put to rights, they all sat down with yet another cup of tea and a plate of leftovers.

'That was a job well done,' James commented.

'Yeah, bully for us,' Pam agreed.

'It's been such a lovely day,' Mrs Kershaw said with a sigh.

Lillian looked at them as they all sat with their feet up, munching sausage rolls and sandwiches with aprons over their wedding finery. She felt far more at ease with the Kershaws than she did with her own family. Pam and Mrs Kershaw asked questions about her life as a dancer and listened attentively as she told them about it. They seemed genuinely interested in her. She talked more about herself to them in half an hour than she had ever done to her lot.

'How long are you home for, Lindy?' James asked.

'A month. That's if they renew my contract.'

'A month! That's good. Tell you what, why don't we go to the Kursaal one evening? I can show you how good I'm getting at dancing.'

'Oh—!' A shaft of pure delight lit Lillian's heart. 'Yes—yes, that would be wonderful.'

'Right, we'll do it. How about Wednesday?'

'Wednesday would be fine.'

The sun had come out on her time at home. She looked ahead to a month of days rimmed with gold.

After the upheaval of the wedding, life at Sunny View settled down into the usual routine. Lillian caught up with Janette and the rest of her old school friends, but most of her time was taken up with doing the housework so that her mother could have a much-needed break. That would not have been so hard if it hadn't been for Gran inspecting her work every half hour or so. After a week of it, Lillian had had enough. The fact that she was going to escape again gave her courage.

'Why can't we have a proper washing machine?' she demanded.

Gran looked at her with amazement. 'We've got a copper,' she pointed out.

'Yeah, a copper and a mangle, for all those sheets and stuff! No wonder Mum's worn out.'

'It was good enough for me, so it's good enough for you,' Gran told her.

'It was all right when there wasn't anything else. People have got machines now. You can fill them up with a hose and they whirl the clothes round, then after you've got them out and wrung them and rinsed them, the water pumps out all by itself into the sink. Just think what a blessing that'd be for Mum!'

Gran snorted. 'And just how much does one of these wonderful things cost?'

'Sixty-five pounds,' Lillian admitted. She had looked at the ads in the local paper.

'Sixty-five pounds! You're off your head, girl. Where am I going to get money like that?'

'You can get them on the never-never for five and seven a week.'

Gran gave her a withering look. 'Neither a borrower nor a lender be,' she quoted, and stalked off.

'How about a vacuum cleaner, then?' Lillian asked her retreating back. 'You can get one of them for only six guineas!'

Gran did not deign to reply.

Disgruntled, Lillian picked up the dustpan and brush and went to clean the stairs. If ordinary housewives had these wonderful aids, why shouldn't her mother have them to help her run a guest house? She had ten times more to do than someone like Susan or Wendy. Wendy didn't even have fires to light and clean out, as the flat above the amusement arcade had lovely warm, clean electric fires, and on top of that she had every electrical gadget known to womankind.

Not that she was going to be in the flat for much longer. In a fortnight's time, she and Terry were moving into a big detached house in Thorpe Bay with five bedrooms, three living rooms, a huge kitchen, a separate bathroom and toilet and, luxury of luxuries, another toilet downstairs—not an outside one, but a proper tiled indoor one with its own wash hand basin!

Lillian spent a couple of days with her sister trailing round furniture stores looking for suitably ornate pieces to put in this palace. Wendy kept exclaiming over sofas and dining tables and elaborate cocktail cabinets but, whenever Lillian suggested she bought something, she always said that she would have to ask Terry. Even equipment for the nursery had to be referred to him.

'But why can't you buy a cot for the baby?' Lillian asked. 'It's your baby.'

'It's Terry's money, though,' Wendy told her.

'What about "With all my worldly goods I thee endow"?'

'What?'

Wendy seemed really dozy. It was difficult to have a sensible conversation with her.

'The wedding service,' Lillian prompted.

'Oh—that.'

'Yes, that. Doesn't he give you any money?'

'I've got housekeeping.'

Lillian could ask as many questions as she liked, but nothing could change the fact that Wendy could look but not buy. Terry held the purse strings. It made Lillian anxious, as did her mother's ill health and her lack of household equipment, but nothing could cloud her joy at spending time with James.

The first evening at the Kursaal was followed by evenings at various pubs featuring up-and-coming rock'n'roll bands. Lillian was in heaven as they danced to the compulsive beat, their two bodies in perfect harmony. She couldn't remember ever having been so happy.

They didn't go out more than a couple of nights a week, as he had to spend some time with Maggie, plus he was busy with an increasing work load and often worked well into the evening. Lillian went round to Kershaw's Auto Repairs one evening to see what it was all about.

'So this is your kingdom,' she said, standing in the entrance. All she could see of James was two feet sticking out from under a big blue car.

'Lindy!' The feet moved and James emerged, lying on a board with castors under it. He smiled up at her, his teeth white in his dirty face. 'This is a nice surprise. What are you doing here?'

'I've heard so much about this place. I wanted to see it for myself.'

She breathed in the smell of grease and oil. It brought back those days when she'd cycled home from school the long way round just to go past Dobson's when he worked there.

'Not a lot to see, really,' James said.

Lillian didn't explain that that wasn't the point. She needed to be able to picture where he was and what he was doing when she wasn't with him.

'No, but it's nice to see what there is. Are you busy? Can I help?'

'You can make us some tea.'

As she waited for the kettle to boil, the phone rang. She answered it, relayed the message to James and wrote the customer and his requirements into James's work diary. Then she passed him various tools that he needed for what was turning out to be a more difficult job than he had anticipated. By the time he had finished, her hands were almost as oily as his and there were black smears on her jeans.

James was apologetic. 'Look at you! You've ruined your clothes.'

Lillian shrugged. 'It doesn't matter. It's only what I wear to do the housework. Not that Gran likes me wearing jeans, but she has to lump it. You're not going to see me in a flowery pinny.'

James laughed. 'No, that's not your style, is it? But even so, it's going to be hard to get that grease off. Maggie won't come within a hundred yards of this place in case she gets dirty.'

Lillian hated it when he referred to his girlfriend. For long stretches of time she could forget that Maggie existed, but then, just when she was enjoying herself, her name would come up again.

'Well, I'm not Maggie, am I?' she said.

'God, no. You couldn't be more different.'

She wasn't sure whether this was meant as a compliment or not but, before she could ask, James had changed the subject.

'You've been a real help this evening, Lindy. The bloke'll be round to collect his car in ten minutes and I wouldn't have got it done in time if you hadn't been here. Look, are you doing anything on Sunday afternoon? Maggie's out for the day visiting relatives so I've got some free time. We could go up the pier or something.'

Lillian went through a painful roller coaster of emotions in the course of a few seconds—pleasure at being considered a help, anguish at being second choice after Maggie, delight at the prospect of an afternoon with James.

'That'd be lovely,' she said. 'I haven't been up the pier since I left the show.'

'That's settled, then. I'll call for you at two. That OK?'

It was more than OK. Lillian was walking on air for the rest of the week.

Sunday was cold with a wet wind gusting off the sea, tipping autumn over into winter. But nothing could dampen Lillian's spirits. She raced through clearing up the Sunday lunch, looked out her winter coat and put on the red woolly hat and scarf she had knitted backstage during the summer in intervals between appearances.

'Sure you still want to go?' James asked when he arrived at Sunny View.

'Of course! I've been looking forward to this,' Lillian told him with masterly understatement.

They marched up the mile and a quarter of timber walkway with the wind buffeting their faces and seagulls crying overhead.

'It's good to be out in the fresh air,' James said, taking exaggerated deep breaths. 'Gets all those petrol fumes out of your lungs.'

'It's glorious!' Lillian cried, intoxicated just to be out with him. She skipped around, her arms wide to catch the wind. 'Come on, race you to the next hut!'

They pounded along, dodging families and older couples and occasional groups of young people all out to walk off their Sunday lunches. James caught up with Lillian well before the little shelter they were heading for, grabbed her arm and swung her round. Shrieking with laughter, Lillian broke away and ran off again. They collapsed, panting, on the bench seat of the shelter.

'It's fun being out with you,' James said. 'You know how to enjoy yourself.'

It was easy to enjoy herself when she was with James. She had been happy simply passing tools to him while he'd worked under a car.

'It's fun with you too,' she said. 'Everything's fun with you.'

The pressure to open her heart was suddenly almost too much to bear. She yearned to tell him how much she had missed him while she had been away, how much she longed to be with him every minute of the day, but she was terrified she might spoil everything if she did. She jumped up.

'Come on,' she said, 'it's about to rain. Let's get to the end before it catches us.'

They spent a happy afternoon wandering round the pier head, playing the machines on the amusement arcades, marvelling at the tropical fish in the aquarium, laughing at their reflections in the hall of mirrors. Then James bought them both tea and buns in the café and they sat looking out over the grey water of the estuary.

Lillian asked about his plans for the exhaust business and James told her all about it—how he was looking for new premises so he could run both businesses in tandem until the exhaust one took off, how he needed to advertise heavily so that people knew he was there and saw the point of a while-you-wait specialist fitter, how he would be taking on staff but didn't need fully qualified car mechanics to do just one task, and how he would have to run up a credit account with the suppliers until he got the business off the ground.

'The whole thing's a great big gamble. If I get this wrong, if no one comes, then I'm going to be in big financial trouble.'

'If anyone can make it work, you can,' Lillian said.

James gave her arm an affectionate squeeze. 'Thanks, Lindy. It's really good to have you on my side. Most of the time I'm confident it'll be a success, but I do wake up at night sometimes worrying about it and there's nobody I can really talk to about it, except for you. So thanks for listening.'

Lillian glowed with happiness. 'It's a pleasure,' she said with complete honesty.

It was the crowning moment of a wonderful afternoon.

The days rushed by. Bob and Susan returned from their honeymoon and took up residence in their own little home. Wendy and Terry moved into the Thorpe Bay house. Lillian could hardly believe that three weeks of her break had gone already. The post brought an offer to renew her contract with the dance troupe, starting with pantomime in Leeds. Lillian dithered. If she stayed at home, she could carry on seeing James, and maybe, just maybe, something closer would grow out of it. A letter the next day from Diane enthused about the panto, saying what a big production it was, and how there might be scope for solo spots. Lillian didn't know what to do. If she was going to accept the contract, she needed to reply right away. Her mother found her frowning over the letters but did not appear to even notice them, asking instead if the vegetables were done for dinner.

'They're all ready. You've only got to put them in water. Mum, they want me to go to Leeds for the panto season,' Lillian told her.

'Oh—!'

At last, she had her mother's full attention. She sat down heavily in a chair across the table from Lillian and ran a thin hand over her head. 'So soon? I thought… I don't know how I'm going to manage when you're gone, I really don't.'

Guilt dragged at Lillian's insides. She really ought to be more of a help to her mother.

'The season's over now, Mum, and when I've gone it'll only be Frank and Dad and Gran to look after,' she pointed out.

Her mother sighed. 'Yes, yes, I suppose you're right.'

It didn't make her feel any better. She knew she was being selfish, going off and doing what she wanted.

'I had a go at Gran and told her you ought to have a washing machine and a vacuum cleaner and a fridge. Other people have them.'

Her mother looked frightened. 'Oh, I wouldn't know how to work any of them.'

'You'd soon learn.'

Not that it was worth arguing about it. It seemed very unlikely that Gran would ever agree to such expense.

She worried about her mother for the rest of the day, read through the chatty letter from Diane several times and finally went round to see James at his workshop. As luck would have it, he was just finishing a job.

'Good timing,' he said. 'Stick the kettle on, Lindy, and I'll be right with you.'

But, before Lillian could embark on her dilemma, James had something he wanted to talk about.

'Have you been to see Wendy's new place?' he asked.

'Yeah, I took her a present yesterday. It was difficult to know what to give when she's got everything anyway, so I bought a vase and some flowers. I did offer to help on moving day, but she said Terry had everything arranged.'

'Seems to me that bastard's got her right under his thumb— beg your pardon, Lindy—I mean, did you notice how she was at Suse and Bob's wedding? She hardly opened her mouth.'

'I know what you mean,' Lillian agreed. 'She doesn't seem to be able to do anything without asking him. It's like she's some sort of robot, with him pushing the buttons.'

'He calls her "doll." I hate that. But then I hate the bastard anyway—sorry—he doesn't deserve a lovely girl like your sister.'

'No,' Lillian said sadly.

'And another thing—do you think your Frank's been acting oddly?'

'Frank?' Lillian couldn't quite follow the change of subject.

'Yeah. I've been meaning to speak to you about him. He's still got that motorbike of his, hasn't he?'

'Yes.'

Frank's motorbike was his pride and joy.

'Well, quite a while ago—last year some time—he tried to touch me for a loan. He said he owed money on the bike and if he didn't pay up it was going to be repossessed. I told him I couldn't lend it to him but he could earn it working for me, but he didn't like that. He said he was going to ask Dempsey and I told him he didn't want to be owing a man like that any favours, but I think he might well have ignored me. I didn't really think much more about it. Well, Frank's a grown man, isn't he? What he does is his business. But the other day I saw him hanging around with a couple of Dempsey's heavies.'

'Oh—' Lillian felt she could do without adding Frank to her list of people to worry about. 'I don't know. He never says anything about what he's doing. He does spend a lot of time down on the seafront, but that doesn't mean he's in with Terry's lot.'

'No, you're right. Forget I mentioned it. Was this just a social call or did you want to tell me something?'

Lillian began to explain about the new contract and her dilemma, but she had hardly started when the phone rang.

James held a long conversation with someone about rents and conditions.

'My new premises,' he explained. 'Sorry about that. You were saying?'

'Well, it is a good production, but my mum—'

'Is this a private party or can anyone join in?'

They both looked up. A large man was standing in the entrance.

'Wondered if you had a moment to look at my handbrake, Jamie-boy? Only it's flaming useless and the wife wants to have the motor tonight.'

'Right you are, Mr Jessop. Leave it with me and I'll see what I can do. Come back in a quarter of an hour or so.'

James turned to Lillian. 'I'm sorry, Lindy. Maybe this isn't the right time to have a serious talk.'

'It's all right. I shouldn't be bothering you at work. Perhaps we could meet up some time? This evening, perhaps?'

She longed to get him by himself for a heart-to-heart.

James sighed. 'Not this evening, I'm afraid. I promised Maggie I'd take her to the pictures and I'd better not blow her out. She's been getting a bit restless lately. Says I'm seeing too much of you! Stupid, I know, but you girls do go getting the wrong end of the stick sometimes. I said to her that you and me have known each other for ever and you're like my little sister, but she wasn't having it. She seemed to think there was something to worry about. Daft, isn't it?'

Lillian just gaped at him as the hope she had dared to nurture shrivelled and died. Her throat was so choked that she could hardly reply. 'Yes,' she managed to whisper. 'I—I'll leave you to it, then.'

'OK. We'll have a chat another time. 'Bye, Lindy—see you soon.'

She held the tears back until she had reached the corner, where they burst out in heaving sobs. Somehow, she stumbled blindly home with those damning words echoing round and round her head. *Little sister—little sister—little sister.*

When she had finally cried herself out, she found a pen and wrote accepting the new contract with the dance company.

CHAPTER 23

'GOODBYE, good luck! Remember to invite me to the wedding!'

'As if I'd forget you! You've been my best pal ever since Sheffield.'

'Three years—it seems longer than that. All those horrible digs—'

'All those greasy breakfasts—'

'All those smelly dressing rooms—'

Lillian and Diane were standing on the platform at Crewe. The last passengers were climbing on board.

'Oh, Lindy—I'm going to miss you!'

They threw their arms round each other and hugged. They had been through so much together.

'And I'm going to miss you too. It won't be the same without you.'

Diane gave her one last squeeze. 'Remember, kiddo— you're going to be a star. I want to see your name up in lights.'

'And you're going to be a married woman. You're a lucky girl, Di. He's a smashing bloke. You mind you look after him.'

'I will, don't you worry.'

At the end of the train, the guard blew his whistle. Lillian released her friend and gave her a little push towards the open door of the carriage.

'Go on, get in, it's about to leave.'

Diane climbed up, pulled the door shut behind her, let down the window and leaned out.

''Bye, Lindy! Break a leg!'

The train started, snorting into the smoky air of the big station. Lillian stood waving as it drew away.

''Bye, Diane! Be happy!'

She watched till her friend was out of sight, then turned and walked slowly back down the platform. She felt quite hollow. It was going to be really strange without Diane. They had managed to get jobs and digs together through three years of pantos and variety tours and summer shows, until she could hardly imagine working without Diane there with her good sense and sunny temper and Yorkshire sense of humour. It didn't help that she envied Diane the ease with which the next stage of her life had fallen into place. On her last 'rest' between engagements, she had met a new pal of her brother's and they had fallen in love. Just like that. No problems, no hiccups, they had hit it off from the start and now, six months later, they were engaged.

Thinking about them as she left the platform, Lillian let out a great sigh. If only it could happen like that with her and James. Fat chance. She tried to shake herself out of her gloom. She had over an hour to wait for her train, so she went to the buffet and bought a cup of coffee and an iced bun and leafed through a magazine. But the stories and articles couldn't hold her attention. In the end she sat pushing crumbs round the plate, thinking of Diane and her fiancé, and of James. He had been full of ideas when last she was home. He was running the repair business and While-U-Wait Exhausts and juggling two girlfriends. Lillian had told him off over this.

'If you're worried about one finding out about the other, don't come to me for sympathy. You shouldn't be two-timing in the first place.'

'I know, but they will start getting too serious. You take a girl out for a couple of months and, before you know where you are, she starts dragging you over to look in jewellers' windows. I'm not ready to settle down yet. I've got too much to do.'

Which was some sort of comfort. If he would persist in seeing her as a little sister, at least he hadn't given his heart to anyone else.

It was a slow journey to Nottingham, giving Lillian plenty of time to make herself stop thinking about what might never happen and focus on the audition ahead of her the next day. She had been taking acting lessons and ballet classes for the last few months and had set her sights on being one of the good fairies in *The Sleeping Beauty*. If she got the job, it meant being in the chorus line for most of the time, but in the christening scene there would be a solo for each fairy and some lines to say. She really wanted this. It was a step up the career ladder.

When she arrived at the theatre, it was the usual chaos of people all hoping for a decent job to carry them as far through the winter as possible. It felt odd arriving on her own, but Lillian soon recognised actors and dancers she had worked with on other productions and joined in with the kissing and shrieking.

'Lindy, darling! Lovely to see you. Didn't know you were coming for this one.'

'Cathy, you're looking wonderful, what have you done to your hair?'

'Oh, just look who's here—where have you been since Leeds?'

It made her realise just how far she had come from that shy little girl who'd first turned up at the theatre in Sheffield, knowing nothing and nobody. She was a seasoned performer now, with years of experience. There was gallons of gossip to catch up on—who was with whom, who had broken up, who was on their way to stardom and who had fallen by the wayside. As she talked, Lillian tried to find out who else was auditioning for the three good fairies. Quite a crowd, as it turned out. Enough to fill the chorus line with unsuccessful applicants.

'Anyone know anything about the producer—what's-his-name? Paul Fuller?' she asked.

'Pauly-boy? He's OK. Knows what he's doing. Puts on a real good show.'

'Does he like boys or girls?' someone else asked. It always helped to know.

'Oh, girls, darling,' a girl called Dawn replied. She gave a knowing smile. 'He adores girls. Blondes mostly, although he will go for brunettes occasionally.' She patted her platinum curls.

Some of the dancers groaned. They could do without being groped while they were trying to rehearse.

'I did say I'd only work for queens from now on. You know where you are with them. But I suppose I'll give it a go now I'm here,' somebody said.

Dawn gave her a disparaging look.

'For God's sake, darling, don't be so stupid. If you've got what he wants, use it.'

The stars of the show had been cast weeks ago and were up on posters around the city already, and the supporting roles had been chosen the day before. Today was the turn of the small parts, the players who would be courtiers, villagers and huntsmen, along with the dancers and the good fairies. By late morning it was the turn of the fairies. Lillian changed into her dance gear, did her make-up and hair and warmed up. There were more than forty of them going for three parts. Lillian avoided Dawn, retreating to a corner to go over her audition poem in her head. It was the first time she had tried for a speaking part, and nerves were really getting to her. The dancing part didn't bother her. She knew that however bad she felt beforehand, once the music started, she would be all right. But she had no idea whether her voice would behave itself when it came to the point.

Lillian was in the third batch to be sent to wait in the wings. The girls coming back from the first two lots had no idea whether they had been chosen or not.

'He's playing it close to the chest, waiting till he's seen all of us.'

Which wasn't much help for those following.

Dawn was in Lillian's group, and the first of them to go on. She walked to the front of the stage, announced that she was to recite Wordsworth's *Daffodils* and launched into what Lillian thought was a rather showy rendition. Was that what the producer was looking for? Then she danced to part of The Dying Swan. Lillian could see immediately that her technique wasn't brilliant, and wasn't that impressed with her interpretation either. No potential rival there, then. But she smiled and whispered congratulations as she came off because that was the thing to do. Next went another girl whom Lillian didn't think was that wonderful, and then it was her turn. She walked out into the spotlight, exuding every bit of charm and confidence she could muster.

'*Stopping By Woods on a Snowy Evening* by Robert Frost,' she announced.

She had liked the poem from the moment she'd read it and had worked hard on it with her acting teacher over the summer. Now she put all that she had learnt into practice. To her relief, she didn't squeak or growl or forget any of the lines, but it was a relief to get it finished and perform her dance piece, the Sugar Plum Fairy.

'Thank you, dear,' came the producer's voice from the stalls. 'Next!'

She could deduce absolutely nothing from his tone of voice. It was very unnerving.

Back in the dressing room, a lot of the dancers felt the same.

'He's trying to keep us keen, the bastard,' one commented.

When the last batch had done their stuff, a lunch break was announced. The prospective fairies groaned and howled in protest.

'What, is he going to keep us waiting for another hour?'

'Bleeding masochist.'

'What's wrong with him? Why can't he just make his mind up?'

Some of the girls decided to go out and find a café. Lillian, as an old hand, had brought sandwiches and a flask with her. Dawn stayed in the theatre as well, but Lillian steered clear of her and went to speak with a couple of the girls she hadn't seen since her first summer in Blackpool. They were just sighing over poor Brenda when an assistant stage manager came and tapped her on the shoulder.

'Miss Parker?' he murmured, so low that the other girls couldn't hear.

'Yes.'

'Mr Fuller would like to see you.'

'Oh! Right—' Lillian jumped up but, even as she did so, unease set in. 'Did he say what for?'

'No.' The ASM looked distinctly sheepish. 'Only to keep it quiet, like.'

'Hmm, well—' She turned to the other girls. 'Got to see a man about a dog. Won't be a sec.'

Paul Fuller had taken over one of the star dressing rooms. A florid man in his forties with longish hair beginning to thin on top, he was sitting at the dressing table surrounded by lists and notes. He smiled as Lillian entered.

'Ah, Lindy-Lou. Come in, my sweetheart, come in. Shut the door.'

Lillian did so, but stayed standing next to it.

'Was there something wrong with my audition?' she asked.

'No, darling. On the contrary, you're a lovely little dancer, lovely. And a nice speaking voice too. Very clear and plenty of colour. This your first speaking part, is it?'

She felt that she had strayed into the wrong panto. She was Little Red Riding Hood and this, if she wasn't very much mistaken, was the Big Bad Wolf.

'No,' she lied, since it never did to admit to being a tyro.

'But stepping out of the chorus line and getting a solo is a big step forward, right?'

Lillian shrugged. 'Not really.'

Paul Fuller grinned.

'Come on, I know ambition when I see it. And I know talent when I see it too. You've got what it takes, Lindy. You could go far.'

Despite herself, Lillian lapped up this comment. 'Thanks.'

'But I have a little problem, you see. Only three roles. I've got definites for two of them, but the third—well—the third is more difficult. It's the biggest one, you see, Lindy. The fairy who promises to soften the spell after the bad fairy's cast hers. An important part, Lindy, one you could shine in.'

She could do it, Lillian knew. She wanted to have the chance, wanted it more than anything.

'Glad you think so, Mr Fuller,' she said.

'So you see, I thought we'd better get together and—er—discuss it further.'

'Discuss?'

'Yes. You see, Lindy, you're not the only one I could give this part to. I'd like to choose you, I really would. I just need you to—er—persuade me that you're right for the job.'

She had to make sure that he really was saying what she thought he was.

'Persuade you?' she said, acting the innocent.

'Oh, come on, darling, we both know what I'm talking about. Naughty but nice, eh? And don't try and pretend you're giving away something precious. I know you dancers. You're at it all the time. Why waste it on some spotty youth when I can help you with your career?'

Lillian felt cheated, used, overwhelmingly angry. She really, really wanted this part. For a moment she even found herself considering his bargain, before stamping on it, disgusted with herself.

'You want me to have sex with you before you give me the role?'

'If you must put it as baldly as that, yes. That's the deal.'

'I am the right person for this job,' she burst out. 'I'd be damn good at it. You know that and I know it but—'

'So, what's the problem?' Paul Fuller interrupted, holding out a hand to her. 'You give me what I want; I give you what you want. It's easy.'

'Not for me, it isn't. I don't want it that much,' she told him. Paul Fuller shrugged.

'Suit y'self, sweetie. There's plenty more here that'll be more than happy to take your place.'

'They're welcome to it,' Lillian cried, and slammed out of the room.

She ran down the dim corridor, choking back tears of anger and humiliation. How dared he think she would do that? How dared he? She found herself at the stage door and burst out into the damp street, her chest heaving. It was so unfair. He had all the power and he sat there playing with it, making other people dance to his tune.

'Not me, matey,' she said out loud. 'Not me. Nobody owns me.'

She marched round the block, muttering to herself, oblivious to the fact that she was still dressed in her dance clothes and people were giving her funny looks. She considered just giving up and going home. But this was the last of the calls for large scale pantos. She had waited for this one because of the chance of a solo role, and now that man had ruined it for her. She walked a bit further and, when she finally calmed down a little, began to take in something of her surroundings. Nottingham was a great city. It would have been nice to do a season here. Still fuming, she went back to the theatre to pick up her things.

She sidled in to find the dancers gathered in a group on the stage. An ASM, the same one who had run Paul Fuller's message for him, was standing in front of them with a list in his hand. She joined the back of the group. One thing was for sure, Paul Fuller wasn't going to give her a job now.

'What's going on? Have they announced the fairies?' she asked the girl nearest to her.

'You just missed it. It's those three over there,' the girl told her, nodding at a group standing downstage left. Lillian looked at them. One of them was Dawn.

'Stupid bitch,' she muttered.

'I beg your pardon?' the girl next to her said.

'Not you.'

A couple of dancers turned round and glared at her. 'Shh!'

'—and these people are in the chorus line—' the ASM said and read out a list of names.

To Lillian's amazement, she was on it. She stood quite still, an island of quiet in a sea of chattering girls, some pleased, some angry, all disappointed at not getting the solo roles.

'—some decent digs, if you're interested.'

'Er—what?' She realised that one of the other dancers was talking to her.

'I said, I was here last year and I know some good digs.'

'Oh. Right. Thanks.'

Should she stay? It meant swallowing her pride. It meant watching that Dawn take her place in the spotlight in every single performance. The whole thing stank. But the alternative was appearing in a second-rate show, and she was worth more than that. She had earned her place in a big production. Very reluctantly, she pulled herself together and managed to smile at the girl who was talking to her.

'Sorry, I was thinking something through. Yes, I'd love to take a look at these digs. Get them off the theatre list and you never know what you're getting, do you?'

Her course was set.

The annoying thing was, Paul Fuller was an excellent producer and a talented choreographer. The panto was a real spectacular, with a big cast and orchestra, magical special effects, slick comedy scenes and great dances. In other circumstances,

Lillian would have been delighted to be part of it. But, every time she saw Dawn perform, she felt sick with anger and a sense of powerlessness. She knew she could put far more life into the lines the good fairy said and, as for the solo, she could do it one hundred per cent better. Dawn was proficient enough, but she had no soul.

She went home for a flying visit at Christmas, as usual. Even though it was the second Christmas with both Bob and Wendy settled in their own places, it still seemed strange without them around. She was surprised at how much she missed both of them. Bob, Susan and the Kershaws all came round to Sunny View for tea on Christmas Day, which livened things up no end, but Wendy and Terry stayed away as Terry's family had joined them for the day. As she ran about preparing dinner, Lillian wondered how Wendy was getting on coping with a baby and a toddler and cooking for all her visitors. Terry would be sure to want to show off and have the table groaning with food and drink. She didn't have time to find out before she had to rush back to Nottingham.

The panto opened on Boxing Day and played to packed houses all week. Then, for the matinee on New Year's Eve, four of the cast who were sharing digs called in sick. They had all gone down with a virulent stomach bug. One of them was Dawn, another was the girl who was understudying the fairies. Paul Fuller was pulling his hair out. He burst into the female dressing room.

'Marilyn—' he grabbed the arm of the girl nearest to him '—you're a nice little dancer. This is your big chance. Have you been watching what Dawn's doing?'

Marilyn went quite pale. 'I can't do it without a rehearsal, Mr Fuller. Not in a million years.'

Paul Fuller gave a growl of frustration. 'For God's sake—'

He cast about the room. His gaze lit upon Lillian. 'Lindy, I know you could do it.'

Lillian's heart beat fast. This was it. Her *A Star Is Born* moment. But she was not letting Paul Fuller off the hook. Oh, no. She stared back at him, stony-faced.

'Yes, I could do it. Standing on my head.'

Relief flooded his face. He was all smiles.

'Great, great, wonderful. What a trouper! Come along; we've just got time for one quick run-through, then Denise can have a go at your costume for you.'

Lillian did not respond. She stayed sitting on her stool, looking at him. 'No strings?' she asked.

Paul Fuller flushed. 'Strings? What strings? I don't know what you're talking about.'

Around her, the other dancers sniggered. They all knew what was going on with him and Dawn.

'And it's not just understudying—I get to do the role for the rest of the run?'

He looked quite shaken. 'I…I don't know about that—'

Lillian shrugged. 'That's the deal, take it or leave it.'

'Well—I—'

He looked around at the rest of the dancers, hoping for a break. Lillian held her breath. If some cow cut the ground from under her by offering to stand in just until Dawn came back, she would strangle her with her bare hands. But Dawn was not popular with the rest of the company. They just looked from Paul Fuller to Lillian, waiting avidly to see who was going to win.

'All right, then,' he conceded.

'Good,' Lillian said with a gracious smile. She stood up. 'We'd better have that run-through, hadn't we?'

As she followed him out of the dressing room applause broke out behind her. It was almost as sweet a moment as when she'd stepped into the spotlight for the very first time.

CHAPTER 24

'WHAT'RE you having, Lindy? Tea or coffee?'

'Oh—tea, please. And an Eccles cake.'

Lillian and a couple of the other girls from the company bagged a table in the crowded café while Marilyn went to get their drinks. It was a rainy afternoon in Nottingham and the January sales were in full swing, so the place was full of shoppers with bulging bags. Underneath the pleasant aroma of food there was a whiff of wet woollen coats that reminded Lillian of school cloakrooms. The other two discussed whether Nottingham was better than Leeds for shopping as they waited for Marilyn. Lillian got out the present she had just bought for her little niece's second birthday, a baby doll in a nightie and frilly cap. She hoped little Coral learned to love it and maybe be a little less jealous of her new baby brother. More than that, she hoped Wendy would be pleased. Her sister had been very subdued when she had last seen her, back in November.

'What d'you think, Lindy? Leeds or Nottingham?' one of the girls asked.

'Oh—I don't know. Here, I think. It's nearer home so it was easier to get back for Christmas.'

'Here we are!' Marilyn plonked a loaded tray down in the middle of the small table. 'Help yourselves. Eccles cake for you, Lindy Lulu, and doughnuts for the rest of us.'

They all tucked in. Dancing made them ravenous.

'You meeting that lad of yours before the show?' Marilyn asked.

Lillian shook her head and swallowed a mouthful of cake. 'Not today.'

'Why not? You ought to hang on to him, he's dishy.'

'He's all right, I suppose.'

What with all the travelling that they did, boyfriends came and went. Some of the girls managed to maintain long-distance relationships. Some even got married and left the company. Lillian never had any trouble attracting men, and the fact that she played it cool only made them all the keener, but she never kept any of them beyond the run of each production.

'You're too picky by half, you are,' one of the girls said. 'Me, I'm getting fed up with all this moving on. If some lad asked me to marry him I'd say yes like a shot. Nice little place and a nice man to keep me warm, that's what I want.'

They all laughed and teased her.

Lillian looked idly beyond her to the next table. A woman of about thirty was staring back at her with wide eyes and an expression of shocked amazement. Their eyes met and Lillian looked away, faintly embarrassed. Was there something wrong with her hair? Did she have crumbs all over her face? She brushed her hand over her mouth and, as she did so, recognition tugged at her memory and made her look back. There was something very familiar about the woman. She was still staring as if she had seen a ghost.

Vaguely disturbed, Lillian turned her attention back to her cake. Who *was* that woman? After more than three years now, moving around doing pantos and summer seasons and weekly variety in between, dozens of people had moved briefly into and out of her life. She couldn't remember all of them.

'…isn't that so, Lindy?'

'What?' She hadn't heard a word her friends had been saying.

'You're still hanging on for Mr Perfect.'

'Yeah, yeah.'

She was tired of being teased about James. That was partly why she went out with other boys, just to escape from being nagged about the stupidity of saving herself for someone who was never going to be hers.

'Excuse me.'

She looked up. The strange woman was standing next to her.

'I… It's silly, I know, but I heard your friends say your name and…well…you do look a bit like…but it was all so long ago…'

Now it was Lillian's turn to wonder if she had seen a ghost. That face—that voice—

'It's not—?' she whispered.

'—so I wondered—only I had a little niece once called Lindy-Lou. Lindy-Lou Parker.'

'It is!' Lillian breathed. She stood up, her knees shaky beneath her. 'Aunty Eileen? Is it you?'

'Lindy! Oh, Lindy, it is you!'

Laughing and crying, they fell into each other's arms.

'I can't believe it,' they both repeated, pulling away to study each other's faces. Eileen did look different in some ways. She was no longer a slim young girl, for she had put on weight all over, and it showed on her face, giving her the start of a double chin. Her hair was now backcombed and lacquered into a fashionable beehive but her merry eyes and her infectious smile were just the same.

'Of all the cafés in all the world—' Lillian misquoted. 'Are you living here, in Nottingham?'

'Not in the town. I only came in to go to the sales, and I found you! Oh, Lindy, I thought of you such a lot. What are you doing now? Why are you here?'

'I'm in the panto, I'm a dancer. I followed my dream, just like you said.'

There was so much to catch up on, neither of them knew where to start.

'I can't stay. My kids'll be coming in from school. They can let themselves in, but I don't like them being on their own in the house too long. Look, you must come out and see us,' Eileen insisted.

She explained which bus to catch and how to find her house. They arranged to meet the next morning and then she was gone, leaving Lillian dazed and elated.

'My Aunty Eileen,' she kept repeating. 'That really was my Aunty Eileen. I never thought I'd see her again.'

Concentrating on the show was really hard that evening, sleeping afterwards even more difficult. Lillian was awake again at six, and up long before any of the others at her digs. Nine o'clock saw her waiting at the bus station for the bus out to the village where Eileen lived. It turned out to be an ugly place dominated by a vast slag heap and the winding gear of the coal mine. A cloud of coal smoke hung over it, coiling up from the chimneys of rows of identical pit cottages. Eileen lived in a flat-fronted terraced place that let straight on to the street.

'Come in, come in,' she cried, giving Lillian a big hug and a kiss. 'Let me look at you. D'you know, last night I thought I might have dreamed it all, but here you are. It really is you.'

Lillian found herself in a small square room with the three-piece suite arranged around the TV set. So this was Aunty Eileen's home. It felt so odd to be here. She walked over to the mantelpiece above the coal fire, where there was a row of family photos.

'Are these your children?' she asked, studying them.

'Yes—' Eileen's voice softened with love. 'That's our Tommy, he's nine now, and that's Lindy, she's nearly seven.'

'Lindy?'

'That's right. It's Linda, but we call her Lindy. After you.'

'Oh—' tears swam in Lillian's eyes '—that's so lovely.'

'I never forgot you, you know. I didn't want to leave you. But you do strange things when you're in love, don't you? You're off your head, really. D'you know what I mean? You're how old now? Nearly twenty? You must have been in love.'

'Yes,' Lillian said. It did do strange things to you. It stopped you from getting serious about anyone else, for a start.

'I was so crazy about that man, I would of done anything for him. I was so stupid then. I knew nothing about life at all. I just thought that I couldn't live without him.'

'Is that him there?' Lillian asked, nodding at a picture of Eileen and a man with his arm round her shoulders at the sea-side somewhere.

'Oh, no! That's my Neil. No, it all ended with the other one in less than a year. I got to realise that he was never going to leave his wife, and then I found out that he was seeing an-other girl as well. He had three of us on the go! I was heartbroken, I can tell you. Cried my eyes out for weeks, I did. I suppose I should of gone home then, but I was too afraid. I didn't know what Mum would say if I came back. I thought she might just throw me out.'

'Well—she was very cut up when you went,' Lillian said with massive understatement.

Gran had never uttered Eileen's name again, to the best of her knowledge. If she did refer to her it was as 'That Girl'.

'That's what I thought. I mean—creeping out in the middle of the night like that. If Lindy was to do that to me when she gets bigger, I'd just die of a broken heart.'

It was hard to imagine Gran dying of a broken heart.

'I'm sure she won't. You must be a lovely mum,' Lillian said. 'So when did you meet your Neil?'

'A year or so after it all finished with the other one. It was quite different with him. Like—we're best pals as well as husband and wife. We've hardly ever had a row. It's like we're sort of in tune with each other.'

'You're so lucky,' Lillian said with a sigh.

'You sound sad. Have you got a boyfriend?' Eileen asked.

'Yes, but it's a long story. Tell me about Neil first. Does he work down the pit?'

'No, thank God. It's so dangerous down there. You'll never believe what he does, though—he's a butcher! It's a joke, isn't it? I leave home with a commercial traveller and I end up married to a butcher, just like my mum. It must be fate or something.'

'A butcher? You're kidding!'

They looked at each other, smiles tugging at the corners of their mouths. And then they were both laughing fit to burst. They collapsed onto the sofa, tears running down their faces.

'I don't know why it's so funny. It's a perfectly good job,' Lillian gasped.

'I know, I know. Stupid, isn't it? Look—come into the kitchen and I'll make us some tea. I want to hear all about everything that's happened at home.'

There was so much to say. They sat across the red formica kitchen table from each other, drinking tea and munching biscuits while Lillian brought Eileen up to date with the family's lives.

'Bob's married now, to a really nice girl called Susan. They did it all very sensibly. They saved up for a little house in Southchurch and then waited another couple of years before starting a family and now they're expecting their first baby in March.'

'Bob, a married man? Well, that doesn't surprise me. He was middle-aged when he was seventeen. What about Frank? Is he still the wild one?'

'Yes, he's never really settled to a job. He works down the seafront in the summer and gets factory jobs in the winter, and he's got this motorbike he goes roaring around on, and he goes about with a bunch of leather boys.'

'That sounds like Frank. And Wendy? What's happened to pretty Wendy?'

'Oh, well, Wendy—she could of married anyone. They were all after her, all the boys. She had them lined up. But she had to go and choose a right nasty bit of work.' Lillian explained about the Carnival court and Terry Dempsey and the rushed wedding. 'So she got to marry a man with money, and much good it's done her. She's living in this huge house but she hardly sees anyone, as far as I can make out. Mum never goes further than the shops and Gran hardly goes out at all, so they don't visit her and she hardly ever goes to visit them. Susan drops in from time to time, but she's nervous of Terry and you never know when he's going to be there. It's not like he works regular hours like most men. I go round there whenever I'm home, but it's really hard work talking to Wendy. It's not just the babies crying and needing feeding and changing and all that. It's Wendy herself. You can't get any reaction out of her. It's like she's a zombie or something.'

'Some women do go like that after they've had a baby,' Eileen told her. 'It happened to a friend of mine. The doctor put her on the happy pills, and then she couldn't get off them. Terrible, it was.'

'Mmm, maybe that's it, but I think it's more Terry and the hold he's got on her. And then there's Frank as well. James— that's Susan's brother—thinks Frank may have borrowed quite a lot of money from Terry, which is bad news, 'cos Terry's the sort of bloke who calls in favours.'

She felt a blush wash over her as she spoke James's name, but Eileen was too interested in finding out more about Wendy's husband to comment. They chewed over the family news for some time, then Eileen wanted to know about her old home.

'What about Sunny View? Blimey, what a name, Sunny View! There was never anything sunny about it. Has it been done up at all?'

'Not a lot. I mean, it's had the odd lick of paint, but nothing's been really changed since you left. The really dreadful curtains in some of the PGs' rooms have been replaced, and they've all got one of Gran's rugs in, but otherwise you'd not notice the difference. Gran's got a telly in her room, and Frank's got a record player in his, but poor Mum hasn't got a washing machine or a Hoover or a fridge to help her with looking after the PGs.'

'Are there still PGs? I mean, I wouldn't stay at a place like Sunny View, not when there are nicer places. It's not like it was just after the war, when nobody had any money and a weekend in Southend was a treat. It's all "You never had it so good" now, isn't it? People go away for a fortnight now. They go in their cars. Or even on planes. Someone I know went to Jersey. Just fancy—going on holiday in an aeroplane!'

'Wendy and Terry went to this place called Le Touquet on a plane for their honeymoon. It's in France and it's got a casino and a big sandy beach,' Lillian said. 'But yes, you're right, people don't stay in Southend so much any more. They come for day trips, but they don't stay and, if they do, it's not at Sunny View.'

'I'm not surprised. Like I said, I wouldn't take my family to somewhere where you had to get out after breakfast and you weren't allowed back till teatime. And I wouldn't like somewhere all gloomy like that, either. You want fun when you go on holiday, not people telling you what the rules are.'

They were still talking when young Tommy and Linda arrived home from school for their midday meal. Lillian had a quick talk to them, then rushed off to get the bus back for the afternoon's performance, promising to return as soon as possible.

It was the start of four happy weeks. Every Sunday Lillian travelled out to spend the day with Eileen and her family, enjoying one of their massive roast dinners and going for a drive or a walk together. At least one day a week Eileen would come into town and they would meet up for a coffee and a chat and a look round the shops. She got tickets for the family to see the show, and took them backstage to meet the performers and the theatre staff. They were enchanted to find that they were related to someone in show-business, while Lillian revelled in being included in their close and loving family.

And then, on a freezing day in February, her landlady called up the stairs to her, 'Lindy! Phone for you!'

She clattered down to stand in the chilly hall. 'Hello?' she said.

It was her father. Lillian was instantly alarmed. Her father never phoned her.

'What is it? What's wrong?' she asked.

'It's your mum. You got to come home, Lillian. Your mum's been taken bad. She's in hospital.'

The cold hand of fear clutched at her. 'In hospital? Why? What's wrong with her?'

'Well—you know—women's problems.' Her father sounded acutely embarrassed.

'Oh, my God.'

Guilt mixed queasily with the fear. Her mum had complained about 'her usual' for years, but still managed to recover and carry on, refusing to see the doctor. Along with the rest of the family, Lillian had got so used to it that she hadn't thought it might be anything serious.

'So you got to come home,' her father insisted.

'Yes, yes, of course I will, Dad,' she agreed, already planning what she had to do in the way of packing, letting the theatre know, ringing Eileen.

'Only you can't stay away at a time like this.'

'I know, Dad. I said I was coming and I am.'

'There's no need to take that tone with me, my girl.'

Lillian clenched her teeth with frustration. Why did her dad have to turn everything into a row? She forced herself to speak with reasoned calm.

'I'll get the first train I can to London, OK? It's nearly midday now, so I'll be home some time this evening.'

'Huh. Well, I should think so too.'

A frantic hour later, she was on her way.

CHAPTER 25

TIRED and anxious, Lillian arrived at Southend Victoria, not expecting anyone to be there to meet her, since nobody knew which train she would be arriving on. She slung her duffel bag over her shoulder and heaved her heavy suitcase down onto the platform. It was bitingly cold away from the stuffy heat of the carriage. She pushed her hair out of her eyes and braced herself to carry the case.

'Here, let me take that.'

She gasped and looked up, hardly able to believe her ears. Like a dream come true, there he was, the one person in the world she most wanted to see.

'James! Oh, James, how did you know——? Oh, it's so wonderful to see you!'

He smiled and kissed her lightly on the cheek. 'Well, it was worth the wait to get a welcome like that.'

'Have you been here long? It's freezing. Far too cold to be hanging around on a station.'

'I'm well wrapped up—look, one of Susan's scarves. Come on, let's get you home.'

He picked up the suitcase as if it weighed nothing at all and strode along the platform. Lillian trotted alongside him.

'Have you heard anything about my mum? Have they said how she is?'

'I don't know, Lindy. She's not been well for a while, but this morning she collapsed in the street and was taken to hospital, and they've kept her in. The last I heard they were doing tests.'

'Oh, my God. I should have been home to help her.'

'You're home now. That's what counts. You couldn't have come any quicker.'

It was small comfort. Lillian felt she had failed as a daughter.

Outside, James unlocked a small green car and shoved her case onto the back seat. Lillian was momentarily distracted.

'Oh, you've got a Mini!'

James patted its roof. 'My new baby. Good, isn't it? They're an amazing design, really revolutionary, and great fun to drive. I'm going to tune it up and go rallying in it. Come on, get in.'

If it hadn't been for the circumstances, Lillian would have enjoyed the drive home, roaring round the streets in the Mini with James beside her at the wheel. In no time at all, they arrived outside Sunny View. James carried the case to the front door for her and waited till it was opened.

Her father let her in. 'Ah. So you're back,' he said, then looked at James and said somewhat grudgingly, 'Thanks, son.'

James gave Lillian's arm a brief squeeze. 'We'll catch up later, eh?' he said, and left.

Lillian ignored the cool welcome.

'How's Mum? What's the latest? When can I see her?'

Her father didn't answer. Instead, she was hustled into Gran's room. A fire was blazing in the grate and the television was blaring in the corner but, as ever, the most imposing presence in the room was Gran herself. She sat in her wing-back chair with yet another half-completed hooked rug over her knees and stared at Lillian over the top of her steel-rimmed spectacles as she came into the room.

'So. The wanderer has returned.'

It was hard not to feel just like a little girl again, hauled up before her grandmother for some misdeed. Lillian took a deep breath in through her nose, trying to slow the racing of her heart. She looked coolly back.

'Hello, Gran. I came as fast as I could. What's the latest news of Mum?'

Disappointingly, Gran didn't seem to know any more than James. They were to phone tomorrow after the doctor had done his rounds and would be told what was to happen next.

'In the meantime, you'll have to take your mother's place. Your grandmother can't be expected to look after the house,' her father said.

It was only then that Lillian realised why she had been summoned in such haste. It wasn't because her mother needed her, it was because the rest of them needed a cook and housekeeper.

'Right,' she said. 'Well, I'll go and unpack, then.'

The next day, she took the bus out to the hospital. Her mother had been transferred to the gynaecological ward. Lillian walked down the double row of beds, clutching her bunch of carnations. She stood still with shock when she got to her mother. A deathly pale woman with wispy grey hair and a sunken face looked listlessly back at her for a moment, before recognition dawned. She lifted a hand briefly and dropped it again.

'Lillian. You're here. Thank God.'

It was worth all the coldness of the rest of the family to be wanted by her mum. Lillian stepped forward and kissed her on the forehead. Her skin felt papery beneath her lips.

'Hello, Mum. How are you?'

Nettie caught at her arm and held on with surprising strength. 'They're going to take it all away,' she whispered, fear gleaming in her eyes.

'Take what?'

'My—you know—women's bits. A hys—something.'

'Hysterectomy?'

'That's it. Yes, I got to have an operation.'

Now that she thought about it, Lillian wasn't surprised. As well as the four children, her mother had had three miscarriages and a stillbirth.

'I expect you'll feel better after, Mum.'

Nettie was still clinging to her arm. 'I don't want them to cut me open.'

Unwanted, the image of Brenda floated before Lillian's eyes. She tried to banish it. This was quite different. Her mother was going to have a proper operation carried out by proper doctors. It was quite safe.

'They wouldn't do it if it wasn't necessary, Mum. You know how bad you've been for ages. Once this is done, you'll be OK again.'

'No, no, you don't understand. Once they get in there, they might find anything.'

'What? What do you mean?'

'Anything—you know—something dreadful.'

Lillian didn't follow her. She changed the subject, talking

about Wendy and the babies. It was on the tip of her tongue to tell her about Eileen, but her aunty had made her promise not to say anything yet.

When the bell rang for the end of visiting hour, Lillian kissed her mother goodbye and went to tell the ward sister of her fears. The sister was brisk.

'Your mother is in very good hands, Miss Parker. Now, no visiting tomorrow as she will be recovering. You may phone at six o'clock to ask how it has gone.'

Lillian could only thank her and go.

All the next day she found it hard to concentrate. The morning wasn't so bad as she had a lot to do, what with cooking and clearing the breakfast, making the beds, sweeping out and relaying Gran's fire, doing the shopping and making the midday dinner. But the afternoon dragged. All she could think about was her mother. Had she had her operation? Was she all right? It was hard to eat her tea when the clock was ticking away towards six. As soon as it struck, she went out to the phone box on the corner of the next street and rang the hospital. The answer was unsatisfactory. Her mother was reported to be 'comfortable', but the doctor needed to discuss her case with her next of kin, and no, it was not possible to do so over the phone. Lillian went home to report back to the rest of the family.

'How am I supposed to get to speak to a doctor in working hours?' her father asked.

'You'll have to take the morning off work,' Lillian told him.

He looked at her as if she had suggested he rob a bank.

'I can't do that.'

'Yes, you can. Someone else can operate the lift. It's not as if you need five years' training to do it.'

Her father went red in the face. 'I'll thank you to show some respect, my girl!'

But the next morning he came down to breakfast wearing his suit and tie rather than his work uniform.

'You coming out to the hospital with me, then?'

It took a few minutes for Lillian to realise that her father was afraid of hospitals and nervous of doctors. He did not admit it, but he needed her moral support. Lillian sighed and agreed.

'I'll get some sausages on the way back. They'll be quick to do for dinner.'

It was a good thing they had each other there for the interview because the doctor had bad news. A malignant growth had been found in Nettie's uterus. They didn't think it had spread to any other organs, but they couldn't be sure. She was to have further tests.

Susan and Bob came round in the evening to discuss what should be done.

'Of course, I'll help in any way I can,' Susan offered.

Lillian hugged her. 'That's really sweet of you, but you're going to have your hands full soon.'

'I know—' Susan rested a hand on top of the eight and a half month bump under her maternity smock. 'But I'll do what I can. And I'm sure my mum will as well.'

'What about Wendy?' Bob asked.

'She's got her own house to run,' Gran interrupted. 'Lillian can manage. She's a strong girl.'

'She's got nothing better to do,' said Frank, who had been dragooned into staying and listening to the family conference.

To Lillian's surprise, it was Bob who defended her before she could open her mouth to protest. 'It means that Lillian has to give up her career. Is that all right by you, Lillian?'

Gran snorted. 'Career! Girls don't have careers! Very good thing to stop prancing around on a stage and do something useful, if you ask me.'

'Lillian?' Bob said.

It had been obvious to Lillian from the moment she'd arrived back that this was to be her role. She just hadn't been sure how long she was going to be needed. A few weeks didn't matter, career-wise. The panto was nearly at the end of its run and, though she would usually have been looking now for something else to fill in, there wouldn't be many jobs available till the summer season started. Now it looked as if it might not be just until her mother recovered from the hysterectomy. The future looked very unsure. But what could she say? She couldn't just walk out.

'Of course I'll stay home and look after Mum. For as long as it takes,' she said.

Nettie was still in hospital when Susan's baby was born. Bob travelled from the maternity hospital to the main one to tell his mother that she now had another beautiful grandson. Nettie tried to be pleased, but it was obvious to all her children that she was very low. She had expected the worst when she had her operation, and being told about the tumour had confirmed her fears. She took it as a death sentence.

When she was allowed home, Lillian tried to persuade her to have one of the guest rooms, which were lighter and more spacious. But Nettie only wanted the familiarity of the attic room that had always been hers. Lillian toiled up and down the stairs with dishes to tempt her mother's appetite, with magazines to interest her, with flowers to cheer her up. None of them worked. She got the family to club together to buy a small radio for her mother to listen to, but she couldn't be sure that she enjoyed having it on. She certainly never commented on it. Susan brought baby Neville to see her and Wendy called in with Coral and little Terrance. Nettie smiled sadly at them and stroked their soft heads, but after they had gone she said to Lillian that she wouldn't live to see them grow up.

By then it was April. It was all too obvious to Lillian that she was going to be needed at home for a good while longer. She had hoped that her mother would make a good recovery and perhaps be back on her feet again by the summer, but anyone with half a brain could see that that was not going to happen. Someone was needed to look after Nettie and the guest house, and the only someone available was her.

'It's so unfair!' Lillian raged out loud. 'Just when I got my solo!'

It wasn't just that she would be losing one summer season. Once you dropped off the radar, there were plenty of other young hopefuls there to take your place. And she had worked so hard to get where she was. Guilt and frustration chased each other round and round her head.

Lillian channeled it all into a fight about the annual spring clean.

'I'm not doing it all by myself,' she told Gran, folding her arms and looking rebellious.

'You'll have Frank to help you, and your father.'

'Huh! A fat lot of good they are. Besides, this place needs more than a clean. It needs redecorating from top to bottom.'

She had been putting a lot of thought into this, and she had discussed it at length with James. If the guest house was to have even a chance of making any money, it had to change radically.

'It needs bright colours and a comfortable lounge and another bathroom. People have nice houses now. Why would they want to come away and stay in a place like this? And we've got to be more welcoming too, make them feel at home instead of turfing them out every morning, rain or shine, and reading them a lot of rules.'

'It all sounds very sensible to me,' James said.

'It should do. I've stayed in enough places myself now to know what it's like from the other side of the fence, so to speak. And I've seen how it works in Blackpool, and which places are successful and which aren't. Personally, I'd like to close down the guest house altogether and convert the top floors into flats and let them. It'd be a much better way of making money. But Gran wouldn't even consider that. The guest house was her idea and she's going to stick with it whether we have guests in it or not.'

'You could use the flats idea as a bargaining tool,' James suggested.

'What?'

'Tell her that it's the only possible way to make a living out of the place, then back down and say you'll carry on with the guest house as long as it's done up. Your gran might not like it, but she knows that she's got to rely on you to do it, so you've got some leverage.'

'Yes—' A slow smile broke out over Lillian's face as she considered this. 'Yes, that could work. That's very clever.'

'It's the way to negotiate—start from an extreme position and work towards a compromise.'

Together they went all over the house, writing down what needed to be done and making a rough estimation of what it would all cost, so when Gran brought up the subject of the spring clean, Lillian was ready for her.

She tried the flat conversion gambit. Gran took the bait.

'What? Have strangers living over the top of us? Over my dead body! Whatever were you thinking of, you stupid girl? There's a good living to be had from a guest house, if only there was someone in the family willing to put their backs into it and make a go of it.'

Lillian told her that flats would be a good steady income all year and much less work than having paying guests for the summer. She kept up the argument for as long as she could, resorting to repeating herself when she ran out of things to say.

Gran got increasingly angry. 'I am not having this house made into flats. Never! Do you hear? Never! You're a stupid ungrateful little girl that knows nothing about the world, and you'll do what I say in my house.'

Lillian stood silent, letting her rant on. When she had finally run down, satisfied that she'd shouted Lillian into submission, Lillian produced what she hoped would be her winning shot.

'OK, Gran. So you don't like that idea. But if you want me to run Sunny View for you, then it's got to be done up, because nobody's going to want to stay in it like it is now.'

Gran was still in full fighting mood. 'You don't know what you're talking about. Not want to stay here? Of course they do.'

'So how many weekends were we full last summer?'

'All of them.'

'Really?'

'Of course. We're always full.'

Lillian let that slide. She knew it wasn't so, but Gran wasn't going to admit it.

'And what about weekdays? How many people came Saturday to Saturday?'

'Plenty.'

Lillian just stood and looked at her. She wasn't going to accuse her grandmother of lying.

'Gran, would you mind coming outside with me for a moment?' she asked, her voice all gentle reason.

It took a bit of persuading, but Gran did consent. Lillian led her down to the corner of the street by the seafront.

'Now,' she said, 'look up our road. Which properties stand out?'

Four of the other guest houses in the road had been redecorated in modern colours.

'That ridiculous pink thing, for a start. And the yellow one. Looks like a fairground.'

'People like bright colours now, Gran. It's not pensioners that come and stay with us, it's young people and families, and they want something modern. I agree about the pink— it's hideous. I was thinking of a nice smart blue and white.'

'Hmph. Well. If we did have it done, that might not look too bad.'

'It does have to be done, Gran. The paint's peeling. If people see peeling paint in the outside, they're going to think the inside's just as bad.'

'I'm not standing out here arguing in the street with you.'

'OK. We'll go in and I'll make us a nice cup of tea.'

She didn't win all at once. It took two more sessions to get Gran's consent to the outside being changed, and many more before she agreed that the inside was less than perfect. And then there was the question of money.

'You have to speculate to accumulate,' Lillian said.

'What sort of a silly thing to say is that?'

'It's what successful businessmen say. If we haven't the money, we'll have to borrow it.'

This produced another huge tirade from Gran on the subject of banks and how wicked they were.

'We could always raise a mortgage on the house,' Lillian suggested, sweetly innocent.

'Mortgage? That's the first step to giving them the roof over your head!'

And then Gran did something that took Lillian's breath

away. She produced a small key from her handbag and un-locked the door to the heavy old dresser in the corner of the room. Bending stiffly, she got out a shoe box and opened the lid. Inside were bundles of pound notes. Lillian just stared at them, astounded.

'Wasn't going to let those devils at the bank get their hands on this,' Gran said. 'You can get this work done, but I want every penny accounted for, d'you hear me? Every penny.'

'Whatever you say, Gran,' Lillian agreed.

But the work had hardly begun before Nettie was back in hospital again.

CHAPTER **26**

THE doorbell rang just as Lillian was about to take a cup of tea up to her mother.

'Damn,' she muttered, taking off her apron. She had hoped for half an hour or so of peace to sit with her mother and keep her company. She felt guilty about all the hours she lay upstairs there in the attic by herself.

She checked her hair in the hall mirror and pasted a welcoming smile on her face before opening the front door. A young couple stood there. A lifetime of assessing potential guests told her that they weren't married.

'Good afternoon,' she said brightly, acutely aware of Gran's door just behind her. If Gran came and stuck her nose in now, these two wouldn't have a chance.

The young man looked at a point over her shoulder. The girl looked at her feet.

'Oh—er—afternoon. Right—er—you got a room for to-night, like? I mean, like, a double room?' the man asked.

They definitely weren't married. Married couples just assumed they would be given a double room.

'Yes, we have. Would you like to see it?' Lillian asked.

'No, no, that's all right. Anything—I mean—'

'I'm sure it's nice,' the girl said.

Lillian led them upstairs to the second best bedroom. Two rooms let on a Tuesday. That wasn't bad for June. She showed them where the bathroom was, explained about breakfast times and gave them their keys.

'I'll leave the guest book on the hall table. Perhaps you could sign it before you go out?' she said. She wasn't going to embarrass them by standing there watching while they wrote down *Mr and Mrs Smith*.

'Right, yes, thanks,' the man said.

'Thanks,' the girl repeated.

They were obviously just dying for her to go and leave them alone.

'Enjoy your stay,' Lillian said, and shut the door behind her.

As she started back down the stairs, she could hear them burst out laughing. Lillian envied them. How lucky they were to have each other.

Gran's head appeared round her door as Lillian reached the hall.

'Who were those people? Did you let them have a room? They didn't look respectable to me.'

'Yes, I did. They were a perfectly nice young couple,' Lillian told her, poker-faced, thinking as she did so that it was a good thing there were plenty of rooms available, and she hadn't had to put them in the one above Gran's.

'I don't know about that—'

'Well, I do. We can't go turning away good money,' Lillian said firmly. 'I'm making some tea. Do you want some?'

'About time too.'

Lillian left one cup and some biscuits with Gran and took the tray up to the attic. She tapped on the door. As usual, there was no answer. She went in anyway.

'Mum?' she said softly. 'You awake?'

There was a sigh and a faint, 'Yes,' from the bed.

'Come on then, sit yourself up. Nice tea and biscuits for you.'

She pulled her mother gently but firmly into a sitting position and rearranged the pillows so her back would be supported. Then she put the cup into her hands and sat down herself.

'I just let number two. That's good, isn't it? One room let all week and now a casual as well. Not bad for a Tuesday, is it? And there's still time for another one to turn up on the doorstep.'

'Shouldn't think so,' Nettie said.

'Well, you never know. Wendy'll be here soon to see you. That'll be nice, won't it?'

'Mmm,' Nettie said.

'It's good now she can let us know by phone. I can't get over how wonderful it is not to have to go to the box any more.'

'Terrible noise. Makes me jump,' Nettie commented.

'It is a bit noisy, yes. But ever so useful.'

She chattered on for a while, not getting much reaction from her mother. Since her second operation, Nettie had retreated even further into herself.

'Mum, why don't you come down this evening and sit in Gran's room for a while? You wouldn't have to get dressed, just put your dressing gown on and your slippers, and Frank and

I could help you down the stairs. Then you could watch the telly. That'd be nice, wouldn't it?'

There was no reaction on her mother's face. 'Too tired,' she whispered.

'But I'm sure you'd feel better for a change of scenery, Mum. And there's sure to be something nice to watch. A variety show or something.'

She liked variety shows herself. It was worth having to sit with Gran in order to see the dancers and assess how good they were. Last week there had been a live broadcast from Blackpool. As the camera had panned along the row of bright-faced girls, Lillian had recognised three people she knew. She groaned aloud. That could have been her, live on the telly.

But her mother was not interested. 'No.'

'The doctor said you shouldn't be just lying here all the time. He said you ought to get up each day, even if it's only for a bit.'

This time her mother didn't even answer. The half drunk tea-cup wobbled in her hand. Lillian jumped up to take it from her.

'You've not had your biscuit, Mum. It's rich tea, your favourite.'

'Not hungry.'

Nettie never was hungry. She hardly ate more than a nibble of any meal. Lillian had to resort to giving her invalid food like Benger's and Lucozade to try to build her up.

Lillian chattered on for a while, but was guiltily relieved when the phone rang. She ran down the stairs and snatched up the handset.

'Sunny View Guest House.'

'Madam—you have good beds for my four wives and stable for my camel?' asked a deep voice with a peculiar foreign accent.

Lillian's spirits soared. 'Certainly, sir. Four hundred pounds a night,' she said, laughing.

'Is cheap at the price.'

'You bet it is. Those camels take a lot of clearing up after.'

James dropped the accent. 'How's it going, Lindy? Giving the Ritz a run for its money?'

'Just about. And you?'

'It's frantic here. Haven't stopped all day. Listen, Lindy, I've been thinking. It's about time you learnt to drive.'

'Me, drive? But I haven't got a car, and not likely to have one, either.'

'You never know. And, anyway, I can always lend you one. Just think how useful it would be if your mum had to go into hospital again, not having to wait for buses.'

'You're right there.'

The way things were going, it looked very likely that her mother would be back in hospital again before the year was out.

'Of course I am. You busy this evening?'

There were plenty of things she had to do. A pile of ironing, for a start. But that could wait if James had other plans.

'Well—'

'I'll be round at half-seven. Wear some sensible shoes.'

'OK—'

'Gotta go. See you this evening!'

Lillian put down the phone with a squeal of delight. James and a driving lesson! The world was suddenly a brighter place.

Just as she turned to go back to the kitchen, the doorbell rang again. This time it was Wendy, heavily made up as usual, beautifully dressed and her hair newly styled. The children were both expensively got up and Coral carried a doll that was almost as big as she was. Behind them at the kerb was Terry's second best Jaguar, with one of his sidekicks in the driving seat. Lillian took them all up to the attic, then went to tackle the ironing. Twenty minutes or so later, Wendy came down to join her in the kitchen. Lillian made more tea, gave Coral biscuits to eat and saucepans to play with and settled down with baby Terrance in her arms. He was a sweet little thing, despite looking alarmingly like his father. She hoped he wouldn't grow up to be like him in character.

'She's no better, is she?' Wendy said, glancing up at the ceiling to indicate their mother.

'No.' Lillian sighed. 'I can't get her interested in anything. She likes it when you come, though, and the babies. It's a pity you can't come more often.'

'Oh—well—it'd mean asking Terry for the car.'

'You ought to learn to drive,' Lillian told her. 'I am. James is going to teach me.'

'I don't think Terry'd like that.'

'Why ever not? He could afford to buy you a little car of your own, and then you wouldn't have to use one of his drivers.'

'I know. I just don't think he'd like it, that's all.'

As Wendy talked, Lillian studied her face. She was sure that under that make-up there was a big bruise.

'Have you hurt yourself, Wend?' she asked.

Her sister's hand flew to the place on her jaw. As she did so, the long sleeve she was wearing slipped back to reveal another bruise on her arm.

'Oh—that. I tripped and fell against a door. These stupid stilettos.'

'You caught your arm as well, did you?'

'What? Yes.'

'You weren't carrying Terrance at the time, were you?'

'No. No, thank goodness. He was—er—in his pram. Look, I'd better go and see Gran. Would you mind the kids for me? She doesn't like their noise.'

Lillian was glad to oblige, but her vague fears about Wendy were beginning to crystallise into something more definite. She decided to study her sister more closely when she saw her. Her family was nothing but a worry. Thank goodness she had this driving lesson to look forward to.

'See you later, Mum!'

James gave his mother a wave and went out of the front door, conscious of the lightness in his step. He was looking forward to teaching Lillian to drive. She was always fun to be with, and he was sure she would get the hang of controlling a car easily enough.

Sunny View looked a different place now that she was practically in charge. It was easy to see why they were getting more customers. She had a good head for business, did Lindy.

'I'm really excited about this,' she admitted as she opened the door to him.

'Me too,' he agreed.

They smiled at each other. She had a lovely smile, with just the right hint of mischief in it.

He drove her out to one of the industrial estates at the back of town, making a running commentary on what he was doing as he went.

'…right turn coming up—mirror, indicate, hand signal, move over, clutch and brake, change gear, check behind….'

'It all sounds very complicated.'

'It does at first. But you'll soon get the hang of it; you're very bright. Once you can control the car, then you can concentrate on the roadcraft,' he told her.

'I just hope I don't damage your baby.'

James patted the steering wheel. 'I'm sure you wouldn't dare.'

Just as he had hoped, the roads round the industrial estate were deserted. He showed her the controls, demonstrated moving off, slowing down and stopping, then sat her behind the wheel and got her to adjust the seat and mirror.

'Right, now you do it.'

Lillian nodded. She did look a bit nervous now but she followed his instructions to the letter. The car began to move.

'I'm doing it! I'm driving!'

'Good, good—don't get overexcited—slow down now, brake *and* clutch. Well done!'

He got her to do it again, this time getting into second gear. Up and down and round the empty roads they went for nearly an hour. She kangaroo-started two or three times, nearly forgot to turn a corner as she searched for a gear and once he had to grab the steering wheel as she narrowly missed a lamp post. But with each try she was a little more in control.

'That was brilliant. You're a natural,' James told her. 'Did you enjoy it?'

He could see that she was shaking from the effort and concentration.

'It was terrific.'

'Just wait till you can go out on your own. Do you remember what it was like when you first had a bike of your own?'

'I do. It was wonderful, just being able to get on and whizz off wherever you want, with the wind in your hair and everything. And so fast, compared with walking.'

'Driving a car is all that and more,' he assured her. 'Get yourself a provisional licence, then we can go out on the proper roads. Now, how about fish and chips on the seafront?'

'Perfect,' Lillian agreed.

She was so easy to be with. A girlfriend would say that chips made her fat, or she'd already eaten or something.

James drove down to the Golden Mile and they sat on a bench facing the sea with the fish and chips on their knees. Lillian tucked in with gusto.

'It's so nice to get out in the evening,' she said. 'Just to see life going on all around you, you know? It's so samey stuck indoors all the time. It's only the PGs who liven the place up a bit.'

She told him about the young unmarried couple who had arrived that afternoon.

James laughed. 'So your Gran didn't scare them off, then?'

'Gran doesn't have it all her own way any more. It's like you said back in the spring; she knows that she's only got me to rely on. That really got me thinking, that did. I don't stand any nonsense, and she doesn't argue with me half as much as she used to.'

'Good for you. You're making a real success of Sunny View. I thought how different it looked now when I picked you up this evening.'

'It's OK. I don't know about success. But it's early in the season yet, there's time to get more people in.'

'You must miss your old life, though.'

'Oh, I do, terribly. I miss the girls and I miss the challenge of learning new dances and I really, really miss the buzz of performing.' Her voice was full of longing.

'It must be really hard. But you'd never be able to live with yourself if you upped and left your mum.'

Lillian sighed. 'I know. There isn't a choice. I have to be here.'

'From a purely selfish point of view, I'm glad. It means I get to see more of you,' James told her.

Lillian flushed. 'There is that,' she said.

He had finished his chips and she had nearly got to the end of hers. She chased the last little bits inside the greasy paper.

'What about you?' she asked. 'How's your big dream coming on? It sounded like you were busy today.'

'We were, very.' James screwed up his chip paper and lobbed it into a nearby litter basket. This was what had been occupying his thoughts for some time now. Like Lillian, he had found that his big dream was not quite what he had thought it would be. He had his workshop and it was very successful, and While-U-Wait Exhausts was building up well, but now he realised that this was just the start. There were difficult decisions to be made.

'I've been turning it over and over in my head and I can't quite make my mind up what's for the best,' he admitted.

Lillian turned to him, clearly interested.

'What's the problem?' she asked.

It was so good to be able to lay it all out before her. She was more than a handy sounding-board; she had good judgement. He knew he could trust her to give an honest opinion.

'Well, there's at least three alternatives,' he told her. 'I could close the auto repairs and use both workshops just for exhausts, but that would mean either putting Tony out of work or employing him fitting exhausts, and he's too skilled a man to want to do that all day long.'

Lillian nodded. She had met Tony, a reliable older man who did a lot of the general repair work while James made sure the less skilled fitters were putting the exhausts on correctly and oversaw both businesses.

'Or—?' she prompted.

'Or I could leave Tony in charge of repairs and move the exhausts to a bigger premises somewhere else.'

'That sounds sensible.'

'Yes. Well, that probably is the best solution—'

He had considered doing that. It was the safe thing to do. But the prospect of bigger things lured him on.

'So what's the third idea?' Lillian asked.

This was what had him waking up sweating in the middle of the night, the thought that if he had the balls to try it, he could make it really big. He took a breath. This was the first time he had told anyone else. Supposing she thought he was out of his mind?

'The third idea is to think beyond just one little local enterprise. I was right about the exhausts. There is a market for on the spot specialist fitting, and if there's a market in Southend, then it's the same elsewhere and I should get in there before someone else steals it. What I'd like to do is to open up Kershaw's While-U-Wait Exhausts in other towns. Chelmsford next, maybe, then Benfleet, Grays, into the outer suburbs, up into Colchester and Ipswich—the sky's the limit, really.'

'Wow!' Lillian's face was alight with an excitement that matched his own. 'If anyone can make it work, you can.'

James glowed. 'Thanks.'

'I mean it. But—' She frowned, thinking. 'It's the finance, isn't it? You haven't got a gran with a shoe box of notes hidden away and, anyway, it would need a pretty big shoe box for what you're thinking of.'

Trust Lindy to get to the heart of the matter.

'Yup. You got it. Though I think I could get a bank loan if I show them my books,' he said. He was confident that his bank manager would back him on this. He'd proved himself as a good bet so far.

'So what's the problem?'

There wouldn't be a problem if he was on his own. He could take risks and if it all came crashing down round his ears, he could always go back to repairing cars again. But he wasn't on his own. He had his mother to consider. If his dad had lived, his mum would be living in a nice house of her own by now and, for as long as he could remember, it had been his ambition to make that up to her.

'If I do that I can't buy a house, which I could do if I carried on with the business as it is at the moment,' he explained.

'Ah.'

There was a silence. They both watched a green and cream tram trundling down the pier.

'Mmm,' Lillian said. 'Difficult. Look—let's leave Tony and your mum out of it for now. If it was just you, which way would you want to go?'

'Expand. Definitely,' James said, without hesitation.

'And that could make lots of money?'

'That's the idea, yes. It could all go belly-up, though. That's the chance you have to take.'

'OK—' Lillian spoke slowly, evidently thinking her way through it. 'Now, is your mum happy where you are now?'

'Well, yes. She likes the flat and the neighbours are nice and it's not too much for her to manage,' James admitted. 'But that's not the point—'

'It is the point. If she likes it where you are, then she won't mind waiting a bit longer, will she? And if you make lots of money in a few years' time, you can buy a house then.'

'Well—yes—'

It was as if a light had been shone through the fog in his mind. At first he couldn't believe it was as simple as that, but the more he thought about it, the more obvious it became.

'Yes, you're right. I had it so fixed in my mind that I should buy a house as soon as I could afford it, that I couldn't see another way round it. Mind you, if I expand and it fails, I'll never be able to buy a house.'

Lillian smiled at him. 'But you're not going to fail, are you?'

He smiled back, lifted by her faith in him. 'Not if I can help it.'

'Now, about Tony—'

He had to laugh. 'Blimey, Lindy, have you got an answer for him too?'

'Possibly. How about making him manager of While-U-Wait in Southend while you're setting up the next one? You know you can trust him to do a decent job.'

'Lindy, you're a genius!' James grabbed her and planted a kiss on her cheek. 'A total genius! What would I do without you?'

Lillian leaned into him. He could feel the softness of her body against his, the swell of her breasts, the pressure of her thigh. She was warm and pliant and wholly desirable. His own body responded with a surge of need. Embarrassed, he pulled back. He had to put a lid on this. This wasn't right. He had girlfriends. Lindy was more important than a mere girlfriend. She was supposed to be his best mate, little sister, even. He jumped up and pulled her to her feet.

'Come on,' he said. 'We're going to have a drink to celebrate the success of Sunny View and the expansion of While-U-Wait.'

CHAPTER 27

'AND where did you get to last night, young man?' Gran asked.

Frank shrugged. 'Just out.'

'It was three o'clock in the morning when you came in. I heard you.'

'Wasn't me. Must of been one of the PGs.'

Lillian doubted it. All the people they had in at the moment were families or older couples. They weren't likely to be out to that time. She slid fried eggs onto plates already loaded with bacon, tomatoes and fried slices.

'Can you bring the toast, Frank? I got my hands full here,' she asked.

'What d'you think I am, a flaming skivvy?' Frank growled.

To Lillian's surprise, Gran came to her defence.

'Don't leave your sister to do everything, boy. And stop slouching. Stand up straight and put your shoulders back. Nobody would think you'd been in the army.'

Frank gave her a look that would have shrivelled a lesser woman, got to his feet and picked up the loaded toast racks. As they went along the corridor from the kitchen to the guests' breakfast room, Lillian hissed, 'I know damn well it wasn't the PGs coming in at three. What's it worth for me to keep quiet about it?'

Frank glared at her. 'Sweet FA, sis. I don't give a toss what the old bat thinks. I'm going to be out of here before long.'

They reached the breakfast room door before Lillian could ask how he was going to manage to leave home, so she just said, 'Good.' Once inside, she was too busy to give her irritating brother another thought. As well as taking orders, delivering breakfasts and clearing used plates, some of the guests wanted information, one couple had a complaint about noise and others just wanted to chat. Lillian did the best she could for all of them, hurried back to the kitchen with the dirty dishes and got going on the last two full English breakfasts.

'Any chance of food for the rest of us?' her father grumbled as she threw bacon and tomato into the pan.

'Yeah, yeah, I'm onto it. I'm doing yours with this lot,' Lillian told him. 'And yours, Frank, so don't start, right?'

As she did so, it occurred to her that she would never have spoken to her father like that a year ago. Frank, maybe. She had never given in to her brother. But her father's word had always been next to Gran's in the house.

'PGs come first,' Gran said, backing her up. And then she said something that really astonished Lillian. 'Three quarters full in the first week of September is good. The girl's not doing a bad job.'

From Gran, that was high praise. Lillian nearly dropped the egg she was cracking. Her father and Frank realised this as well and went quiet.

'Th-thanks, Gran,' she stammered.

'Hmm. Well. Don't let it go to your head,' Gran told her.

Lillian turned it over in her mind as she hurried through the day's chores. Once the PGs were fed she went to see if she could coax her mother into eating anything, then helped her out of bed and onto the commode she now used, assisted her in washing, changed her nightdress, made her bed and helped her back into it.

'Gran actually said I wasn't doing a bad job. Isn't that amazing?' she said as she gently brushed her mother's thin hair.

'Mmm,' Nettie agreed.

It was about as much reaction as Lillian was going to get. She still found it very frustrating not being able to get through to her mother.

'I thought I might go over and see Wendy today,' she persisted. 'She said Terry was going away on business for a couple of days, so it'll be safe.'

This time there was no answer at all. Lillian chattered on a bit longer, put the radio on and made sure the little brass bell was within reach.

'Now, remember to ring if you need anything. I can pop up any time,' she said.

'Right,' her mother whispered. Her eyes were already closed.

Lillian sighed and went down to get on with the rest of her jobs. Once the kitchen was cleaned, there were the bedrooms and bathroom to see to, the hall, stairs and PGs' dining room, and then Gran's room. Then there were Gran's errands to run and the shopping to get for the family's midday dinner. Her father only had a bare hour to get home, eat and get back to work again, so the meal had to be on the table on the dot of ten past twelve. When that was cleared away and washed up, she was finally free for two or three hours until prospective guests might be expected to start calling. Lillian checked that Gran and her mother were both all right and went to get her old bike out of the shed.

As she cycled along the seafront, she felt her spirits rise. It was a beautiful late summer's day, the tide was in, the sea was sparkling and the sun was warm on her back. Despite her hard morning's work, energy surged through her legs as she pedalled along, revelling in her brief freedom. Good old bike. She had James to thank for this. She wondered how he was getting on today. He was over in Chelmsford, looking at premises for his new branch of While-U-Wait Exhausts.

Beyond the Halfway House pub, the seafront opened up, with gardens and tennis courts and bowling greens on the inland side of the road. Cheerful Southend was behind her and she was in sober, well-heeled Thorpe Bay. She turned up a tree-lined side road and again into Wendy's street. Big detached family houses stood on each side, with driveways and front gardens with trees in and big bay windows and fancy porches. Unlike the houses on Lillian's street, every one was different and all had plenty of space around them. She leaned her bike against the porch of Wendy's house and rang the bell.

No one came. Lillian tried again, wondering as she did so if she should have phoned beforehand. Maybe Wendy was taking advantage of Terry's being away by going out. Still nobody came to the door, but from somewhere inside the house she could hear a child crying. Lillian tried one more time and backed it up by opening the letterbox and calling through it.

'Wendy! It's me, Lillian. Come and open the door!'

This time she heard footsteps and saw the silhouette of her sister through the thick stained glass. The door opened a crack.

'Lill? It…it's not a good time—'

There was a thudding of small feet, a cry of 'Mummy!' and what sounded to Lillian like a gasp of pain from Wendy. Lillian pushed at the door, opening it enough to put her head round and catch a glimpse of her sister. She cried out with shock. Wendy's face was swollen and bruised, her eyes blackened.

'My God, Wendy! What on earth happened?'

'It's nothing—'

'It is not nothing.'

Lillian slid round the door and closed it behind her. Wendy curled defensively round her small daughter, vainly trying to hide her injuries. Little Coral wriggled and struggled in her arms while Wendy muttered, 'It's all right, darling. It's all right.'

'It bloody isn't all right,' Lillian said.

She took Coral from her sister, swinging her onto her hip and promising her biscuits. Then she put her other arm round Wendy, who flinched at her touch.

'Come on,' she insisted. 'Into the kitchen.'

Wendy looked even worse in the bright light of the kitchen. Lillian sat her down at the big table, put the kettle on and found biscuits for Coral. Looking out of the back window, she saw that baby Terrance was safely asleep in his pram in the garden. She made coffee and set a cup before Wendy, who was now quietly crying.

'Now,' she said, gently but firmly. 'Tell. What's been going on? And don't say that you fell or that you bumped into a door. Terry's done this to you, hasn't he?'

Wendy nodded, tears falling from her poor swollen eyes and running down her battered face. Upset, Coral started crying too. Lillian took her onto her lap, but kept her eyes on Wendy.

'He never meant to—' Wendy sobbed.

'That's rubbish, Wend. You can't not mean to do damage like this.'

'I annoy him—'

'Maybe, but he doesn't have to hit you.'

'I deserve it. I'm stupid—'

'No one deserves this. Wendy, you look dreadful.'

This only produced more tears. 'Not…pretty…any… more…' Wendy sobbed.

Lillian realised that she had said the wrong thing. Wendy had always put so much store on her good looks.

'You are still pretty, Wendy. You're more beautiful than ever, without the bruises. It's not you. It's him that's done this.'

Slowly, the tale came out. Terry hit her because she let him down, said the wrong things, didn't run the house correctly, looked at his friends the wrong way.

'I can't do anything right,' Wendy sobbed. 'I'm so stupid.'

'You're not stupid, Wend.'

'I am, I am. He wishes he'd never married me.'

Guilt dragged at Lillian's guts. She was partly responsible for this. She had persuaded Wendy to tell Terry about the baby.

'Do you wish you'd never married him?' she asked.

Wendy shook her head. 'No, no. I love him.'

'But—'

Lillian was dumbfounded. How could her sister possibly still love a man who did this to her?

'You can't let him get away with this,' she decided, standing up. 'I'm going to phone the police.'

'No, no!' Wendy made a grab for her arm. 'Don't! I don't want you to!'

'But we've got to stop him, Wendy.'

'No, please, please, you mustn't—'

Wendy was panic stricken. She held on to Lillian's arm with
manic strength. Coral started wailing again. And, as if sens-
ing the family feeling, outside in the garden little Terrance
started to cry. Wendy stood in the middle of it all, looking
from one child to the other and back to Lillian, not knowing
what to do first.

'You go and get the baby,' Lillian said.

'No, not if you're going to phone the police. You mustn't
phone the police.'

'No p'lice, no p'lice!' Coral repeated in her ear-splitting voice.

'All right, all right,' Lillian said. 'Look, I'll get the baby.'

Gradually, she managed to soothe everybody. By the time
she did so, the clock on the kitchen wall was showing nearly
four. Lillian was torn. She had to get home and see to her
mother before making family tea.

'I've got to go,' she said. 'Are you going to be all right,
Wendy?'

'Yes, yes. But promise me you won't phone the police.'

By now it had occurred to Lillian that it would be no use
anyway. The police did not interfere in what went on between
man and wife.

'All right. I promise,' she said.

Wendy gave a great sigh of relief. The tension went out
of her body.

'But what can I do to help?' Lillian wanted to know.

'Nothing. And don't tell no one. Promise? I couldn't bear
it if you told. It's all right as long as nobody knows.'

Reluctantly, Lillian agreed to this as well, but made a mental note that it was only until she had decided what was the
best course of action.

'I'll come back tomorrow and see if you're OK,' she said.

'No!' Instantly, Wendy was trembling again. 'No, Terry might be back. He wouldn't want you to see me like—'

She broke off. No, Lillian thought grimly, she wasn't surprised that Terry didn't want anyone to see her looking like that. He ought to be ashamed of himself.

'OK. But look, you phone me when it's all right to come round.'

This time it was she who extracted the promise.

James drove back from Chelmsford with his head whirling with plans. This was the start of the big time. It was both exhilarating and terrifying, and what he needed was someone to share it all with. Fleetingly he considered calling round to see Bob and Susan, but he dismissed the idea as soon as it came into his head. Neither of them would understand what he was aiming at. They would just think him irresponsible to be risking so much. It was no use talking to his latest girlfriend either. She was a pretty thing, and very nice. Too nice, really, for he knew that she would just listen wide-eyed and make all the right noises but not have anything of substance to say. So he did what he'd known he was going to do all along. He stopped off at the next phone box he came to and rang Lillian.

'Sunny View Guest House.'

'Hi, Lindy! Your friendly neighbourhood exhaust man here.'

'Oh—James—'

She did not sound especially glad to hear from him. Disappointment dragged at his insides. This was all wrong. Lillian was always happy when he rang.

'What's the matter, Lindy?'

'Oh—nothing—'

'You need to get out more. Listen, how about a driving lesson this evening? It's about time we put you in for the test.'

'I don't know, James—'

'Oh, come on. There's something I want to show you. Half-seven all right?'

'OK, yes. Half seven. Got to go now; my mum needs me.'

He needed her too, James realised, then reproved himself for being so selfish. Poor Lindy. She had her mother to look after, her grandmother to appease, that useless lump of a father and slimy brother to feed and clean up after and the guest house to run. She could do without him leaning on her as well. He would take her out somewhere nice some time soon, give her a treat. She deserved it. And in the meantime he would make sure she passed her driving test.

He tied the L-plates on the Mini and arrived at the door of Sunny View dead on time.

'You're looking pleased with yourself,' Lillian said.

'I'm on my way, kiddo. And all due to you.'

'Really?'

'Really. Talking to you helps me sort my ideas out. Now, let's see if you can pull away without me reminding you what to do.'

For the next fifteen minutes or so, he gave her directions and corrected her driving. Then Lillian began to realise that they were not taking their usual route round the town.

'What are we doing here?' she asked as she drove along the main road out of town.

'We're going to Chelmsford,' he told her.

'Chelmsford! What for?'

'We're going to look at two possible places for While-U-Wait. I need your opinion.'

'Oh—'

'So now you can take her up to sixty. It's safe enough here.'

'Sixty! I've never been that fast before.'

'You'll be fine. You're a natural.'

By the time they got to Chelmsford, Lillian was shaking and making silly mistakes. She pulled over and stopped the car.

'You take over. I can't concentrate.'

It wasn't like her to give up. James was worried.

'What's up, Lindy? You're not yourself this evening.'

'Nothing. At least—no, nothing really. Just family. You know.'

James did know. 'They don't deserve you,' he said. 'Slaving away for them all.'

'It's not that, it's—' She hesitated.

'What?'

'Nothing.' Lillian got out of the car and came round to the passenger side. 'Go on, get in the driver's seat. Where are these premises of yours?'

James showed her the two places he had chosen out of those available. They chewed over the pros and cons of each one until he came to a decision. It was the one he had preferred all along, the more expensive one. Answering Lillian's questions made him certain that the investment would be worthwhile.

They went for a drink.

'Here's to the Exhaust King of Essex,' Lillian said.

They clinked glasses.

'I'll either be a king or a bankrupt. I'm really going out on a limb with this,' James said.

'It's a brilliant idea. You're going to be a huge success,' Lillian assured him.

Warmed by her faith, James talked on for a while about his plans, until he realised that her attention had wandered.

'—or I could give it all up and be a pig farmer,' he said.

'Well, yes, you could—what? Pig farmer? What are you talking about?'

'You're not with me, are you?'

'I am, honest.'

'Something's bothering you.'

Lillian sighed. 'I'm worried about Wendy, that's all.'

'Wendy? What about her?'

'I said I wouldn't—it's just that Terry. I don't think he's treating her right.'

It didn't come as any surprise to James. 'I never did think the bastard was good enough for her. What's he done now?'

Lillian's eyes slid away from his. 'Oh, well—you know— Wendy never seems happy these days.'

How could she be happy, married to a man like that?

'Poor girl. She deserves better. Look, Lindy, I don't know what I can do to help—I mean, she's not going to leave him, is she?'

After all, wives did not leave their husbands when there were children to be considered.

'No. She says she still loves him.'

James frowned into his drink. It frustrated him that this was one problem to which he couldn't see a solution.

'There's not a lot to be said then, is there? I don't have any influence over Dempsey. I don't know who has. He's a law unto himself. But listen, Lindy. If ever you feel there's something I can do, don't hesitate to ask.'

'Thanks.' She smiled at him. 'I'll remember that.'

After he had dropped her back at Sunny View, James drove down to the seafront and sat for a while looking at the crowds swirling along the Golden Mile. The illuminations were better than ever this year, thousands of lights forming starbursts and flowers and moving cartoon characters. People came down from London in the hundreds on trains and coaches to see them, to drink in the seafront pubs and spend their money in Terry Dempsey's amusement arcades. And, as he contemplated this, James realised that he no longer felt the searing jealousy that he once had of Dempsey. He loathed and despised the man, but he didn't envy him his possession of Wendy. The spell was broken. All he felt for Wendy was sadness that such a lovely girl should be shackled to a man who made her unhappy.

CHAPTER 28

'OI!'

Lillian jumped. She was folding a pile of towels at the kitchen table and thinking about James and his latest girlfriend, and now here was this furtive face looking round the back door.

'Your Frank in?'

He was a thin-faced young man with a shifty look to him. Lillian was transported back to that long-ago time when James had rescued her from Frank's cronies.

'No, he didn't come home last night,' she said.

Gran was furious about it. She did like to know where everyone was.

'You sure?' the young man asked.

Lillian put down the towel and turned to face him. 'What's it to you?' she countered.

The young man gave her a filthy look. 'Don't you go giving me no lip, see? I want to know, that's all.'

Lillian wasn't taking any of that. She wasn't a kid any more. She'd dealt with types like him before. 'Well, I want to know and all, so we're quits, aren't we? Now, you can just get out of my kitchen, OK?'

'If I find you been lying—'

Lillian took a step forward. 'You trying to threaten me? Who are you? What's your name?'

He didn't like that. 'None o' your bleeding business,' he said, and left.

'Good riddance,' Lillian muttered to herself. When Frank came home, she was going to kill him.

He didn't appear till early evening, when Lillian was once again in the kitchen, washing up the tea things.

'Where've you been?' she asked. 'You better watch it— Gran's after your hide.'

'So what? She can go boil her head. Any grub going?'

'There's bread. You can make yourself a sandwich.' She wasn't going to start cooking for him.

Frank grumbled a bit, then slapped some marg and jam on a couple of slices of bread and took a massive bite. 'Gotta go,' he mumbled through his mouthful, and made for the door.

'Where are you off to now?' Lillian called after him.

The slam of the door was the only reply.

Lillian stared out into the gloom of the back yard. She didn't like this. Something was up. She was proved right an hour later when there was loud knocking at the front door. She hurried to open it and found herself confronted by the police.

A plain clothes policeman stepped forward and waved his ID in front of her face.

'Detective Sergeant Phillips, miss. Frank Parker live here?'

'Yes,' Lillian said. 'Why?'

'We'd like to speak to him.'

He made to step inside. Lillian stood with one hand on the door and the other on the frame, blocking the entrance.

'He's not in.'

'Then we'll have to search the house, miss. We have a warrant—' A piece of paper was briefly held up.

Lillian was horrified. A search warrant! This didn't happen to people like them. Only criminals had their houses searched. The unease that she had been feeling escalated into a sense of doom. Shaking, she stepped back and opened the door. The hall seemed to be filled with large bodies in navy uniform. At that moment, Gran appeared round the door of her room, closely followed by Doug, who had been watching the television with her.

'What's happening? What are all these policemen doing in my house?'

'Searching the premises, madam. We'll start here, if that's all right with you. And miss, would you show me Frank Parker's room?'

Lillian left Gran arguing with two police constables and led the detective and another uniformed man upstairs. She remembered the shoe box full of notes. What if Gran had another one stashed away? She wouldn't put it past her. Would the police believe that it was an old woman's life savings, or would they think it was the result of whatever Frank had been up to? Her stomach churned. And what about her mother? Surely they wouldn't search her room?

'Can you be quiet, please?' she asked as the men clumped up the stairs behind her. 'My mother's very ill and she's in bed in the room next to Frank's. I don't want her frightened by all this.'

Then another thought came to her. If Frank had hidden anything since last night, it wouldn't be indoors. He had only got as far as the kitchen. Her mind whirred, grappling with the conflicting loyalties. She had to protect her mother, she didn't want the house turned upside down, but, on the other hand, she didn't want to direct the police straight to something that might incriminate her brother.

She watched, appalled, as the men ripped the sheets off the bed, turned over the mattress and started pulling the drawers out of the chest and turning them out. This was awful, awful. Were they going to do the same to her room? Were they going through Gran's like this? She put her head round the door of her mother's room. Nettie had the bedspread pulled up to her chin with both thin hands. Her terrified eyes looked back at Lillian.

'It… It's all right, Mum,' Lillian said, trying her hardest to sound reassuring. 'Just some men looking for something in Frank's room. Nothing to worry about, really. They'll soon be gone.'

Nettie said nothing, but a small whimpering noise came from her throat.

Lillian closed the door and stood at the threshold of Frank's room. She had to stop them from frightening her mother.

'Wait—listen—' she said.

The detective looked up. 'Just doing our job, miss.'

'I know, I know,' she placated. 'But I just thought—Frank called in for just a few minutes earlier this evening. He hadn't been in for—oh—twenty-four hours before that. But, the thing is, he only came into the kitchen and then he was away again, so whatever you're looking for, it might be in the sheds in the yard.'

'That so, miss?' the detective gave her a hard look. 'Only just remembered that, have you?'

Behind him, the uniformed man was now rifling through the wardrobe.

'Well, yes—I didn't think—look, I don't want you going through my mother's room like this. She's really sick—'

The detective looked sceptical. 'So you said, miss. You stay right there, right? Where I can see you. Then, when we've finished here, we'll look outside.'

It took her several minutes to realise that he didn't trust her not to go and move whatever Frank might have hidden. She felt sick with humiliation and anger. He thought she was some sort of—what was it?—accessory to a crime. She hardly knew whether she most wanted to cry or scream or get hold of Frank and shake him until he rattled. How dared he bring this on his family?

Nothing untoward was found in Frank's room, so they went downstairs again. As they went past Gran's room, Lillian could hear her berating the policemen and them being very polite in return. She smothered the start of a hysterical giggle. Trust Gran to hold up, whatever the situation. If it came to a contest between Gran and a young police officer, her money was on Gran.

It was cold and damp outside in the yard. Lillian shivered and wrapped her cardigan more firmly around her as the policemen shone powerful torches first in the old wash house with its copper and stone sink and mangle, then in the shed where she kept her bike. They had hardly been in there half a minute before the uniformed man gave a shout of triumph.

'Look at this, sir.'

It was a large cardboard box full of cartons of cigarettes.

Lillian was filled with helpless fury. How could Frank be so stupid as to put them there? A further search produced a crowbar.

'This yours, miss?'

'No. Never seen it before,' Lillian said.

When she got hold of her brother…and then she fetched up against another dreadful dilemma. What was she going to do when Frank made another appearance?

She didn't have very long to make her mind up. Just five minutes after the police left, Lillian was making a soothing pot of tea for everyone when Frank turned up at the back door again.

'They gone?' he asked.

'Frank! What the hell—?'

'Shut up, sis. I had enough trouble for one day. I'm going to bed.'

'You are not!'

All at once, she knew what she was going to do.

'If you think I'm going to protect you, you've got another think coming. I only just stopped them from going all through Mum's room. Just think what that might have done to her!'

Frank stared at her. 'You're not going to shop me, are you? Your own flesh and blood?'

'No, but I'm not going to lie for you either. You go now and hole up with one of your fine friends, and I won't tell the police you've been here. But you're not to come back, do you hear? I won't have you back here making Mum even sicker than she is already.'

Frank couldn't believe she was serious. Lillian resorted to walking up the hall towards the phone.

'OK, if you won't go, I'm calling 999.'

From Gran's room, the TV was blaring. Lillian prayed it was covering the noise of her row with Frank. Her hand hovered over the receiver.

'You bitch!' Frank spat. 'All right, I'm going. Bleeding traitor! You're no sister of mine.'

'And no brother of mine is a thief and a liar!' Lillian hissed back.

It was the last thing she was to say to him for some time.

Three days later they heard he had been arrested along with two others for breaking and entering a tobacconists and using threats and violence against the shopkeeper, who had come down and found them emptying his till. Gran and Doug railed against Frank and his cronies, whom they blamed for leading him astray, and wondered how he had turned out like this when they had brought him up with all the right values. Lillian sat huddled on a chair in a turmoil of anger and dread. The shame of it! She was related to someone who would tie up a helpless old man and threaten to hit him with a crowbar. What was it going to do to her family when all this got out? What was she going to say to her mother? Already she was asking where Frank had gone. Bob and Susan—they were going to be horrified, and so ashamed. And Wendy—there she came to a stop. She cut through what her father was saying.

'I bet that Terry Dempsey is behind this,' she said.

Doug and Gran stopped talking at each other and looked at her.

'How do you mean?'

'I don't know, it's just a feeling. Everyone says Terry's got a protection racket going on the seafront, and I know he bailed Frank out when he couldn't pay the HP on his motorbike—'

'How do you know that?'

'James told me, ages ago. At least, he said that Frank said he was going to go to Terry for a loan, and he's still got the motorbike, hasn't he? So he must have got the money from somewhere. I bet Terry put them up to it to frighten the old man into paying.'

'You ought to tell the police, then,' her father said.

'I know, but—there aren't any facts, are there? Nothing I can really tell them.'

'You can tell them what you just told us.'

It was very tempting. If it could be proved that Terry was the moving force, he might be put away, and then Wendy would be safe from him for a while. But it was all so hazy, nothing but hearsay and supposition. She worried about it all through a sleepless night and the next long morning. She desperately needed someone to talk to and there was really only one person whose judgement she trusted. James. Up till now she hadn't told him about Frank as she was too ashamed of her brother, but he was going to have to know some time. Directly after midday dinner, she rang him and arranged to meet in twenty minutes at the coffee bar nearest to While-U-Wait.

She arrived first and sat at a shiny yellow Formica table sipping a frothy coffee in a shallow clear glass cup. Somebody put *Cathy's Clown* on the jukebox. The heartrending voices of the Everly Brothers soared through the steamy atmosphere, chiming perfectly with her mood. She stared out of the window, longing for James to arrive.

When he did, he ordered two more coffees and sat down opposite her, his face concerned.

'Whatever's the matter, Lindy? You sounded really agitated on the phone. Not like you at all.'

It was wonderful to know that she always had him to turn to.

'Oh, James, it's so good of you to come straight away like this. I don't know what to do. It's Frank—he's been arrested.'

And, to her horror, her voice broke on the last few words and she burst into tears. James came round to her side of the table, sat next to her on the bench seat and put an arm round her shoulders, holding her and talking to her.

'It's all right, Lindy. It's not the end of the world, we'll think of something—'

'I'm so sorry—' Lillian sobbed.

'Don't worry, you cry if you want to. Here—' He handed her a fresh handkerchief.

Lillian managed to get the tears under control, wiped her eyes and blew her nose.

'Better now?' James asked.

She nodded.

'Now, tell me what's happened.'

Lillian explained.

James nodded, his eyes narrowed in thought. 'Has he got a solicitor?'

'I don't know. I shouldn't think so. We've never had anything to do with them.'

'Everyone's entitled to legal representation. They'll have given him the duty solicitor if he hasn't anyone of his own. We'll go and see the firm I go to. They handle criminal cases as well as business stuff.'

Lillian was impressed. She hadn't realised that James was now the sort of person who knew about solicitors.

'I'm not sure he deserves it. I'm still so angry with him. But he is my brother, so I suppose we've got to get him all the help we can,' she said. 'But there's something else—'

She outlined her theory about Terry Dempsey's involvement.

'Mmm. I'm with you, I wouldn't be at all surprised if he's behind it. But it's hardly what you might call evidence, is it?'

They discussed it for some while and came to the conclusion that they should take their suspicions to the police and let them make what they could of it.

'We'll go straight away,' James decided.

'But you're supposed to be working!'

'It can wait. What's the point of employing people if you can't leave them to it in an emergency?'

They were lucky. DS Phillips was at the station. Lillian told him what she knew, James backed it up with the tale of the HP payments. Phillips looked unimpressed, but gave nothing away. Their statements were written out and they signed them. They walked out of the station, both feeling flat and disappointed.

'He didn't buy it, did he?' Lillian said.

'No, well, we did think it was a long shot. But look at it this way, Lindy—each statement against Dempsey is one brick. If they get enough of them, they might be able to build something. Now, let's go and see about getting Frank some legal help.'

Lillian might normally have been a bit intimidated by the brown building, solid furnishings and solemn air of the solicitor's office, but James breezed in and chatted to the stiff-looking lady at the reception desk, who melted into a smile.

'You need to see Mr Allenby. Now let me see—' she ran a finger down the page of an appointment book '—as it happens, he's free at four. Would that be convenient?'

'Absolutely,' James agreed, before Lillian could say a word.

'But you're going to be away from the garage all afternoon at this rate,' Lillian objected as they walked out of the building.

'Don't worry, Lindy. Tony's got it all in hand. You were dead right about him, he's a good manager. When While-U-Wait Chelmsford opens next week, I'll be spending most of my time over there, leaving him in charge here, so everything's OK, see? Now, I think you deserve a really nice cake.'

Lillian didn't know whether she wanted to laugh or cry.

'I don't know what I would have done without you,' she said.

James made a dismissive noise. 'What are friends for?'

They ate huge slices of creamy cake at a tea shop and discussed what else could be done for Frank, before going back to the solicitor's office to talk to Mr Allenby. To Lillian's surprise, he turned out not to be a crusty old man, but a sharp young one, hardly ten years older than herself. He took all the details and smiled at Lillian across his shiny desk.

'It's a first offence, so that's got to be in his favour. Don't you worry, Miss Parker, I'll get going on this case straight away. If there's a way out, I'll find it.'

They all shook hands and Lillian left feeling she had done all she could for her brother.

'Now all we've got to do is tell the rest of the family,' she said. 'I don't know how Bob and Susan are going to take it.'

'I'll go and break it to them, if you like,' James offered. 'You get back to your mum; she'll be needing you.'

It was the start of a long anxious time of waiting and wondering.

CHAPTER 29

So THIS was what a courtroom looked like. Lillian had seen them on TV programmes, but it wasn't the same as actually being in one. It was smaller, more cramped, and much more frightening. Up here in the public gallery, you could look down on the proceedings as if you were at a play. But this was no piece of entertainment. This was Frank's freedom and the Parker family honour at stake. She glanced along the row. Gran had come out for the occasion and was sitting beside her, very stiff and upright, dressed entirely in black with a hat and veil. Bob was on the far side of Gran. He had taken the day off work and was looking pale, his hands fiddling with his cufflinks. On Lillian's other side was James. That was it. Just four people here to show their support for Frank and make sure that justice was done. Susan had volunteered to look after her mother-in-law for the day, and Wendy had said she would come but hadn't showed up.

The worst thing was that their father had been called as a witness for the prosecution.

'I bet Terry stopped Wendy from coming,' Lillian murmured to James.

'You're probably right.'

'I'm so grateful to you for coming. You didn't have to, you know. I know how busy you are with the new fitting shop.'

James had been working all hours to get While-U-Wait Chelmsford off the ground. Lillian knew he could ill afford to take time off.

'Of course I had to. I couldn't leave you to face this by yourself, could I?'

His concern ran over her like warm sunshine, partly quelling the churning nerves in her stomach.

'I've been dreading this,' she admitted.

It was a terrible moment when Frank and the other two defendants were brought in. Frank looked white and drawn. Lillian sat with her hands clasped tight in her lap, willing him to look up and see that his family were here for him, but he kept his eyes on his feet. She recognised the defendant on his right. It was the weasel-faced man who had come looking for him that evening the police had searched the house.

She studied the jury members as they were sworn in. Frank's fate depended on these people. Could they be trusted to see it the right way? Some looked very solemn and earnest, others slightly bewildered. One or two just seemed bored.

The proceedings got underway. All three men in the dock pleaded Not Guilty. The lawyer for the prosecution outlined his case. Lillian listened with a growing sense of doom. The tobacconist had identified all three defendants in a line-up. Their fingerprints had been found at the scene. Cigarettes and other goods from the shop had been found, not only at Sunny View but at the houses of the other two.

James leaned towards Lillian and muttered in her ear. 'How can they have been so stupid? Why didn't they wear gloves, and something over their faces? You only have to watch films to know basic stuff like that.'

'I know,' Lillian said.

It all looked very grim.

Witnesses were called. Lillian leaned forward as the defence at last had the chance to cross-question. Under pressure, the tobacconist admitted that the men who had raided his shop had been wearing hats and scarves.

'And you say that your spectacles were knocked off in the scuffle?'

'Yes, sir. Smashed, they were. I had to buy another pair.'

'And how well can you see without them?'

'I can't read, that's for sure.'

'So everything is a bit of a blur without them?'

'Well—'

'Yes or no?'

'A bit, yes.'

'Can I ask you to take your spectacles off for me now? I'm going to hold two pictures up, lifesized photographs of faces. Can you tell me which is the young man and which is the young woman?'

The woman in the photograph had a gamine haircut like Audrey Hepburn, and wore no make-up. Both people wore open-necked shirts.

'That's clever,' James commented.

The tobacconist had some difficulty in telling them apart and, although he did finally choose correctly, the lawyer had made his point. The man's sight was not reliable without glasses.

'So he's going for mistaken identity,' Lillian whispered.

'It's about all he can go for,' James answered.

But when DS Phillips and his superior were called, the evidence started stacking up. The fingerprints and the loot were impossible to explain away. Then relatives were produced to confirm that the three men had not been home on the night of the robbery. Lillian wanted to curl up and die when her father took the stand. She hated herself for it, but she just knew he was going to be made to look small by these smart-tongued figures of authority. Down in the dock, Frank looked up from the floor for the first time and stared at his father with accusing eyes.

'Tell me, Mr Parker, what time did your son get home on the night in question?'

Doug shuffled his feet and mumbled. He was asked to speak up.

'Don't remember,' he said.

Lillian squirmed inside. Why didn't he just admit the truth? Unless he was going to lie under oath, it was going to be drawn out of him one way or another.

'You don't remember him coming in at all?'

'No—yes—I mean—'

'What do you mean, Mr Parker, no or yes?'

'I—er—'

'Well, Mr Parker, did your son come home that night?'

Doug avoided everyone's eyes by doing what Frank had done—looking at his feet. 'No,' he admitted.

'He was out all night?'

'Yes.'

Lillian heard a small groan beside her. It was Gran.

'Hopeless,' she muttered.

Lillian wasn't sure whether she meant her son or the case. The defence lawyer tried to prove that it was not unusual for Frank to be out all night and that he could have been any-where in town or even out of it, on his motorbike. It did not sound very convincing. She looked at the jury's faces.

'Do you think they believe him?' she asked James.

'We can only hope.'

He was being tactful, Lillian knew. Only a very stupid jury member would fall for the defence's arguments.

She brightened up just a little after the lunch break, when the defence started to put its case. But the preamble was hardly halfway through when there was a small disturbance at the back of the public gallery. Two heavyweight men with cropped heads clumped in and made their way to the front, where they stood for longer than was necessary before taking their seats.

'I know them!' James hissed at Lillian. 'They're Dempsey's men. They're the ones who tried to warn me off Wendy.'

Down in the dock, one of the defendants had spotted them. He elbowed the other two and they all looked up. There was no doubt that they too recognised the men.

'That's the end of any chance of accusing Dempsey of being behind it,' James said.

Any spark of hope that the case might take a dramatic turn for the better died at that moment. The barrister that James's solicitor had engaged did his best to establish an alibi for Frank, producing two witnesses to say that he had been at a bikers' café up till eleven o'clock, but they admitted under cross-questioning that, though Frank had said he was setting off for the new M1 motorway, they didn't know for sure whether he had gone there. They even admitted that Frank was known to make empty boasts about what he had done and where he had been on his motorbike.

As it happened, there was no need for Dempsey's men

glaring down from the public gallery. The defence did not even try to suggest that the defendants had been put up to it. Lillian guessed that Frank and his friends had already denied that one and the lawyer knew it was no use going down that road.

The judge did his summing-up, the jury retired. The Parkers and James gathered in the corridor outside the courtroom, stretching their legs and discussing the case.

'That stupid boy. How can he do this to us? I'll never be able to hold up my head again,' Gran said.

'I don't know what they're going to say at the bank when all this comes out. Supposing they assume that I'm tarred with the same brush?' Bob said.

'Will it all come out?' Lillian asked.

'Of course it will. Didn't you notice the reporter sitting there writing it all down in his notebook?'

Lillian hadn't.

'I suppose there's no chance of some sort of reprieve?' she said.

Bob gave a sigh of impatience. 'This isn't *Perry Mason*, Lillian. It's real life. Like the judge said, that old man could have had a heart attack and died when they left him tied up like that.'

'I know,' Lillian said miserably.

She was so ashamed of her brother. She almost wished James wasn't here to witness all this.

They didn't have long to wait. The jury took just fifteen minutes to decide. Everyone assembled in the courtroom again. The foreman of the jury stood up. The judge asked for their verdict.

'Guilty.'

The word fell like a stone into Lillian's heart. She had been expecting it, but it was still a dreadful moment. She felt a warm hand close round hers. It was James.

The judge told Frank and his cronies what a despicable deed they had done. The only factor in their favour was that this was their first offence. Frank stood in the dock stony-faced, his eyes still on his feet.

'Eight years,' the judge decided. 'Take them down.'

Lillian gasped. Eight years! Down in the dock, Frank at last registered emotion. Shock was written clearly on his face. But it was too late now for any reaction. He and his partners in crime were escorted out by policemen. The door to the cells closed behind him, and he was gone from the everyday world.

'You all right, Lindy?'

James's voice was concerned. Lillian nodded. She felt very strange. Unreal. This could not be happening to her family. They were not criminals.

There was a low groan beside her. Lillian turned. Gran was still staring at the dock. Her face was set and grim, but she could not quite control the trembling of her chin. To her horror, Lillian realised that Gran, the hard rock, the immovable force of their family, was struggling to hold back tears. For the first time in her life, she put an arm round her shoulders.

'Come on, Gran, there's no more to be done. Let's go home.'

Gran was still staring at the empty dock. 'Who would have thought that the Parkers could sink so low?' she said, almost to herself. 'Thank God his grandfather isn't here to see this.'

There was no respite when they reached home. Susan met them at the door with her baby on her hip, her face pinched with anxiety.

'I'm so glad you're back,' she exclaimed. 'Poor Mother's so restless. She knows something serious is going on. She keeps asking for Frank.'

Lillian went to run up the stairs, but stopped with one foot on the bottom step.

'What are we going to tell her?' she asked the family in general.

Up till then, they had been maintaining a story that Frank had got a job up north.

'We can't tell her the truth. It would break her heart,' Bob said.

There was a murmuring of agreement.

'We'll just have to carry on saying that he's working away. There's no point in changing the story now,' Doug decided.

'For eight years?' Lillian questioned.

Silence greeted this. Everyone looked down, unable to voice the obvious: Nettie was not going to live for eight years. She probably wasn't going to live eight months. She was never going to see her son again.

Lillian swallowed. 'Right,' she whispered. 'Shall I go and see her now, or does someone else want to?'

'You go,' Bob suggested. 'It'll look more like normal.'

Lillian hesitated. She looked at her father. 'Dad?'

'Yes, you go,' he agreed, ever one to get out of a difficult situation.

With a heavy heart, Lillian climbed the stairs, up and up to the cramped attic bedroom under the eaves. Her mother looked frailer than ever, her thin face white against the white pillow.

'Frank?' she said, her voice clearer than Lillian had heard it for a long time. 'Where's Frank? Why doesn't he come to see me?'

Lillian's powers of acting nearly deserted her. It was so hard to lie, so hard to carry on as if nothing had happened.

'Now, Mum, you know he's—' her voice cracked; she fought to keep it under control '—he's got this job up north. Like I did, you know? I was working up north for ages, wasn't I? I had a lovely time there. I expect Frank is as well. He'll be earning good money, too.'

Nettie did not look convinced. But the effort of speaking had almost been too much for her. '—goodbye,' she whispered.

'What?' Lillian knelt down at the bedside and put her head close to her mother's.

'—say goodbye.'

'He didn't come and say goodbye? Well, he did, Mum, but you were asleep, and he didn't want to wake you.'

She hoped fervently that she would be forgiven for lying to a sick woman. But how could she possibly tell her the truth? Looking ahead, she could only see more lies, piling one on top of the other. She was overwhelmed with anger at her brother. How could he do this to his mother? She wanted to get him by the throat and squeeze every last breath out of him.

Nettie closed her eyes. Lillian knew the signs. She wasn't asleep, she just didn't want to speak or be spoken to. Reluctantly, Lillian left her and went down to join the gloomy family group below.

Bob and Susan went soon after, as Susan wanted to feed the baby at home. Then James took his leave.

'Remember, you only have to lift the phone if there's anything you need, or anything I can do,' he insisted.

Lillian made a tea that nobody had the appetite for. Just three of them were left now.

'The family's falling apart,' Gran said.

'Bob and Wendy have only gone because they're married,' Lillian pointed out.

'Hmm, well, at least Bob's keeping the standards up,' Gran commented.

Lillian felt deeply hurt. She knew it was no use looking for praise from Gran, but she would have liked to at least have some recognition that she wasn't letting the family down. But there it was—she was just Lillian, the eternal dogsbody.

'I'll clear this away, if nobody wants any more,' she said and began to gather up the used plates.

Gran and Doug said nothing, but just let her carry on.

Lillian envied her father going off to work the next day, even though he was only going to spend it going up and down in a lift. At least he was going to be in contact with normal everyday people. The house was beginning to close in around her, and there was little chance of any PGs turning up with the season well over. So she was glad when the phone rang. Any tidings from the outside world were welcome.

'Lillian?' a thready voice asked.

'Yes?' For a moment she couldn't think who it was.

'Can you come over?'

'Wendy? Is that you?'

'Please, Lillian—'

'Of course. But what's up?'

'Just come. Please.'

Dread gripped Lillian. Something terrible had happened.

'OK, I'm coming. Just hold on.'

Already her mind was racing. This was when she needed a car. What was the use of having passed her driving test if she didn't have anything to drive? She wondered about contacting James, then remembered that he was in Chelmsford today. So it was bike or taxi. This was an emergency, she decided, so it had to be a taxi. She would pay for it out of the housekeeping and reimburse it out of her savings. She lifted the phone again to order one, then went upstairs to make sure that her mother was all right. Finally, she put her head round Gran's door, told her where she was going and went before any questions could be asked.

Travelling along the seafront in a depressing drizzle, she

tried to imagine what was awaiting her. Terry must have hurt Wendy again. How much of this was Wendy going to take? How bad was it this time? She had sounded dreadful over the phone. The taxi driver tried to talk to her, but she answered him in monosyllables as various possibilities went through her head, each one worse than the last.

'Wait there,' she said on impulse as they arrived at Wendy's house. 'I might need to go somewhere else.'

It was a vain hope, but perhaps she could persuade Wendy to leave.

She rang the bell. There was a sound of small footsteps inside the house, and Coral's high-pitched voice calling, 'Mummy, door!' If the circumstances hadn't been so grim, Lillian might have smiled at hearing her sister being shouted at the way she used to be. The door opened a crack. Lillian cautiously pushed from her side until there was enough space to get in. What she saw shocked her. Wendy did not appear to be bruised, but her face was drawn with pain and she looked as if she hadn't slept for a week.

'Wendy—'

She went to hug her sister, but Wendy flinched from her. She was cradling one arm with the other.

'Don't—'

'Aunty Lilli!'

Coral flung her arms round her legs. She was still in her pyjamas. Upstairs, little Terrance started crying. Lillian picked up the toddler and cuddled her.

'What's happened?' she asked Wendy.

'It's my arm—I think it's broken.'

'Wendy!' Despite her imaginings in the taxi, Lillian was still horrified. 'Did he do it?'

Wendy avoided her eyes. 'I fell,' she said.

'Oh, yeah? Well, never mind that now, we've got to get you to hospital.'

'But the children—'

'We'll drop them off at Susan's. They'll be fine with her. I'll go and get Terrance. Is he still in his cot?'

Wendy nodded, tears oozing from her eyes. 'I couldn't pick him up. I had to feed him in the cot.'

'All right, don't worry. Just tell me what I've got to fetch for him. Nappies? Change of clothes? Bottles?'

'Yes, yes—oh, Lillian, I'm so glad you've come.'

'Everything's all right now,' Lillian said, wondering how big a lie that was. She hurried round, collecting things for the children. It took a while for her to realise the significance of the fact that Wendy was dressed. How could she have done that with a broken arm?

'When did this happen?' she asked, fetching a coat to put round her sister's shoulders.

'Last night,' Wendy admitted.

'Last night? Why on earth didn't you call me sooner?'

'I thought he might come back.'

'Good God—!'

She had to get her sister away from this monster. But, for now, she just had to get her injuries seen to. With the baby in one arm, a bag over her shoulder and the toddler holding her other hand, Lillian managed to shepherd her little flock out to the waiting taxi.

They stopped off at Bob and Susan's house.

'Don't tell her!' Wendy begged.

Lillian wanted to tell the world how badly her sister was being treated, but now was not the time to argue the point. She told Susan that Wendy had had an accident, left the children in her capable hands and went on to the hospital. The housekeeping just about covered the fare. It was an hour before they were seen. Lillian used the time to try to persuade Wendy to do something about her situation.

'You can't go on like this,' she said. 'It will only get worse. This time it's a broken arm; what will it be next time? Supposing you have to stay in hospital? What would happen to the children?'

'I don't know,' Wendy said miserably. 'It's all my fault. He loves me really, but I just make him angry.'

'Loves you! And this is how he shows it? Gives you a broken arm, then goes out and leaves you and the children to fend for yourselves? Funny sort of love.'

'But he does—'

'You've got to do something, Wendy. Tell the police. Or leave him.'

'Leave him?' Wendy sounded amazed.

'Yes, leave him, before he does something really dreadful to you.'

'I couldn't do that.'

'Why not?'

Lillian persisted, but all Wendy could do was say, 'I don't know.' In the end, she started sobbing. 'Stop getting at me, Lillian. Please. Just stop it.'

Reluctantly, Lillian gave in. It was obvious that she was getting nowhere, and only succeeding in upsetting Wendy.

At last Wendy's name was called. Once she was being attended to, Lillian was faced with a dilemma. She wanted to stay here and make sure that her sister was all right, but her mother would be needing her at home. There was nobody but Gran there, and she couldn't run up all those stairs and help Nettie on and off the commode. And, whether she went now or later, she still had to get home somehow, and she had spent practically all her money. Never had she felt her lack of income so much.

'Look,' she said to Wendy, 'I hate to leave you here but I've got to get back to Mum. It'll take too long to walk, so I'll have to get another taxi and hope that Gran won't make too much of a fuss about paying it. Can you do the same when you've been fixed up? Get a taxi and come back home?'

Wendy nodded.

'Promise? That you'll come back home?'

Wendy nodded again. 'Thanks, Lillian. I don't know what I would of done without you.'

Gran reluctantly doled out the exact fare without any tip for the driver. 'Where on earth have you been? You can't just go running off like that, leaving me and your mother. Where's your sense of duty?'

'Wendy broke her arm. I had to get the children looked after and take her to hospital.'

'Broke her arm? How did she do that?'

All the secrets she was keeping suddenly reared up and faced Lillian. Secrets and lies—about Wendy, about Frank, about Eileen. She hated them.

'It wasn't her. That Terry did it to her. He beats her up.'

There. It was out. Now there was no going back.

Gran drew her mouth down at the corners, pulling her face into severe lines. 'Well,' she said, 'she made her bed. Now she has to lie on it.'

Lillian was dumbfounded. She stared at her grandmother. Was that all the support that Wendy could expect?

'I'm going to see to Mum,' she said, and ran up the stairs.

Wendy did not call back at the house. When Lillian rang Susan to find out if she still had the children, she learnt that Wendy had come straight to her from the hospital, borrowed some money and gone back to her own place.

Lillian put the phone down and sank onto the bottom stair.

She felt utterly defeated. Frank was in prison, her mother was terminally ill, her sister was living with a man who beat her up, and she felt helpless. There seemed to be nothing she could do to change any of it.

'Oh, James—' she said out loud.

How she yearned to have him here, to feel his arm around her shoulders. But James thought of her as a little sister, or a good friend. It was all quite hopeless.

CHAPTER 30

IT TOOK Lillian a long time to get to sleep that night. Everything churned around in her head—the trial, Wendy, her mother—until there seemed to be no quiet place to rest her thoughts. Wherever she looked, there were insurmountable problems. She tried thinking back to the carefree days of touring with the dance company, to the fun and close sisterhood of the girls, the squabbles and the dreadful digs, the stage fright and the sheer thrill of performing. But it all seemed so far away now, a different world. She could hardly believe that then all she had to worry about was getting her dancing shoes repaired and making sure her hair was clean. She finally managed to chase the overwhelming worries of the present away by going through in her mind some of the dances the company had done. Making sure that each step was correct, listening to the music in her head, she calmed herself enough to fall asleep.

But she had hardly slid down into oblivion before something dragged her back up again. Her shoulder was being shaken. A voice was urgent in her ear.

'Lillian! Lillian, wake up!'

'Mmm—what—?'

She felt heavy and drugged. She desperately wanted to sleep.

'Lillian, it's your mum.'

'What? Mum? What's the matter?'

Wide awake now, she realised that her father was leaning over her.

'She's taken a turn for the worse. I'm worried, Lillian. Come and see.'

Lillian slid out of bed and pulled on her dressing gown. Every limb was aching. Across the landing, the bedside light was on. Her mother was groaning and moving her head from side to side on the pillow.

'Mum? Mum, what's wrong? Does something hurt?'

She put her hand to her mother's forehead. It was cold and clammy.

'I think we'd better call the doctor,' she decided.

'Yes, yes, you're right. I'll do it now,' her father agreed.

For what seemed like an age, they waited for the doctor. Lillian sat on her mother's bed and talked to her, saying anything that came into her head. There was no reaction, but she had long ago ceased to expect one. If anything, she was talking for her own benefit, to keep fear at bay. When the doctor arrived, he shook his head and said it was time for her to go back into hospital. An ambulance was called.

'Are you going with her?' Lillian asked her father.

Doug looked horrified. 'What, me? I got to go to work in the morning.'

She might have known. Lillian just had time to pull on some clothes and pack a bag for her mother before the ambulance arrived.

Once at the hospital, there was more waiting around while the right person was found, so it was eight in the morning by the time Nettie was settled in a ward. Tests were to be done, Lillian was told. Now her mother must be allowed to rest. Feeling dazed and hollow, Lillian found her way down the echoing corridors to the hospital entrance. It was only then that she realised that she had come out without any money. She hesitated. A taxi or call James? The need to see him overcame all sensible thoughts. She picked up the phone in the call box and put in a reverse charge call to While-U-Wait Southend, praying that he was there. He was.

'Oh, James, I'm so sorry to do this, but can you possibly come and pick me up? Only I haven't any money with me—'

'Of course I will, Lindy. What's happened? Where are you?'

'I'm at the hospital. It's Mum—'

'Stay right where you are. I'm on my way.'

Just ten minutes later, there he was, smiling and cheerful in his green Mini.

'You look dreadful,' he commented as he opened the car door for her.

Lillian nearly burst into tears on the spot. Instead, she tried to turn it into a joke. 'Thank you very much.'

James was contrite. 'I didn't mean it as a criticism, Lindy. But you look as if you've been up all night.'

'It feels like it.'

As they drove out of the hospital grounds, he said, 'I suppose you haven't had breakfast?'

'No—oh, God! I wasn't there to cook breakfast for Dad and Gran!'

'Well, it'll be too late for that by the time you get home. Let them cope on their own for a change. It won't hurt them. I'm taking you for a Full English.'

She did try to protest. 'What about work?'

'That can cope on its own as well. No arguments, OK?'

'OK.'

It was bliss to let someone else take charge. James drove them to the nearest café and ordered the works. Lillian sat at a cramped table, breathed in the smell of frying and relaxed for the first time in days. She was surprised to find that she was ravenously hungry.

'Now,' James said, 'tell me what's up.'

Through mouthfuls of egg and bacon, Lillian told him all about her mother and then about Wendy. Across the table, James's hands curled into fists.

'That bastard,' he spat. 'Surely she doesn't love him?'

'She says she does. She says he loves her. It makes me want to scream. When she just sits there looking helpless and saying it's her own fault, I want to shake her until her teeth rattle, so what does that make me? As bad as him.'

'But you don't actually do it. He does. I just don't understand it, Lindy. How can a man hit a woman like that? His own wife, the mother of his children. How can he take it out on people who are weaker than him? It's despicable. I always loathed Dempsey, but now I despise him as well. He's the lowest of the low.'

They talked round it for ages, but came to no solution. Unless Wendy agreed to leave him, there seemed to be nothing they could do. They couldn't very well kidnap her and the children.

'But there is one thing I can do to make your life a bit easier,' James said.

Lillian stared at him, amazed to find any bright spot in the dark. 'There is? What?'

'Wait and see. You finished there? Come on then, I've got something to show you.'

More than that he refused to say. They drove round to While-U-Wait Southend.

'Just wait there a minute while I make a phone call,' James said, leaving her in the work bay while he went to the office area at the back.

Lillian looked idly around. Three cars were up on hydraulic lifts with fitters underneath them putting on new exhausts and in the corner there was a grey Morris Minor Traveller with its distinctive round nose and wood-trimmed body. She presumed that it was waiting for its owner to come and pick it up. James came back with a set of car keys.

'Here you are,' he said, handing them to Lillian. 'All fixed. I've got a buyer coming for it in a couple of weeks, but it's insured for you to drive until then.'

Lillian just stood and stared at him, the keys resting in the palm of her hand. 'What?'

'The Traveller. Tony's been keeping his hand in doing it up. You'll be needing something to take you out to the hospital.'

'You're lending me a car? Just like that?'

'Of course. You need one and it's just sitting there doing nothing.'

'But—'

He reached out and closed her fingers round the keys. 'Go on—get in it.'

She did as she was told, adjusting the seat and the rear-view mirror, making sure she knew where the gears were. Then she started it up. The engine sprang into life.

James leaned down and spoke through the open window.

'There you are—sweet as a nut. You'll find it a bit clumsy after the Mini, but it's a good reliable car. Off you go—just let me know if you have any problems.'

He brushed aside her thanks and stood back to let her drive out of the garage. Gingerly, Lillian put it in gear, released the handbrake, let out the clutch. The car moved forward. She squeaked with a mixture of alarm and pleasure. This was the first time she had driven all by herself. But she kept her head, negotiated the back streets of Southend and emerged on to the seafront. Now she had got the hang of manoeuvring the car, she was beginning to enjoy herself. It was a grey chilly day, but she was protected from the weather. The promenade road was practically empty. For the first time in weeks she felt the weight of dread lift from her heart as she passed the end of her road and carried on towards Thorpe Bay, the engine humming happily, the car obeying her, the scenery whizzing by. She was in Shoebury before she knew it.

If only she could just keep on and on driving, back past Southend and on to anywhere, leaving her responsibilities behind her. She thought of Eileen and the cosy welcome of her little home up there in the midlands. How lovely it would be to go and visit her. But she could not. Already she had stayed out far too long. Gran would want to know what she had been up to. She turned around and drove home, her brief freedom over.

It was much easier getting to the hospital now she had a car. The next day, as she was sitting at her mother's bedside, Wendy turned up. She had make-up over her bruises, and of course she still had her arm in a sling.

'Look,' she said brightly, too brightly, thrusting her good hand in front of Lillian's nose. 'Terry bought me this. Isn't it beautiful?'

A new ring flashed on her middle finger, a ruby flanked with diamonds.

'It's big,' Lillian said.

'You see—he loves me. A man doesn't buy a ring like that for anyone.'

Their mother lay between them in the hospital bed, her eyes shut, seemingly unaware of their presence.

'Not unless he's feeling guilty about something,' Lillian replied.

Wendy's pretty mouth twisted. Hot-eyed, she rounded on Lillian. 'You like to make out you're so clever, but you don't know anything about anything,' she said. 'Look at you, you've never even had a proper boyfriend. You're just jealous because I've got a rich husband. You've always been jealous of me.'

'I wouldn't want your Terry if he was the last man on earth,' Lillian said.

There was a faint sound from the bed. Both of them shut up and looked at their mother. She was looking back at them with fear in her eyes.

Lillian took her hand. 'It's all right, Mum. You know Wendy and me. Just a little squabble, that's all.'

'Yeah,' Wendy agreed, bending over to kiss Nettie's white cheek. Don't take any notice of us. You just get better as soon as possible, all right?'

Nettie focused on Wendy's sling. 'Arm?' she whispered.

'What? Oh, this—I tripped over. Silly me. Look, Mum, look at this lovely ring Terry gave me to make it feel better—'

They managed to behave themselves until the end of visiting time but, the moment they were ushered out of the ward, Lillian grabbed her sister by her good arm.

'Wendy, how can you be so stupid? Letting yourself be bought off with a bit of flashy jewellery.'

Wendy twisted out of her grasp. 'Shut up, Miss Goody Two Shoes! I'm fed up with you telling me what to do. You don't understand nothing about what it's like to be me. So just put a sock in it, right? I don't want to hear no more preaching from you, not never.' And she set off along the corridor as fast as she could totter in her four-inch stilettos.

Lillian overtook her in just a few strides. 'OK, if that's what you want. But don't come running to me next time he knocks you about.'

She marched ahead of her sister and emerged into the late afternoon gloom. Outside the front entrance, Terry's driver had the Jag parked in a space reserved for doctors as he waited to take Wendy home. Angry, resentful, worried, Lillian hurried past, found where she had parked the Traveller in the street and climbed inside. For several minutes she just sat in the driver's seat with her hands at the top of the steering wheel and her head resting on them. She felt safe in here, with the solid little car between her and the troubles of the outside world. She breathed in the smell of it. The scent of cars and petrol were always associated with James. He had sat here. He had held the steering wheel, touched the gear lever. Try as she might, she couldn't get Wendy's mocking words out of her head. *You've never even had a proper boyfriend.*

'I've had loads of boyfriends,' she said out loud.

But she knew that her sister was right. She might have gone out with plenty of boys during her dancing days, but none of them had been sweethearts. There wasn't one whom she regretted leaving behind. Right from the moment they had met, all those years ago, it had only ever been James.

'Why can't you see me?' she asked.

But she knew the answer. He did see her, but not as a woman. He did care for her. The car was proof enough. Lending her this had been so considerate. He had seen what she needed and provided it. But he didn't love her the way she loved him. He simply didn't think of her in that way. She sighed deeply. Like everything else in her life at the moment, she couldn't see a solution. All she could do was to plod on, coping with each thing as it presented itself. She started the car up and drove home to report back to Gran and see what she needed. There was sure to be something.

It was as she was making the tea later on that afternoon that she realised with a jolt that she hadn't written to Eileen in ages. There was just so much bad news that she hadn't known where to start. She'd told her a bit about Wendy and Terry, but nothing about Frank, and now there was her mother back in hospital as well. She didn't want to burden Eileen with it all but, on the other hand, she knew that her aunty would be cross if she kept it from her. Eileen did like to hear what was happening in the family after being out of touch for so long, and Lillian still hoped that one day she would be able to bring them all together again once more. She decided to sit down that evening and write a nice long letter and felt a bit better. Writing to Eileen wasn't the same as speaking to her, but it would help.

At tea time her father wanted to know about her visit to the hospital.

'The sister said they were still waiting for the results of the tests,' she told him.

'Ah. Right,' Doug said.

'She didn't seem any brighter, though, did she?' Gran prompted.

'Not really,' Lillian admitted.

'So you better go and visit her this evening,' Gran decided.

'What, me? I been at work all day,' Doug said.

'Won't hurt you to go and visit your wife. Lillian's got that car. She can drive you out there.'

Doug shifted uncomfortably in his chair. 'I hate hospitals.'

'So does everyone. You can go directly after Lillian's washed up.'

Lillian just sat there wrestling silently with a mass of conflicting emotions. She was disappointed at seeing her letter to Eileen slide away, glad to see her father being forced to do his duty, guilty at feeling that way when she should be simply concerned about her mother, tired of always being the one who had to run around after everyone else, and guilty again at being so selfish. She stood up and started to clear the plates away.

'I'll be fifteen minutes or so, Dad,' she said, not bothering to keep the edge out of her voice.

Doug just made a noise in his throat, lit a cigarette and waited till she was ready.

The days passed by, dominated by trips to the hospital. Susan, Wendy and James's mother all visited as often as they could, but Lillian made sure she went every day as well. Each time she saw her mother, she seemed to have shrunk a little more, retreated even further from the world. Lillian woke each day with dread in her heart. Although she never said it out loud, she knew it was only a matter of time. It was a clash with Gran that brought matters to a head.

'She's no better, I suppose?' she asked when Lillian served tea one day.

'No.'

Her mother had not acknowledged her presence at all that afternoon.

'She never did have much go to her.'

Lillian thumped the pot down on the table, slopping tea out of the spout onto the cloth.

'Careful!' Gran snapped.

'I think you better be careful what you say about Mum. She slaved away for you all those years with never a word of thanks from anyone and now look at her—she's dying.'

There was a sharp intake of breath from both Gran and Doug. She had said the forbidden word. A wild vindictive part of Lillian was glad. It was about time they faced the truth.

'You're a wicked, wicked girl,' Gran stated.

'I'm just saying what's true. And, what's more, it's about time you made the effort to go and see her, before it's too late.'

'Me? Go to the hospital?' Gran looked as if she had suggested flying to the moon.

'Why not? I can take you in the car and, if you can't walk at the other end, I'll get you a wheelchair.'

'I'm not sitting in no wheelchair.'

'OK, suit yourself, but I think you ought to go and see her.'

'Don't talk to your grandmother like that,' her father snapped.

Lillian rounded on him. 'And you ought to go and see her more often, too. You only go once a week, and then only because I force you to. She's your wife—don't you care at all?'

Her father looked down, fiddling with the crumbs on his plate. 'It's upsetting,' he admitted, his voice gruff.

Lillian was far too upset herself to recognise any pain in his words.

'Oh, and I enjoy watching my mother fade away in front of my eyes, do I? I find it fun? That's why I go every day and make sure she knows that someone cares about her?'

'That's enough,' Gran barked.

'No, it's not enough. I'm tired of shutting up just because you don't like what I say. Both of you ought to go and see Mum, because she's sinking fast. Don't worry, you won't have the bother of doing it many times more, she's not going to be here very much longer.'

'How dare you speak to me like that? After all I've done for you—' Gran began.

Lillian ignored her. She looked at her father, challenge in her eyes.

'So—are you coming with me this evening, or not?'

'I'll come,' Doug mumbled.

'Good.' She turned to Gran. 'And when are you going to go? I won't have the car for much longer. James has already put the new owner off once.'

'I'll go when I'm good and ready,' Gran told her.

'Well, don't leave it too long.'

In the event, Gran consented to go the next day. She sat at the bedside in silence while Lillian attempted to chatter to her mother and Nettie lay there, seemingly unaware of their presence. After fifteen minutes or so of this, Gran hauled herself to her feet, leaned over and placed a cold kiss on Nettie's brow.

'Goodbye, Nettie. You been a good wife to my boy,' she said, and walked stiffly out of the ward.

Lillian stared after her. How could she do that? She could hardly believe her ears. She was never sure whether her mother did hear what was said to her. In this case, she fervently hoped she hadn't.

'Well, that was typical, wasn't it?' she said, as matter-of-fact as possible. 'Bet that cost her something to be even halfway nice to you, the bad-tempered old bat.'

She talked on a bit longer, deliberately making Gran wait, then kissed her mother gently on the cheek. 'See you tomorrow, Mum.'

Gran was sitting in the day room. 'She's not long for this world,' was the only comment she made.

Lillian was too angry to reply.

It was that evening that James called round. He took one look at Lillian's tight face and told her to put her coat on.

'I'm taking you out for a drink. You look as if you need it,' he said.

Lillian was more than willing to agree. She felt like walking out of the house never to return.

'Do you want to talk about it?' he asked as they made their way along the road towards Leigh.

'No.'

If she told him about the last couple of days, she knew she would start crying and not be able to stop.

'OK, you choose what you do want to talk about.'

'Tell me about how things are going in Chelmsford.'

James entertained her with tales of awkward customers. It was such a relief to hear about the world outside of Sunny View and the hospital that she wouldn't have cared what he talked about really.

They chose one of the pubs in the old fishing village. James bought their drinks and they sat in a cosy corner close to a blazing fire.

'Isn't it Thursday today?' Lillian asked. The days were all so similar now that they tended to get tangled up in her mind.

'Yup. Why?'

'Don't you usually go out with Julie on Thursdays?'

Julie was his latest girlfriend.

'Oh—I gave her the push. She was getting too clingy.'

Lillian couldn't suppress a little spurt of pleasure. Another one gone.

'You hadn't been going out with her for long.'

'I know, and she was already trying to pin me down. I can't be doing with it.'

She knew it was silly to be pleased. There would soon be another one. There was no shortage of girls wanting to go out with James. He was good-looking and fun to be with, and now he was turning into a successful businessman. No wonder Julie wanted to pin him down.

'So you thought you might as well see me as there was no one else around?'

She regretted the words as soon as they were out of her mouth. They sounded like the sort of thing one of his jealous girlfriends might say.

'No, I blew her out so that I could see you.'

Lillian flushed. She was feeling far too raw to be having this conversation. She should never have started it. Another couple of steps and she was going to have no control at all. She took a deep breath and moved away from the edge.

'Oh—well—thanks. So, apart from the awkward squad, things are going OK in Chelmsford, are they?'

James took his cue from her and talked for a while about the business, and then about the rally he had entered and what he was doing to prepare himself and the Mini for it. Lillian listened, fascinated as ever by every detail of his life, but, instead of being soothed, she became increasingly uneasy. It seemed as if James was slipping away from her. He was no longer a lanky boy with a dream, he was a man on the threshold of success. One day soon he was going to meet a woman who was sleek and sophisticated, as befitted his new status. Someone whom he wouldn't ditch after just a few weeks. And then where would she be? Utterly alone.

The evening passed all too quickly. Soon they were whizzing back along the promenade again towards Southend. The dark water beside them was gleaming under the fitful moonlight and, far away on the other side of the estuary, flames were burning at the tops of the oil refinery chimneys. Lillian looked at James's profile, relaxed and happy as he always was when driving, and was overwhelmed with such a wave of yearning that she couldn't trust herself to speak.

James pulled up outside Sunny View and switched off the engine. 'Home again. Thanks for a nice evening.'

'Thank *you*,' Lillian managed to say, forcing the words from an aching throat. 'I think I'd of gone mad if you hadn't taken me out.'

James half turned in his seat. 'Look, I know it's difficult at the moment. Well, pretty impossible really. But you shouldn't be stuck in like this. Get out more. Go dancing—you must miss it. There must be blokes lining up to ask you, surely?'

The emotional pressure that had been building up inside her all evening suddenly burst out. She couldn't control it. Hot-eyed, she faced him, the man she had loved for so long.

'I don't want anyone else. It's just you, James—only you. I've never loved anyone else from the moment I met you. So now you know.'

And she wrenched open the car door, jumped out and fumbled for her front door key. Behind her she could hear James calling for her to wait, but she couldn't bear to look at him, sure that if she did she would see only brotherly concern in his face. She got the door open, slammed it behind her and ran upstairs to the privacy of her bedroom, where she flung herself on the bed and wept as she had never done before.

CHAPTER 31

LILLIAN DIDN'T KNOW how she was going to get up and face the next day. She had blown the one bright hope in her life. James would avoid her now. He wouldn't want to be lumbered with a lovesick girl in place of his undemanding little sister. She was awake most of the night regretting those hasty words. Why had she done it? If she could just have kept her mouth shut for a few more minutes…but she knew deep down that she had been incapable of holding back. For a sweet fraction of time, it had been so wonderful to let it out.

She was turning it over with an aching heart for yet another time when the phone started ringing in the hall. A jolt of dread went through her. There could only be one place that would call this early. The hospital. Propelled by fear, she leapt out of bed, grabbing her dressing gown and pulling it on as she ran downstairs. She grabbed the handset.

'Hello, yes?'

'Miss Parker?'

'Yes.'

Her heart was hammering in her chest so hard that it was difficult to breathe.

'Sister Morgan from Anderson Ward. Miss Parker, I think you had better not wait till afternoon visiting to see your mother. In fact, you should come as soon as possible.'

It wasn't quite the worst words, but bad enough. Even though she had been expecting this call for days, still it was a shock to have it actually happen.

'Right—' she gabbled. 'Yes—thank you—I'm coming—thank you—'

She ran upstairs again two at a time and hammered on her father's door.

'Dad? Dad, get up. We got to go to the hospital now, this minute!'

The real fear in her voice must have transmitted to Doug. For once he didn't argue or prevaricate. Both of them pulled on the first clothes that came to hand. As she arrived back down in the hall again, Lillian put her head inside Gran's room. The fug of coal ash and cigarette smoke hit her. It was too dark to see.

'Gran? We're going to the hospital. I don't know when we'll be back.'

There was a faint grunt from the bed, but Lillian wasn't waiting for anything clearer. Five minutes after the phone call, she and Doug were in the car. It was dark and drizzling, a morning as depressing as her mindset. Thankfully, there was hardly any traffic on the roads, but still the journey seemed to take twice as long as usual. There was silence in the car. Lillian couldn't formulate any clear thoughts; her head was simply full of the need to get where she was going as soon as possible.

She knew the moment they arrived at the ward that it was too late.

Sister Morgan got up from her desk to meet them at the door. 'I'm sorry—' she said.

Lillian failed to take in anything else of what she said. In a blur, she followed the nurse to the curtained-off area round her mother's bed. She didn't know what to expect. For a week now she had got no response at all from her mother, not so much as a flicker of an eyelid, so she hardly knew whether there would be much difference. But the moment she looked at her, she saw the change. What was lying there was no longer the woman who had given birth to her. She had gone.

Some distant part of her knew that she ought to be feeling something, doing something, but she felt totally numb. Stiffly, she approached the bed and bent to kiss the cold forehead.

'Goodbye, Mum,' she whispered.

Her father was still standing just inside the curtain, a look of total bewilderment on his face. Lillian was overtaken by a burst of anger so strong that she only just stopped herself from hitting out at him, the nearest person. It was all so unfair, so very unfair. She pushed past her father and ran blindly out of the ward and into the day room, sobbing with rage and grief. Her mother hadn't had much of a life and now it was gone. Something was very wrong somewhere. Lurking there too was a sense of unfinished business. There had been that one moment when her mother had said, 'Lillian. You're here. Thank God.' But since then there had been nothing, no sign that she was wanted or valued. The small child in her still longed for a word of love from her mother, and now it would never come. The gaping hole inside her would never be filled.

That evening, there was a knock on the door. Wearily, Lillian got up to answer it. She had spent the afternoon providing tea and cakes for Wendy, Bob and Susan and Cora Kershaw and she was just about wrung out, physically and emotionally. She opened the door to find James standing there.

'Oh—' She just stood and gaped at him, a deep flush of embarrassment washing over her.

'Lindy, I'm so sorry about your mother.'

'Yes—thank you—'

She felt paralysed. Her last words to him the night before seemed to lie between them like a huge black barrier. Where before she had always said whatever she thought to him, now she didn't know where to start.

'I know she was ill, but it must still be a terrible shock.'

'Yes.'

'She was such a—a gentle person.'

'Yes, she was.'

James looked awkward in the face of her brief responses. 'I…er…I don't want to take up your time. I mean, it must have been a difficult day. But I just wanted you to know…well, to know that I was thinking of you, and how hard it must be for you…'

At last it got through to Lillian that she was keeping him standing on the doorstep, when in the past she would have welcomed him in.

'I'm sorry—come in—'

'You've had enough to do today, Lindy. You look all in.'

She couldn't let him go, not like this. The need to keep him there forced her into speech. 'No, please, don't go away. It's awful in here with just them. Come in, just for a bit.'

She stepped back, opening the door wide, until he couldn't refuse. Lillian nodded at Gran's room. The noise of the television was pounding through the heavy door.

'With a bit of luck they won't hear. Come through to the back.'

They sat in the kitchen over cups of coffee and the remains of the Swiss roll that Lillian had fed to the afternoon visitors. She found herself tongue-tied again. After her confession, nothing was easy between them any more. Then she remembered the car.

'Mum said it happened early this morning?' James said.

'About the car—you must be wanting it back,' Lillian said at exactly the same moment.

They both stopped. In the past, they would have laughed. Now they were both carefully polite.

'You say—'

'No, you.'

James waited for her. Lillian repeated her question about the car.

'Oh, don't worry about that. The sale fell through, so you keep it as long as you need it.'

'I don't want to take advantage.'

'You're not, really. It would only be taking up space.'

'If you're sure—'

'Of course I am.'

The conversation limped along. They talked about Lillian's mother a bit. James finished his coffee.

'I'll go now. I just wanted to make sure you were…well, not OK, you're not going to be OK, are you? But…you know…'

'Yes. Thanks. It's been really nice to see you.'

She couldn't think of anything to make him stay longer. In the hall, he hesitated. 'I suppose I'd better speak to your gran.'

He went and gave his condolences, then said he had to get

back to his own mother. As Lillian opened the door again, he paused. Then he placed a hand on her shoulder and kissed her cheek.

'Call me at any time, OK?'

'OK.'

Lillian stood on the step and watched him out of sight, the imprint of his lips still warm on her face.

While Lillian found it a huge effort just to get through each day that followed, Gran was on top form. She had a funeral to arrange. The Parker family honour was at stake. Lillian was bombarded with lists of food to buy and prepare for the funeral tea and, when not attending to that, she was needed to taxi Gran to and from the funeral director, the florist, the church and even the shops. Gran might not have bought a new outfit for either of the weddings, but she seemed to think that it was necessary for Nettie's funeral. Lillian stood miserably by in shops dedicated to old ladies while Gran looked at shapeless coats and ugly hats, grumbling loudly all the while about the cost of things these days.

'And what about you? What are you going to wear?' Gran asked when her own choice was finally made.

'I don't know,' Lillian said.

She had a black skirt and jumper. They would have to do.

'You'd best start thinking about it, girl. Do you have a black coat and hat?'

'No.'

'Well, get some, and hurry up about it. You've only got two days now.'

It was all very well for her to say that. The anger at the whole situation that had been simmering under the surface all week came to a head.

'What with, Gran? I haven't been paid a bean since I

stopped working back in the spring. The last of my savings went on the petrol that's now in the car. You tell me how I'm supposed to go shopping for new clothes.'

Gran just looked at her as if she was stupid. 'You only have to ask. There's no need to be so rude.' And with that she delved into her vast handbag, opened her purse and thrust a handful of notes at Lillian. 'There—get yourself something respectable. Can't have you letting us down.'

Lillian managed to mumble an ungracious, 'Thank you.' She would almost have preferred not to have been given the money so that she could have a good row about it.

The day of the funeral dawned. Susan and her mother came round early to help with the last minute sandwich making. Susan put her arms round her and kissed her cheek.

'You poor darling. I don't know how you can stand it. You're so brave.'

Cora Kershaw gave her a warm hug. 'I know I can never replace your mother, dear, but I'll always be here as a sort of aunty.'

Their kindness dissolved Lillian's anger into tears.

'Thank you,' she sobbed. 'Thank you. You're so nice. I'm so glad I've got you.'

The two women sat her on a chair in the kitchen, put a cup of sweet tea in her hands and proceeded to get on with the preparations.

'You just have a rest, dear,' Cora told her. 'You've done enough already. Let us do this.'

'Yes, it's about time someone did something for you,' Susan agreed.

Lillian tried to protest, but was outvoted. In the end, it was lovely to let go for a while and let someone else take charge. It wasn't just the physical help, it was having someone consider her and how she might be feeling. The only other person who ever did that was James.

The trays of sandwiches were covered with clean damp tea towels, Susan, Cora and Lillian changed into their formal clothes, the family began to gather. Bob arrived, having dropped baby Neville at one of Susan's friends. James arrived, and went round shaking everyone's hands, stirring the gloomy atmosphere a little. The London relatives turned up. Lillian wondered over and over whether she should have pushed harder at Eileen to come. Now might have been just the right moment.

'Wendy not here yet?' everyone asked, for something to say.

Nobody mentioned Frank. It was as if there was a large hole in the room, around which everyone skirted.

Just five minutes before the hearse was due, the phone rang. As usual, Lillian answered it.

'Oh—Lillian—'

'Wendy? You better get a move on. The hearse'll be here any minute.'

They had hardly spoken to each other since the row over Terry and his guilt offering.

'Well—er—Terry and me will meet you at the church, all right?'

'Not really, no. Gran expects you to be here.' She lowered her voice to a stage whisper. 'It's bad enough not having Frank here.'

'I know—I'm sorry, only—look, I'll see you there—'

'Wendy—!'

But the line was already dead.

Lillian went slowly back into the front room to tell Gran. The old lady's face set a little further into its severe lines.

'The family's falling apart,' she said.

The funeral procession drew up outside the door. Lillian's eyes were drawn inexorably to the coffin. Leaning along one side of it and dwarfing all the other wreaths and bouquets was the word MOTHER done in pink roses and white lilies. As they walked across the pavement to get into the cars, Gran glared at it.

'Who gave that thing? Makes it look like a didicoi funeral.'

'It shows somebody's love, Mrs Parker,' Susan said soothingly.

Lillian guessed that it was Terry's choice.

Wendy and Terry were at the church when they arrived. Wendy was wearing a black feathered hat with a heavy spotted net veil down over her face and was already dabbing at her eyes underneath it. Apart from the Kershaws and the London relatives, the congregation was horribly thin. Once more, Lillian regretted not trying harder to persuade Eileen to come. The service ran its inevitable course, the small band of mourners struggling to sing the hymns, muffled sobs coming from various throats. Lillian sat through it in a state of numbness, not quite believing that it was really happening. It was only at the graveside that she finally broke down. While Gran tutted at her, Cora Kershaw and Susan put their arms round her.

'There, there, dear. She's gone to a better place,' Cora murmured.

Lillian hoped she was right.

Back at the house, she busied herself with plates of food and cups of tea and glasses of sherry and whisky. She offered a sherry to Wendy, who was still wearing the hat.

'You can take that off now, you know,' she said.

'Oh—no, it's all right,' Wendy said, pushing the veil up as far as her eyes and downing the sherry in one. She put the glass down and reached for another. 'How's Gran taking it that Frank's not here?'

'Badly,' Lillian told her. 'She can't keep lying to the London lot and saying he's working up north. She's telling them now he's got a job abroad. I don't think they believe her.'

As she spoke, she studied what she could see of her sister's face. There were bruises under her heavy make-up again.

Wendy realised she was looking. 'Better go and talk to the Kershaws,' she said, and moved across the room.

Lillian stared after her. Wendy could still turn heads. Her voluptuous figure was tightly cased in a matt satin suit with a pencil skirt and her legs looked great in sheer black stockings and stilettos. Black wasn't really her colour, but it contrasted well with her pale skin and the bright blonde hair curling down to her shoulders. She watched as James spoke to her, concern in his face. Even now, with a brute of a husband who knocked her about, Wendy could still outshine her. She turned away and went to offer drinks to the rest of the guests.

At last everyone started to leave. Lillian was gathering plates of half-eaten food when James cornered her in the kitchen, two trays of almost untouched sandwiches in his hands.

'Did you see Wendy?' he asked.

Lillian sighed. 'Yes, but I'm not talking to her about it any more. If she wants to pretend everything's all right and flash her diamond rings at me, what can I do? All I get is a mouthful of abuse from her.'

'I know, it's impossible at the moment. But look, if ever she does say she wants to escape from him, I've had an idea about where we could take her.'

'You have? Where?'

Even as she asked, the word 'we' shone out like a beacon of hope. But that moment, his mother came in with a tray of dirty cups and saucers.

'There you are, dear. I'll stay and help clear up, if you like.'

James gave her elbow a quick squeeze. 'We'll talk about it later. It's not urgent.'

Lillian flashed him a grateful smile. On the worst day of her life, he was still there. Maybe she had not completely ruined everything between them, after all. Perhaps they could keep pretending that they were just good friends. It was a whole lot better than nothing.

C H A P T E R   32

WHAT now? That was the question that nagged at Lillian. She seemed to have lost all her energy and drive, dragging herself through the dull December days and dropping into bed exhausted, only to find sleep hard to come by.

'It's not as if there's much to do at the moment,' she told Susan when she made the effort to go and visit her. 'There's only the three of us to look after, and the very occasional PG, but it all seems so difficult. I can hardly lift an iron.'

'It's not surprising,' Susan said. 'You've just been through a very difficult time, nursing your poor mother through her illness, and seeing her pass away. That was bad enough, and then you had all that business with Frank as well.'

Lillian sighed. 'It's his visiting day coming up soon. I suppose it will have to be me that goes. I'm dreading it, having to go into the prison.'

The very thought of high walls and bars and locked doors

made her feel sick inside. She just knew that walking in there was going to take away a bit of her humanity.

'Well—' Susan frowned, thinking. 'Look, I could come with you, if that would help. I'm sure Mum would look after Neville for me. I think they only let one person in, don't they? But I could wait outside for you, so you had someone there to talk to when you came out.'

Lillian could hardly believe she had said that. If she was appalled by the very thought of prison, then Susan, staid conventional Susan, must feel it even more. But still she had volunteered to come along.

'Oh, would you? That would be wonderful. It would make all the difference not to have to go by myself. I'm really grateful, Susan. You're so sweet to me.'

The Kershaws always had been so much nicer than her own family.

'You're my sister, or nearly my sister,' Susan said, as if that explained everything. 'And you're a very nice person, too.'

Lillian flushed. 'Thank you,' she said. But it was a bittersweet compliment. *A sister* was how James thought of her as well. She bit her lip, thinking of that last time they had been alone together. She had not seen him since the funeral.

'It's not just this prison visit that's worrying you, is it?' Susan asked.

It came as a shock to find herself so easily read. Had James been talking to her? Did she know? Susan's sympathetic expression led her on. She desperately needed someone to confide in

'No,' she admitted. 'It's—'

She was a breath away from confessing just how she felt about James. But somehow it was too precious to talk about. Deep inside was the fear that if she admitted it to James's sister, the whole thing would be somehow diminished. She side-stepped into the other thing that possessed her thoughts.

'It's…well…everything, really. I look ahead and I can't see my way…'

She paused. It sounded feeble, put like that.

'You mean, what you should do next?' Susan prompted.

'Yes. You see, I always had this dream of becoming a dancer, ever since I was a kid. It probably looked pretty impossible to other people, but I did it, I became a real professional dancer and I did all those pantos and summer shows and tours and there was always something new, something happening. And then I came back home and made Gran have Sunny View done up and looked after Mum, and now she's gone and…well…I don't know what comes next. It's like…like a fog. There's no way through. All I can really see is sticking here and looking after Gran and Dad and trying to keep Sunny View going.'

It was a depressing prospect. Even if she wanted to run Sunny View, it was like swimming against the tide. Fewer and fewer people wanted a guest house holiday, not in Southend. They came to the town for day trips, not whole weeks.

'And you don't want to do that?'

Lillian shook her head.

'Bob and I were talking about this the other day. He thought you ought to stay and look after your gran and your dad, but I said that wasn't fair, why should it always be you that your family leans on? You have your own life to lead.'

Lillian just stared at her. It was the second time that day that Susan had taken her by surprise.

'Th-thanks,' she stammered.

'So what would you like to do? Go back to dancing?'

That was just it. She wasn't sure whether she did want to

dance any more. So much had happened since last she'd performed that it seemed like a different world, one that she could hardly imagine going back to.

'I don't know,' she admitted.

Lying awake in bed that night, she felt better for having aired her problem, felt closer to Susan after having spoken to her about something so personal, but knew that she had got no further forward. Here she was with the rest of her life to live, and she didn't know what to do with it. She was adrift. And the one person she really wanted to confide in, the one who could put the meaning back, had not spoken to her for over a week.

And then, a couple of days after her conversation with Susan, he phoned.

'Lindy, are you all right?' he asked.

All right! She was very far from all right. But just hearing his voice again jolted her out of her listlessness. She couldn't have said whether it was more painful or pleasurable to speak to him, but there he was, on the end of the phone, and she felt alive again.

'I'm OK,' she said. 'No need to worry about me.'

'But I do worry about you,' he said.

Her heart twisted in agonising hope.

'Look,' he said, 'I need to see you urgently. I've just had a call from Susan, about Wendy.'

The hope plummeted.

'Wendy. Right.' She couldn't keep the disappointment out of her voice.

'Of course, I want to see you as well,' he added hastily. 'But I've got the beginnings of a plan, and I thought we ought to get it all in place for when Wendy changes her mind and says she wants to get away from that bastard.'

'Right,' Lillian said again. She gave a great sigh. Talking to him about Wendy was better than nothing. 'OK. This evening then, if it's that important. It's not as if I'm doing anything much.'

They agreed to meet at a coffee bar.

It was a relief just to get out of the house for the evening. She managed to get a parking place right outside and, as she went in at the door, there he was waiting for her, the man she loved, smiling at her in welcome. Her chest felt so tight she could hardly breathe. This was the first time they had met since the funeral. Just how were they going to react to each other?

'Here—' He pushed a coffee across the table towards her. 'It's hot. I've only just arrived.'

Lillian concentrated hard on stirring the froth into the brown liquid.

'So,' she said without looking at him, 'what's all this about, then?'

Wendy, he explained, had been round to Susan's that afternoon. She had been in a very emotional state, and had finally confessed that Terry beat her. What was more, he was now threatening to take the children away from her if she tried to get away.

'I was surprised when Susan said she'd told her. I thought you said she didn't want anyone to know what was happening,' he concluded.

Lillian sighed. She leaned her head against one hand and continued playing with her coffee with the other.

'I suppose it's because of that big row with her up at the hospital,' she confessed. 'She was going on about how much she loved her precious Terry and how he loved her and she'd never leave him, so I said she'd better not come to me next time he hit her.'

'Oh, I see. Yes, you said something about not talking to her at…at the funeral. That explains it. Well, she can be pretty annoying, the way she keeps changing her mind.'

'Annoying! She's infuriating. She drives me mad. But I guess I shouldn't have shut the door in her face like that, so to speak. She is my sister, after all, and we ought to stick together.' Guilt over rejecting Wendy was another thing that added to the weight on her mind. 'The family's getting like that song we used to sing as kids—you know, *Ten Green Bottles*? First Frank, then Mum, and now Wendy's sort of tottering, about to fall off. And it makes me feel so—so powerless. What can I do about it? That's why Wendy makes me so angry. She won't be helped.'

Despite herself, there was a catch in her voice and the hand gripping the teaspoon shook a little. This was dreadful. She mustn't break down in front of him.

'It is frustrating, I know. I feel just the same. Maybe I shouldn't have rung you. Susan said you had quite enough to worry you without taking this on as well.'

But at least he was here, talking to her. If it hadn't been for Wendy, and then Susan, maybe he wouldn't have broken his silence.

''s all right,' she said. 'Anyway, I have been thinking about it, and I've had this good idea about where Wendy and the children could run away to.'

'You have?' James said. 'So have I. If she does go, she's got to get right away, to somewhere Dempsey will never find her.'

'Yeah, or there will be hell to pay, for her and the person she goes to. That's why I thought I'd ask—'

'Aunty Eileen,' they both said together.

Their eyes met and, for the first time that evening, something of the old spark kindled between them.

'Great minds,' James said with a laugh.

And from then on it was easier. They were conspirators, planning a break out. It all had to be thought out, down to the last detail, so that nobody was implicated. Neither of them wanted to be responsible for Terry Dempsey's wrath to be visited on anyone near to them. They agreed on a list of things to do.

That done, there was an awkward pause. James was looking at her. She knew he was weighing his words in his head.

'Look, Lindy…' he began.

Lillian stood up. Now that things were a little mended, she couldn't bear to break it all up again.

'I better be getting home now.'

He caught her hand. 'About what you said—'

Terrified of losing what they had regained that evening, she snatched her hand away. 'Just leave it, right? I shouldn't have said anything. Just forget it. Please.'

'Lindy, wait—'

She hurried to the door.

James followed her out into the winter's night. 'Don't go like this,' he pleaded.

The Traveller was waiting for her just outside. She unlocked the door. 'Please,' she repeated, with desperation in her voice. 'Just forget it.'

She got in, slammed the door, started the engine and drove off, leaving James on the pavement, staring after her.

CHAPTER 33

'I SAW you, you bitch, out there in the garden, giving him the glad eye. What d'you think I am? An idiot? Do you think I don't see?'

Wendy cowered before Terry's anger, her stomach churning with fear.

'I was only passing the time of day, Tel, honest.'

She knew as she said it that it was useless to reason with him. She had only been chatting over the fence to the man next door, but Terry didn't see things the way other people did.

Crack! His hand smashed into the side of her head, making it ring. Through the noise, she could hear Coral wailing.

'Don't lie to me!'

'I'm not! I'm not lying. He's our neighbour, Tel. I have to speak to him. I can't just ignore him.'

'You say good morning and that's all, d'you hear me? All. You—do—not—lead—him—on— Gottit?'

Wendy wrapped her arms round her head, trying to ward off the blows. 'Yes—yes—I'm sorry—I'm sorry—'

'So you bloody well should be. You're my wife, and don't you ever forget it!'

As if she ever could.

'I won't, Terry, I won't. I promise.'

'You're not to go out to the garden while he's there, d'you hear me?'

'Yes, Terry. I do. I hear you.'

'Good. You just better.'

Wendy remained where she was, crouched on the floor of the kitchen, as he marched out of the house. She heard Coral's sobs and felt her small arms go round her neck and gathered the child to her, seeking comfort from her soft little body.

'It's all right, darling,' she said automatically. 'It's all right now. Mummy's got you.'

They clung together as Wendy listened for the front door and then for the car starting up. It wasn't until she heard it go out of the driveway that Wendy allowed herself to relax. He was gone. Now there would be an interval of peace. Until the next time. Painfully, she straightened up. At least this time it hadn't gone on for long. Just a small outburst really. Nothing at all. She heaved Coral onto her hip, put the kettle on and took some aspirins for her thudding head. Then she sat down with tea and cake and thought it through out loud.

'What am I going to do, darling? I can't leave him, can I? He does love me, really. And he loves you and Terrance. But I don't know how—it's like a prison. Now we can't even go in the garden when he's around.'

Coral was still looking shaken. 'Don't like Daddy shouting.'

'I know, darling. I know. He doesn't mean it, not really.'

But he did mean it. If he caught her speaking to their neighbour again, there would be hell to pay.

'Uncle James says he can take us away, somewhere safe, but we couldn't do that, could we? Leave our lovely home?'

The house she had always wanted, in the best part of town, with everything in it new and expensive. Except that she had got it right the first time—it wasn't a home, it was a prison. A dangerous prison.

She went listlessly about her day's tasks. Mrs Riley still came to clean, but with the bigger house and the babies around, there was more for Wendy to do. And they very seldom ate out together now. Wendy made a meal each night but usually ended up eating it on her own.

It was Mrs Riley's day for scrubbing out the kitchen so, to keep out of her way, Wendy went upstairs and started tidying the bedroom. Like the rest of the house, the furnishings had been shiny and new when they'd moved in. There was spindly white and gold French-style furniture, a white carpet, fur rugs and gold satin sheets and bedspread. When first she had moved in, she had adored it all, spending hours sitting at the kidney-shaped dressing table, doing her face and hair and nails and moving the triple mirrors to study herself. Now she sat down on the padded stool with her back to the mirrors and stared at the range of wardrobes. They were full of clothes, expensive clothes that Terry had bought her. If she had to go, what would she take with her? Her fur coat. She couldn't leave her fur coat behind. But what about all her lovely ballgowns? She got wearily to her feet and opened the wardrobe in the corner. A rainbow of dresses hung there, satin and chiffon, full and straight and fishtail, trimmed with lace and sequins and crystals. Neatly arranged below them was a row of stilettos, dyed to match the gowns. Wendy stroked the fine fabrics, enjoying the sensuous feel.

'I don't know,' she sighed, 'I don't know.'

From Coral's room she could hear the little girl playing. She was talking to her dolls. Wendy gave up trying to make a decision and padded along the landing to peep in at her daughter. Coral plonked a toy teacup in front of one of her teddies. 'There. Nice cuppatea.'

Wendy smiled painfully. She sounded just like Susan.

But then Coral pounced on the bear and snatched it up, shaking it with frightening fury.

'You stupid bitch! You broke it! You bad, bad stupid bitch!'

Holding the bear with one hand, Coral punched it repeatedly with the other, before throwing it down on the floor and stamping on it. Frozen to the spot, Wendy just gaped at her, horror trickling through her veins. It was only when Coral dropped the bear, flopped down on the floor beside it and started to cry that she managed to go to her on shaking legs.

'There, darling, there,' she murmured, gathering the child into her arms. Together they sobbed amongst the scattered toys.

Who could she tell? Who could she confide in? If she spilt it to Lillian, she would only nag her to leave Terry. She had no real friends left, only the wives of Terry's colleagues, and she couldn't possibly speak to them. And now that her mum was gone, she didn't even have the excuse of going to visit her. Not that she'd ever said anything to her either, but at least it had been a reason to get out of the house. Even Terry couldn't stop her going to see her sick mother. She lit upon Susan. Terry didn't mind her going there. She decided to try to set it up while Terry was still in his calm phase.

'I thought I better go and see Susan,' she said next morning over breakfast. 'Only I haven't seen her much since the funeral and everything.'

She held her breath. You just never knew with Terry which

way he might take something. He grunted as he swallowed a mouthful of fried egg and bacon.

'All right, doll. I'll run you over there this afternoon. The other car's in dock.'

It wasn't quite what she wanted. She would rather have just pushed the children over to Southchurch in the pram. But she knew better than to make any objections.

'Oh. Thanks, Tel. That'd be lovely.'

When it came down to it, she found she couldn't tell Susan about Coral's behaviour. She just couldn't get the words out of her mouth. It was too horrible. But it was soothing just to be in Bob and Susan's home. Compared to hers, it was small and shabby. Some of the furniture was second-hand, they only had a little rented TV and you could hear the children next door when they pounded up and down the stairs. But there was so much love and contentment in the place that it calmed Wendy's wounded heart just a little.

'You're so lucky,' she said to Susan when Terry turned up at the door to pick her up again.

'I know,' Susan said. She kissed Wendy and stood for a moment, holding her by the shoulders and looking into her eyes. 'If there's anything I can do—you know? Anything at all—'

Wendy could hardly trust herself to answer.

'Thanks,' she whispered, and tottered down the short front path with Terrance in his carrycot in her hands and Coral clutching her skirt.

She put the carrycot on the back seat and sat beside Terry with Coral on her lap.

'Crappy place, that,' Terry commented as they drew away.

'Mmm,' Wendy agreed.

'Not like ours, eh, doll?'

'No.'

'Nah, we come a long way, we have. But not as far as we can go. Oh, no, not by a long chalk. I was thinking of something bigger. In the country, maybe. Might even have a pool. What d'yer think of that, eh, doll? Fancy a place with a swimming pool?'

'That'd be lovely, Tel.'

But inside, she quailed. Live in the country? She really would be cut off from everyone then.

Halfway home, he drew up outside a tobacconist's. Without saying anything, he got out of the car and went inside the shop. Wendy expected him to be out within a couple of minutes with some cigarettes, but he was gone some time. Coral got bored and slipped out of her arms, climbing between the front seats into the back of the car.

'Don't wake the baby,' Wendy said.

Coral was quiet in the back and Wendy sank into a reverie, going over and over her impossible situation in her head. It suddenly struck her that Coral was a bit too quiet and she peered round to see what she was doing. The child was tugging at something that was stuck down the back of the seat. Something long, black and metallic.

'Mummy help?' she asked.

Wendy stared at what she was holding, unable to believe her own eyes. She twisted round and reached into the back of the car. She was not mistaken. It was the barrel of a shotgun.

'Put it back!' she squealed.

She stretched further into the car, prised Coral's hands away and pushed the horrible thing back into its hiding place. Coral began to howl with annoyance at having her toy taken away. Wendy hauled her back into the front seat, sat her on her knee and opened her handbag.

'Ooh, look, what's in Mummy's bag?'

Not a moment too soon. Terry came out of the shop. Wendy's heart was thumping so loudly that she was sure he would hear it.

'What's all this row about?' he asked. He sounded positively cheerful. He thrust a lolly into Coral's hand and a huge heart-shaped box of chocolates into Wendy's. 'There y'are, girls. Watch your waistlines.'

'Oh!' Wendy had to use all her limited acting ability to sound delighted. 'How lovely. Chocs. My favourites.'

As ill luck would have it, Terry chose to eat at home that evening. Wendy's hands shook as she served up steak and kidney pudding followed by Bakewell tart. Terry ate it all with gusto.

'Very good,' he said. 'Not quite up to my old mum's, but not bad at all.'

'Thanks,' Wendy said.

'You hardly touched yours. What's up? You're not in the pudding club again, are you?'

'No, no—'

Heaven forbid! That really would be the end.

'Well, I gotta see a man about a dog. Bye, doll.'

'Bye.'

To her vast relief, he left the house. Wendy forced herself to clear the table and wash up. She was feeling so feeble and shaky that it took her over an hour, but it had to be done because Terry didn't like things to be left. Her mind tried to shy away from what she had seen, but she could not blank it out. A gun. Terry had a gun. All the time she had known him, people had been trying to tell her that he was a crook and she had always denied it. Terry was a businessman. People were jealous of him because he was successful, so they told lies about him. Now, at last, she had been brought face to face with the truth. An ordinary businessman did not keep a shotgun hidden down the back seat of his car.

And, just as she finally admitted that to herself, she remembered something else. For the last three weeks the local paper had been full of an armed robbery in the High Street. A shop assistant had been wounded in the chest. The men had been masked and the police were appealing for sightings of the getaway car. Could that have been Terry? Was that the gun that had been used in the raid? Nothing was certain any more. She was adrift on a sea of anxiety.

For the next two days, her every waking moment was taken up with brooding over the gun, her new view of Terry and Coral's outburst with the teddy bear. To make it worse, the only people she spoke to, apart from Terry and the children, were the butcher, the greengrocer and Mrs Riley. Towards the end of the second afternoon, she cracked and phoned Lillian.

Her sister didn't sound especially pleased to hear from her.

'Oh, hello, Wend. How's things?'

'You were right,' Wendy gabbled.

'What?'

'You were right—he is a crook, Terry. I see it now. And Lillian, it's horrible, I've been so worried. The other day I saw Coral playing and she was hitting her teddy, like, punching it really hard in the head and she was saying "*Bitch, stupid bitch*" and stamping on it. I didn't know what to say, it was just so horrible seeing her do that, just like, just like…'

'Just like her father?'

'Yes,' Wendy whispered.

There. It was out.

She waited for Lillian to say *I told you so*. But, to her surprise, her sister was sympathetic.

'It must've been dreadful for you. Coral's a sweet little thing really.'

'She is, she's the loveliest child, an angel—'

'But having all that going on round her must be doing her harm.'

'I know,' Wendy admitted.

'And what's going to happen when Terrance is old enough to take in what's happening? You don't want him to do the same to his wife when he grows up.'

Wendy was appalled. She hadn't thought of that. 'But he won't be like that.'

'How do you know? If he thinks that's how husbands treat their wives, he'll just do the same.'

'Oh, my God—'

Her mind skidded about helplessly, trying to avoid taking this on board. While she was still floundering, Lillian struck out on a different tack.

'What's brought all this on, Wend? What's made you sure Terry's a criminal?'

'Well I...he's...'

It was all too much to cope with. She couldn't tell Lillian about the gun, not on top of what Terry was doing to Coral and Terrance.

'I just do,' she said.

'Something must have changed your mind.'

'I...I can't tell you, not really, please...'

'Well, whatever it was, I'll tell you something else, Wendy, I wouldn't be surprised if he was behind Frank's being sent down.'

'What? What's that? Frank?'

So many mental blows were making her punch-drunk.

'Yes. It was no use saying anything to you before, because you wouldn't listen, but James and I think your Terry had some sort of hold over Frank over money for his motorbike, and he got him to do some of his dirty work for him.'

'But, but—' Now she really couldn't think straight. 'What am I going to do?'

Back came the answer she knew she would get.

'Leave him, Wendy. Leave him before anything worse can happen. Do you want to be killed in front of the children?'

Shocked, Wendy gave a gasp. 'Lillian!' she managed to squeak. 'Don't say that!'

'Then do it. Be brave. All you got to do is give me the word, and James and I will come and take you away.'

'I can't,' Wendy whispered.

And exasperated noise came down the line. 'For God's sake! Or at least for the children's sake. Think of them, Wend.'

'I know, I know—'

In her delicate state, she couldn't stand any more nagging.

'Terrance is crying,' she lied. 'I got to go.'

Another few sleepless nights, and she finally accepted the fact that there was only one choice if she wanted to be safe, and to keep the children safe. But she couldn't quite face admitting it to her sister. Instead, she phoned James.

'All right,' she whispered down the phone. 'I'll do it.'

CHAPTER 34

'WE'RE off!'

James's voice rang down the phone line. For a moment, Lillian was so pleased just to hear from him that she didn't grasp what he was talking about.

'What?'

'We're off. Wendy's agreed.'

'She hasn't? What, just like that?'

Lillian couldn't believe it. Wendy had been hanging on for so long that she'd almost given up hoping she would ever be brave enough to leave.

'Yup. I don't know what's happened, she didn't say, but, whatever it was, it was enough to make her jump. So are you ready?'

'You bet!'

'OK, then. See you at half past nine. We've got to give Dempsey enough time to get out of the house, and then we've got to get in there and get Wendy out before that cleaning woman arrives.'

'Right—but James, does Wendy know what she's got to do? About not letting Terry find her packing and all that?'

'I've told her. She seemed to understand. I mean, it's not that difficult, is it?'

'No—'

It wasn't difficult for James or herself to grasp, but Wendy seemed so dozy. It was hard to know what was going on in her head, if anything.

'Till tomorrow, then! Operation Rescue Plan is underway!'

The lethargy that had gripped Lillian ever since the funeral dropped away like magic. Here at last was something positive, something active that she could do. She rang Eileen's neighbour to ask her to pass the message on that they would be coming tomorrow, then started setting up a cover story about going to see Janette in Colchester. It was like breaking out of a cocoon.

They met up the next morning in a side road in Southend that had a phone box on the corner. James was waiting in a big rover.

'Ready for anything?' he asked. His face was alight with excitement.

'I suppose so.'

Now that it had come to the point, Lillian was feeling nervous. Supposing Wendy was wrong, and Terry came back before they could get away? The consequences didn't bear thinking about.

'Eileen knows we're on our way,' she said.

'Good. I've just rung Wendy, and Dempsey left half an hour ago. We're all set. Great, this, isn't it? I've been looking forward to showing Dempsey that he can't get away with whatever he likes. I just wish I could be there to see his face when he finds out she's gone.'

That was the last place Lillian wanted to be.

'D'you think she'll really go through with it?' she asked as she got into the car.

'She will, even if I have to tie her up and kidnap her,' James said.

They put on their disguises. Lillian had a short black wig. James a peaked cap and a heavy pair of glasses. Lillian had to laugh. He looked so strange.

'You do look daft,' she said.

'Hark who's talking! Just promise me something.'

'What?'

'Never dye your hair black.'

'Why ever not? I rather like it.'

Joking helped her deal with the tension as they drove out to Thorpe Bay.

Wendy was looking sick with fear as she opened the front door to them.

'Are you ready?' Lillian asked, kissing her cheek and trying to sound more confident than she felt. 'Have you got your bags packed?'

'Yes—well—no. Sort of. It's so difficult—I don't know, Lillian. Is this really the right thing to do?'

'Absolutely. Look at you! It's the only thing to do. It's all organised and, once we're on our way, I'll tell you where we're going. You'll be so surprised! Now, come on, I'll help you get things together.'

Between them, she and James ushered Wendy upstairs.

'Valuables,' James instructed. 'Have you got all your jewelry and anything else that's small and saleable? Pity he never let you have a joint account.'

Wendy's face crumpled. 'I'm going to be poor. The children are going to be poor. How can I do that to them?'

'How can you let them stay here with a father who beats their mum up?' James said.

'But it's nearly Christmas—'

'Best time to go.'

While Wendy dithered, Lillian grabbed winter clothes and stuffed them into Wendy's half-filled suitcase and James patrolled the house picking up anything he thought might bring Wendy some cash.

'It's so hard to decide. I tried to last night, but I kept changing my mind,' Wendy said.

Alarm bells rang in Lillian's head. 'You didn't leave a case where Terry could see it, did you?'

'No, no—at least—no, he never goes in the spare room—'

'Wendy?'

There was no point going into it now. She noticed that Wendy had at least packed the children's things, including food and bottles and nappies for the journey.

'Have they got their favourite books and toys?' Lillian asked. 'It's going to take us quite a while to get there. What about their Christmas presents?'

Wendy filled yet another bag.

'That's enough,' James decided, looking at the pile he had loaded into the car. 'Come on, let's go.'

Wendy looked anguished. Lillian glanced at James. They mustn't let her back down now. Mrs Riley would be here any minute. Together, they ushered her and the children into the back of the car. Lillian and James got in the front and they pulled out of the driveway. Once they were moving, Lillian's heart slowed a little and the sick feeling in her stomach subsided. They had done it. They had got Wendy and the children out of the house.

'Now, just guess where we're going?' she said in an effort to distract her sister from the enormity of what she was doing.

'I don't know,' Wendy said dully. She was sitting hunched up in the back seat with her babies in her arms, her pretty face pinched and hollow with misery.

'Aunty Eileen's!'

Wendy just looked vaguely puzzled. 'Who?'

'Aunty Eileen. Our Aunty Eileen. I found her. Well, no, she found me, actually. We were in the same café when I was on tour, and she heard someone call me Lindy-Lou, and she recognised me! Isn't that amazing? After all this time.'

'Mmm. Amazing,' Wendy said in the same flat tone.

Lillian chattered on about Eileen, bringing Wendy up to date with everything that had happened to her since she'd sneaked out of the house all those years ago. She did not succeed in lifting her sister's spirits, but by the time they got to Basildon, she found that she had lifted her own. Talking about her favourite aunt made her keen to see her again.

Wendy didn't seem to be listening. She had tied a scarf over her head and kept glancing out of the back window. 'D'you think he's following us? I thought I saw a Jaguar.'

'There's plenty of them about. Your Terry's not the only man in town with money,' James said.

'I don't know—' Wendy wailed. 'P'raps I shouldn't of done it. P'raps we ought to go back. There's still time.'

After all they had done to plan this for her!

'For God's sake—' Lillian muttered.

But James seemed to have endless patience with her. 'No. You're doing the right thing, Wendy. If you go back now, one day you could end up dead, and then what would happen to the children?'

He knew her well, Lillian realised sadly. He had hit upon the only argument that cut any ice with Wendy. She glanced round. Her sister was kissing the top of Coral's head.

'It's all right,' she was murmuring. 'Mummy's always going to be here to look after you.'

How odd it was. Three years ago she would never have thought that her sex bomb sister would be the least bit interested in children, but here she was, the devoted mother. Her children meant more to her than the clothes and the cars and the film star life she had always craved. Wendy's dream had turned out to be a false alley as well. Of the three of them, it was only James who was still forging ahead with his ambition of being a successful businessman. Only last week he had taken on another fitter at While-U-Wait Chelmsford, and he was already talking about where he should open the next branch.

It was a slow journey. The traffic round the North Circular was dreadful, with roadworks holding things up. By midday they were still in London and Terrance needed feeding and Coral was getting grizzly.

'We'll have to make a stop,' Lillian said. 'Look, there's a café over there.'

'I don't know. Maybe we should just keep going,' James said.

He sounded tense. The excitement of the morning had died. Lillian put it down to the difficulty of driving in traffic with Wendy moaning in the back.

'You need a break as much as anyone,' she said.

As she spoke, a van pulled away from right outside the café. James braked and swerved into the gap.

Wendy had to be coaxed out of the car, still convinced that the moment she showed her face then one of Terry's cronies would recognise her. But once they were all fed and watered and the children were happy again, she seemed to relax a little.

'Fancy you finding Aunty Eileen,' she said. 'Where did you say she was living?'

Lillian told her all over again. James fiddled with his teaspoon.

'Come on,' he said, 'we haven't got time to hang about.'

He chivvied them all out again. Lillian watched as he helped Wendy into the back seat, holding the door for her, supporting her elbow, making sure she was comfortable before closing the door carefully. Something in his gestures, a quality of care, of tenderness, brought a jolt of pure jealousy that made Lillian gasp aloud. And then, as if a curtain had been drawn back, it all became horribly clear. There was more to this than just rescuing Wendy. Once she was away from Dempsey, there was a good chance she would one day be a free woman again. And who had been obsessed with her from the first moment he'd clapped eyes on her? James.

How could she have been so blind? Lillian stood staring at the pair of them, stunned. An incident from way back slid into her mind. She and James were in the yard at Sunny View, mending her bike, talking nineteen to the dozen. She was totally happy, basking in the warmth of his interest. And then suddenly his attention switched off, leaving her cold, leaving her on the outside. James was staring over her shoulder and, even without looking, Lillian knew who had come into the yard. Wendy. It had always been Wendy for him. Just as it had always been James for her. Why else had he never got serious about any of those girlfriends of his? Because he was waiting for this moment. Waiting for Wendy.

'Come on, Lindy,' James said. 'Stir yourself. We've got miles to go yet.'

Like a puppet, Lillian got into the car. She hardly noticed the next stretch of the journey, nor the fact that both James and Wendy had gone quiet. She was too absorbed with her own gloomy thoughts.

At last they reached the new M1.

'It's like something out of the American movies, isn't it? Two lanes and a hard shoulder each side all the way, no roundabouts, no crossroads, no traffic lights. Just these slip roads feeding traffic in and out,' James said, like a courier pointing out the sights. 'See the cars going over the bridge? Nothing to hold you up at all. We should make good time now.'

'Good,' Lillian said, since he seemed to expect an answer.

She looked at him as he drove. As she did, she realized that he was only acting being cheerful and trying to interest them in the wonders of the motorway when all the time he was uneasy about something. He was usually a relaxed driver, but now his hands were clamped tight to the wheel and his jaw was tense. She waited till Coral was taking Wendy's attention and she could speak without being overheard.

'What's the matter?'

'Nothing.'

'Yes, there is. You've been worried for quite a while.'

'I'm not. Everything's all right.'

'Don't treat me like a kid. I know you. What's up?'

James said nothing. He glanced in the rear-view mirror. Lillian leaned to one side to look in the wing mirror. They were going down a slight slope, so she could see the cars behind clearly. Four or five back was a two-tone Jaguar.

'It's not, is it?' she whispered. 'I mean, it can't be. We're miles and miles away from home.'

As James had said to Wendy, Terry wasn't the only man rich enough to own a Jag. There were plenty of them about.

'It is. I thought I was being paranoid at first, but it's been there all the way. I was finally sure when we came out of the café and he picked us up three streets on.'

'Oh, my God.' Fear coursed through her, seizing up her mind. 'What are we going to do?'

'I'm not sure. As long as we're where there are lots of people, he won't be able to do much. We were OK in that café. It is only him, thank God, and not a bunch of his heavies. I've an idea that he wouldn't want them knowing that he can't control his own wife.'

'But how did he know?'

'Search me. Maybe something Wendy said or did made him suspicious. Maybe it was just bad luck. What matters is that we've now got him on our tail, and we're leading him towards Eileen.'

'Could we stop somewhere and phone Eileen's neighbour and get her to call the police?'

'They won't be interested. They don't interfere in domestic arguments.'

'How about if we drove to a police station and asked for protection for Wendy and the kids?'

'I considered that, but I'm not sure how Wendy would react if he went in and demanded that she went back with him. She might just give in and agree.'

This seemed only too likely.

'Before then, though, we need more petrol. We're practically out. I'll have to stop at the next service station.'

They pulled in and James got out to fill the car. Wendy made to open the rear door.

'I'll just give Coral a little run round. She's been good so far.'

'Stay in the car,' James told her.

'But—'

'I said stay in the car!'

Wendy's face crumpled. 'What's the matter?' she wailed. 'Why can't I—'

'It's for the best, Wend. Just sit there now, eh? James knows what he's doing,' Lillian said.

James went to pay. As he did so, a space became available at a pump diagonally opposite to them and a car drew into it. A two-tone Jaguar. Lillian noticed it first and began talking at top speed, trying to distract Wendy with whatever came into her head. For a minute or so it worked. But then Coral tugged at her mother's jumper.

'Daddy's car!'

'What? No, it can't be, darling, he's—oh, my God!' Wendy's voice rose to a terrified squeak. 'Lillian, Lillian, it's him, it's Terry! What are we going to do? He'll kill us. He'll kill us all!'

Lillian was frightened enough already, without Wendy getting all hysterical and setting Coral off.

'For God's sake, Wendy, shut up! He can't do anything here, not with all these people around.'

'He can, he can! Oh, what are we going to do. What—?'

'Are all the doors locked? Check them, Wendy—look, press that knob down now, quick—'

James came running back and leapt into the driver's seat.

'James, James, he's there! Terry's right there!' Wendy shrieked.

'I know.'

He started the engine and shot out of the filling station.

As they passed the Jaguar, Terry looked right at them, raised a hand and grinned. It was not a pleasant smile.

'Just hold on tight,' James said. His voice was calm and level. 'Get the map out, Lindy. We've got a bit of time while he fills up and pays. If we can make it to the next exit before he does, we might be able to lose him.'

He powered the car into the outside lane, with Wendy and now both children crying in the back, while Lillian struggled with the map. It didn't help that she wasn't sure just where they were. Frantically, she ran a finger up and down the blue line of the motorway, trying to remember which towns they had passed. To her relief, one of the big blue signs showed in the distance. But, just as she was thinking she might regain some control over the situation, she heard James curse under his breath. She looked sharply at him.

'Bastard must've made off without paying,' he muttered.

If he hoped to keep it from Wendy, he failed. She was craning round to look out of the back window.

'He's behind us! James, go faster, he's catching up!'

'I can't outrun a Jaguar,' James stated. 'I hoped to get to an exit before he saw where we went, then we might have lost him on the side roads.'

Lillian glanced at the speedometer. They were already doing over ninety.

'Can't you still turn off?' she asked.

The exit was coming up fast.

'I'm not doing high speed chases on country lanes, not with two kids in the back.'

'Then, what—'

'Oh, please, please, go faster!' Wendy begged. 'He'll kill us all. He's got a gun.'

'*What?*' Lillian shrieked.

'It's in the car. Coral found it. I think he shot that girl, you know, in that robbery?'

'Bloody hell, Wendy, why didn't you tell us that before?'

'I thought we'd got away.'

'But if we'd known we could've got the police onto him. We could've phoned from the filling station, even. Now we can't stop.'

'I'm sorry, I'm sorry. I didn't think—'

'How can you not think about a gun, for God's sake?'

Still speeding down the outside lane, they passed the exit. James eased off a little. The Jaguar did the same. Wendy was still apologising and trying to soothe the crying children in the back.

'We've got to go to the police. They'll listen to us now. It's not just a domestic,' Lillian said.

'You're right,' James agreed. 'I'm not trying to deal with a gunman with women and kids around. How far are we from Eileen's turn-off?'

Lillian frowned at the map. 'About fifteen miles.'

'Is there a police station where she lives?'

'Yes. It's called a village but it's quite a big place.'

'Right—' He raised his voice. 'Wendy, can you please pipe down? I'm trying to think here.'

The noise in the back went down to a less ear-splitting level.

'It's quite simple, hardly a plan at all,' James said. 'We just need to be ready to move quickly. No panicking, OK? Lindy, write down the number of the Jag. We must get the bastard nailed.'

Now that they weren't just running blind, Lillian felt a calm spreading through her. They just had to hold on. She spoke reassuringly to Wendy and the children, who were all still whimpering quietly. Off the motorway they went and onto the B road. After the speed they had been doing, they hardly seemed to be moving at all.

'Is he still there?' Lillian asked, peering in the wing mirror.

'Oh, yes. He wants to know where we're going. He's not giving up now.'

They passed the sign for Eileen's village. Lillian almost cheered.

'Left here and straight up the main street,' she directed. 'It's on the left-hand side. Look—there—'

'Pass Coral over to Lindy,' James said to Wendy. 'And have Terrance ready. Sit on Lindy's side, remember.'

Lillian could hear Wendy making small noises, trying to stop herself from crying out loud.

'Is it unlocked? Have you got your hand on the door handle?' she asked as she clasped Coral firmly to her.

'Yes—' Wendy squeaked.

'Right, get ready,' James said.

He swerved into the police station, making the driver behind him hoot in anger. Lillian had her door open as the car slowed and was out as it stopped. She grabbed Wendy's arm as she emerged and together they raced up the steps and through the heavy doors, leaving James to see what Terry did.

Behind the desk was a solid-looking man in a sergeant's uniform.

'Please,' Lillian begged him. 'You've got to help us—'

CHAPTER 35

OUTSIDE the police station, James got back into the car. Dempsey had stopped when they did and backed down the street to wait where he could see the entrance. Now they were like two cats staring at each other, waiting to see who blinked first. The engines of both cars were still running.

The minutes ticked by.

'Come on,' he muttered.

What was going on in there? Had the girls not been able to persuade the police to do anything? His confidence began to seep away. Two women running into a police station in a quiet little town claiming to be pursued by a man with a gun was a bit of tall story. What were they going to do if that story was dismissed? Then another thought struck him. Supposing the gun wasn't there any more? Dempsey might have got rid of it since Wendy had found out about it, in which case the police would have nothing to hold him on. The whole thing was looking more and more flimsy. Now they had led Dempsey practically to Eileen's door and they didn't have a Plan B.

Suddenly there was movement. Four police officers were coming out of the station. At the same moment, Dempsey saw them and began to move off. The policemen leapt forward, shouting at him to stop. James stamped on the accelerator, shot out of the forecourt and rammed into the Jag as it passed. There was a crash of splintering glass and crumpling metal as the impact jolted through his body. And then the policemen were swarming all over the Jaguar and hauling Dempsey out. For a moment his eyes met Dempsey's. James allowed himself a smile of triumph.

'Got you, you bastard,' he said.

As two officers held Dempsey, a third emerged from the back of the car with a sawn-off shotgun.

'This yours, sir?' James heard him say.

'Never seen it before. Dunno how it got there. Someone must of planted it,' Dempsey claimed.

He was led away into the station. The fourth officer approached James.

'That was a very dangerous thing to do, sir,' he said.

'Yes,' James agreed. 'I know.'

But he didn't care. They'd got Dempsey. That was all that mattered.

It was ages before they were able to leave the station. Eileen's Neil came to meet them with a neighbour's van which they used to ferry all Wendy's possessions. When they finally got to their house, two small faces appeared beside the Christmas tree in the window, then they disappeared and a moment later the door opened and there were Eileen and her children, smiling and waving.

James slung an arm round Lillian's shoulder.

'We did it,' he said. 'Well done us.'

There was a happy tangle of huggings and kissings and introductions.

'Come in, come in,' Eileen said. 'The tea's just mashed. You poor things, what a terrible time you've had; you must be worn out—'

She ushered them into the front room, festooned with paper chains and tinsel, and hurried out again to fetch the tea while James and Neil brought in all Wendy's things. It was such a cosy, welcoming place. It was all slightly surreal to James after the events of the day. The coal fire glowed in the hearth, the television warbled in the corner, the budgie squawked and chirped in its cage and the children were soon laughing and tumbling together. There were Christmas cards jumbled together on every available surface. He looked at Wendy, who was taking it all in. Eileen's was a world away from Wendy's place in Thorpe Bay. It was small and crowded, the furniture was worn and the wallpaper faded, but surely she would like it here, until they knew what was going to happen with Dempsey.

He finished taking all the bags upstairs and collapsed onto the sofa beside Lillian.

'Isn't this nice?' he said. 'You'll be fine here, Wendy.'

'Yes,' Wendy said doubtfully.

Eileen came in with a tea tray and orange squash for the children.

'We'll have tea proper in a minute. What a time of it you've had, and ending up at the police station. Oh, but it's so lovely to see you all! Just look at you, Wendy! You were just a kid when I ran away and now you're a mum. And such beautiful little ones too, one of each, just like mine. And this is James— I've heard so much about you.'

Had she? He wondered just what Lillian had told her.

'I hope it was good,' he said.

'Ooh, I'm not telling! But Wendy, you poor darling—' She went to perch on the arm of Wendy's chair and put her arms round her. 'How you must have suffered. But you'll be all right now, I promise. We'll look after you. You'll be safe with us.'

The tension seemed to drain out of Wendy. She leaned against Eileen and a tear slid down her cheek.

'Thank you,' she whispered.

Eileen planted a kiss on the top of her head.

'There, there. We'll have lots of good long talks and you can get it all out of your system,' she promised. 'But, in the meantime, what are we going to do with you all? James and Lindy can't get home tonight now you've crashed the car.'

'Not only that, the police want to speak to us again in the morning,' James told her. 'Perhaps there's a guest house or something we can put up at?'

Eileen laughed. 'What, a Sunny View? Not likely! Not when we've got neighbours what'll find you a bed.'

Neil wanted to hear more about their journey and Dempsey's pursuit. James described their day, calling on Lillian and Wendy for collaboration every now and again. Reliving it brought it home to him how close to disaster they had been. If Wendy hadn't told them about the gun they might still be trying to get Dempsey off their tail.

Eileen and her family listened open-mouthed.

'Blimey, it's like something off the telly,' Eileen said. 'But what am I thinking of? You must all be starving and I promised you tea. Lindy, love, come and give us a hand, will you?'

Lillian had been sitting listening to James talking, feeling utterly drained. She got up and let herself be dragged out to the kitchen. Eileen closed the door behind them.

'Here, I can see why you're bonkers about him,' she said,

putting the kettle on to boil again. 'He's scrumptious! If I wasn't married to my lovely Neil I'd fight you for him. I've done a great big cottage pie; d'you think that'll be all right?'

'What? Oh—yes—lovely—' Lillian tried to get her thoughts together. 'What do you want me to do?'

'Oh, nothing. You just sit there; you've done enough for one day. I just wanted a word in private. Your James—so handsome and so capable too. Sort of man you can rely on to get you out of a tight corner. And so nice with it as well, doing all this for Wendy.'

Lillian nodded. He was all that and more. Her throat ached with tears of longing.

'That's just it,' she blurted out. 'He's doing it for Wendy. He's always wanted her.'

Eileen stopped in the middle of heaping chopped cabbage into a saucepan of boiling water. 'Are you sure?' she said. 'Only—'

The door opened and James put his head round. 'Anything I can do?'

Eileen flapped him away. 'No, no, we're all under control here.'

It was hopeless trying to have a private conversation when the tiny house was full to bursting. Wendy gave Terrance his bottle, then they all ate the cottage pie, then various neighbours turned up as the story spread down the street. Just as Eileen had predicted, beds were found for James and Lillian. As Wendy and Eileen battled to get overtired children off to bed, James sat down by Lillian again.

'D'you fancy a walk?'

'What?'

It was the last thing she had expected.

'I know you must be exhausted, but I just wanted a bit of quiet and fresh air, and I thought you might as well.'

Now that he suggested it, it was exactly what she wanted. They found their coats and slipped out of the front door.

It was cold out in the street. Frost was forming on the pavements and their breath made clouds in the chilly air. All along the rows of houses, front curtains were parted a little to show brightly lit Christmas trees and families gathered round the green glow of televisions.

Lillian couldn't trust herself to speak.

James broke the silence. 'We did it, then. Who'd have thought it would all work out like this?'

'I know,' Lillian said. 'I suppose Wendy could go home straight away really, or as soon as we know that Dempsey really is going to be remanded.'

'Yes, she looks so out of place at Eileen's, doesn't she? Not that I'm saying anything against your Aunty Eileen. She's a lovely person. But Wendy was a bit like—oh, I don't know— an orchid amongst daisies.'

A spurt of anger propelled Lillian away from the despair that had been threatening to overtake her. 'You talk as if she's some sort of princess. She's a Parker. She was brought up at Sunny View, same as me.'

'I know that, Lindy. That's not even what I meant—' He paused, frowning. 'I don't know what I meant, really. It's been a bit of a day, hasn't it? Everything changed so quickly. D'you think we did the right thing, forcing Wendy to leave him?'

Lillian stopped still. 'What are you talking about? We didn't force her; she said she wanted to go.'

'Yes, yes, you're right, of course you are.'

James's hand closed round hers. It felt warm and strong and secure. A glow spread through her as they walked on down the street.

'You see—' James said slowly, 'if anyone was to take you away from me, I don't know what I'd do.'

For several moments, Lillian couldn't believe she had heard that. She wanted to. More than anything else in the world, she wanted to. But she hardly dared ask him to repeat it, in case she had got it wrong.

'Lindy?'

She swallowed. It was difficult to speak.

'I thought—' she started. Her throat was all croaky. She cleared it and tried again. 'I thought you'd got Wendy away from Dempsey so that you would have a chance with her.'

'Wendy?' James gave a short incredulous laugh. 'Whatever made you think that?'

'You've always been obsessed with her.'

'I was once, I suppose, but I got over that ages ago. No, I wanted to get her away from Dempsey because no one should be treated like he treated her. And because she's your sister, and you were so worried about her.'

'Oh,' Lillian said. Deep inside, a small flame of hope had kindled.

'Lindy, when you said that—when you said you'd always loved me—'

James turned to face her, taking her other hand.

'You really shook me up, you know. Until that moment...well...it was like I had blinkers on. I thought... well...I thought it was just a kid's crush and you'd got over it ages ago. Like me with Wendy. I mean, you had lots of boyfriends when you were on tour, didn't you? But when you said that, I was totally confused. You've always been very important to me, you know. You're the woman I always turn to, more than Susan or my mum, but suddenly you weren't my little sister any more, and I didn't know where I was. And then your mum died and there was the funeral and everything, so it hardly seemed like the right time to be talking about you and me. And then all this business with Wendy. I wanted to talk to you that evening at the coffee bar—'

'I know,' Lillian said.

That had been a horrible moment. She had been terrified that he was about to say he could only ever be her brother.

'I've got brothers. I didn't want another one,' she said.

'And I've got a sister, and I don't really need another one. Not the way I need you, Lindy. I realise now why I never got the least bit serious about any of my girlfriends. None of them measured up to you. They weren't as bright or kind or clever or funny as you, and they certainly weren't as pretty as you. In fact, there's no one quite like you—'

Lillian was gazing at him, drinking in his words, watching his face, watching his lips as he spoke. All the time he was speaking, an almost painful excitement was building and building inside her.

'Lindy—darling—'

They moved into each other's arms as easily as breathing. Their lips met, gently, tentatively at first, a kiss of discovery, then deeper and more passionate, sending Lillian spinning into a breathless spiral of pleasure. When they finally broke apart they smiled at each other in wonder, not quite believing what was happening. James ran a gentle hand over Lillian's cheek, smoothing back her hair, running his fingers across her ear.

'My sweet girl,' he murmured. 'Why didn't we do this before?'

Lillian just smiled and kissed him again, wanting nothing but to be close to him, to feel his eager mouth on hers and his hands caressing her body. The tensions of the day evaporated until there was just the two of them at the hot centre of their own small world.

'Funny that Wendy sort of brought us together. I've always been so jealous of her,' she admitted.

'Jealous? Of Wendy?' James sounded genuinely surprised.

'Yes. She was always so much prettier than me. And you were besotted with her. I hated her for that.'

'Daft girl. Wendy's just a—a—an iced cake. All pink and sugary on the top and nothing much underneath. You're so much better in every way. And, now that we've found each other, I'm never going to let you go.'

Lillian smiled. 'Found each other? You mean you found me. I always knew that you were the one.'

'Yes, well, you're obviously much brighter than me. It took me a lot longer.'

It was so amazing and wonderful but, now that it had happened, it seemed inevitable.

'I love you,' she said.

There was a deep happiness in saying that, and knowing she could say it safely.

'I love you too. I think I have for a long time. I've been an idiot. A blind idiot.'

Lillian traced the line of his jaw with her fingers. 'It's all right. I forgive you.'

The ugly streets of the little town were transformed into a place of magic and wonder as they wandered along with their arms round each other, talking about the past and the future, and stopping every so often to kiss and look into each other's eyes. It was only when the church clock struck eleven that they realized how long they had been out. Around them, lights were going out downstairs windows and on in bedrooms.

'I suppose we'd better get back to Eileen's. She'll be wondering where we've got to,' James said reluctantly.

'Mmm—' Lillian laid her head against his shoulder. 'We'll have to tell her how we've been taking her advice.'

'About following our dreams? Yes, I think we'd better do as she says about that one,' James agreed.

As the Battle of Britain rages
over the Essex coast, two teenagers
fall in love…

On the bleak family farm on the Essex marshlands,
Annie Cross slaves all day for her cruel father. The one
thing that keeps her going is her secret meetings
with Tom Featherstone.

But war steals Tom from her when he joins the RAF.
Annie would love to do her bit but, stuck on the farm,
she lives for Tom's letters – until they stop coming.

When, against the odds, her beloved Tom returns,
he finds a different, stronger Annie to the one he
left behind. But he also finds the girl he loved
is carrying another man's child…

www.mirabooks.co.uk

It's 1953, Coronation Year and everybody is celebrating…

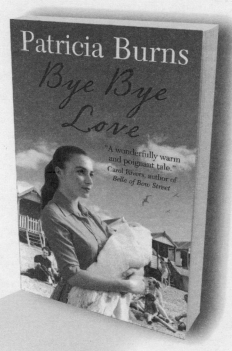

Everybody except Scarlett Smith.
After losing her mum and her home, she and her
father are adrift in Southend. Scarlett's only
happiness is her innocent romance with Tom.

When Tom leaves to do national service, Scarlett
discovers the Saturday night dance hall. There she
forgets her troubles with a rock 'n' roll ban
singer – with disastrous consequences…

www.mirabooks.co.uk